Praise for the novels of Rachel Reid

"Rachel Reid's hockey heroes are sexy, hot, and passionate!
I've devoured this entire series and I love the flirting,
the exploration and the delicious discovery!"

—#1 *New York Times* bestselling author Lauren Blakely

"It was sweet and hot, and the humor and banter gave it balance.
I'm really looking forward to more from Rachel Reid."

—*USA TODAY* on *Game Changer*

"Reid's hockey-themed Game Changers series continues on
its red-hot winning streak.... With this irresistible mix of sports,
sex, and romance, Reid has scored another hat trick."

—*Publishers Weekly*, starred review, on *Common Goal*

"The Game Changers series is a game changer in
sports romance (wink!), and firmly ensconced
in my top five sports series of all time."

—*All About Romance*

"*Role Model* proves that you can take on sensitive topics
and still deliver a heartfelt and sexy sports romance.
Grumpy/sunshine at its best."

—*USA TODAY* bestselling author Adriana Herrera

"It's enemies-to-lovers with loads (and loads, literally)
of sizzling hot hate sex and hot hockey action and it's
all tied up in a helluva sweet slow-burn love story."

—*Gay Book Reviews* on *Heated Rivalry*

TIME TO SHINE

Rachel Reid

carina press®

Recycling programs for this product may not exist in your area.

ISBN-13: 978-1-335-45853-7

Time to Shine

Copyright © 2023 by Rachelle Goguen

For questions and comments about the quality of this book, please contact us at CustomerService@Harlequin.com.

Carina Press
22 Adelaide St. West, 41st Floor
Toronto, Ontario M5H 4E3, Canada
www.CarinaPress.com

Printed in U.S.A.

This book is for Matt, Mitchell and Trevor.
Thank you for your support and patience.

Time to Shine contains depictions of grief related to the past death of a close family member.

Chapter One

Landon Stackhouse had been expecting the call, but his heart still caught in his throat when his phone rang.

"They need you in Calgary," his team's general manager, Chris Ferguson, said. Five words that Landon had been waiting to hear for over two years.

"Yes, sir. I can drive myself there." It was a six-hour drive at least from Saskatoon to Calgary, and since it was November there was a decent chance of snow happening somewhere during it, but if Landon left now...

"Nah, you're booked on the next flight out of Saskatoon. Leaves in two hours. You've got a room waiting at a hotel near the arena. Someone from the Outlaws should be in touch soon with more info."

"Right," Landon said, barely stopping himself from asking how he'd get his car to Calgary. He wouldn't need it. It was fine, it was fine. He'd probably only be there for a couple of days anyway. Maybe a week. He saw the game last night, and saw the Outlaws' backup goalie, Gilbert Morin, get run over by a Dallas player. The injury didn't look good; Morin had needed to be helped off the ice.

"You know this is good news, right?" Landon could hear the smile in Ferguson's voice. "Getting called up to the NHL?"

"Yes."

Ferguson laughed. "I'll miss these sparkling conversations, Stackhouse. Good luck in Calgary. You've been outstanding for us, so go show the big guys what you've got."

Landon doubted he'd be showing them much more than his door-opening skills while sitting on the bench, but he said, "I will."

"And try to enjoy yourself for god's sake."

"Thank you, sir."

After the call ended he sat on his bed with his hands on his knees, pressing his fingers into the soft material of his sweatpants. "Okay," he said quietly into his empty bedroom. "Okay."

He tried to put the situation into perspective. Yes, he was going to the big leagues. Yes, he would be teammates with actual superstars, including his hero, Antton Niskanen. Yes, this was what all his hard work was for. This was different from the training camps where he was always inevitably cut early. Calgary *wanted* him.

But also, he was about to go from being Saskatoon's starting goaltender to sitting on the bench in Calgary. Realistically, he was barely going to meet any of his big-league teammates before hopping on a plane straight back down to the farm team. This would be a cool experience, but it wouldn't change his life. He could be sure of that.

"I should probably tell Mom and Dad, huh?" Landon said out loud to someone who wasn't there.

He sent a text to his mom, who was more reliable about checking her phone: Got called up. Heading to Calgary now. After a moment, he added, Flying, not driving, to reduce her anxiety.

He packed quickly and efficiently, the same way he would for a roadie, not as if he was moving to a new home. Because he wasn't.

Should he wear his suit? This was the big leagues. He should wear his suit.

He removed his basic navy suit from the garment bag he'd carefully packed it in. Minutes later he was inspecting himself in his full-length mirror, which he stood far away from by necessity to fit his entire six-four frame into the glass. He ran a hand over his clean-shaven face, and unnecessarily smoothed his short brown hair.

The last time he'd been in Calgary was over two months ago for the Outlaws prospects training camp. He'd known then that he'd had no hope of making the team; Calgary's goaltending duo was the envy of the league. Antton Niskanen was a future Hall of Famer, no question, and Gilbert Morin had once been a star goalie for Buffalo and was now a solid backup for Niskanen. Landon had worked hard in the AHL and had established himself as the best-of-the-rest. He could probably expect to see a lot more of Calgary as inevitable injuries and illnesses happened. Calgary wanted to rely on him in a tough situation, and Landon needed to show them that they could.

The man in the mirror looked reliable, he thought. Responsible. Probably too skinny but that was unlikely to ever change. At least he was tall. Coaches and general managers liked tall.

Landon didn't particularly enjoy looking at himself. He didn't like being seen, and only truly felt comfortable when he was wearing fifty pounds of goalie gear. Outside of his shell, he was all limbs and sharp angles and vulnerable skin and bones. He had to talk to people, and think about things that weren't hockey. It was the worst.

Mom replied to his text just before he left his apartment to start his new adventure: **Congratulations! That's amazing and we're so excited for you. Love you. Be careful!**

Landon grimaced at the "be careful," though he couldn't blame his parents for worrying. Just like he didn't blame them for not watching his games. The limited support they were able to give him was already more than he deserved, and the usual wave of guilt swept over him as he wrote back, **I will. Love you too.**

★ ★ ★

Landon was sitting in an NHL locker room directly across from Antton Niskanen. Antton fucking *Niskanen*.

He'd met him before, at training camps. But there had been lots of goalies at those, and Niskanen hadn't been present for most of the practices and scrimmages. Superstars rarely were. So far, Landon's conversations with his idol could be described as short and embarrassing. Last time Landon had attempted to talk to him, he'd clumsily stopped himself from gushing about what an honor it was to meet him by complimenting Niskanen's shoes and asking where he'd bought them. Niskanen had said, "Milan," and then had turned to talk to the Outlaws captain, Lee Ramsay. Landon had walked away, mentally kicking himself with his own Marshall's dress shoes.

Things could only get better, right?

When he'd first walked into the arena, Landon had met with Andy Bates, the goalie coach, and learned that he'd arrived during a hectic week. After the game tonight, there would be a short practice and video meeting in the morning, then the team would be flying to St. Louis to start a four-game road trip.

A real NHL road trip. With airplanes and everything.

Landon was glad he'd be busy. He knew himself, and if he wasn't kept busy, he would spend every hour not at the arena alone in his hotel room. The travel would be good for him.

So far Landon had been met with polite greetings and nods by his temporary teammates; the exact sort of welcome one could expect from coworkers who knew there was no point in trying to get to know you. In the locker room now there was chatter and laughter and the easy camaraderie of men who were together nearly every day and night. Landon had made a bee-line for his own stall when he'd first entered the room, keeping his head down, letting everyone here know that he was here to do a job, and didn't mind being ignored.

As he was fastening the straps of his right leg pad, a pair of skates with neon pink laces stepped between his wide-spread legs. He glanced up and saw the smiling face of Casey Hicks, Calgary's young star left winger.

"Hey, Stacks. Good to see you again," Casey said, as if they were old friends instead of two guys who had barely spoken to each other during training camp. "How's Saskatoon been treating you?"

"Uh. Good. Team's had a strong start."

"Thanks to you." When Landon's face must have shown surprise, Casey added, "Yeah, I follow that shit. I've got lots of friends in the AHL. I saw that epic save you made last month. The one where you were all—" Casey stretched his arms out and lifted one leg. Landon knew the save he was talking about, and it had looked nothing like that.

"That was a tough one," Landon agreed.

Casey put his arms and leg down and kept smiling at him. Landon went back to fastening his straps.

"What's your wingspan?" Casey asked. "It must be like a mile long, right?"

"About six-nine."

"Nice," Casey replied automatically, then laughed. "For real, though. That's killer."

Casey had dimples when he laughed. Combined with his shoulder-length dark blond hair, unusual blue-green eyes, and pink lips, it was understandable why he was a fan-favorite for reasons beyond his hockey skills. He was…cute.

"Thanks," Landon said, because he wasn't sure what else to say.

Casey nodded. "Well, welcome to Calgary. Everyone's cool here. I heard the postgame meal is gonna be subs. Try to grab one of the chicken parm ones. They go fast, and they are fuck-ing awesome."

As if Landon was going to elbow his way to the front of the food line on his first night with the team to get the good sand-wiches. In front of players who had *actually played*.

"Oh, and avoid the third shower stall on the right because it's all fucked up."

"Okay."

Casey's tone turned gravely serious. "No. For real. Don't use it."

Landon stared at him. "I won't."

The easy smile returned to Casey's lips. "Cool. Let me know if you need anything, 'kay?"

Landon couldn't imagine what he could possibly need from Casey Hicks. If he required anything at all during his short stay in Calgary, he could probably find someone more appropriate to ask than an all-star.

Even if the all-star in question was a year younger than Landon.

Still, though. The offer was nice. "I will. Thanks."

A few minutes later the team took to the ice for warm-ups. Antton Niskanen dropped to the ice in his usual spot to stretch, and Landon found a spot far away from him. He knew Antton didn't like to talk before games. He knew everything about him. Landon didn't like to talk much either, so he stretched in silence and tried not to be obvious about the glances he was stealing of his idol. Antton's mask was a new variation on the same design he'd had for years: a team of demonic horses breathing fire, mounted by skeletons wearing cowboy outfits. This year the mask had "NISK" written like a brand on the chin of the mask, the letters still smoking. It looked dope. Landon was wearing his Saskatoon Bandits mask, which thankfully matched the Calgary team colors.

Lee Ramsay took a knee on the ice beside Landon. "Hey, I didn't get a chance to welcome you earlier. Sorry. I was getting some treatment."

"No worries," Landon said, because he was totally chill and not at all starstruck. Lee was in his fourteenth season of an incredible career, and had been Calgary's captain for seven of those seasons. He was often described as a natural leader, the kind of captain every team wants. He was also often described as handsome, which he absolutely was with his warm brown skin, tall, muscular build, and his Hollywood smile.

"You know anyone here?" Lee asked him.

"I've met some of the guys before at training camps."

"Gotcha. So no friends on the team?"

"Uh no. Not yet," Landon said, as if he would be making friends any minute now.

"Rossi is a good kid. Leandros too. They're tight, though. Definitely come as a package."

Landon wasn't sure how to react to Lee Ramsay trying to suggest potential friends for him. Lee was ten years older than Landon and married with kids, so of course Landon didn't expect him to volunteer for the job himself.

"Hicks is about your age," Lee said, then laughed. "But you'll never get a moment of quiet with that guy."

Landon glanced across the ice where Casey Hicks was standing between two other forwards. Casey was talking, and the other two men were laughing. Casey was several inches shorter than either of them. He was, Landon knew, the shortest player on the team by about two inches. His official listed height was five-nine, but Landon suspected that number had been stretched a bit.

Lee tapped Landon on the shoulder and said, "We'll talk later," before standing and skating away. Landon's gaze followed him to where the Calgary players were lining up to take shots on the net. There were so many star players on the ice, both on Calgary's half of the ice, and down in the Los Angeles end. Landon tried to ignore his own nerves about it, like he tried to ignore how much bigger this arena was than the one in Saskatoon. How much louder it was already, even though the seats were only partially full for the warm-ups.

He watched Niskanen stop rapid-fire shots from his teammates. The veteran goalie's movements were quick and confident. Efficient, just how Landon had modeled his own style of play. Not that he was comparing himself to Niskanen.

Holy shit, he was teammates with Antton Niskanen. And Lee Ramsay. And Casey Hicks. And Ross MacIsaac. The list went on and on.

And now he had to take his turn in the net.

Antton nodded at Landon as he passed him. He may have said something, but Landon didn't hear. He was entirely focused on settling his nerves. It was *warm-ups* for fuck's sake, not the playoffs.

He got in position, exhaled and waited. When the first puck slammed into his blocker pad, he smiled behind his mask. He could do this. The Calgary Outlaws open-fired on him, and Landon welcomed every thud against his body like a friend. He loved this. He knew it wasn't normal to enjoy being bludgeoned with pucks, but god, he lived for it. He loved being in a headspace where nothing mattered but making sure he didn't let anything get past him.

Of course, some pucks got past him. No goalie stopped every shot during warm-ups, but enough pucks thudded off of him to quiet his brain. By the time he headed back to the locker room with the rest of the team, he felt calm.

Calgary's head coach, Greg Patrick, was waiting for them in the locker room. He kept his words brief, reading out the lines for the game and reminding his players of a few key things about the L.A. team. Everyone listened intently, including Landon. Patrick was unusually soft-spoken for a hockey coach, known more for his intelligence and sharp attention to detail than his ability to intimidate and shame. He was the style of coach Landon responded best to.

"I'd like to welcome Landon Stackhouse to the team," Coach said, and suddenly all eyes turned to the new goalie. Landon wished he still had his mask on. He held up a hand, not quite a wave. More of an acknowledgment that, yes, he was Landon. He was here.

"Hi, Stacks!" Casey Hicks called out cheerfully. Some of the other guys laughed.

"Let's show the new guy how we win in Calgary, all right, boys?" Coach said. There were whoops of agreement, then everyone stood to shuffle into the hall.

In the hallway that led to the ice, the guys were loud and excited. Calling out nicknames, performing pregame rituals with each other. Niskanen was crouched at the end of the line, staring at the wall, focused. Hicks was doing a ridiculous little dance with his linemate, Clint Noseworthy. Landon stood near the back, but not all the way at the back because Ross MacIsaac, Calgary's 37-year-old defenseman, was famously superstitious about being the last one to step on the ice.

It felt both surreal and normal at the same time, waiting to go on the ice. The home crowd in Saskatoon loved their team, so being greeted by a full house of cheering fans wasn't new for Landon; the house was just twice as big in Calgary. But in Saskatoon, Landon was the star. People wore his jersey there, and he often got the loudest cheer when the starting lineups were announced before games. He'd played a huge part in making the Saskatoon Bandits a Calder Cup contender last season, taking them deep in the playoffs last spring.

Here, Landon felt like a ghost floating among these stars. Or like a kid who'd won a prize to hang out with his heroes for a day.

He glanced down at his chest, almost shocked to see that he was wearing the same uniform as everyone else around him. The iconic red, white, and golden yellow of the Calgary Outlaws.

"Doesn't feel real, right?" said a cheerful voice. Landon realized two things at once as his head jerked up in surprise: that Casey Hicks was suddenly standing beside him, and that Landon had been caressing the Outlaws logo on his own chest with his blocker glove.

"My first game I was like…" Casey bugged his eyes out and pulled his mouth into an exaggerated cringe. "Y'know?"

"Yeah," Landon agreed, because that basically summed up how he was feeling.

"It's just hockey," Casey said easily. "And we're good at hockey. If they wanted us to go out there and do, like, opera, I'd be fucked. But hockey? Pfft. No problem."

"Right." Landon was starting to feel more confused than nervous.

"What about you?"

"What about me what?"

"Could you sing opera if you had to?"

Landon stared at Casey for a long moment, trying to decide if he was making fun of him or not. He got sidetracked along the way by Casey's dimples. Finally he just said, "No."

Casey gently bumped his glove against Landon's chest. "Aw. But imagine if you'd just, like, started singing perfect opera at me. That would have been epic."

Landon could not imagine it. At all.

He also couldn't look at Casey's dimples anymore, so he focused instead on the floor. Casey's famous pink skate laces gleamed up at him. They clashed horribly with the tomato-red uniform socks, but Landon was sure Casey didn't care.

"Here we go, boys!" someone yelled from near the front of the line.

Casey let out a scream like a hawk in reply, and Landon hoped he didn't have permanent hearing damage.

A few minutes later, Landon was seated at one end of the bench, watching an NHL game. It was fucking *awesome*. Even if he was only in Calgary for one night and he never again returned to this league, he'd have this. He'd have gotten to watch Antton Niskanen shut down the Los Angeles team in a way that seemed effortless, but Landon knew was pure unmatched skill. L.A. was a good team; they'd taken Calgary to game seven in the first round of the playoffs last season, but just like in that seventh game, Antton wasn't giving them an inch tonight.

Calgary's top line of Lee Ramsay, Clint Noseworthy, and Casey Hicks was incredible to watch this close as well. The crowd was obviously in love with Casey in particular, cheering every time he had the puck, and exploding in celebration when he scored the first goal of the game. Landon spotted a ton of jerseys in the crowd with Casey's name and number on them.

Casey's father, Dougie Hicks, was in the Hockey Hall of Fame after a long, outstanding career. He hadn't played for Calgary—he'd started his career in Toronto and then played for Tampa Bay for his final eight seasons—but he must be an Outlaws fan now. Landon's dad, a lifelong Toronto fan, had loved Dougie Hicks.

Dougie's son was almost as impressive already, but had a very different style of play. Where Dougie had been intimidating and physical, Casey seemed to have fun, skating around opponents and making them look bad.

Calgary had a great team. It was an interesting mix of players who gelled well together. Lee Ramsay had played his entire career in Calgary. Ross MacIsaac, the most senior defenseman on the team, had joined the Outlaws on a two-year contract after an incredible fourteen seasons in New Jersey. There were a bunch of young, talented players, which, added to the fact that the farm team in Saskatoon was currently at the top of their division, boded well for Calgary's future.

Landon wondered if he would be a part of that future. Obviously that was the dream, but it didn't seem very likely. He *was* a star in Saskatoon, though, so if he never truly made it past that level, well. There were worse things.

But when Niskanen made an unreal save, and the crowd of over twenty thousand Outlaws fans roared their excitement, Landon couldn't help but think there were better things too.

Chapter Two

Casey wedged himself between Clint Noseworthy and West Ackerman, placing a hand on each of their shoulders. "I don't know about you guys, but I could use a beer."

West stepped away from him. "Not tonight, Case."

"Gotta rest up for the roadie," Clint agreed.

"I'm wired, though," Casey said. "No way am I getting to sleep anytime soon. Come on. One drink. I'm buying." He pointed at Clint. "We can go to that country bar you like."

Clint shook his head. "I'll let you buy me a beer another night."

Casey would not be defeated. He turned to Ross MacIsaac, who was shrugging on his coat, ready to leave the locker room. "How about you, Mac? Beer, wings?"

Ross laughed. "The night before a road trip? Mandy would kill me. I promised the kids I'd make pancakes in the morning, and they get up fucking early."

"Yeah, okay," Casey said, trying not to sound too dejected. The locker room was emptying fast. He made a last-ditch effort and raised his voice so the whole room could hear him. "Anyone want to come to my place? Have a beer? Hang out for a bit?"

The only response was some assorted muttering, none of

which sounded enthusiastic about his offer. Things were looking bad for Operation: Avoid Going Home Alone.

He spotted the new guy, Landon, standing in one corner,
frowning at his phone. He was wearing a long, black wool coat
that accentuated how tall and slim he was. He had a backpack
slung over one shoulder, obviously about to leave.

Casey was walking toward him before he'd bothered to think
about it. "Hey, Stacks. You got plans tonight?"

Landon blinked at him. His eyes were huge and dark brown,
framed by long lashes. Pretty. His thick, straight eyebrows
bunched together as he said, "Plans?"

"Yeah. You wanna go out, get a beer or something? Or we
could go to my place. I've got all the movie channels. Or we
could just, y'know. Chill." Whoops. He laughed and held up
his hands. "Sorry, not, like, *chill* chill. I'm not saying we should
have sex. That's not what this is. Not that you're not—fuck.
Okay. I thought you might want something better to do than
go back to that hotel room. We could go to a bar."

He forced himself to stop talking because Landon's cheeks
had turned pink. He was clean-shaven and had very pale skin,
giving his blush nowhere to hide.

"Thank you," Landon said after a weird few seconds, "but
it's been a long day and I need to sleep."

Damn. "Cool," Casey said as cheerfully as he could manage. "Totally get that. Forgot that you woke up in Saskatchewan this morning. You're probably zonked. Did you get one
of those chicken parm subs?"

"No."

"Shit. You should have told me I would have made sure.
Unless you don't eat meat. Or dairy. Or bread."

"I eat all of those things," Landon said seriously. "I need to
eat a lot. Can't afford to be choosy."

Casey laughed. "I'll bet, Slenderman." He'd hoped the gentle
teasing would get a smile out of Landon. It didn't. "Hey, you
gonna be at the gym here tomorrow morning?"

"I was planning on it."

"Nice, yeah. I'll be here." Casey completely forgot where he was going with any of this, so he just smiled at Landon and hoped the other man would think of something to say.

"Okay," Landon said finally.

"Dope."

"I'll see you tomorrow, then."

"For sure. Have a good sleep. You can text me if you change your mind. I'll be up for a bit." *Jesus, Casey.* "That sounded wrong. I don't mean, like, 'u up?' I—" Casey pressed his lips together to stop any more words from spilling out.

Landon glanced away, clearly uncomfortable. "I get it. Goodnight." He turned and almost ran toward the exit. Casey couldn't blame him.

Well. Casey could do the responsible thing and go home. Alone. He really should try to go to bed early so he wasn't exhausted or hungover for his morning workout.

Decision made, Casey congratulated himself on his maturity, and strode toward the players' parking lot.

Casey regretted his decision to be responsible the minute he walked in his house. His large, dark, empty house.

He considered getting back in his Jeep and driving to one of his favorite bars. He considered the long list of reliable hookups he could send messages to. It was past eleven thirty on a Sunday night, but someone would be up for coming over, right?

Those would be the easy things to do. The things he always did. Last season, before he'd bought this house, he'd loved going home after games. Home had been a rented house shared with two teammates, Pete Leandros and Gio Rossi, and the evenings would be full of movies, video games, beer, weed, bars, and sex. Not with each other, though Casey wouldn't have been opposed to that. Gio and Petey both seemed pretty committed to heterosexuality, so Casey had never gone there.

He missed having roommates. His teammates knew he'd

happily share his house with any of them, no charge, but so far no one had taken him up on the offer. Casey got it. He knew he was kind of a lot.

He made his way to the kitchen, turning on every light as he went. He hated how his pulse kicked up when he was alone at night. How he couldn't help constantly checking over his shoulder, or how he studied every door suspiciously. How he couldn't look at the dark windows at all. It was beyond ridiculous, and there was absolutely no reason for it. Just his brain being stupid.

Why the fuck had he bought this house?

A loud clattering noise made him nearly jump out of his skin before he realized it was the ice maker in his fridge doing its thing. "Jesus. Chill out, Hicks," he muttered as he grabbed a glass from his cupboard. He shoved it under the ice dispenser to prove he wasn't afraid of it. It dropped two ice cubes, then made an angry whirring noise.

"Hunk of junk," Casey grumbled. Every appliance in his house was super high-tech and none of it worked right. He opened the fridge, grabbed a plastic bottle of lemonade and a silver container labeled *Sunday Night Snack*. He hoped it was cake but knew it wouldn't be.

He brought his glass of lemonade and his snack to the massive leather sectional sofa in his living room. He called out to the AI speaker thing to turn on the TV, and was ignored.

"Thanks," he said as he searched for the remote, eventually finding it at one end of the sofa under an unwashed sweatshirt. He made a show of turning on the TV, as if the AI unit could learn from watching him. If he had to be alone, he could at least pretend he wasn't.

He flipped through channels and ended up watching wrestling while he ate his snack (grain salad and two hardboiled eggs; disappointingly dissimilar to cake), vaped some weed, then watched a bit of one of the *Mission: Impossible* movies while he

idly scrolled through his favorite hookup apps. It didn't hurt
to *look*.

A text from his sister, Brooke, interrupted his careful consideration of a dude with a nice chest and two pierced nipples:
Sweet goal tonight.

Casey: made yr bf look like dogshit

**Brooke: He's not my boyfriend because SOMEONE won't in-
troduce me.**

Casey laughed. Brooke was hot for one of the L.A. defense-
men, but Casey was pretty sure the dude was engaged.

Casey: idk him just know how to deke around him

Brooke: Did Dad tell you about the Christmas plan?

Casey: yep. renting a cabin near Banff

Brooke: Lol. "Cabin." It's a fucking mansion. 8 bedrooms!

Casey: 2 for each of us!!!

Brooke: Nice math, college boy.

His family liked to roast him for being kind of stupid. It
didn't bother Casey because, well, he *was* kind of stupid. Not
about everything, but about a lot of things. His teammates
roasted him for the same thing, as had his friends in college,
so Casey owned it.

He and Brooke texted back and forth for a while until she
said she was going to bed. The weed had done a decent job
settling Casey's nerves, so he decided to try going to sleep too.

He left his food container and empty glass on the coffee table to be dealt with when the kitchen was less dark and creepy, and headed upstairs.

Tomorrow night he'd be in a hotel room in St. Louis, hopefully with someone hot he'd met at a bar. He wouldn't have to be alone in this house for almost a week.

He turned off the overhead light in his bedroom before he climbed into bed, leaving the lamp on his nightstand on, as always. He watched videos on his phone until he couldn't hold his eyes open anymore, then fell asleep hoping he didn't wake until morning.

Chapter Three

"Do you think that we're the closest thing to knights these days?" Casey wondered aloud. He basically wondered everything aloud.

Lee paused mid-abdominal crunch and stared up at Casey from the floor. "Knights? What the fuck are you talking about?"

"What is he *ever* talking about," Clint teased as he picked up a kettle ball.

"Like," Casey explained, "we wear armor kind of and fight for our cities. Kind of like kingdoms. I know it's not the same. It's not like there are dragons to kill anymore."

"Wait." Lee sat all the way up. "Did you just say *anymore*?"

Clint was laughing so hard he had to put the kettle bell down.

"Hey!" snapped West. "Is anyone spotting me right now or what?"

"Sorry," Casey said, and returned his focus to the man lying on the weight bench in front of him. The gym was busy that morning, even though it was an optional workout before their flight to St. Louis.

"You know that dragons never existed," Lee said slowly. "Right?"

"I'm spotting Westy right now!"

"Barely," West grumbled.

"I need to hear you say those words, Hicks."

"Yeah. Okay. Dragons aren't real."

"And were never real."

"Dinosaurs were real," Casey argued. "Those were basically the same."

Clint was howling as he staggered toward the bathroom. "I can't! Holy fuck."

"Didn't you go to *college*?" West asked.

"Yeah, but I wasn't learning about that stuff." Truthfully he hadn't learned much of anything beyond hockey skills during his two years of college, except that he really liked sex and didn't like tequila.

"What stuff?" Lee asked. His eyes were wide and almost fearful. *"Dragons?"*

"No, like...history?"

Lee fell back to the floor with his arms outstretched like he was dead.

"Aw, Casey," West said sadly, "even for you, this is bleak, dude."

"I was going to argue that we're more like gladiators than knights, but my brain just shut down for its own protection," Lee said.

Ross MacIsaac paused on his journey across the gym to stare down at Lee. "You okay, Captain?"

"Hicks thinks dragons are real."

Ross's brow furrowed. "Like, fire-breathing dragons?"

"I don't think dragons are real!" Casey was desperate for this conversation to be over. "I just thought...forget it. Fuck you guys."

Ross shrugged and walked away.

"Hey," West said, "if it isn't too much trouble could you help me rack this fucking barbell, Hicks?"

"Right. Sorry." He grabbed the barbell and eased it into the rack. He wasn't *embarrassed* exactly. After years of unintentionally saying stupid shit to basically everyone he met, he was more or less immune to embarrassment. He only wished he was better at keeping the random stuff in his head *in his head*.

West sat up and swung his legs to sit sideways on the bench. "You doing another set?"

"Uh," Casey said. His gaze had fallen on a treadmill in the corner of the room where Landon Stackhouse was running at an impressive clip. Landon stared straight ahead, stone-faced and focused, seemingly ignoring everyone around him.

He was wearing shorts, and his legs looked a mile long.

"Hicks?" West asked, breaking the hypnotic state Casey had been entering watching Landon run like he was punishing himself.

"I'm good," Casey said. "I'm gonna…" He walked away without finishing his sentence, and kept walking until he was standing next to Landon's treadmill. Landon didn't seem to notice him, or if he did, wasn't interested in turning his head to acknowledge him. That was fine since Casey had no idea why he was standing here.

He got on the stationary bike next to him, just to appear normal. Now he could see Landon's reflection in the mirror in front of them. He tried to meet his gaze, and offered a smile, but Landon kept staring straight ahead, lips pulled tight in a frown. It was intense—he wasn't even wearing earbuds.

Casey pedaled for a while, and did his best not to stare at Landon's reflection. He wasn't sure why he found the man so fascinating to look at. He was handsome, but most of the guys in the room were. Maybe it was simply the novelty of Landon being new. Of being someone who didn't know how stupid Casey was yet.

Landon didn't seem stupid at all. Casey would bet he read books for fun and kept up with the news and shit.

After about ten minutes, the pounding of Landon's sneakers slowed to a walk. He exhaled loudly, but he didn't seem as wiped as Casey would certainly be if he'd been running at that pace. Casey was in great shape, but distance running was definitely not his thing.

"Did you catch him?" Casey asked Landon's reflection.

"Catch him?"

"Whoever you were chasing. Running like that."

"Oh." He sniffed. "Funny."

Casey stopped pedaling and turned to face him. "You get some sleep? In the hotel?"

"Some."

"That's good. I sleep well in hotels usually. Not sure why." He knew exactly why: hotels were full of people, and the rooms weren't cavernous spaces full of dark corners. "Hey, you excited for your first NHL roadie?"

Landon stopped the treadmill. "Sure."

"Sweet. This one's not that cool, but the next big one we go to Vegas and that's always fun. You ever been to Vegas?"

"No."

"Oh, man, you'll love it. It's exactly like in all the movies. It's all lights and people and fun. It's awesome."

"I'll probably be back in Saskatoon by then."

Shit. "Yeah. Right. I guess probably." Casey wasn't sure why that made him feel sad. It's not like he was hoping Morin's injury was serious.

"I'm going to do my stretches," Landon said, then stepped off the treadmill.

"Of course. Yeah. Gotta keep that goalie body all bendy."

Landon's dark eyebrows pinched together. "Right." He began to walk away, then paused. He took a step toward Casey, then bent so their faces were close and quietly said, "Dragon lizards exist."

It took Casey a moment to realize Landon wasn't making fun of him. Then another moment to get over the shock of learning that Landon had been listening to the whole dragon conversation while seemingly being focused on destroying a treadmill.

Finally, Casey smiled and said, "Dragon lizards! Right! What are those?"

Landon's lips curved up slightly. "It's type of lizard. There are a bunch of different kinds. Like Komodo dragons and bearded dragons."

"Bearded dragon," Casey repeated as an image of a lizard with a Santa beard filled his head. "Dope."

Landon hovered for another moment, his big brown eyes locked on Casey's, then turned and walked away.

Chapter Four

Landon was trying really hard not to look like a total bumpkin, but he was probably failing.

Between the private plane, the fancy food that was served on the plane, and the luxurious hotel the team was staying at, Landon was a little overwhelmed. No long bus rides on icy highways, no stops at a Subway for dinner, no off-ramp-adjacent cheap motels. It had also been the first time Landon's legs had actually fit in front of his plane seat.

He could get used to this.

The roommate he'd been assigned, a second-year defenseman named West Ackerman, seemed less impressed. "None of the outlets have USB ports? Jesus, nice hotel, St. Louis."

Landon, who had never been to St. Louis in his life, turned from where he'd been staring out their twenty-fourth-floor window. "I brought a plug you can borrow."

"I have one," West said grumpily as he grabbed his backpack off the floor. "Somewhere."

West wasn't quite as tall as Landon, but was much broader with wide shoulders and huge muscles everywhere. His blond hair was short, and neatly styled, making him look like an all-American superhero. He was, in fact, American, which Landon decided to try as a conversation topic.

"Are you from...near here?"

West didn't look away from his backpack. "What? No, I'm from Hartford. Where the fuck is that plug?"

End of conversation.

Landon sat on his bed and stretched his legs out. It was a nice bed. Firm, and not creaky at all. On roadies with his usual team, Landon always roomed with the other goalie, Felix Lavoie. They had a good thing going because they were both quiet, had similar routines, and gave each other as much space as possible. When they did talk, it was mostly about goaltending and never got too personal. It was perfect.

Landon's phone lit up with a message, and it seemed West's phone did the same. Team group chat, then. Landon hadn't contributed to the Outlaws group chat yet, still mostly focusing on the Saskatoon Bandits one. Not that he had much to say in that one either.

Casey: whos in? The text was followed by a link to a local bar's website.

West huffed out a laugh. "That didn't take him long."

A new message popped up, from West: I'm in. But no shots this time.

Casey: totally chill. game tmrw

Lee: It BETTER be chill. I'm staying in, and I don't want any of you idiots to be hungover tomorrow.

More messages flooded in. Landon noticed that it was mostly the younger players who were agreeing to go out.

"This happens a lot?" Landon asked. "Hicks planning stuff?"

"Yeah," West said. "He's the social director for sure. Don't know why he bothers inviting anyone. He always finds someone to hook up with in like two minutes. Hicks lives a charmed fucking life."

"Does he?" Landon asked, even though obviously, yes.

"Are you kidding? He basically grew up in this league. His dad is a legend, and loaded. All of this—" West waved a hand around "—is, like, normal for Casey. Like it never occurred to him that he wouldn't play in the NHL."

"Right."

"He makes it hard to resent him, though. He's a good guy. Chatty as fuck, but fun. Small doses, y'know?"

Even after the short interactions Landon had had with Casey, he could tell the guy would probably get exhausting quickly. He also wasn't surprised Casey had no trouble finding people to hook up with. Not only was he pretty, he seemed to not even consider the fact that someone might not like him, which would make it a lot easier to shoot his shot.

Basically the opposite of Landon, who would rather die than attempt to chat someone up in a bar. He'd honestly have no idea what to do next if the person he'd managed to flirt with suggested they go have sex somewhere. Even imagining that scenario made his stomach hurt and his pulse speed up.

Landon typed out: I'm staying in.

He hesitated before hitting send, because did anyone even care if he went out or not? He sent the message and put his phone down on the bed beside him.

"You're not coming out?" West asked, eyebrows raised.

"Nah," Landon said, hoping he sounded relaxed and cool. Then something occurred to him. "Unless…did you want me out of the room? Are you planning to bring someone back here?"

"Don't worry about it. I've got a girlfriend. Though I may ask for an hour or two to FaceTime her one of these nights."

"Right. Got it. No problem." In Landon's experience, having a girlfriend or even a wife at home didn't necessarily mean hockey players weren't going to hook up with strangers on the road. If West really was faithful to his girlfriend, that would make this road trip a lot more comfortable for Landon.

"Found it!" West triumphantly held up his phone charger. "We've got two hours before dinner. Gio and Petey have a PlayStation set up in their room, if you wanna come check that out."

It was a nice offer, and Landon appreciated it but, "I think I might try to nap," he said. "Thanks, though."

"Okay. It's Room 2417 if you change your mind." With that, West left, phone and charger in hand.

Landon stood and went back to the window. The sun was low in the sky, the beginning of what looked like a beautiful sunset.

He thought about calling his mom. He brought up her number on his phone and hovered his thumb over it. He hadn't spoken to either of his parents in over a week, beyond a few texts, and he hated himself for that. In the past year or so, their conversations had been lighter, reminding him more of the way his family had been before tragedy had torn them to shreds, but he was still on edge whenever he spoke with them. Lately all he wanted to say was "I'm sorry" a million times, but not over the phone. Right now, he just wanted to hear their voices, and to attempt to convince them that he was thriving.

The sun was a lot lower by the time he finally called them. Mom answered right away. "Landon! Is everything okay?"

He winced. He really needed to call them more often. "I'm fine. I'm in St. Louis and just...wanted to call you."

Mom exhaled slowly. "It's nice to hear from you. We watched the first period of your game last night. Sorry we couldn't stay awake past that."

"It's fine. I wasn't playing anyway." Halifax was three hours ahead of Calgary, which made watching the games live difficult. Especially for people like his parents who had to be up early for work.

"They showed you, though. On the bench. You looked handsome."

Landon smiled wryly. "Well. That's the important thing."

An awkward silence fell between them, as it often did. They

stood in for all of Landon's unsaid apologies, all of the resentment he was sure his parents carried, and all of their mutual pain and grief.

"Oh!" Mom said. "Dad just got home. I'll put you on speakerphone."

"Okay."

A few seconds later, his dad said, "Hi, Landon. How's Calgary?"

"Good. I haven't seen much of it. Mostly the arena and the hotel."

"He's in St. Louis now," Mom said, in an impressed tone that made St. Louis sound like Paris.

"Did you see the big arch?" Dad asked.

"I saw it, yeah. It's hard to miss."

"Are they treating you well in the big leagues? Making friends? How about Niskanen? It must be hard to believe you're teammates with him!"

Landon huffed out a laugh at Dad's excitement. "It is. It's surreal. I think I'll be back in Saskatoon soon, but for now it's an experience for sure." He skipped over the question about making friends. He'd never been good at that, but they didn't need to know it.

"So you don't think you'll actually be playing in any Outlaws games?" Mom asked. Landon was sure he could hear relief in her voice. Or maybe he was imagining it.

"Probably not."

"Saw it was snowing in Calgary this morning," Dad said.

"Yeah. A bit."

"We haven't gotten any snow here yet."

"Oh. Soon probably." Landon tried to think of something—anything—interesting to say. "Going to Nashville next. Maybe I'll see some country stars."

"Erin would have been so jealous," Mom said. Another heavy silence fell between the three of them, then she gave a nervous little laugh and said, "Anyway. Nashville's exciting. Where else are you going?"

"Chicago. Then home. Calgary, I mean."

"We wish you were coming home," Dad said. "It would be nice to see you."

"I know. I miss you guys." In that moment, he really, really did. He barely ever spent time in Halifax anymore, which he knew was his own doing. He kept busy during the summers, training and taking part in goaltending clinics. He'd spent most of last summer in Minnesota.

He'd been selfish for so long now he didn't know how to stop.

"I should probably get going," he said, even though he had nowhere to be at all. He didn't like the way his heart was turning to lead. "I just wanted to say hi, and, um. Let you know I was okay."

"We appreciate it," Dad said. "Be safe. And have fun."

"We love you," Mom added.

"Love you too. Bye." He ended the call, then stared at the empty hotel room. After a moment, he turned the lights off, then sat on the edge of his bed to watch the sun set.

He dug his fingers into his knees and wished he had a goalie mask with him. He knew it was weird, but it settled him sometimes, wearing it.

What would Erin say, if she were here? Would she tease him for being weird? Would she quietly enjoy the sunset with him? Would she urge him to go to the bar with his teammates? It was hard to know, because he could only guess at the adult she would have become. He knew Erin wouldn't like seeing her younger brother being so mopey, especially after achieving his dream of playing (sort of) in the NHL. She'd always been the sunniest member of the family.

"You think I should go to the bar, don't you?" he said to her now. "I probably won't. Sorry."

Maybe he should go down to the room with the PlayStation

and pretend to be normal and fun for a bit. Or maybe he really should take that nap. He'd slept like shit last night.

His thoughts were interrupted by a loud knock on the door. He stood and went to open it, finding Casey Hicks on the other side. He was wearing black shorts, a T-shirt with a cartoon drawing of an anthropomorphic hot dog on it, and Adidas slides. His hair was loose around his shoulders and looked slightly damp. Landon was still wearing most of his suit from the plane.

"Hey, Stacks! Oh shit. Sorry. Were you asleep?"

Landon turned to look back at the dark hotel room. "No." He immediately wished he'd said "yes" because that would have made the dark hotel room less weird.

Casey didn't seem bothered by it. "Cool. So why aren't you coming out tonight?"

Landon blinked at him. He'd never had to explain his absence at team outings before. His teammates in Saskatoon never expected him to go out. He did, sometimes, when he felt like it, but his default mode was antisocial homebody.

"I don't know," is what he finally came up with for an answer.

"Dude. You are so coming out. Mind if I come in for a bit? I'm bored."

"Uh. Sure." Landon stepped back and turned on the lights. Casey glided in, immediately kicked off his slides, and threw himself onto West's bed.

"Where's Westy?"

"In the PlayStation room."

"That's cool. I'm banned from the PlayStation room."

"Why?"

"Because I suck at video games. And Gio says I'm distracting. And, okay, one time—" he held up a finger "—*once* I spilled a can of Coke on the PlayStation."

Landon could easily imagine all of that. "Ah."

"I bought him a new PlayStation. He needs to let it go. We

used to live together. Petey too. So. They probably got their fill of me."

Landon didn't reply, so Casey kept talking.

"We're still friends. I'm not saying we're not. We hang out all the time. Like, away from the rink I mean. Obviously we hang out all the time for hockey reasons. So what's your deal?"

Landon had not been expecting the question and had no answer ready. "My deal?"

Casey grinned. "Yeah. Where're you from? What are you into? You got a partner?"

Landon sat on his own bed, facing Casey. "I'm from Halifax. In Nova Scotia," he clarified.

"Sweet," Casey said. "Is that a cool place?"

"It's okay. I'd never lived anywhere else until I played junior, so I don't have a lot to compare it to."

"I lived all sorts of places," Casey said. "I was born in Toronto when Dad played there, so I'm technically Canadian, but I mostly grew up in Tampa. I did hockey camps and schools in Michigan and Wisconsin mostly, then ended up at Minnesota State for college. Then Calgary."

Landon nodded, trying to keep up.

"Question two now," Casey said. "What are you into?"

"Besides hockey?"

"Dude. Of course besides hockey."

Landon struggled for a moment to think of one single thing. "I like to cook."

Casey seemed to like that answer. He beamed and said, "Yeah? I fucking suck at cooking. What can you cook?"

"All sorts of stuff. I got into it after—" He paused, and redirected. "I like watching cooking shows and YouTube videos. It's relaxing."

"Do you read? You seem like someone who reads."

Landon huffed out a surprised laugh. "What does that mean?"

"You seem smart. I dunno. You knew about dragon lizards, which, by the way, I googled the shit out of and they are fucking rad. Though I was hoping the bearded dragon would have more of a beard. So you don't read?"

"I read," Landon said, somewhat defensively. "Sometimes. I prefer watching videos. I retain information better that way."

"Yeah, same. I'm shit at reading. Like, I *can* read, but it's so fucking boring. My mind wanders."

Landon hoped he wouldn't regret asking this. "What are you into?"

"Oh, shit. I don't know. Everything. Having fun, meeting people."

Well. The meeting people thing probably explained why Hicks was here. Not the having fun part, though.

"You know those videos where they show you how something is made in a factory?" Casey asked.

"I think so."

"Super into those right now. I watched one today where they showed how pool balls are made. Like, billiard balls. Not beach balls. It was fucking neat."

"Was it on YouTube?" Landon asked, not because he cared, but because it seemed like a friendly thing to ask.

"I don't remember. Somewhere. Mind if I turn on the TV?"

So he was staying, then. "Go ahead."

Casey flipped through the channels, landing on a show about ice road truckers. It kept him quiet for about a minute and a half, and then he said, "So. Partner?"

"Partner?"

"Yeah. Girlfriend, boyfriend." He waggled his eyebrows. "Both?"

Good grief. "No."

"Me neither. I'm just having fun, y'know?"

"Meeting people."

Casey grinned. "Yeah! You get it. No reason to tie myself down yet."

Since Casey was all of twenty-three years old, Landon agreed. As for himself, a romantic relationship wasn't something that was even on his radar and "Emotionally mangled weirdo with an intense work schedule" wasn't a great dating app profile.

"So the bar we're going to tonight is totally chill and fun. It's not a club or anything. More like a sports bar kind of? I always try to go there when we're in St. Louis."

"I'm going to try to get to bed early."

"Yeah, yeah. But come out for a bit. One drink. Or no drinks, if you want. Do you drink?"

"Sometimes. A bit."

"One drink. Get to know some of your teammates. We're totally nice. How's Westy treating you?"

"Fine. Seems cool."

"I love Westy. He can be a dick sometimes but he's just, y'know, focused. He wants to be a star. I think he will be."

Landon thought of a real question he could ask Casey, but he wasn't sure if it was rude or not. Finally, he just blurted it out. "Are any of the guys ever jealous of you, do you think?"

"Why? Because I'm hot?" Casey flashed another easy smile. "They should be."

Landon's ears felt hot. "Because of your dad, I meant."

Casey's face scrunched up as he considered the question. "Mm...yeah. Maybe. I get chirped about it on the ice a lot, but then I just take the puck and score a goal. Hard to give Dad credit for those."

Landon found himself suddenly very curious about what it would be like to have a celebrity father. He tried to come up with a coherent question, but Casey beat him to it.

"I don't even think my game is anything like Dad's. For one thing, he's like three inches taller, which sucks for me. Where the fuck did those genes go, right? He was way more physical. I'm fast."

"And creative," Landon added, because it was what Casey Hicks was best known for. Flashy, highlight-reel goals and passes.

Casey tapped the side of his own head. "Hockey IQ. I've got it. Good thing because I am fucking stupid besides hockey."

"You're not stupid," Landon said automatically, even though he hadn't been provided with a ton of evidence to support that. Still, he didn't like Casey putting himself down.

"Nah, it's fine. I know myself pretty well, and I am for sure not smart."

Landon wasn't sure how to argue with him, so he didn't. Instead he watched a commercial that reminded him the holiday season had begun. It wasn't, historically, his favorite time of year. If it were up to Landon, there wouldn't be a break in the hockey schedule for Christmas so he could avoid having three days with nothing to do but wallow in guilt and loneliness.

"You gonna change out of that suit for dinner?" Casey asked.

Landon welcomed the interruption to his misery spiral. He turned his gaze back to Casey. "I thought maybe we had to wear the suits to dinner?"

Casey laughed. "Fuck no. Wear whatever you want. It's like a buffet in a fucking conference room."

"Oh."

"Get changed. Wear something comfy. Or something slick for going to the bar later."

"I'm not—" Landon sighed, then stood and took one step toward his suitcase on the floor. "I really didn't pack any clothes for going out."

Casey studied him for a moment, his eyes raking up and down Landon's tall frame. Then he smiled and said, "Well, you can't borrow mine."

A breathy squeak escaped Landon's lips. He immediately covered his mouth and pretended to cough. It didn't work.

"Was that laughter? Is that what you sound like when you laugh?" Casey asked, clearly delighted. "Dude, that's cute."

"No!" Landon said, still squeaky. He took a breath. "No. Shut up."

"I hear that a lot. Never works."

Landon pressed his lips together.

"Seriously, though," Casey said, "just wear jeans or something. Did you pack jeans?"

Landon had packed most of the clothes he'd brought from Saskatoon to Calgary, which didn't amount to a whole lot. "I have one pair of jeans. Black ones."

"Perfect! Wear your tightest T-shirt and you're good."

Most of Landon's T-shirts were either branded with the Saskatoon Bandits or the Calgary Outlaws, and he may not have much game, but he knew wearing your team's gear to a bar was pretty weak. "I think I have a plain gray one."

Casey frowned.

"What?" Landon said flatly. "Sorry I didn't pack my fucking cartoon hot dog shirt."

It was probably too soon for Landon to reveal how bitchy he could be, but Casey cracked up. Actually curled into the fetal position on the bed laughing. It was alarming and kind of adorable.

"I like you, Stacks," he finally said. "You're hilarious."

No one had ever accused Landon of *that* before.

Casey stayed curled on his side on the bed and watched TV while Landon put together an outfit of sorts. Black skinny jeans, his high-top black sneakers, and a V-neck dark gray T-shirt that he normally only wore under other shirts. He examined himself in the full-length mirror beside the TV. He didn't look fashionable, but he didn't look like he was heading to the gym either.

"Damn, dude. Look at how hot you are!" Casey said.

Landon froze. "What?"

"You. Look hot. Those jeans look tailor-made. Were they tailor-made?"

Landon huffed. "None of my clothes are tailor-made. And I'm not trying to look hot. I just want to go to dinner without looking ridiculous."

"Sorry, Stacks. You're hot. Live with it."

Landon turned back to the mirror and tried to will away

the heat that was flooding his cheeks. Why was Casey saying any of this? Why was Casey even here? He was an all-star who surely had lots of friends on the team. Landon would be back in Saskatoon in a few days. There was no reason for them to get to know each other.

Was it possible that Casey Hicks was lonely?

Landon dismissed the idea immediately. Like Casey had said himself, he liked meeting new people. Landon was a novelty. Something a tiny bit interesting on an otherwise dull afternoon.

Casey hopped to his feet suddenly. "Well, I should get changed too. See you at dinner. You know where it is?"

"I'll find it." Landon assumed he could just follow everyone else.

"Cool. Hopefully the food is decent. And if it sucks we can eat at the bar later."

Landon was ninety-eight percent sure he wouldn't be going to the bar, but he nodded and watched Casey slip his feet back into his sandals.

"Later, Stacks."

And then he was gone, leaving Landon alone to wonder what the hell any of that had been about.

Chapter Five

Casey loved road trips.

A lot of the guys groaned about them—Casey's dad had complained about them all the time—but Casey usually enjoyed himself on the road. He liked visiting different cities, trying new restaurants and bars, meeting new people. He liked spotting the Calgary fans in every arena they went to. He liked days off in cities that were a little more exciting—or warmer—than Calgary in the winter. He liked nights out, and he liked hotel sex.

But most of all, he liked that he was never alone.

He didn't have a roommate anymore; that had ended after his second season. Most guys were psyched to get their own rooms, and Casey could definitely appreciate that the privacy was nice for *some things*, but most of the time he was lonely and bored.

Which was why he spent as little time alone in his room as possible. He visited his teammates' rooms, he organized outings, he invited people he'd just met back to his room for sex.

People like the woman who was in his hotel room right now. She was sitting on the edge of his bed, her back to him, finger-combing the mess that Casey had made of her long, strawberry-blond hair.

"You should stay," Casey said, meaning it. Tess was fun.

The sex had been great, and they'd laughed a lot. A perfect night, really.

"No way," she said with her adorable Georgia accent. "I'm not doing a walk of shame in the morning in front of all your teammates."

Her tone was teasing, but Casey knew she meant it. She'd told him she was new to St. Louis, starting a job. Casey couldn't remember what the job was because he hadn't really understood it when she'd explained it to him. Jobs like mailman and baker he could understand. Jobs like "data quality specialist" and "logistics and integration manager" were mysteries to him. But he genuinely listened to people when they talked about themselves, even if he didn't always understand what they were saying.

"I don't like that saying," Casey said. "Walk of shame. There's nothing to be ashamed of. Not if you had a good time." He propped himself up on an elbow. "You had a good time, right?"

She glanced at him over her shoulder and smiled. "I did."

"Because I can probably do better. Sometimes I need a practice run, y'know? Second time will rock your world. And the third time—"

"Oh my god." She laughed and tossed a pillow at him. "I can't stay. I was only supposed to have one drink at the bar tonight and go straight home. I have work in the morning."

"Boooo."

She leaned over, then kissed him. He sighed happily and deepened the kiss, hoping it might convince her to stay. Her arguments were valid, though. Being on time for a job you'd only started recently, and had moved to a whole new city for, was probably more important than another round of sex with a hockey player.

She broke the kiss, smiled a little sadly at him, and said, "You're cute. Sorry I have to go. Maybe next time you're in St. Louis you can DM me."

"For sure," Casey said, though he knew that would be next season sometime. It was still a nice offer.

She gathered her clothes from the floor and carried them to the bathroom. Casey fell back against the pillows and smiled at the ceiling. Road trips were awesome.

He hoped the guys he'd gone out with had all had good nights too. It had been a small group: only Gio, Westy, and Petey had gone. Landon hadn't come out. Casey had been disappointed, though he'd only been half expecting him to go. After dinner, Landon had claimed he was tired. Casey had texted him before they left for the bar, one more attempt at an invite, but Landon had replied with Staying in. Thx.

Casey had enjoyed talking to him, earlier in Landon's room. Maybe Landon had hated it. A lot of people found Casey annoying. He knew it. Except there had been that laugh. Or that sound that was close to a laugh. Casey needed to hear it again, to make sure it was as cute as he remembered.

Tess emerged from the bathroom, wearing the tight black pants and bright blue top that had caught Casey's eye in the bar. He hopped out of bed and went to grab his phone from the dresser across the room. "I'll get you a cab."

"Thanks," she said, then laughed. "It's always so weird after, when you're just, y'know, naked."

Casey looked down at himself. He was extremely used to being naked around other people for lots of reasons, but he decided to cover his crotch with one hand to be polite.

"So much better," she said, still laughing.

"Good thing I have huge hands," Casey joked. His dick was not big by anyone's measure, and he knew it.

"Mm."

"The car will be here in five minutes," Casey said. "I can walk you to the lobby, at least, if you give me a sec to—"

"No," she said, stepping close to him. "I'm fine on my own." She kissed him. "Thanks for a fun night. And good luck with your hockey game tomorrow."

"Aw, thanks." They'd established early on that she had no idea who he was and had never watched a hockey game in her life. Casey didn't mind that. The hero worship he got back in Calgary, and sometimes on the road, was nice too, but it was good to know people found him attractive for reasons other than his fame and money.

Tess left after one more kiss at the door. Casey turned on the overhead lights, then went to the bathroom to get cleaned up. He left the door open, and the fan off, and cleaned himself with a facecloth rather than taking a shower. He'd do that in the morning.

He left the bathroom light on, as well as his bedside lamp, when he was finally ready to sleep. He reminded himself that he was surrounded by his teammates, and that the only thing he had to be afraid of was how much Clint was going to complain in the morning about having to listen to Casey having sex.

When he felt brave enough, he turned off the lamp. The room was still lit by the bathroom, but shadows loomed everywhere.

"You're fine, Casey," he muttered to himself. "Grow the fuck up."

Casey didn't have many secrets, but he fiercely protected this one. He loved his teammates, but they would absolutely roast him if they knew he couldn't stand to be alone in the dark. To be alone at night at all, really. It was the sort of weakness that could be exploited for laughs. Casey had been around hockey long enough to know that sometimes a group of men who spent too much time together got bored. Sometimes they got mean. Sometimes they made bad decisions and hurt people.

Casey could withstand being teased, and maybe even being embarrassed, but he knew if his teammates ever did anything to really hurt him, the worst part wouldn't be the humiliation, or the disappointment. It would be the loneliness.

Chapter Six

"Morin is out," Coach Patrick announced before their first practice back in Calgary, five days later. "He'll be gone until January at least."

There were groans throughout the locker room, some frustrated, some sympathetic. Casey immediately looked across the room at Landon.

As usual, Landon's face gave nothing away. His mouth remained a tight, flat line, and his eyes were dark and attentive, though Casey guessed he must have a million things going through his head. Casey felt bad for Morin, but this was a big fucking deal for Landon. Two months was a long time. Two months could launch a career. It was different for goalies. Casey knew that. Landon may only get to start a couple of games in those two months; Antton was known for not needing many nights off. But still. This was huge.

As soon as Coach left the room, Casey crossed over to Landon and sat in Ross MacIsaac's abandoned stall next to him. "Sounds like you're sticking around," he said, then nudged Landon's arm.

"Yeah," Landon said quietly, staring straight ahead. "Sounds like it."

"That's cool. I mean, sucks about Morin, but good for you. I will warn you, it gets cold as fuck in Calgary in the winter."

Landon's gaze slid over to Casey. "Saskatoon isn't exactly tropical."

Casey laughed. "Right. Duh. So I don't have to tell you to get a good parka."

Landon didn't answer. He looked a million miles away.

During practice, Casey was distracted by thoughts of Landon being sad and alone in his hotel room for two months. Maybe he'd find a short-term rental somewhere, but he'd still be alone, and Casey sensed that Landon could use a friend. Somewhere between power play drills and a neutral zone transition drill, Casey was struck by a great idea. At least he was pretty sure it was a great idea. Sometimes he thought ideas were great and they turned out to be terrible, like the time he stirred peanut butter into his coffee.

He waited until practice was over, and then killed some more time messing around with a puck while Landon stayed in front of one of the nets, talking to the goalie coach, Andy. Finally Andy patted Landon on the shoulder and left the ice. Casey swooped in.

"I have an idea."

Landon's dark eyes fixed on him from behind the mask. "What?"

"Live with me."

"What?" Landon said again.

"You need somewhere to live, right? I have a whole huge house and you can have your pick of the guest rooms. I have a full gym and a sweet TV setup. It's a bit of a drive to the arena, but we can commute together and I can show you the city. There's a Thai restaurant near my house that is fucking delicious, and if you don't like Thai there's—"

Landon held up his blocker pad. "You don't need to do this. I'm sure I could find a short-term rental somewhere."

"Yeah, but why? You heard the part about the gym, right? It even has a treadmill you can destroy."

Landon was quiet for a long moment, and Casey braced himself for rejection. Then Landon said, "I like Thai food."

Casey beamed. "You can move in anytime. Today, if you want. You got much stuff? I can help."

"No, I barely had time to pack anything. I don't have my car either."

Casey waved a hand. "We'll be carpool buddies, and I've got a second car you can borrow if you need one."

"That's..." Landon appeared to be conflicted, which seemed ridiculous to Casey. Finally he said, "You really wouldn't mind?"

"Of course not!"

Landon's mask tipped down as he fixed his gaze on the ice. "I should warn you, I'm not a ton of fun."

"Dude, you're not there to entertain me."

"I can pay rent."

"Absolutely the fuck not." Casey almost wanted to tell him that he would benefit from this arrangement too. That having another person in the house every night would chill him out like a thousand percent. Instead he said, "The house is way too big for one person. You'd be doing me a favor."

Landon's eyes were skeptical when he glanced back up. "Doing you a favor how?"

Casey shrugged one shoulder. "By making me feel like less of a dick for buying such a big house. Now there's a reason for it."

"To house a temporary backup goalie you don't even know?"

Casey tapped Landon's left leg pad with his stick blade. "Yet. But I'm gonna get to know him, and it's gonna be awesome."

"Home sweet home," Casey announced as they pulled into his driveway.

Landon realized his mouth was hanging open, so he shut it. Casey had not been kidding about the size of his house. He hadn't even left the passenger seat of Casey's neon-blue Jeep and he was already in awe. The house was not only enormous, it looked very new and modern, all gray slate siding, dark wood, and glass.

Casey hopped out of the Jeep and ran around to the back, presumably to get Landon's bags for him. Landon snapped out of it and exited the vehicle.

"I'll get it," he said.

"No worries. It's not that much. You should see how many suitcases my parents travel with. You'd think my dad would be good at traveling light, but that man loves his outfit options."

Landon wouldn't mind having a few more outfit options. He needed to get to a mall ASAP. He grabbed his small carry-on suitcase because Casey was already carrying the larger, heavier duffel bag toward the front door. The duffel had been packed so haphazardly before Landon had left Saskatoon that he barely knew what was in it. He'd made sure to toss his "thinking" mask in there, his winter boots, his parka, a few odds and ends from around his apartment like hand cream and, embarrassingly, an Antton Niskanen hockey card that he'd thought he might ask him to sign. Back when he'd thought this would be a short trip.

The first thing Landon noticed when he stepped through Casey's front door was how *open* the house seemed to be. The entrance, living room, dining room, and kitchen all formed one giant space, and the second floor wrapped around it, mezzanine-style. You could see almost every room in the house from the front entrance. Landon briefly worried about the lack of privacy, then pushed the thought away. This offer was incredibly generous. As much as he cherished his alone time, he didn't want to spend two months in a hotel room.

Casey's house was a definite upgrade from the hotel room or from Landon's apartment in Saskatoon. Everything looked bright and new and *expensive*. The walls were all painted white, and the floors were a light-colored wood, all reflecting the abundant sunlight that streamed through the house's many large windows.

"Holy shit," Landon said.

"You like it? I just bought it in the summer, so it's new to me too. I still can't figure out half the fancy appliances. The kitchen is a mystery. Come on, I'll give you the tour."

Casey dropped the duffel bag by the door and started walking. Landon followed. "Consider this your house, okay? Go wherever you want, use whatever you want. You don't have to ask. So this is the living room. The TV is kind of complicated, but the picture and sound are amazing. I've got full cable, all the movie channels and sports channels." He started counting off on his fingers. "Netflix, Disney, Prime, all that shit. There's a PlayStation and a Switch too. You like video games?"

"Sure," Landon said, even though they'd never been his thing.

"Cool. Maybe we can play later."

The large sectional sofa was littered with objects: a hoodie, a massage gun, a PlayStation controller, a pair of sunglasses and, most confusingly, three oranges. There was a dirty glass on the coffee table, and a pair of sneakers on the floor underneath.

Landon followed Casey to the kitchen, which was like the ones he'd always dreamed about, with a Viking gas range, a huge butcher block-topped island, and a farmhouse sink.

"Full disclosure," Casey said, "I don't cook. I've used that stove, like, once and it was to burn some eggs. So. Go nuts in here, I guess. If you want." He opened the fridge, revealing stacks of small boxes and containers, all labeled. "I get my food delivered by a service that caters to athletes. It's, like, tailored to my body or whatever, but I can ask them to send double of everything."

That sounded expensive as hell. "No, it's fine. I can get my own food."

"Good call. This food is kind of gross, not gonna lie. Healthy, though. And easy." He closed the fridge door and pointed to the touch screen on the front. "This screen does stuff but I don't know what. I mean, it's a fridge. It keeps my food cold. I don't need it to do more than that, right? Oh, and the ice maker is fucked. Good luck with it."

He started opening cupboard doors. Some had dishes, some were empty. "There's...stuff up here. And down below. My mom bought all of it. She was optimistic about what I was gonna do in here, I think. There's a bunch of things that I have no clue what to do with. There's a pantry over here." He opened two double doors that ran almost floor to ceiling. It was packed with food. "Help yourself."

"I'll buy groceries," Landon said quickly. "I won't eat your food."

"You can if you want, but I'm not gonna eat all this myself."

Landon wanted to ask why he had it all, then, but it seemed rude.

"There's a coffee maker," Casey said, slipping past Landon to one corner of the countertop. "I actually managed to figure this one out. Coffee is next to it. Oh, and in here—" he grabbed a yellow canister from the back of the counter "—are edibles." He opened the canister and pulled out various silver bags, holding them up for Landon to see. "Different levels of THC, different highs. Ask me if you want a recommendation. I've got oil and, y'know, regular weed too."

Landon wasn't sure how he'd gone from being an undrafted goaltender living in a small apartment in Saskatoon to being offered weed in Casey Hicks's home in a few short days. But he knew better than most how quickly life could change. "I don't usually. Very often," he said. "But thanks. Some of my teammates use it for pain, or as a sleep aid. Do you find it good for that?"

Casey grinned. "Yeah. It's also good for getting me really fucking high."

Landon felt like such a dork, and he felt even dorkier when a nervous laugh escaped him.

"Aw, it's my favorite laugh again," Casey said.

"Shut up." Landon turned his face away, to hide his blush.

"For real, though, I find it's good for, like, postgame adrenaline. Helps me sleep for sure. Here, I'll show you the rest of the house."

Casey took him to the basement first, showing Landon the impressive gym he'd set up down there, including the promised treadmill. The gym was also a trophy room, displaying Casey's own memorabilia and awards, like his Rookie of the Year trophy, his Team USA jersey from the World Junior Championships, and his gold medal from the same tournament. Some of Casey's father's jerseys hung on the wall as well, along with photos commemorating some of his accomplishments, like his two Stanley Cup wins with Tampa.

Landon had his AHL Goaltender of the Month plaque sitting on his dresser back in Saskatoon.

Adjacent to the gym was a full bathroom (one of five bathrooms in the house, Casey explained) and a large bedroom (one of four). "I don't think anyone has ever slept in here," Casey said. "It's, like, the dungeon guest room."

They went up to the top floor and Landon peeked inside the other three bedrooms. Each had their own bathroom and was large enough to be the main bedroom, but Landon could tell which room was Casey's by the unmade bed and the clothes strewn around the floor.

"The cleaners come tomorrow," Casey said, a bit sheepishly. "They come once a week, so you don't have to worry about chores."

Landon was starting to get the picture that Casey didn't have to worry about *anything*.

They ended the tour downstairs, on the enormous deck that looked over the fenced backyard. It had a barbecue, lots of outdoor seating, and looked perfect for parties, if the weather was warmer.

"I might get a pool," Casey said, "but I dunno. I travel a lot in the summer, and a pool is kinda pointless here the rest of the year."

"Right," Landon said distantly. What would it be like to live like this? What would it be like to give his parents a house like this? Or even one half this nice? He would be earning more money for however long he stayed in Calgary than he did back in the AHL, but nothing like what Casey earned.

Landon was generally frugal. He knew it wouldn't take much for his hockey career to be over, and then even the AHL salary would disappear. An injury, a bad season, or even just a better goalie showing up in Saskatoon could end it all.

He knew Casey's career could be ended suddenly too, but earning eight million dollars a year probably helped alleviate some of the stress around that. Having rich parents probably helped too.

"So," Casey said when they were back in the living room, "which room do you want?"

Landon didn't hesitate. "The basement one. If that's all right."

For the first time since Landon met him, Casey's face fell. He quickly covered it with an unconvincing smile. "Sure. Yeah. That's cool. You sure, though? There's way more light upstairs, and the rooms are nicer, I think."

"I like to be alone," Landon said, then mentally slapped himself and added, "I just mean that I can be...weird. To live with. I think it's better if I give you as much space as possible."

"I don't mind you upstairs with me, but I get it. Privacy and all that."

He sounded so dejected, which Landon couldn't understand. Why would he want Landon any closer than he needed to be?

"Well," Casey said with an enormous amount of forced cheerfulness, "let's get your stuff into your room."

He went to retrieve Landon's suitcase and duffel from where they had been left by the front door. Landon quickly took the duffel from him and followed him down the stairs. He felt that he had already made things awkward between them, which had to be a new record even for Landon.

★ ★ ★

Casey tried not to be disappointed that Landon had chosen the basement room, or that he'd mostly stayed in the basement since he'd moved in that afternoon. It was obvious that Landon was a private person, and he probably just wanted a quiet room to relax in after a hectic week. It made sense.

But he needed to eat.

Casey was about to go downstairs to check on him, but he stopped himself and sent a text instead, asking if Landon wanted to order a pizza.

Landon emerged from the basement a moment later, barefoot and wearing sweatpants and his dark gray T-shirt. His short brown hair was a mess.

"Were you asleep?" Casey asked.

"I was awake when you texted, but yeah. I conked out. That's a comfortable bed."

Casey smiled, even though he'd been hoping the basement bed was horrible and that Landon would choose a different room.

They ordered pizza from Casey's favorite place, and he'd waved away Landon's offer to pay. They ate on the couch, because that's where Casey ate most of his meals, and watched the second half of an action movie. Casey probably talked too much during the movie, while Landon quietly consumed half of a large pizza. He'd apparently not been kidding about eating a lot.

When the movie ended, Landon began cleaning up, taking the mostly empty pizza box to the kitchen along with their dirty glasses. Landon had seemed surprised when Casey had offered him lemonade, but one thing he was going to learn really fast by living here was that Casey fucking loved lemonade.

"There's a dishwasher," Casey said as he followed Landon. "It's hidden really well, but here." He pulled on the handle of a square panel that matched his wooden cupboards, revealing the dishwasher behind it. "I swear to god I didn't know I had a dishwasher for the whole first month I lived here."

"Yeah," Landon said. "That's...fancy."

When the mess was cleaned up—far more thoroughly than if Casey had been alone—Casey said, "So. You wanna do something?"

Landon's anxiety was immediate and obvious. "Like what? We've got practice in the morning."

"Yeah, yeah. I didn't mean hit the clubs. We could play video games, or watch another movie. I swear I'll try not to talk through the whole thing."

"I um. I think I might hang out in the gym downstairs, if that's all right. I need to do my stretches, and maybe get some meditation in before bed."

"Meditation," Casey repeated. "Cool. You do that a lot?"

"I try to."

"I am so fucking bad at it. Maybe you could give me some tips sometime."

Landon was already edging toward the basement stairs. "Maybe."

"If you change your mind, I'll be chilling on the couch for a while." Casey realized he was starting to sound desperate. "Or whatever. I'll see you tomorrow, okay?"

"Okay." Landon sounded relieved. "Goodnight."

"Goodnight, Stacks."

Landon hurried down the stairs, and Casey felt exactly as alone as he had last night.

Chapter Seven

"Heard you tricked poor Stackhouse into living with you," Clint quipped during a hydration break at practice.

"Hey." Lee sternly pointed his water bottle at Clint. "That was a nice thing Hicks did."

"Yeah," Casey said. "I didn't *trick him*."

"I know, buddy," Clint said. "It was nice of you. I'm just being a dick. How's it working out? He seems quiet."

Casey gazed down the ice to where Landon was talking to the goalie coach. His mask was flipped up, showing off his sharp jawline and serious expression. "He's not super chatty, but he's cool. I like him."

"I remember when I was called up," Clint said. "I was fucking terrified. Fitzy let me live with him until I found my own place. Remember that guy?"

Lee nodded and Casey didn't because he was far younger than either of them.

"Made a big difference," Clint continued. "Made me feel like less of an outsider, driving to practices and stuff with him. So, yeah. Good on you for helping Stackhouse out."

Casey's heart swelled at the praise. "It's nothing. I have plenty of room, y'know?"

Lee laughed. "Yeah, no shit. Your house is bigger than mine and I've got two kids."

"I probably should have bought something smaller," Casey agreed. "But Dad said it was a good investment, and I dunno. It's a nice house."

"If Dougie Hicks wants to give me investment advice, I'm all ears," Clint said.

"Yeah, same," Lee said. "I know Ross has a buddy who's looking for investors for his business. Ross is talking it up like it's the next Amazon, but I dunno."

"I can tell you right now that Dad's advice would be to not invest in anything your buddies think is a sure thing. He taught me that early." Dougie Hicks was nearly as famous among hockey players for being smart with his money as he was for his legendary hockey career. His intelligence was the other thing, besides his height, that Casey hadn't inherited.

Coach Patrick blew his whistle and announced that they were going to end the practice with breakaway drills. Some of the guys cheered because breakaway drills were fun.

Lee put his gloves back on and tilted his head in Landon's direction. "Let's see what your boy's got."

Casey had suspected, during previous practice drills, that Landon might be a decent goalie, but during the breakaway drill he decided he was better than decent; Landon was really fucking good.

"Jesus Christ," Clint bellowed after being denied by Landon for the third time. "You can retire, Nisk. We don't need you anymore."

"Good," Antton said from where he was standing by the boards. "I'm sick of you assholes."

Casey felt...proud. He knew he had no right to—he barely knew Landon—but he was definitely rooting for him. When it was his turn to shoot, he decided to try out a tricky move that he'd managed to beat Antton with once.

Landon stopped him cold.

That really got the boys hollering. Everyone was having fun now.

"I thought we were friends," Casey teased as he bumped his glove against Landon's blocker pad.

Behind the mask, Casey saw the faintest suggestion of a smile.

Casey watched from the centerline as Landon stopped shot after shot, never with more movement than was necessary. Anyone who knew hockey could tell he based his style on Antton Niskanen. It was kind of cute. And impressive.

When it was Antton's turn to go in the net, Casey met Landon by the boards. "So, no big deal, but you just fucking destroyed this whole team."

Landon flipped his mask up. "As if."

"Seriously, dude. That was sexy."

Landon's gaze dropped to the ice, and he shuffled his skates. "Thanks. I guess."

"You want Thai food tonight?"

Landon glanced over at him. His brow was pinched, as if he'd forgotten that they lived together now. "Sure. Sounds good."

"Cool."

"But, um," Landon said, "my treat, okay?"

"Aw, you don't have to—"

"Please."

Casey could tell this meant a lot to Landon, so he nodded. "Okay. Thanks."

"And could we stop at a grocery store? Or maybe a Walmart? I need some things."

Casey laughed, because Landon needed more than a few things. "I've got an even better idea. Where's Nosey?"

What was supposed to be a quick stop into a store for Landon to get a few groceries and some extra socks and underwear ended up being a group outing to Costco after practice. Apparently Clint Noseworthy had a membership and loved any excuse to go there.

"Why is this place exciting?" Landon asked as he pushed a very large shopping cart down a very wide aisle.

"Dude, look at how huge it is. It has everything," Casey said with his arms spread wide.

"And it has free food samples," Pete Leandros said. "Have you never been to a Costco before?"

"Once or twice."

"Oh fuck yes," Clint said, and then dumped a giant Nerf gun set into his cart. "For my kids. For Christmas," he explained.

"Sure," said Pete.

In total, there were six of them: Landon, Casey, Clint, Pete, Gio, and West. Landon noticed they were getting a few stares from other shoppers, but so far no one had approached them for autographs.

"So what do you need?" Casey asked.

"Clothes, mostly," Landon said.

Casey wrinkled his nose. "This is not the place."

"Are you kidding?" Clint said. "This place rules for clothes. Cheap, functional, totally nice stuff."

"If you want to dress like a divorced lumberjack," Casey chirped. Gio, Petey, and West laughed, and even Landon smiled because Clint was currently wearing sweatpants, a plaid shirt unbuttoned over a T-shirt with the Caterpillar logo on it, and a mesh ball cap.

"Eat shit, Hicks," Clint said.

"I just need some basics," Landon said. "I'm sure I'll find something here."

In no time at all, the cart he was sharing with Casey was full. Some of it was the clothing and groceries Landon had grabbed, but most of it was a random assortment of whatever had caught Casey's eye, including a bunch of Christmas decorations.

"I need them," Casey argued. "My house doesn't have any. It's sad. Ask Nosey, he's the Christmas king."

Clint grunted in agreement from where he was carefully considering a pair of heated work gloves.

"It's true," Gio said. "His house looks like Santa's fucking workshop."

"I have kids," Clint argued. "When you guys are adults, you'll understand."

"I'm not even getting that much stuff," Casey said. "Whoa! What's a hot chocolate bomb and why does that sound amazing?"

"It's just chocolate that melts into hot milk," Landon said. "To make hot chocolate."

"I gotta see that!" Casey said, and tossed the package of—good grief—eighteen hot chocolate bombs into the cart.

Landon needed to get back on track. "Does this place sell deodorant and stuff?"

"It sells *everything*."

They followed the other guys into one of the snack food aisles. West was video calling his girlfriend. "Babe, what are the nuts that I like?"

Gio, Pete, Clint, and Casey cracked up.

"Oh god, West," said the voice on the phone. "Did you just ask that in front of your teammates?"

West scowled at all of them. "Forget them. Was it the macadamia ones, or the hazelnuts? They're both round."

"Hi, Allison," Casey called out.

"Hi, Casey," the woman sighed. "Please be nice to my boyfriend."

"I'm always nice. And we need closure on this nut situation."

"Macadamia," Allison said. "And get some olive oil while you're there."

"Okay, I love you," West said, and it was obvious from the way he was smiling at his phone that he really meant it.

"Allison is rad," Casey told Landon. "Clint's wife, Theresa, is super cool too. You'll meet all the wives and girlfriends at the team Christmas party."

"When's that?"

"I forget. Nosey's hosting it. Hey, Nosey, when's the Christmas party?"

"You weren't supposed to know about it," Clint chirped.

"Fine. Then I won't give you the gift I got you."

"Is it hot chocolate bombs?"

"Maybe. If I don't like them."

"The party is December 17. And that's firm because it was a whole thing arranging for the kids to stay with Theresa's parents that weekend."

"Shit, that's soon," Casey said. "What's the theme? We doing ugly sweaters? Semiformal?"

"I literally don't care," Clint said.

"Please not formal," Gio groaned.

"The theme is getting drunk at Nosey's house," Petey said.

"Fucking right," West agreed as he tossed three bags of macadamia nuts into his cart.

A team Christmas party sounded like a great place for Landon to be very, very awkward. He was already dreading it.

In the pharmacy section, Landon got deodorant, Advil, and probably more dental floss than he would ever use in his life. He was considering several gallons of mouthwash when he noticed Casey dump an enormous box of condoms into the cart.

"Holy shit," Landon blurted out.

"It's a good deal," Casey said enthusiastically. "You should get some! Unless you need a special size, which maybe you do since..."

Landon managed to not drop the mouthwash, thus preventing a flood. "What—what are you talking about?"

Casey leaned into him and dropped his voice. "I wasn't, like, *looking*, but I caught a glimpse in the locker room and, y'know. Damn, Stacks."

Landon felt hot everywhere. "It's not that big."

Casey grinned. "I've seen a few dicks in my day, pal. That's a doozy you've got there."

It's not like Landon didn't *know*. Yes, fine, he seemed to be a little larger than average, but he was also taller than average, and had longer arms and bigger hands than average. Having a dick on the large side made sense, but unlike his other attributes, it didn't improve his ability to stop pucks, so he didn't care much about it.

"It's a normal size," he mumbled.

"Sure. So do you want me to grab you a box?"

"No." Landon certainly didn't need five thousand condoms, or however many were in that crate. "I'm good."

"Okay. If you ever need to borrow one, let me know. Or, not borrow. I don't want it back after. You can keep it." Casey laughed. "That would be really weird."

Everything about this conversation was really weird, so Landon changed the subject. "Do you usually go home for Christmas? To see your parents?"

"They usually come to me. Mom and Dad rented a cabin near Banff this year, so we'll all go there. My sister, Brooke, will be there too. She's in L.A., so we don't see each other all that much. That doesn't stop her from having tons of opinions about my life, though. Big sisters, right? What are you gonna do?"

Landon tightened his grip on the shopping cart. "Right."

"So yeah, it's always fun to hang with the whole family at Christmas. Hey! You should come too!"

"To your…family Christmas?"

"Totally! There's lots of room. You can meet my folks and Brooke and my grandma! She's my dad's mom. Grandpa died a few years ago, which was awful. My other grandparents do Christmas with my mom's brother, which is fine because all of those people are dicks. Anyway, you should come to the cabin."

"It, um. Maybe it's a bit early to be inviting me to your family's Christmas," Landon said carefully.

"Why?"

"I just moved in yesterday. And maybe your parents don't want some random guy at their Christmas holiday."

Casey waved a hand. "Of course they will. And you're not random. Holy, look at the size of that bottle of Tums!"

Landon felt like he could use that entire bottle of Tums right now. "I'll think about it," he said, because it was an easy way to back out of this invitation. Casey would probably forget about it anyway.

"There you guys are," West said as he came around a corner. Gio and Pete were behind him. "I think Nosey wants to leave and he's the one with the membership, so."

"I'm done," Landon said, embarrassed that he'd been holding Clint up.

"Wait," Casey said, pointing at West's cart. "Where did you get those cookies?"

"In the automotive department," West said. "Where the fuck do you think?"

"I want some."

"No, come on," Landon said. "Clint is waiting."

"You're no fun."

"I did warn you about that."

Casey smiled at him. "I'm just kidding. You're rad. And I can steal one of Westy's cookies."

"The fuck you can," West said.

Landon shook his head and pushed the cart purposefully in the direction of the checkout area.

Oh hell yes. Casey's living room was looking festive as fuck.

"Check it out," he called to Landon. "Looks like Christmas Town over here."

Landon was sitting at the island in the kitchen, eating the last of the Thai food they'd ordered. "Nice," he said. "What's holding those lights up?"

Casey looked at the multicolor lights that he'd outlined the living room window in. "Just, like, tape." It would probably hold, right? How else did people do it?

He'd also lined the floating shelf under the television with a fake evergreen garland and more lights, and rested a Santa-shaped pillow on the sofa.

"Hey, maybe we should get a tree!"

"You're not even going to be here for Christmas," Landon pointed out.

"Yeah, but there could still be a tree."

Landon didn't answer. He was looking at his phone while chewing another mouthful of food.

"Since you're all napped up," Casey said, "wanna do something?"

Landon stared at him, swallowed, and said, "You don't rest much, do you?"

Casey smiled. "Not much, no. And we could just watch something. Unless you feel like going out. I'm up for whatever."

Landon glanced down at the plaid pajama pants and Saskatoon Bandits T-shirt he was still wearing after his post-Costco nap. "I'm gonna stay in."

"That's cool. I'm down with that."

Landon stood and began carrying the empty take-out containers to the sink. He sprayed them off, then neatly stacked them.

"I usually just throw those out," Casey said.

"Oh. You can reuse them."

"Reuse them for what?"

"Putting food in. Like, leftovers and stuff."

"But I get new containers every time I order food, so the leftovers just go in there."

"I meant if you cook something." Landon seemed to realize what he'd just said. "Well. I'll use them."

"Sure." Casey still didn't quite understand, but whatever made Landon happy.

Landon crossed to the living room and leaned on the back of the sofa. "You can go out if you want. You don't have to, like, entertain me."

"What do you mean?"

"You've been hanging out with me all day. And last night. You probably have lots of friends, and I know I'm not super fun."

"I like hanging out with you," Casey said, which was absolutely true. Landon wasn't wrong about not being a ton of fun, but Casey still enjoyed being around him.

Landon's dark eyebrows shot up. "Why?"

"Jeez, what a question. I don't know, I just do."

Landon seemed to consider this, then said, "Okay. But if you want to go out—"

"I don't. I want to watch dumb shit on TV with you," Casey said quickly.

Landon's lips curved up on one side. "Watch any good factory videos lately?"

Casey grinned. "Oh, buddy. Have you ever seen how a marble is made? Buckle up."

Chapter Eight

Casey slammed the door as he got to the bench. "Fucking Hoffman!" he yelled. At least Landon was pretty sure that's what he yelled. He was sitting at the opposite end of the bench from Casey, and the Calgary crowd was very loud.

It was only the second period, but Landon already understood why Casey didn't like Tristan Hoffman. The Vancouver forward had been antagonizing Casey all night, even drawing a bullshit penalty on Casey by taking what anyone could see was a dive.

Anyone but the refs, apparently.

A minute ago he'd very obviously crosschecked Casey's shoulder, and had somehow gotten away with it.

"Nosey's going to end Hoffman's life," West said. He was sitting next to Landon.

"I think Casey might do it himself," Landon said.

West spat, then said, "Nosey won't let him. Lee either. Casey is shit at fighting."

Landon hoped West was right; he didn't want to see Casey get hurt.

The score was 2-1 for Calgary, and the game hadn't turned into a brawl like the last time the two teams had met, but it didn't seem like an impossibility either.

West went out for his shift, and Ross MacIsaac replaced him

on the bench. "This game is a fucking powder keg," Ross said as he grabbed a water bottle.

"Seems like it."

"I barely ever played against Vancouver when I was with Toronto. Were they always this goony?"

Landon huffed. "You're asking me?"

Ross smiled. "Right. I can't believe we've gotta play these assholes again on Sunday. The ice is gonna be soaked in blo— Hey! What the fuck, ref! Is slashing not a penalty anymore or what?"

A few shifts later, all hell broke loose. Hoffman whacked Casey in the back of his ankle with his stick blade, and Casey lost it.

"Oh shit," West said. He was back on the bench beside Landon, but stood up when Casey got in Hoffman's face. "Don't do it, Case."

Landon was frozen in place by a weird numbing blend of horror and fascination. Was Casey seriously going to drop the gloves and fight this guy?

Yes. Yes, he apparently was.

Casey's gloves hit the ice and Hoffman didn't have a chance to even be surprised before Casey had grabbed him and started swinging. The crowd went bananas. In seconds both men were on the ice, Casey unfortunately under Hoffman.

Landon's heart was in his throat. He couldn't see any part of Casey except for his legs, but he could see Hoffman's right fist rising in the air and landing in the vicinity of Casey's face.

The refs broke it up quickly, likely knowing that Casey had no business trying to fight this guy. Landon finally regained control of his body and stood to get a better view of Casey. God, was he okay?

Hoffman was hauled away, still yelling at Casey over his shoulder. Casey hopped to his feet immediately, to Landon's relief. Casey's mouth was bloody, but he grinned all the way to the bench as the crowd cheered him on.

Everyone on the bench was cheering him on too, bang-ing their sticks on the boards in the traditional hockey player version of applause. Landon didn't have a stick to bang, so he half-heartedly rapped his glove against the top of the boards as he watched Casey go down the tunnel for medical attention.

West's heart didn't seem to be in it either. "That was really fucking stupid, Hicks," he muttered, and Landon decided that he liked West a lot.

"That was really fucking stupid," Landon said later, because he hadn't thought of a way to improve on what West had said.

"He deserved it," Casey said, though it came out a bit muffled because his lip was swollen. He was in the passenger seat and Landon was driving because Casey's knuckles were also swollen.

"Maybe," Landon conceded, "but you're not the guy for the job."

"I can fight my own battles," Casey snapped. It was the angriest Landon had ever heard him. "I'm not useless."

"No shit. That's exactly why you shouldn't fight. You're important."

"Aw."

"To the team, I meant."

"Whatever. Maybe he'll stop bothering me now."

"I doubt it. He kind of won the fight. Don't know if you noticed."

Casey was silent for about ten seconds, then he mumbled, "I got some good shots in."

"I know. That's why you can't drive right now. How's your head?"

"Hurts a bit. It's fine, though. They checked me for concussion."

Landon pressed his lips together.

"You've never fought anyone?" Casey pressed. "Come on. I'll bet you have."

"I've shoved guys a bit. I've never dropped the gloves and mask and gotten in a real fight."

"I recommend it. Makes you feel alive."

Landon huffed. "Except he nearly killed you."

"He wishes. Take a left up here."

They were silent for the rest of the drive, which was good because Casey ought to be resting his mouth. When they got in the house, Landon went straight to the freezer and grabbed an ice pack. "Go to the sofa," he instructed. He had no idea where this need to take care of Casey was coming from, but he couldn't stop himself.

Casey let out a groan as he stretched himself out on the sofa. "Fuck, okay. Everything hurts."

Landon sat on the coffee table and faced Casey. He could have just handed him the ice pack, but instead he said, "Let me see your hand."

Casey held out his right hand, which was definitely in worse shape than his left. Landon held it carefully, letting it rest in the cradle of his own palm, then gently pressed the ice pack to Casey's knuckles.

Casey hissed.

"Serves you right," Landon said.

"You're a shitty nurse."

"You're a garbage patient."

Casey laughed, and then moaned. "My mouth hurts when I smile."

"Good thing I'm not funny."

"Ow. Stop making me laugh."

Landon glanced away from the ice pack, and when his gaze met the softness in Casey's eyes, he suddenly became very aware that he was holding Casey's hand. He fought the urge to pull away.

"Why are your hands so soft?" Casey asked, which only made things weirder.

"I moisturize," Landon muttered. "Here." He guided Casey's hand onto the sofa and rested the ice pack on top. "You want to watch something?"

"Yeah. Okay. And could you get me some lemonade? With a straw? And an edible?"

Landon frowned. "What painkillers did they give you already?"

"Nothing. Just some ibuprofen, I swear."

"Fine." Landon turned on the TV and found the Discovery Channel after some helpful guidance from Casey because the remote really was confusing. He left Casey watching a show about competitive Christmas decorating and went to the kitchen.

"Do you even have straws?" he called out as he poured a glass of lemonade.

"Yeah. In one of the drawers."

Landon began opening drawers. In the sixth one, he found a battered package of plastic straws next to way too many packages of cocktail umbrellas. He brought Casey's drink and the canister of cannabis gummies to the living room.

"Which one do you want?" Landon said after he opened the canister. He held up one of the packages.

"No," Casey said.

Landon held up three more before Casey said yes. "You should have one too," Casey offered. "These ones are super mild."

"I'm okay," Landon said automatically. Then, realizing that he could already tell he'd be fighting insomnia tonight, said, "Actually, sure. Okay."

They ended up watching TV together for over two hours. Landon had made himself a sandwich during one of the commercial breaks and refilled Casey's lemonade glass. He'd offered to switch the ice pack for a fresh one, but Casey insisted he was okay.

A show about Alaska came on, and Landon said, "We should go to bed." He felt relaxed and heavy, like he could sleep for a week and only have good dreams.

"Probably," Casey said. His eyelids were drooping.

"Flying to Seattle tomorrow."

"Mm. Short flight." Casey curled onto his side, tucking

his knees up. Even with the split lip and bruised knuckles, he looked adorable.

"I've never been to Seattle."

"It's like Vancouver but..." Casey yawned and his eyes closed. "More."

"More what?"

"More Vancouver."

Landon laughed. "That doesn't make sense."

Casey smiled. "You laughed." Then he grimaced. "Ow."

Landon let himself look at him for probably longer than he should. He was oddly fascinated by the inch of exposed ankle between Casey's sock and the cuff of his sweatpants.

"Do you want me to just throw a blanket on you?" Landon asked. "You can sleep here."

"No," Casey mumbled. "Can't sleep here."

"Seems like you can."

Casey opened his eyes and sat up surprisingly quickly. "I can't. I need to...you're not gonna sleep here too, are you?"

"No. Why would I?"

Casey glanced at the window he'd decorated yesterday, then at Landon. "I'll go to my room."

The way he was staring at him made Landon think Casey was going to invite him along. Landon didn't want that, obviously, but he still asked, "Do you need help getting up there?"

Casey got to his feet. "Nope! I'm good. Goodnight, Stacks."

Landon stood too. "Goodnight." He turned off the TV as Casey headed toward the stairs.

"Hey," Casey said from the bottom stair. "You were a good nurse. Not shitty at all. And, um, it would have sucked to be alone tonight. So thanks."

Warmth bloomed in Landon's chest. "No problem."

Casey walked quickly up the stairs, and Landon tried to ignore the weird desire to follow him.

Chapter Nine

Landon shouldn't have been surprised when Casey sat next to him on the plane to Seattle, but he was. Surely Casey could use a break from the guy who'd invaded his life.

Although, Landon found he didn't need a break from Casey either.

They'd had a nice morning together. Landon had made them both omelets and toast for breakfast, which had blown Casey's mind. Landon had been pleased to see the swelling in Casey's lip had gone down quite a bit overnight, and his knuckles didn't look too bad either.

Then they'd driven to the arena for practice, stopping at a café on the way where Casey had flirted with the barista. Landon hadn't loved that part, but it was probably a useful reminder that Casey was not someone he should develop a crush on.

The problem was, Landon *always* developed crushes on unattainable people because it was safe. That way he never had to deal with the complications of that person liking him back.

The other problem was that Landon had stayed awake for a while after going to his room last night, uncomfortably aware that he was more turned on than he'd felt in a long time. He'd resisted the rare urge to jerk off, because he'd known he would think of Casey if he did, and that was a line he didn't want to cross.

If he could help it.

Now they were sitting together on the plane and Landon was keeping his focus on the window, admiring the peaks of the mountains that poked through the clouds. It was safer than admiring the man who was pressed against his side.

Casey wasn't making it easy to ignore him, though.

"Hey, remember the omelets you made? Those were amazing."

"I remember them, yes."

"How do you get them so thin and perfect without burning them? I tried making fried eggs once and burned the shit out of them."

"How high did you turn up the heat?"

"Oh, like, all the way. Huge flames." He was smiling, and even though he looked a bit busted up he still, unfortunately, looked very cute. His hair was tied back in a loose bun, and he was wearing a mint-green suit that made his eyes look unreal.

"Well," Landon said. "There's your problem."

Casey kept smiling at him, and Landon kept staring. In a desperate dimple-evading maneuver, Landon changed the subject. "You got big social plans for the team tonight? A bar or something?" This road trip was a weird one, consisting of back-to-back matinee games in Seattle, and then Vancouver. Tonight was a night off in Seattle.

"Nah, not tonight. I've got a date lined up!"

Landon managed to stop himself from physically recoiling. "A date?"

"Yeah. There's this guy I hooked up with the last couple of times I was in Seattle. He's smoking hot. He wanted to get dinner this time too, which I think is kind of adorable."

Oh.

Oh.

Landon had no idea what his face was doing but he must not look friendly because suddenly Casey was frowning at him.

"That's not, like, a problem, is it?" he asked.

"That you have a date?" Landon asked stupidly, because it weirdly felt like a problem.

"That I'm into guys. I'm bi. Everyone on the team knows. It's not a big deal, unless…"

"It's not a problem," Landon said quickly. "Just a surprise. Sorry, I'm being weird."

It *could* be a good opportunity for Landon to share that he was maybe probably gay. He honestly wasn't sure. Most of the time he felt…not very sexual. But sometimes he crushed hard on someone, and those someones had always been male. That could be more of a proximity thing because he only really got to know other men. The getting-to-know-someone part was important to Landon.

Landon hadn't quite figured himself out yet, so he wasn't ready to share. He also suddenly felt too warm and like he didn't fit in the space he was in. Having Casey this close wasn't comfortable or exciting, it was awful and he needed to get away, if only for a few minutes.

"Excuse me," he said, standing up as best he could. "I need to…"

Casey was still frowning. "Okay. You sure you're not freaked out about—"

"No! I promise. I just need to use the bathroom."

Mercifully, Casey stood and moved into the aisle. "Hey, Petey. How's it going?"

"Not bad, killer. How are those knuckles?"

While Casey chatted with Pete Leandros, Landon made his escape to the bathroom. He generally hated airplane bathrooms because he didn't fit in them at all, but at least he'd be alone.

When the door was safely locked behind him, he leaned against it and closed his eyes. Why did he have to be so uncool about *everything*? Why couldn't he just enjoy the hospitality of a teammate who barely knew him without getting weird about it? Why would he be upset that Casey was going on a date with someone? Obviously—*obviously*—Landon had no right to be hurt. Casey was helping out a teammate, and it was absolutely not his fault that Landon was finding it hard to ignore things he hadn't felt in ages. Things that swirled hopefully in all the empty places inside him.

If Landon were built differently, maybe he and Casey would hook up one night. Maybe one thing would lead to another, and they'd both say, "Hey, why not do this? Might be fun." Maybe it wouldn't mean anything more than watching TV together did; just something to do before bed.

But even imagining that filled Landon with so much anxiety he wanted to tear his skin off. He didn't want to hook up with Casey.

So what the fuck did he want?

He supposed it didn't matter. He wasn't going to get it. He needed to pull himself together, go back to his seat, and pretend to be a much more laidback person than he was.

At least he and Casey would be separated a bit on this trip. They were in different hotel rooms, and clearly Casey had his own plans for their free time. Maybe distance would clear Landon's head.

But when he returned to his seat, and Casey smiled at him and randomly asked if he thought walruses were weird, Landon really doubted it.

Chapter Ten

"Aw, man," Casey said as he bent next to Tristan Hoffman outside the faceoff circle, "the crowd sounds like they'd really like you guys to score a goal. Why are you letting them down like this?"

"Did I not punch you in the mouth hard enough the other night or something?" Tristan snarled.

"When did you hit me? Sorry, I didn't notice."

"You'll notice in about five seconds if you don't shut up."

"Oh, I'll be long gone in five seconds. If you manage to catch up with me, I'll show you how to score a goal."

Tristan didn't get a chance to reply because the puck dropped, and Casey took off, as promised.

And, okay, he didn't score a goal, but he did get the puck back to West at the point and *he* scored a goal, so not bad. It wasn't a *necessary* goal, because the score was now 5-1 for Calgary, but it was an enjoyable one.

All in all, it had been another pretty excellent road trip for Casey. They'd lost in overtime in Seattle, which was annoying, but it had been a hard-fought game on both sides. And tonight's trouncing of Vancouver had erased any pain from yesterday.

Casey's night off had been fun too. He hadn't been on a proper date in ages, and it had been nice having dinner with someone one-on-one. He liked Devon, and if they lived in the same city, maybe Casey would even consider going on more dates with him.

The sex had been top-notch too. Devon was very talented.

So the past couple of days had been decent. The only thing that had been a little off was Landon's mood. The guy was quiet and not the *least* socially awkward person in the world, generally, but he seemed to be intentionally distancing himself from Casey on this trip. Casey tried not to read too much into it, but had Landon already had enough of him? Or was he more bothered by Casey's sexuality than he was letting on?

He hoped not. It would make things weird when they got back home.

During a commercial break a few minutes later, Casey leaned on the boards in front of where Landon was sitting. "We could stop at a grocery store on the way home tonight. If you need anything."

The game was a Sunday afternoon matinee, and the flight home directly after the game was a quick one. Casey found himself looking forward to relaxing at home with Landon.

"If you want," Landon said. He only glanced quickly at Casey, and then away. "We don't have to. I can go tomorrow."

"I don't mind." Casey took a risk and tapped the brim of Landon's ball cap with one gloved finger. "I heard there's a Christmas version of Cap'n Crunch. I want it."

Landon ducked his head, but not fast enough to prevent Casey from seeing the way his lips had curved up. "Are you sure your healthy food delivery service isn't going to send some of that over?"

Casey laughed, both at the joke and from sheer relief that Landon was teasing him again. "I mean, I could ask them."

"Maybe they have hot chocolate bombs too."

"Oh shit! I forgot about the hot chocolate bombs! We gotta try those!"

"I think you need to manage your expectations about them."

"Can't do it. Already sky-high."

"Hey, Hicks," Clint Noseworthy called as he skated toward their defensive zone. "You wanna play some hockey, or what?"

"Yeah, yeah." He pointed at Landon. "Groceries, Christmas cereal, hot chocolate bombs. Our evening is *set*."

Landon waved his giant goalie glove at him. He wasn't quite smiling, but his dark eyes were sparkling. "Go. Hockey."

Casey was grinning when he skated away. "Hey, Hoffman. Have you tried the Christmas Cap'n Crunch yet?"

"Shut the fuck up, Hicks."

Definitely an excellent road trip.

The grocery store only had regular Cap'n Crunch.

"I'm going to ask someone if they have it," Casey said.

"Please don't."

Casey ignored Landon and strode toward a young man arranging boxes of granola bars on a shelf. "Hi! Do you know if you have the Christmas Cap'n Crunch?"

"Uh," the man said, "you might have to check with customer service." He pointed vaguely in the direction the customer service desk probably was.

"Thanks," Casey said, and started walking that way.

"Seriously?" Landon said.

"Sorry, Stacks," Casey said solemnly. "I need to see this through."

A few minutes later he was dealing with the crushing revelation that the Christmas version of the cereal wasn't going to be sold in Canada that year.

"I was just in the States," he moaned as he trailed behind Landon and the cart. "I could have brought a bunch back."

"Christmas is ruined," Landon said dryly.

"It totally is," Casey agreed as he tossed a container of candy cane ice cream in the cart. It joined the festive M&M's, Christmas tree-shaped crackers, and eggnog he'd already put in there, along with the milk, bread, vegetables, and other normal foods Landon had selected.

While Landon was inspecting a carton of eggs, Casey nudged him gently and said, "Hey, I think you're gonna get the start this week."

Landon's body seemed to tighten everywhere. "It's possible."

"More than possible. We've got back-to-back home games and then a Battle of Alberta game on Saturday. Antton is gonna want to be rested up for that one."

"Yep." Landon closed the lid on the egg carton and placed it carefully in the cart. "I do know a bit about how goalies work."

"Are you excited?"

"I don't know." Landon pushed the cart ahead and grabbed some cheese.

"Are you kidding? First NHL game? There's nothing like it."

"*If* I get the start this week," Landon said, "of course I'll be excited. It's been my dream forever."

"You know who else will be excited? Me! Because I want everyone to see how good you are."

Landon huffed. "Okay."

"I want to see you rob guys who *aren't* me."

Landon nodded in the direction of a man wearing an Outlaws ball cap who was openly staring at them while holding a container of sour cream. "That guy wants your autograph, I think."

"Maybe he wants yours."

"Shut up."

"This time next week everyone will want yours, Stacks. Just wait." He waved and smiled at the staring man, who tentatively smiled back.

"Sorry," the man said, "but you're Casey Hicks, right?"

"Yep. No one else is this handsome."

"Can I get an autograph?"

"Heck yeah. You want me to sign your hat?"

Casey pulled a Sharpie from his coat pocket—he always carried a Sharpie because this sort of thing happened a lot—and scribbled his illegible signature on the brim of the hat. "You should get Stackhouse here to sign it too. He's gonna be huge."

The man blinked at Landon as if he'd somehow not noticed the six-foot-four man standing behind Casey. "Oh. Stackhouse. The goalie, right? You were called up to replace Morin."

"Yes," Landon said. "But it's okay. You don't need to listen to Casey."

The man hesitated for a moment, then held out the hat to Landon. "No, I'd like your autograph too, if you don't mind."

Landon glared at Casey as he took the Sharpie from him. After the hat was signed and returned to the man, and Casey and Landon were alone again, Landon said, "I can't believe you just made me ruin that guy's hat."

"As if. By the way, your signature is nice as hell. So fancy!"

"I have a long name."

"It looks like Shakespeare's autograph or something." Casey mimed signing something with a flourish in the air.

"Yeah, well. Yours looks like a drunk baby did it."

Casey cracked up, and even Landon smiled a bit. Casey was struck once again by how handsome he was. How was Landon single? He must have been getting laid like crazy in Saskatoon.

"Are we done?" Landon asked as they got close to the check-out area.

"Yeah. Let's get out of here. This drunk baby needs hot chocolate."

Hot chocolate bombs ended up being kind of a disappointment.

"That's it?" Casey asked sadly as he watched melted chocolate slowly sink to the bottom of his glass mug. A few marsh-mallows bobbed soggily on the top.

"What were you expecting exactly?" Landon asked as he stirred his own hot chocolate.

"I don't know. An explosion?"

"That would be a mess. Here." Landon handed him the

spoon. "It'll taste good. Using hot milk instead of water makes a big difference."

"Damn. Check out Chef Stacks over here."

Landon narrowed his eyes at him.

"You got a YouTube channel I can subscribe to?" Casey teased.

"Maybe I'll go to bed early."

"No." Without thinking, Casey reached out and put a hand on Landon's bare forearm. "I want to hang out."

Landon stared at Casey's hand, then slowly pulled his arm away. "Fine." He went to the living room with his mug, and Casey lingered in the kitchen for a moment, replaying the last few seconds. He shouldn't have touched Landon.

He was going to apologize, but it got caught in his throat when he glanced at the living room. Landon was standing at the window, backlit by Christmas lights, and rubbing the spot where Casey had touched him.

It's not like Casey hadn't had any sexual thoughts about Landon. Casey had sexual thoughts about a lot of people, but they were usually along the lines of "I'll bet it would be fun to have sex with them" or "I'll bet sex would be intense with them" or "I should see if this person wants to have sex again sometime." Looking at Landon now, he was hit by a weird combination of "I want to make him smile" and "I'll bet sex with him would be fun and intense at the same time" and "Oh no I really like him."

He *really* liked him.

And now Landon was staring back at him with a nervous little half smile. "What?"

Casey managed to smile back. "Nothing. The lights look nice."

It wasn't that he was a coward—he had a long history of shooting his shot with just about anyone he wanted—it was that he knew any sort of advance or flirtation would make Landon uncomfortable. Just like how touching him had clearly made him uncomfortable. Casey needed to adjust his typical behavior around him.

"We should watch a Christmas thing," Casey said.

"Sure." Landon sat in the corner of the sectional sofa, his long legs stretched out on the cushions in front of him.

"Wait! I have an idea," Casey said. He turned on the electric fireplace he always forgot about, even though it was directly under the TV and almost as big. "There we go. Christmas movie, hot chocolate, fireplace."

"We're party animals," Landon said.

"Out of control," Casey agreed. He sat on one end of the sofa, far from Landon, and began the process of fighting with his television.

In the end, they watched *Elf,* and Landon fell asleep halfway through it. If it wasn't for the creepy fucking living room window, Casey probably would have fallen asleep too. Instead, he watched the movie, but kept stealing glances at Landon. Asleep, his face softened. His jawline was still razor sharp, but his plush lips weren't pulled into a tight line or a confused frown. His dark eyelashes were fanned out on his pale skin. Every now and again he'd let out a quiet sigh that would make Casey's heart flip.

When the movie was over, Landon woke up. "Oh shit. Did I fall asleep?"

"Yeah. But don't worry, Buddy saved Christmas."

Landon sat up and stretched, exposing a strip of stomach where his T-shirt rode up. Casey looked away.

A few minutes later, as Casey climbed the stairs to his bedroom, he resolved to shut these weird feelings down. They weren't going to do anyone any good. Not him, and especially not poor Landon.

Chapter Eleven

Three nights later, Landon was sitting cross-legged on the floor of his dark bedroom, wearing pajamas and a goalie mask.

Earlier that day, at practice, Landon had learned he would, in fact, be starting against San Jose tomorrow. It hadn't been a surprise—Antton had played tonight against Minnesota, and San Jose was a low-ranked team—but Landon still could barely believe this was happening. He was going to be starting an NHL game tomorrow night in front of the home crowd.

And now he couldn't sleep.

It was, last he'd checked, past three in the morning and he was wide awake. After several hours of staring into the total darkness of his basement bedroom from his bed, he'd moved to the floor, and put on his mask. It was a strange but effective method he'd been using for years to settle his brain.

Tonight, it wasn't working. He felt the passing minutes like weights being added to a belt.

If he didn't sleep, he'd play like shit tomorrow.

He was going to be exhausted and slow and terrible.

He'd be sent back to Saskatoon.

He would let Antton Niskanen down. And his team. And the city of Calgary. And Casey.

It would be his last NHL game.

He needed to sleep.

Insomnia was a familiar enemy for Landon. When he was a kid, he'd shared a room with his sister, Erin. They were close in age, only separated by eighteen months, and their twin beds were close enough together that they could talk quietly at night. Even the nights where they didn't talk at all, the comfort of being close to someone who loved and understood him had always quieted his overactive brain.

When they were teenagers, Erin got the bedroom, and the dining room of their family's small house was converted into a room for Landon. Insomnia began plaguing him again. Some nights he would quietly knock on the bedroom door. Erin would invite him in and he'd lie on the floor by her bed. Sometimes they would talk, sometimes they'd both fall asleep right away. He'd wake up with a few aches from lying on the floor, but at least he'd gotten some solid hours of sleep in. Sleep had been more important than ever, when he was a teen, because being drafted by a junior team had started to look like a real possibility.

When he was sixteen, his hard work paid off. He was drafted by a team in Quebec, and his family had been so proud of him. Erin had just graduated from high school weeks before, and was trying to decide between starting university right away or traveling first. Everything had been exciting and new for the Stackhouse family.

Two weeks later, Erin was dead, and nothing had ever felt exciting again.

Now, on the floor of Casey's guest room in Calgary, Landon squeezed his eyes shut. He couldn't start thinking about Erin or he would truly never sleep. Thinking about Erin meant drowning in guilt, regret, and misery. It meant useless anger and horrible, consuming emptiness. He couldn't invite any of that into his head right now.

He turned his thoughts back to hockey. Hockey was how he'd gotten through the grief and the guilt and the misery the first time. He'd thrown himself into hockey even as it created a wall between himself and his parents. Maybe because it did.

He'd been handed an opportunity to escape the misery that had swallowed his family whole, and he'd taken it.

He'd been so selfish. He *was* so selfish.

He couldn't think about that now.

He closed his eyes and began another round of deep, controlled breathing. He should be able to sleep here. He had all the space and privacy he could possibly want, alone in a basement with a bed large enough to comfortably spread out his long arms and legs. Casey was somewhere in the house, but Landon couldn't hear him.

He huffed into the darkness, thinking about how rare it was to be in the same place as Casey Hicks but to not hear him. It was a relief, of course. Landon liked him, but good god, he was chatty. And if he wasn't talking, he was humming, or laughing at something on his phone or on the television. Sometimes Landon heard him talking to himself, when Casey was a floor above him.

Landon was living in Casey's house for free. He shouldn't be thinking a single negative thing about him.

He shouldn't be *thinking*. He should be sleeping. Fucking hell.

There was a part of him that wanted to fly back to Saskatoon, or maybe all the way to Halifax. There was a part of him that wished Casey was upstairs in the kitchen, talking to himself, just so Landon could feel less alone. Maybe he should have taken one of the upstairs bedrooms.

There was a part of Landon that wanted to knock on Casey's door, lie on the floor beside his bed, and listen to him breathe.

Right. Like that wouldn't be weird as fuck.

With a heavy sigh, Landon removed his mask and set it on the floor. He stood and got back into bed, even though his brain was more active than ever. He rolled onto his side, squeezed his eyes tight against the moisture pooling in them, and tried desperately to shut himself off.

He had left home when his parents had needed him most. He had chosen hockey over everything. The least he could do is not fuck this chance up.

Chapter Twelve

Landon didn't look good.

Casey knew better than to mention something like that to his starting goalie before a game—especially before that goalie's *first-ever* big league game—but, well, Landon looked terrible.

Coach Patrick was standing in the middle of the locker room, offering encouragement in that calm, steady way he had. He announced Landon as the starting goalie, as if it was a secret, and everyone whooped and tapped their sticks on the floor. Landon didn't react, his face rigid and pale, and his eyes sunk into the sharp angles of his face.

"Let's go, Stacks!" Casey called out, hoping to at least get his attention. Landon didn't even flinch, just kept staring into the middle distance.

Goalies were weird. Casey knew this. They all had their own pregame rituals and ways of mentally preparing to get pummeled by pucks and bodies. Casey had his own private ritual, which was to tell himself that tonight was going to be the best game of his life. Usually it wasn't, but until that final siren wailed, Casey played like it was a possibility. If he had a bad game, he shook it off quickly. It was okay because the next game was going to be his *best game ever.*

Landon did not look like he was about to have his best game

ever. He looked like he was remembering every bad thing that had ever happened to him.

He'd been quiet during the drive to the arena, which wasn't unusual. Casey had gotten the vibe right away that Landon did *not* want to talk about the game, so Casey had chatted about whatever popped into his head. Mostly about the nature show he'd watched in bed the night before. It'd been about owls.

Owls couldn't move their eyes. Fucking weird.

Landon kind of looked like he couldn't move *his* eyes, the way he was staring. Most of the guys were standing now, ready to head to the ice and start the game. Landon stayed seated, staring.

Casey couldn't take it anymore. He crossed the room and stood in front of Landon's leg pads. "Hey, buddy," he said cheerfully, "I got good news and bad news."

Landon blinked, and his gaze shifted away from the wall and focused on Casey. "Huh?"

"Good news—we're gonna fucking bury San Jose. I'm gonna score three goals. At least three goals."

"Okay."

"Bad news—you're gonna be fucking bored."

Seeing the slight upward tick of Landon's lips felt like scoring an overtime goal.

"That so?" Landon asked.

"Yeah, dude. You've got the easiest job in the world tonight. They should charge you for a ticket."

Landon stood, which made him tower over Casey. For a moment, he looked like he was going to say something, but instead he only nodded, then grabbed his mask and put it on.

"Let's go, boys!" Casey called out, and some of the guys cheered in response. "Goals for everyone. Let's fuck 'em up."

Landon wasn't bored at all.

It was seven minutes into the first period, and he'd already let in two goals.

On four shots.

"Fucking get it together, Stackhouse," he muttered to himself when the play was at the other end of the ice.

It wasn't different from any other game he'd played. Yes, the crowd was bigger and louder, and yes, the game was being broadcasted nationally, but it was still just a hockey game. It was still just stopping pucks.

The roar of the crowd startled Landon before he realized his team had scored. "Thank fuck," he said.

It was Casey who had scored, god love him.

"We got this," Casey said after he skated down the ice to high-five Landon in celebration.

Landon nodded. He'd given up two easy ones, and he could blame jitters for that, but he'd be solid now. He deserved to be here. He'd prove it.

He stopped the next shot, and the next one, and then completely flubbed an easy save and had to watch helplessly as the puck rolled past the goal line behind him.

The crowd was silent. Or at least it felt that way. Landon tried to shake it off. Tried to believe he could still be of use to his team, even as he wished the ice would swallow him. At least his parents never watched his games live. He could tell them to skip this one.

During a commercial break a couple of minutes later, Landon skated miserably to the bench.

"How you doing, Stackhouse?" Coach Patrick asked.

Landon could be honest and tell him his head wasn't right tonight. Goaltending was a mental game as much as physical, and anyone who understood hockey understood that. He simply wasn't able to focus the way he needed to.

He glanced at Antton, who was watching their conversation with interest from his seat at the end of the bench. If Landon gave his coach an honest answer, Antton would have to go in.

No. Fuck it. There were still over two periods left to play. Landon wasn't going to give up. Antton needed this night off. He was counting on Landon to hold it together for one fucking game.

"I'm good," Landon said. "Just jitters, but I'm settled now."

Coach studied him for a long moment. "Good," he finally said. "Get back out there, then."

Landon raced back to the net, trying to make his strides look powerful and confident. Distantly, he heard the crowd cheering for him, which was nice of them. He'd like to give them something real to cheer for.

The puck dropped, and the play immediately headed in Landon's direction. It was two-on-one, and Landon had to decide whether the San Jose forward with the puck was going to pass or shoot.

Landon sank into the moment. The crowd disappeared, along with the cameras, his teammates, his coaches, Antton Niskanen, all of it. In the span of a few seconds, Landon watched the forward's hands, the puck, his feet, his eyes.

He was going to shoot. He would wait, try to fake Landon out, but he would shoot.

Landon edged his left leg toward the other San Jose player, to make it seem like he was anticipating a pass. When the shot he'd been expecting came, he shut the door, stopping the low shot cleanly and covering the puck to stop the play.

The world came back, and the crowd was cheering. He could hear Casey yelling from the bench over everyone. "Hell yeah, Stacks!"

He handed the puck to the linesman and shook himself off. He could do this.

Unfortunately, he could not do it. After managing to prevent any more pucks from getting by him in the first period, he let in three goals in the first half of the second period, two of them within forty seconds of each other.

And then he was called to the bench and Antton had to go in to replace him. Landon couldn't even give his hero one badly needed night off. He was a joke.

Sitting on the bench for the rest of the game was a nightmare. He felt like everyone in the arena was staring at him. He felt like crying but fought like hell not to because he was sure the broadcast would show close-ups of his face.

Antton kept Calgary in the game as best he could, stopping every shot, but in the end San Jose still won.

Landon didn't talk to anyone in the locker room after. He removed his gear as quickly as he could. He wanted to burn it.

"Hey," said a voice behind him. Landon turned and saw Antton standing there, still in full gear with his mask flipped up.

"Sorry," Landon said, because it was the only word in his vocabulary in that moment.

"They won't all be like this one," Antton said. It was a nice thing to say, but Landon was pretty sure there wouldn't be any more Outlaws games for him. He'd probably be on a plane back to Saskatoon tomorrow. Felix, the next goalie in line, would be happy.

Landon didn't know what to say, since he'd already used up his one word, so he just shrugged and continued to remove his gear.

"Listen," Antton said quietly. "The press is coming in here in a minute. Go take a shower, all right? And stay in there. I'll talk to them."

Landon almost started crying, but he managed to swallow it down as he nodded. He absolutely could not deal with talking to the press right now.

"And that save you made in the first? The two-on-one? Beauty. I thought he was going to pass."

Landon let out a shaky breath. "No way. You would have seen it too. He was shooting."

"It was nice. An NHL save. You should be proud of that one."

"Thanks."

Antton gently nudged Landon's chest with his glove. "You've got talent. Now get naked and get out of here."

Landon nodded, lips pressed together as his eyes burned. Antton left, and Landon made quick work of the rest of his gear, more than ready to shower away his disastrous first—and probably last—NHL game.

Chapter Thirteen

"I don't want to talk about it," Landon said as soon as he and Casey were in the car.

Casey thought it was pretty obvious that Landon didn't want to talk about the game. The way he hadn't said a word in the locker room after—had barely made eye contact with anyone—and the way he'd walked several strides behind Casey on the way to the car.

"That's cool," Casey said. "No problem." He started the ignition. "But. You shouldn't—"

"I don't want to talk about it."

"Yeah, I know. But—"

"Do you ever fucking stop talking?"

Casey flinched, and a heavy silence filled the car.

Landon exhaled. "I'm sorry. Jesus, I'm so sorry. I didn't mean it."

Casey swallowed. It was probably weird for someone who played hockey for a living to be averse to conflict but, well. He didn't need a psychologist to tell him that he had an intense need to be liked.

"It's okay," he said quietly. "I get it."

They drove the rest of the way home in silence. Casey didn't even put on any music. It had snowed a bit during the game, which was something he normally would have mentioned, just to make conversation, but he wanted to give Landon the quiet he needed right now.

The game had been a disaster for Landon, no question. Definitely not the start you want to your big league career. Everyone had bad games, Casey included. Even with the goal he'd scored, he wasn't thrilled with his own performance tonight. But goalies had bad games in an entirely different and more noticeable way than anyone else on the team, and Landon's bad game had been super noticeable.

Landon sniffed loudly beside him. Casey glanced over, but Landon was turned toward the passenger-side window, hiding his face.

Casey opened his mouth, considered a few things he could say, then didn't say any of them. He closed his mouth and kept driving. His left shoulder was throbbing and would need some ice when he got home. He'd gone down on it hard after a heavy hit against the boards. He was sure it was nothing serious, just a bad bruise probably. Regular hockey shit.

When they got home, Landon said, "Thanks for the lift," as if that was necessary, then went immediately to the basement.

Casey stared at the basement stairs for a minute or two after Landon was gone, wanting to follow him and talk to him, but also wanting to give him his space. In the end, he went to the kitchen to get his postgame snack from the fridge and an ice pack from the freezer. Landon's groceries were tucked among Casey's prepackaged meals, the only evidence that Casey even had a roommate.

He sat at his kitchen island to ice his shoulder and eat, rather than heading to the living room. The silence made him anxious, but it was nice knowing that someone else was in the house with him. Even if that person was already sick of Casey.

Casey twisted on his barstool, back and forth, and wondered if Landon was crying. He wondered if leaving him alone really was the best thing for him.

He couldn't do it. He couldn't just go upstairs to bed and leave Landon all alone with his misery. He grabbed a bag of grapes that Landon had bought and carried them down to the basement.

Landon's bedroom door was closed, which wasn't a surprise. Casey knocked softly. "Hey. I brought you some grapes."

There was a long silence, and then Landon said, "What?"

"Grapes. I thought you might be hungry."

"I'm not."

"Oh." Casey felt silly now, standing outside Landon's door, holding a bag of grapes for no reason, but he still didn't want to leave him. "Maybe you will be?"

"I don't need grapes."

"Okay. Well, maybe I'll just put them outside the door here. And maybe I'll sit here with them for a bit."

Landon must have moved close to the door, because his voice was louder when he asked, "Why?"

"I know you don't want to talk to me, or see me, but maybe I'll just be here. For a little bit. So you don't have to be alone."

Landon didn't reply. Casey sat on the floor, his back against the door. He wondered if Landon would mind if he ate one of the grapes. They looked good.

"You don't have to keep me company," Landon said.

"I know. Do you want me to leave?"

There was a light thump against the door, which may have been Landon's forehead. "No."

Casey smiled. "You know what I was thinking?"

"That I'm the worst goalie you've ever seen?"

"Nope. I was thinking that we need to go shopping before we go to Vegas. You need something slick for the clubs."

Landon huffed. "I don't think I'm going to be here long enough for it to matter."

"You think they're gonna send you back to Saskatoon after one rough game?" Okay, it wasn't impossible.

"Yes."

"Is the other goalie in Saskatoon any good?"

"Sure. Yeah." Landon paused, then added, "I think he's a better puck handler than me."

"Sounds like a dick."

A shocked-sounding laugh burst out of Landon. Casey wished he could see his face.

"He's not a dick."

"If you say so."

"I let Antton down."

Ah. There it was. "You think Antton never had a bad game?"

"He had a shutout in his debut," Landon pointed out.

"Yeah, but that was back when hockey was easy."

Another muffled laugh, and then the door shook slightly and Casey was pretty sure Landon had joined him on the floor. Casey tilted his head back against the door without even thinking about it.

"I didn't sleep last night," Landon confessed.

"Kinda guessed that."

Landon let out a long, exhausted-sounding sigh. Casey could picture him closing his eyes, those dark lashes fanning against his pale skin...

Yikes. Okay. Maybe Casey needed to get laid. He realized he hadn't brought anyone home since Landon had moved in, which was kind of a long time for him.

"Sorry," Landon said, breaking Casey's train of thought.

"For what?"

Casey waited for a reply, but it never came. Instead, Landon said, "I would have liked to go to Vegas with you. With the team, I mean."

Casey curled forward a bit and rested his forearms on his bent knees. He realized that he hated the idea of going to Vegas without Landon. "You will. It was one game, and we've seen what you can do in practice."

"It doesn't matter what I can do in practice if I can't—" Landon cut himself off with a frustrated-sounding huff.

Casey ate a grape while he tried to think of something to say. Talking was easy; saying something useful was the tricky part. After a lot of thought (and four more grapes) he said, "What's the best save you've ever made, do you think?"

Landon took his time answering. "It was my first season with Saskatoon. We were playing in Cleveland and they had a power play late in the game. We were up by one. One of their top scorers, Verlander, took a shot from the left circle."

"I played with that guy. He's got a wicked shot."

"He does, but that's not the save. His shot pinged off the post and went straight to fucking Travis Barnes, who's just waiting at the edge of the crease, no one on him."

Casey blew out a breath. Barnes played in the NHL now, and was a skilled sniper. "What'd you do?"

"I didn't have time to think, even though it felt like slow motion. I went down, as low and as wide as I could go. Maybe a few inches past that limit, honestly, and I caught the puck with my toe and tipped it into my glove. Made it look pretty somehow."

Casey laughed. "Is there video of that?"

"Maybe."

"As if you don't know."

Landon huffed. "Yeah. There's a clip on YouTube. I've watched it a million times."

Casey already had his phone out and was typing "Landon Stackhouse Save" into the YouTube search bar. The clip was only twenty seconds long, and it was amazing. "Shit, dude. How'd you get back up again after that? You look like you split yourself in two."

"I almost did."

"You should watch this clip right now," Casey said, as he hit play again. "So you know how stupid it sounds when you talk like you shouldn't be here."

Behind the door, Casey heard Landon sigh heavily. Without really thinking about it, Casey brushed his fingertips along the tiny gap at the bottom of the door. He imagined Landon doing the same thing.

"I need to confess something," Casey said.

"What?"

"I've eaten several grapes."

The door began to wobble a bit, and then there was a giddy, strangled sound and Casey realized Landon was laughing.

"They're really good!" Casey was laughing too. "You sure you don't want any? I could try to mash some under the door."

And then, without warning, the doorknob turned. Casey had just enough time to scramble to his feet before the door opened.

Landon looked exhausted, sad brown eyes sunk deep into his skull. He towered over Casey, but Casey could probably knock him down with one finger right now. All of that would have been concerning, except Casey couldn't focus on anything but the slight upward tilt of Landon's lips.

Landon held out his hand, and Casey stared at it until Landon said, "Grapes."

Casey grinned and handed him the bag.

"Thanks," Landon said.

"They're your grapes."

"Not for the grapes. Thanks."

Casey, for whatever reason, saluted him. "Anytime, Stacks."

Landon looked at the floor, and then glanced shyly at Casey. His bangs flopped into his eyes. Casey's heart began to race.

"Goodnight, Casey."

Casey blinked. "Right. Yeah. Get some sleep."

Landon nodded, then gently closed the door.

Chapter Fourteen

The next morning, Landon went to *work*.

Somewhere between being handed a bag of grapes and turning off his bedside lamp, Landon had decided he was going to fight to stay in Calgary. He *was* a good goalie. With more experience, he could be a *great* goalie. He wanted to stay.

So now he was in the team gym, doing his third set of iron crosses on the floor. He'd walked in with his head held high, locking eyes with any teammate he passed, greeting them with silent but confident nods. He would get better. He would make himself worth keeping.

Would he have felt like this today if Casey hadn't sat outside his door last night? There was no way to know for sure, but Landon didn't think so. He'd been wallowing in his room before Casey had knocked, crying a little, ready to give up.

Landon had received plenty of pep talks over the years: from coaches, from teammates, and from his parents. He'd never had a conversation as weird or as effective as the one he'd had with Casey through that door. He suspected it was something he would remember for a long time.

Maybe more than the conversation, he would remember what he'd seen when he'd finally opened the door. Casey had looked so happy to see him, all dimples and eager eyes. His long hair had been kind of a mess, like he'd been running his hands through it.

Casey wanted him to stay. That made Landon want to stay.

Maybe it wouldn't matter. Maybe Coach Patrick would call him into his office today and tell Landon to go back to Saskatoon. It was possible, but until that happened, Landon was going to believe he belonged here.

Casey was getting a massage and some treatment on his shoulder because apparently it had been bothering him since the game last night. Since Casey had mentioned it during their drive to the arena, Landon hadn't been able to stop thinking about how Casey had been in pain while he'd been comforting Landon through the bedroom door.

Landon hadn't even asked about the shoulder last night. He'd watched Casey get hit, watched him skate to the bench in pain, watched him jump back on the ice for the next shift as if nothing had happened. Landon knew that didn't mean Casey wasn't hurt, but he'd been too consumed by shame and frustration to even ask if Casey was all right during the drive home.

"Do you ever fucking stop talking?"

As embarrassed as Landon was about his performance last night, it didn't come close to how ashamed he was of saying *that*. He'd apologized, and Casey had waved it off like it was nothing. Had kept trying to help him. Had kept being a friend.

Landon finished his set and lay on the floor, arms outstretched, staring at the ceiling. He would be better, for the team, and for Casey.

Lee Ramsay's face suddenly eclipsed the ceiling fan Landon had been watching.

"Coach wants to see you," Lee said. "In his office."

"Okay." So. Back to Saskatoon, then. Maybe that *was* the best thing for the team. And for Casey.

Greg Patrick's office door was wide open, but Landon knocked anyway.

"Stackhouse. Come in." His tone was friendly, which could mean he was trying to break the news gently.

Landon sat in one of the two chairs across the desk from his coach, and waited.

"Rough one last night," Coach said.

"Yeah," Landon agreed. "Sorry."

"I just wanted to check in with you. See how you're feeling."

Landon was feeling confused at the moment. Coach's gaze was locked with his, waiting, and Landon took a moment to consider what he wanted to say.

"I felt like shit last night," he admitted. "I'd been dreaming of getting that chance for so long, and I blew it."

Coach's expression remained neutral. "How do you feel now?"

This time, Landon didn't hesitate. "I want to stay. I'm better than what I showed you last night. I know it's probably too late, but if I'm not sent back down, then I'm going to work my ass off here. If I do get sent back down, I'm going to work my ass off there. I want to be part of this team."

Coach leaned back in his chair, eyes still focused on Landon. "I was talking to Bill this morning," he said, referring to the Outlaws' general manager. "We're keeping you here, for now."

A surge of emotion strangled Landon, and he had to blink back tears. He'd been so sure it was over. "Thank you," he managed to say.

"Thank me on the ice. You taking part in the skate today?"

"Yes. Definitely."

"Good. I'll see you out there."

Landon left quickly, and nearly crashed into Casey in the hall.

"Shit. Sorry, Stacks."

"My fault."

"I was just coming to find you. I—" Casey seemed to suddenly realize whose office Landon had been exiting. His eyes went wide and questioning.

Landon tilted his head toward the end of the hall and started walking. "I'm staying."

Casey beamed like this was the best news ever. "Fucking right!" He grabbed Landon's arm and shook him. "Told you."

"Stop it. You'll make your shoulder worse."

Casey let him go. "Shoulder is all good. Just got a little banged up. Good thing too, because I would be super bummed if I had to sit for a Battle of Alberta game."

The city had been buzzing all week about tomorrow night's game against Edmonton. Even back in Nova Scotia, Landon had known how big a deal these Battle of Alberta games were. This one would be the second meeting of the season between the two teams, and the first in Calgary. Landon was excited to be a part of it.

"Why were you trying to find me?"

"Huh?" Casey said.

"You said you were coming to find me."

"Oh. I guess it wasn't for any reason, really."

Landon lengthened his stride, placing himself slightly in front of Casey to hide his smile.

"So I meant what I said last night," Casey said, "about taking you shopping."

"Oh. No thanks." Trying on clothing wasn't something Landon had ever enjoyed. Absolutely nothing looked right on his stretched-out frame. "Clothes look weird on me."

"You need to shop where I shop!"

"Where? Gap Kids?"

Casey burst out laughing. "Damn, Stacks."

Landon bit the inside of his cheek.

"Well," Casey said, "where do you buy clothes? The fucking...ladder store?"

Landon lost the battle with his smile and started laughing. "Ladder store?"

"That was weak. Let me try again."

"No." He continued down the hall, Casey scrambled after him.

"We can go to Holt Renfrew. Samir never misses."

"Who's Samir?"

"He works in menswear there. He knows his shit."

Landon had vaguely heard of Holt Renfrew. It was a store for rich people or something. "It might be a little beyond my budget."

"Aw, I can—"

"No."

"One outfit? We could call it a Christmas present."

"I'm calling it ridiculous. No way are you buying me clothes."

Casey sighed dramatically. "Fine. But we should still go. For fun."

"Fun," Landon said flatly. But he did enjoy hanging out with Casey. "Okay. Fine. We'll go."

"Sweet. I'll book an appointment for next week."

"An appointment? For shopping?"

Casey grinned at him. "Yeah, dude. This is classy shit. I tell Samir what I'm looking for, and he brings a bunch of amazing clothes to a private fitting room."

That actually did sound extremely appealing. And expensive. Most of Landon's clothes growing up were from thrift stores.

"You're in the big leagues now, baby," Casey said. "Time to live the life."

Landon still didn't feel like he was in the big leagues, but maybe he could indulge a little while he was still in Calgary. Just a tiny bit.

Chapter Fifteen

The following morning, Landon was awoken by his dad calling.

"Hey," Landon croaked. "What's up?"

"I woke you up, didn't I?"

Landon sat up, blinking into the darkness. "It's okay. I should be up by now anyway." It was only seven thirty, and he absolutely did not have to be up yet, but he wasn't going to tell Dad that.

"Sorry," Dad said anyway. "I was just thinking about you. Is it cold there?"

Landon smiled, and he desperately wished he could hug his father right now. "Probably."

"It's not too bad here, for late November."

"Good."

A silence passed that was long enough to make Landon start worrying.

"Is everything okay?" he said at the same moment Dad said, "So, Battle of Alberta tonight."

Landon exhaled. "Yeah. Should be interesting."

"I'll say. What a thing to be a part of. You must be excited."

"Sure, yeah. It'll be cool. I mean, I won't be playing, obviously, unless…" He didn't finish the sentence because he was superstitious enough to not mention the possibility of Antton getting hurt out loud.

"But still," Dad said cheerfully, "front-row seats."

"Yep."

Another silence passed, then Dad said, "Sorry about your game the other night there."

"Oh. Yeah."

"That must have been rough."

"It was, but the team has been supportive. I haven't been sent back to Saskatoon or anything and, y'know, everyone has bad games. Sucks that this was my first one. But the team's been nice about it."

"I'm glad. Good to know that you're doing okay there."

"I am. The team is great."

"So you're liking Calgary?"

"Yeah. It's been good." Because Landon knew the question Dad was really asking, he said, "I'm doing well."

"And Dougie Hicks's son has been treating you okay?"

Landon felt inexplicably embarrassed by the question. All he could think about was Casey sitting outside his bedroom door, making him laugh when Landon had felt like he'd never feel happiness again. "He's cool," he said.

"That's good," Dad said. "I'm glad you're not alone out there."

Something crumbled in Landon's chest. The combination of Dad worrying about him being lonely—when loneliness was the consequence Landon deserved for his choices—and the sudden realization that Landon *wasn't* lonely, thanks to Casey, hit him like a slap shot.

"I'm not alone," he said quietly.

"We're glad to hear it." There was another long silence before Dad said, "Hey. Listen. You can say no to this, but we were thinking about maybe coming out there to visit? Maybe for Christmas, if you're not busy."

God. The suggestion that Landon might be too busy to see

his parents at Christmas if they flew to Calgary was too much. "I'd love that," he said. "If you guys want to. And I can buy the plane tickets."

"Don't worry about that. We both have some vacation time, and we were thinking about coming for a week, if that works for you."

"It works," Landon said, growing excited. His parents barely ever traveled, and had never flown out west to visit him before. Landon had almost invited them to Saskatoon several times, but he only had a small apartment there, and he hadn't thought he'd deserved their limited vacation time anyway. "Our schedule has us at home the week before the Christmas break, so yeah. It'll be great. You can probably stay here at the house. I'll ask Casey, but I don't think he'd mind. He's not even going to be here for Christmas."

"That sounds good." Dad sounded excited too. "We'll talk some more about it, okay?"

"Okay. But you guys should come. I really want to see you."

"We really want to see you too. It would be nice to spend Christmas together."

"Yeah. It would. It will be." He decided to push his luck. "Would you want to come to a game, do you think? I'd probably just be on the bench, so—"

"We'd love to. I know that we haven't—well. We probably have some things to talk about in person. But we'd love to go to a game. We're proud of you."

Landon pressed his palm to his chest. This all felt like too much. Like the three of them were on the brink of stepping into sunshine together after eight long years in the dark. "I'd like that."

"You know," Dad said, "I haven't been to an NHL game since that time we went to Toronto when you were ten. Remember that?"

"Of course I remember." It was the biggest trip they'd ever

taken as a family, and Landon had loved every minute of it. "It was a great trip. We went to the Hall of Fame."

"That's right. You wouldn't touch the Stanley Cup. Not until you won it." Dad laughed. "Erin hugged it."

Landon smiled sadly. "She was laying it on thick, telling me how good it felt."

"Well, maybe you'll find out for yourself one day."

"Maybe."

"Never thought—" Dad paused and cleared his throat before continuing. "Never thought the next game I went to would feature my own son."

Landon blinked rapidly and tried not to complete that thought. *Or that my daughter would be gone.*

"The arena here is cool," he said ridiculously. "Old, but kind of nice that way, y'know?"

"I've heard that. Can't wait to see it." Dad exhaled slowly. "Well, good luck tonight. And have fun."

"I will."

"We'll watch for as long as we can hold our eyes open."

"So, three minutes?" Landon joked. The game would start at eleven in Halifax.

"We'll try to make it five."

"Okay. Love you, Dad. Say hi to Mom."

"I will. And we love you, Landon."

They ended the call, and Landon stayed exactly where he was, sitting on his bed in the dark, for a long time. He stared at nothing and tried to process his feelings.

Eventually, he left the bed and decided to hit the treadmill. A hard run usually settled him. It was something he'd started doing in the weeks after Erin died—an excuse to leave the house, where the grief had been so heavy it had threatened to crush him. He'd pushed himself, running faster and farther every day, his sneakers pounding the streets of Eastern Passage until his head was clear and the burning in his lungs briefly replaced the agony of losing his sister. These days he ran to overcome anxiety, loneliness, insomnia, and, still, that unending agony of loss.

By the time he'd run ten kilometers on Casey's treadmill, stretched, showered, and dressed, he was more or less ready to face other people. He heard Casey stomping around upstairs, so he went up to make breakfast.

He reached the top of the stairs just in time to watch Casey fumble and drop three oranges that he'd seemingly been trying to juggle.

"Hey, Stacks," Casey said cheerfully. "Do you know how to juggle?"

His hair was pulled back in a messy bun, and he was wearing a white T-shirt that was full of holes. The neck was all stretched out, making a display of his collarbones. None of it should have made Landon's mouth go dry.

Landon swallowed, then crossed the room to retrieve the oranges from the floor. At least now he knew why he'd spotted oranges on the couch the day he'd moved in. "Promise to be cool about this?"

"Nope."

Landon sighed and started juggling. He was good at it because he'd spent hours and years practicing the skill after his junior team's goaltending coach had recommended he learn. It promoted hand-eye coordination, focus, and rhythm; all things that were important to goalies. Plus, like running, it had been something to distract him from misery.

"Holy fuck, Stacks! You could be in the circus."

"That's the dream."

"Can you juggle knives?"

"Why the hell would I juggle knives?" Landon asked as he continued to juggle the oranges.

"Because it's badass."

"It's dangerous and stupid."

"That's why it's badass. I would totally juggle knives."

Landon neatly caught all three oranges. "Please don't."

"You're no fun."

"I know." Landon took the oranges to the kitchen and put them in the fridge. "Do you want some eggs?"

"I was just gonna eat breakfast at practice. They have a decent spread, usually."

"Yeah, but…" Landon pulled a carton of eggs and a flat of turkey sausage out of the fridge. "That's not for an hour."

Casey smiled. "Good point. I'll make coffee."

Chapter Sixteen

Battle of Alberta games were the fucking best.

Casey always fed off the energy of crowds, and there was no bigger or louder energy than the Calgary home crowd when their team was facing Edmonton. Casey didn't have any negative feelings about Edmonton personally—he really hadn't seen much of the city beyond the arena, because they were always in and out quickly when they played there—but he was fully committed to destroying their team and making every citizen of Edmonton cry.

Everyone on the Outlaws felt the same way. It didn't matter that one of Casey's best friends from college played for Edmonton, or that Gio Rossi's cousin played for them. Fuck the Edmonton Drillers forever.

"This one is gonna be nuts, I can feel it," Casey said in the tunnel as they waited to charge onto the ice.

"Fuck yeah," Nosey said. "Maybe we'll get a goalie fight again. That happened...five seasons ago? Fucking great."

Casey had seen the footage, but he still couldn't believe Antton had gotten in an actual fight. He'd gotten some good swings in too. "Maybe the backup goalies will fight," he mused. Then he yelled down the line, "Hey, Stacks. You wanna get in a fight?"

Landon narrowed his eyes and sort of shrugged in a *what the fuck are you talking about?* kind of way.

"A backup goalie fight would be fucking wild," Nosey said. "Both of them jumping over the boards and meeting in front of the benches." He laughed. "Can you imagine that shit?"

"Stacks," Casey called out again. "Have you ever seen two backup goalies fight?"

Landon turned his back to him.

"Wow. Your roommate hates you already," Nosey said.

"He does not." Casey hoped it wasn't a lie. He tapped Gio's shin with his stick blade. "What's the best way to annoy your cousin?"

"For *you* to annoy him?" Gio asked. "You could probably just talk to him. That'd annoy anyone."

Casey tapped him harder. "Maybe I'll flirt with him. Do you think I'm his type?"

"Nope." Gio grinned. "He likes 'em tall."

"His fucking loss."

Casey wasn't actually going to flirt with Patricio Rossi, but he was definitely looking forward to flirting with *someone* after the game. He was extra motivated to win tonight because he really wanted everyone to go out after the game. He badly needed to get laid. He'd had a sexy dream last night where Landon was feeding him grapes. They'd both been naked, and Landon had wings. It was weird.

Nosey raised his stick in the air like it was a sword. "For Calgary!"

"For Calgary!" the rest of the team roared back.

Casey silently added *for victory sex* in his head, then followed his teammates to the ice.

"Everyone is going out tonight!" Casey announced from where he was standing on the bench in his locker room stall. "Every fucking one."

The whole team cheered its approval of Casey's plan. Calgary had defeated Edmonton, and that meant it was time to party. Casey was definitely getting laid tonight. He could probably get laid five hundred times if he wanted to. In that moment, he felt like he could handle it.

He hopped down from the bench and darted over to where Landon was removing his gear. "Stacks. You're coming out, right? We talked about this."

"I guess so. Where?"

"I don't know! Somewhere. Everywhere. This city is in love with us right now and I wanna fucking drink it in."

Landon's eyes twinkled with rare amusement. "Okay. Sure. I'm in."

Casey put his hands on both of Landon's shoulders. He squeezed the muscle there through the thin, slippery material of Landon's athletic T-shirt. "Fucking. Right."

Landon stepped back, out of Casey's grip. "Yeah. Okay. Go get showered." He rubbed his own shoulder, clearly uncomfortable.

"Sorry," Casey said. "I forgot."

"Forgot what?"

"That you don't like being touched."

Landon's brow furrowed. "I never told you that."

"You didn't have to." Casey was a tactile guy. Most hockey players he'd met were, but Landon clearly wasn't. And that was cool. Casey could respect that.

"I—" Landon started, then stopped. He nodded and said, "Go shower."

Landon would love bars, if it weren't for all the noise and people and chaos. He wasn't a big drinker, not enough to get to the point where he could relax and enjoy himself in the sort of place he was in right now.

The bar was huge and there'd been a line outside, but Landon and his teammates had been ushered right past it. The people waiting in line had cheered when they'd recognized them.

Loud country music with a driving beat blared throughout the room. The dance floor was packed, partially with Calgary Outlaws. Casey was in the mix somewhere; Landon got occasional glimpses of his long hair from where he was sitting with a few of the older guys, slowly nursing a beer. He'd noticed Casey leaning close to a handsome guy on the dance floor, lips against the man's ear as he smiled and told him something. The other man had laughed, and Landon tried to ignore how jealous he was. The feeling had gripped him so suddenly and so completely, it had been shocking.

Antton was sitting at his table, and Landon was trying to ignore that too. All he wanted was to get through this night without embarrassing himself.

"Why aren't you dancing?" Ross MacIsaac asked.

"I, um. I don't. Dance." So much for not embarrassing himself.

"None of us can dance, but most of us met our wives in a place like this. You should go dance."

Landon couldn't imagine anything he wanted to do less than squeeze between all those writhing bodies and then attempt to make himself sexually appealing. What a nightmare. "I'm fine here."

Ross shrugged and turned to talk to Antton.

Casey had been right, of course. Landon didn't like being touched. It was one of many things that made intimacy of any kind difficult for him. But tonight his attention kept being drawn to the dance floor, and he wished he could be different. He wished he could be *fun*.

He wished he was the one laughing at whatever ridiculous shit Casey was saying. He wished Casey's lips were brushing his ear.

Dangerous thoughts. Dangerous, useless thoughts.

Landon wouldn't know what to do if Casey *did* pull him onto the dance floor, pressed their bodies together, and drawled something sexy into his ear. For one thing, Landon would have to lean way down for Casey to even reach his ear.

He laughed at the thought, just a little huff of air, but Ross noticed. "What are you giggling about? Shit, are you drunk already?"

"No! Nothing." God, Antton was staring at him. "Just thinking about something else."

"Well, I'm thinking about taking a piss and getting more beer."

Ross stood and left, which removed the human barrier between Landon and Antton.

Most of the guys had brought a club outfit to the arena, including Landon, because Casey had insisted: "If we win, we party. Pack something sexy." Antton's club outfit was the full three-piece suit he'd worn to the arena, complete with a crisply folded pocket square. Landon had no idea how he wasn't melting; Landon was wearing a T-shirt and jeans and only had slightly more body fat than a skeleton and he was dying.

But Antton, of course, looked effortlessly elegant, not a hair out of place. Landon rubbed the back of his own neck, which was damp with sweat.

"Good game tonight," he blurted.

Antton studied him with his ice-blue eyes, and Landon wished he could slide under the table without it being weird.

"Yes," Antton finally said. "It was a fun one."

Landon started nodding, and then worried he'd never be able to stop. "Totally. Lots of fun. Looked fun, I mean. Great game. Really good."

Antton smiled, just slightly, then took a slow sip of his beer.

Landon glanced at the dance floor. Casey was still dancing with the handsome guy.

"Who has caught your eye?" Antton asked.

Landon's head whipped around. "What?"

Antton nodded toward the dance floor. "You have been watching someone."

Landon shouldn't have been surprised that Antton fucking Niskanen, the best goaltender of his generation, noticed everything. "I'm not looking at anyone," he lied. "Just watching the dancers, I guess."

Antton's expression let Landon know that he didn't believe him. "Did you know?" he asked. "That Hicks likes men too?"

Landon nearly choked on the sip of beer he'd just taken. "Too?" How the fuck did Antton know that Landon—

"Yes. He likes women and also men."

Oh. "Yeah. He told me. I think it's cool that he's, y'know. Open about it."

Antton nodded. "Good."

They sat in silence for a few minutes, during which Landon purposefully looked everywhere except the dance floor. Ross returned with two pitchers of beer, which made most of the table cheer.

Antton pushed his half-full glass aside and began to stand up. "None for me. I'm driving, and I need to get home before I fall asleep."

Landon spotted Casey without meaning to, still on the dance floor, and now kissing the handsome man. Landon's heart froze. He had no right to feel jealous, and maybe it was shock as much as jealousy. Maybe it was excitement, seeing his teammate making out with a man in the middle of a crowded bar. Whatever was happening inside Landon, he needed to get the fuck out of here.

"Would you mind giving me a lift?"

Antton raised his eyebrows. "You're leaving?"

"Yeah, I uh, I'm pretty tired too. You live near Casey, right?"

"Yes. Do you want to tell Casey you are leaving?"

Landon glanced again at Casey, who was grinning at the man, their noses almost touching. "I'll text him. He won't mind."

Antton tilted his head toward the door, so Landon followed him.

They didn't speak much in the car. Antton drove a black

Lexus SUV with soft leather seats. It was spotless, unlike Casey's Jeep, which frequently had clothing and food wrappers strewn around it.

"You are like me," Antton said, breaking the silence that had lasted for several minutes.

"I am?" Besides both being goalies, Landon couldn't think of a single way they were similar.

"You are old when you are young," Antton explained. "Not a partier."

"Oh. Yeah. I guess I'm not."

"I thought maybe you were shy about fitting in here, but you probably were the same in Saskatoon, right?"

Landon flattened his palms against his thighs and curled his fingertips into the scratchy fabric of his coat. "Pretty much."

"Like me, then. Some advice?"

"Sure," Landon said, probably too eagerly. "Yeah."

"Have some fun. I was so serious when I was your age, I didn't enjoy myself nearly enough."

"You were busy being the best," Landon couldn't stop himself from saying.

"Maybe I would have been even better if I'd relaxed a bit. Had fun with my teammates. Enjoyed the experience."

Landon couldn't imagine a *better* version of Antton Niskanen, but he kept his mouth shut.

"I'm old now," Antton sighed.

"You're only thirty-four."

"Feels like a thousand. My life is amazing. My career, my wife, my kids. It's all perfect, but I wish I'd had more fun in my twenties. Been a little reckless, maybe."

"I don't know if I can do that," Landon said honestly. "I'm not built that way."

"Maybe not. Maybe I'm not either. But I wish I had tried, just a little."

For the rest of the drive, Landon tried to imagine a different version of himself. One who wasn't hollow inside. One who could stand to be touched and seen. One who could dance and flirt and smile.

He wanted it. It felt impossible, but was it something he could work at, the same way he worked to improve his game? He'd never be like Casey, but that didn't need to be his goal. He just wanted to be someone who could be happy.

Chapter Seventeen

"Oh."

It was the following morning, and Landon had emerged from the basement in need of breakfast. He'd heard footsteps upstairs, and thought he'd find Casey in the kitchen but instead he found a stranger.

No. Not a stranger. The man Casey had been dancing with.

The man smiled at Landon now. "Good morning. Sorry if I startled you." He held out his hand. "I'm Zach."

Landon shook his hand, an action he never enjoyed but especially not now. Zach's hand was warm and solid and stupid.

"Nice to meet you," Landon lied. "I'm Landon. Casey's roommate."

"He mentioned you. I hope we didn't wake you last night."

Miraculously, they hadn't. Landon had fallen asleep quickly and deeply after getting home. "Nope. Didn't hear a thing."

An awkward silence filled the kitchen, a mutual acknowledgment of the sorts of noises Landon could have potentially heard, had he been awake.

"I'm making omelets," Zach said. "You want one?"

"No," Landon said, even though Zach was definitely using *his* eggs, cheese, and vegetables to make them. Also, Landon was starving and would actually very much like an omelet.

"I haven't made coffee yet," Zach said apologetically. He looked like he hadn't slept much, but he was still unfairly attractive. Closer to Casey's height, and obviously very fit the way his T-shirt was stretched across his chest. He was white with dark hair, dark eyes, and dark stubble, all a bit rough looking at the moment.

Landon walked past him and began making coffee, just to give himself something to do.

"So you're a goalie, right?" Zach asked cheerfully as he flipped an omelet.

"Yes."

"I don't follow hockey much, but I've heard the goalie for Calgary is a big superstar. Is that you?"

Landon huffed. "No."

"Oh. So there's more than one goalie?"

"Yes." Landon was being an asshole, and he needed to stop. He turned on the coffee maker, then turned to face Zach. "I'm the backup goalie."

"Gotcha." Zach's gaze slid over him, appraisingly, and he smiled. "You're so tall. It must be hard to get pucks past you."

Landon wanted to say something pointed about how there was a lot more skill involved than simply blocking the net with his height, but instead he said, "It helps."

"It probably helps with a lot of things." Zach bit his lip flirtatiously.

Landon folded his arms across his chest. "I can reach things on high shelves."

Zach smiled. "Maybe you can come over sometime and help me put up Christmas lights."

Well. Zach was certainly making a lot of assumptions.

Thankfully, in that moment, Casey finally came downstairs. "Oh, cool, you guys met. Do I smell breakfast?"

"I made the coffee," Landon said quickly, and with too much pride.

"He got here just in time," Zach said. "I was a little lost on how to use your fancy coffee maker."

"Aw," Casey said, then kissed Zach quickly on the cheek. Landon turned to focus all of his attention on the coffee maker, as if it needed to be watched.

"Are you hiding any more hot men in your basement?" Zach asked.

"Only if Landon brought some home."

"No," Landon said quickly. "I came home alone."

"That's surprising," Zach said.

Heat crept up Landon's neck. He needed to exit this conversation. "I'm going to take a shower," he announced, and headed immediately to the basement.

He was in a terrible mood. He took a long, grumpy shower, and then grumpily put on clothes before grumpily heading back upstairs because he really was starving.

"Hey," Casey greeted him from the living room sofa. He was watching soccer. Alone.

"Did Zach leave?"

"Yeah. Do you think maybe later you could help me get my Jeep back from the arena? We can take my other car. The car you keep refusing to borrow."

"I haven't needed to borrow it," Landon said. He went to the kitchen feeling inexplicably lighter than he had a minute ago. There was an omelet on a plate with some apple slices on the side. "This for me?"

"Yup. Zach made it just in case."

Landon wolfed down the omelet, which was delicious despite being a bit cold. It was rude of Zach to be such a decent guy. It wasn't even any of Landon's business who Casey dated. Or hooked up with. Or whatever.

Landon poured himself what was left of the coffee, then went to the living room.

"Did you have fun last night?" Casey asked when Landon sat on the opposite end of the sofa.

"Not as much as you, maybe."

Casey frowned. "If you needed a wingman, I could have helped you out."

"No. I'm fine." He sipped his coffee and pretended to watch soccer.

"You know you're hot, right?"

Landon set his mug on the end table before his hand started shaking. "Zach seemed to think so."

"Yeah! He suggested we have a threesome next time." Casey laughed. Landon didn't.

"I'm not going to do that," Landon said.

"I know. I told him."

"Told him what?"

"That I don't think you're into dudes. We've never talked about it, so maybe I'm wrong but, I dunno. I figured either way you're probably not a threesome-with-your-roommate kind of guy."

Landon swallowed, then swallowed again. "I, um…"

"Oh shit. Did I fuck this up? If you're into that I could tell him and—"

"No! No. I'm not. Into that." Except his heart and his dick were telling him that he was into at least part of that. Probably not the Zach part.

"Got it. I shouldn't assume, though."

Landon was torn between changing the subject and blurting out his whole awkward deal when it came to sex and relationships. He settled on offering one piece of information. "You're right, about me not being into, like, threesomes. But you're wrong about the other thing."

It took Casey a moment to solve the puzzle. "You're into men!"

Landon nodded, once, gaze fixed on the TV.

"Just men?" Casey asked.

"I don't know."

"Oh. Have you, like…"

Landon could lie, or simply change the subject. He could pretend he didn't understand what Casey was asking. There were plenty of ways to avoid revealing the truth to the man Landon was almost certainly crushing on. Plenty of ways to avoid letting Casey know exactly how weird Landon was.

He chose honesty.

"I haven't. No."

There was a long silence, and then Casey said, "I think maybe I'm not understanding you right. I get confused easily. Are you saying—"

"I've never." Landon locked eyes with him. "Had sex."

More silence. Casey's brow furrowed like he was translating the words. "At all?"

"It's not impossible to go without sex, you know," Landon mumbled.

"Yeah, but—"

"I really don't think about it very much."

"Jesus. I do."

"I know."

"But you like guys."

Landon nodded. His face felt so hot. He stared longingly out the window at the gently falling snow.

"So if you see a hot guy, do you just, like, not think anything about him?"

"I find people attractive. Men, mostly. I get, y'know, crushes sometimes."

"Like on Antton," Casey teased.

"No! Absolutely not on Antton. Fuck you."

Casey laughed, then said, "So is it like, casual sex that you're not into or—"

Landon had reached his limit. "I don't want to talk about this."

Casey flinched. "Sorry. I won't ask about it anymore. I think I'm gonna work out a bit in the basement, if that's okay."

He hopped to his feet, ready to move on completely from

their conversation, and Landon wanted to hug him for it. "It's your house. Of course it's okay."

"Yeah, but it's, like, your *zone.*"

Landon stood too. "You're allowed in my zone."

He wished he'd phrased it differently, especially after all the sex talk. Casey just smiled, though, and said, "Hey, I booked that shopping thing at Holt Renfrew for Tuesday."

"Okay."

"I was thinking you'd look good in a dark floral print."

"For *you.* We're not shopping for me."

Casey nodded solemnly. "Totally."

"I might buy a shirt or something but not from your weird fashion doctor."

"Samir is a genius. Just wait. You'll look almost as good as me."

"Almost, huh?"

"Yeah, I mean. Samir is good, but he's not a wizard."

"Go work out." Landon was smiling now. "You can roast me in the car later."

Casey bounded down the stairs, and Landon found he wasn't jealous of Zach anymore.

Chapter Eighteen

For the next two days, Casey's thoughts were always divided. No matter what he was doing, or supposed to be focusing on, at least half of his brain was fixated on one thing: Landon was a virgin.

It wasn't a big deal, he told himself. Obviously it would be super uncool of Casey to make it a big deal. So what if Landon had never had sex? There were probably tons of people who'd never had sex by age twenty-four. Casey didn't know any personally, but in the whole world? There had to be plenty.

So there was no reason to be obsessed with the fact that no one—not one person—had ever laid Landon out naked on a bed, admired those miles of lean muscles, straddled his flexible hips and felt that fucking enormous cock press hard against them.

Boring. Who cared? Not Casey.

Landon was sitting across from him now at Casey's seldom-used dining table, eating the delicious bacon and eggs he'd made for them both. He was reading something on his phone, and Casey was trying not to stare at him. Trying not to wonder how the hell a man this beautiful had never been laid.

Casey had so many questions and he was going to keep every

single one of them to himself. Landon didn't want to talk about it, and it was none of Casey's business anyway.

So instead he asked, "Have you thought any more about Christmas?"

Landon glanced up from his phone. "Hm?"

"Christmas. You gonna come to the cabin with my family?"

"Oh, um. Actually my parents are thinking about coming to visit for a few days for Christmas. I was going to ask if maybe it would be okay if they stayed here?"

"Of course they can! But what if they came to the cabin too?"

"That's...it would be too many people."

"You'd think so, but this cabin has eight bedrooms because my parents don't do anything on a small scale. Invite them! Have they ever seen the Rockies?"

"No. They haven't traveled much."

"Shit, dude. You've gotta bring them. It's, like, an ideal Christmas situation. Mountains, snow, cabin, fireplace. Mom says it's gonna be fully decorated with a tree and everything."

Landon did not appear to be convinced, but he said, "I'll ask them what they think."

"Rad. It's just for two nights anyway. And they can stay here for as long as they want."

"Okay. Thanks. They may not even come, but thanks."

Casey had a bunch of questions about *that* too. What was the deal with Landon's family? He seemed to have an okay relationship with them, but he didn't mention any members of his family much, and his parents seemed oddly disinterested in their son making the NHL.

Again, though, none of Casey's business.

"You ready to shop?" he asked cheerfully. Their appointment with Samir was today.

"I guess."

"We can do some Christmas shopping today too," Casey said. "If you need to get your family some gifts. I haven't bought any presents yet."

Landon looked at him oddly. "What—" Then he shook his head. "Never mind."

"Never mind what?"

"I just...what do you buy your parents? They're so..."

"Rich?" Casey smiled. "You can say it. It's not like it's a secret. They are totally loaded. Mom came from money, too, so there's plenty of it between the two of them. And now I'm making bank, so yeah. There's way too much fucking money in our family. I know it."

Landon didn't say anything. His expression shifted from uncomfortable to interested, though.

"They give a lot to charity but—" Casey rolled his eyes "—I know. That's such a rich person thing to say. Brooke, my sister, she full-time volunteers for an organization that helps low-income families in L.A."

"That's cool."

"She moved out there for college and stayed. She seems really happy."

"So your parents are alone?" Landon asked.

"Hardly. First of all, Grandma lives in their guesthouse, but also they're super social. They're always traveling, hosting parties, going to parties. They're fun, y'know? They love people."

Landon's lips quirked. "Sounds about right."

"I know. Wait until you're surrounded by four of me."

Landon took a sip of his coffee, put the mug down, and said, "Is that supposed to sell me on this cabin?"

"Obviously."

Landon huffed and reached for more toast from the small stack in the middle of the table.

"I guess five of me if you count Grandma. She's a little more chill, though. I think you'd get along great with her."

"Wow. You're comparing me to your grandmother."

"I am not! I'm just saying she's mostly quiet but she has a dry sense of humor that's, like, deadly, and...okay. Yeah. You are basically the same."

"And she's single, you say?"

Casey laughed. "Yeah, but you'll need a really nice shirt to impress her, so let's go shopping."

Landon had left the real world. He'd been transported, via valet parking and a personal escort, to a planet where shirts cost thousands of dollars. And people acted like that was *normal.*

Casey was behind a curtain, trying on his zillionth outfit. Landon was slumped on a plush purple sofa, trying to ignore the way Samir kept frowning at him.

There was a rack of clothes Samir had selected for Landon, at Casey's request. Landon had no idea what Casey had told Samir in advance. *Please find some clothes for my lanky roommate?*

My lanky, virginal roommate.

Landon couldn't believe he had shared that with Casey. He didn't tell *anyone* that. If he could help it, he didn't talk about sex at all. Not because he never *thought* about it, but because thinking about it vaguely and thinking about *actually doing it* made him feel very differently. He watched porn sometimes, jerked off, enjoyed sexual fantasies that didn't necessarily involve himself. There was a sex drive there, but it was one he didn't want to copilot. Sharing himself that way with another person terrified him.

Casey stepped out from behind the curtain and Samir actually gasped.

The suit was emerald-green velvet and shouldn't have looked good on anyone, but Casey absolutely pulled it off.

"Good, right?" Casey said as he assessed himself in the mirror.

Samir dashed over and began fussing with the suit, pulling it in the back so it tightened across Casey's muscular chest and trim waist. "Oh, I think so," Samir purred.

"What do you think, Stacks?"

Landon met Casey's gaze in the mirror. "Good," he said, even though the real word he wanted to use was *dazzling.*

Casey was fucking dazzling in that ridiculous suit. Anyone else would look like a leprechaun, but Casey just looked…fun. Confident. Sexy.

"Why aren't you trying on clothes?" Casey asked. "I want to see you in this sweater." He crossed the room to where the rack of Landon clothes was and held out the sleeve of a light purple cashmere sweater.

"That sweater costs over two thousand dollars," Landon said. Samir gave an unhappy sigh, as if acknowledging the price of things you were expected to buy was rude.

"Yeah, but trying it on is free," Casey said. He removed the sweater from the rack and held it out.

Landon stood. "Fine." He took the sweater and went behind the curtain of the second changing area. It only took a few seconds to remove his hoodie and slip the sweater on over his T-shirt. God, it was so soft. He indulged for a moment, running his hand down his chest and stomach, as if the sweater needed to be straightened out. It didn't. It fit him perfectly, clinging to his muscles slightly, and hanging a bit loose around his waist, an area he was always self-conscious about because he was so skinny. He'd never even considered wearing this color before, but it was…nice. Flattering, maybe.

He stepped out from behind the curtain.

"So it fits I guess," he said.

"Holy shit," Casey said as he walked toward Landon. "Like, holy shit. Right, Samir?"

"It's a gorgeous sweater," Samir said, clearly trying to avoid complimenting Landon the cheapskate. "I have one myself."

"Stacks, buddy. You look so fucking good." He hovered his hand over Landon's chest, then pulled it away when he seemed to realize what he was doing. "Is it soft? It's soft, right?"

Landon bit the inside of his cheek, then held out one arm in invitation. "It's soft."

Casey rested his palm on Landon's forearm and everything just kind of…stopped. The touch wasn't anything—he was feeling the sweater, not Landon—but Landon seemed to forget how to breathe anyway. Casey's fingers drifted up to Landon's inner elbow and Landon had to fight to keep his eyes from fluttering closed.

It felt *so nice.*

"Soft," Casey said quietly.

"Yeah."

Casey pulled his hand away, and was he blushing a little? He glanced at the floor for a moment, and then back at Landon, and his little smile looked almost...shy.

"You look really good," Casey said.

And that was when Landon decided to spend way too much money on a sweater.

"I'm already doubting my mom's gift, Stacks."

Landon swallowed his mouthful of burger and said, "Why? You said she actually asked for it."

He had not understood the appeal of the absurdly expensive designer yoga bag Casey had bought her, but he didn't understand much about anything he'd experienced that day. Including the twenty-five hundred fucking dollars he'd personally shelled out for a single sweater.

Or the way he'd wanted Casey to run his fingers over Landon's sleeve forever. Or maybe even under the cuff, caressing the sensitive skin on the inside of his wrist.

It was a weird thing to be hot and bothered about, but here he was.

"You're right," Casey said. "She'll love it." He cheerfully popped a french fry into his mouth, problem solved.

"Are you going to bring the green suit to Vegas?" Landon asked.

"Nah. It needs to be tailored. I'd like to debut it at home."

Landon huffed. "Debut."

"What? I'm famous for my impeccable fashion, dude. Check the best-dressed lists."

Landon would definitely never do that. "You are a good dresser," he conceded.

"I know. It's because I'm not afraid of color."

"Like your pink skate laces."

"Exactly." Casey pointed a fry at him. "You know why I wear those?"

"No," Landon said, though he'd been curious. "Why?"

"In college my team did one of those gift exchanges where you can, like, swap gifts if you see something you like better than what you got. You know what I mean?"

"I think I've heard of that."

"Right, so one of the guys bought bright pink skate laces as the gift. Like, as a joke, right? Who wants to be stuck with the pink laces?"

Landon nodded.

"It felt wrong," Casey continued. "Homophobic or sexist or both. I dunno. I didn't like it. Anyway, I was the last one to open a gift. I got a poker set. Totally solid gift. But I traded it for the pink laces, and then I wore them for the next game. After that I just kept on wearing them."

"That's…" Landon didn't know what to say. He'd assumed Casey just wore the laces because he was a showoff, or maybe to be obnoxious, but the real reason was almost heroic. "I like that," he finally said. "I never would have been confident enough to wear them, but I would have felt the same way as you about it."

Casey smiled. "I know, Stacks. That's why I like you."

After lunch Landon requested they go to a less-expensive store so he could shop for presents for his parents. He wasn't being cheap; he just knew his parents weren't really the designer yoga bag type.

He wanted to buy them the whole world. They deserved it, and he owed it to them.

Instead he ended up buying his dad some really nice-quality

winter work gloves, along with a scarf and hat, and was now considering a bathrobe and slippers for his mom.

"Dude," Casey said, "how old are your parents?"

"Like, early fifties?"

"Okay, because I thought they were maybe in their early hundreds based on this gift."

Landon sighed. "Fine. What's your idea?"

"I don't know. What does she like?"

It was a simple question, but it made Landon burn with shame. The truth was he didn't really know what his mom liked anymore.

"Gardening," he said, because it popped into his head suddenly. "Or she used to like gardening. Our backyard wasn't big, but it always looked nice. Lots of flowers."

"Okay," Casey said slowly. "I know less than nothing about gardening, but there are probably some dope gifts you could get her."

"Like what? And besides, it's winter. Not exactly gardening season."

"Who cares? Come on. We're going somewhere else."

They ended up at a year-round garden center that Casey had googled. Casey immediately began charming the woman behind the counter, who looked to be about Landon's mom's age.

"So what would you say would be the ultimate gift for someone who loves gardening?" Casey asked. "Like, the very best thing."

The woman, whose nametag said Lori, happily showed them a few high-quality items while Casey reacted with an absurd amount of excitement to each one.

"Stacks! Look at this thing. She can keep all her tools in here and sit on it. It's, like, ergonomic. And you could get her new tools too! Oh, and that hat!"

So Landon walked out of the store with a fancy folding garden stool, a set of gardening tools, leather gardening gloves, a cheerful sun hat, and a rugged apron. He also felt lighter, like he'd maybe done something right by his parents for once.

"Thanks for thinking of that," Landon said as they placed the purchases in the back of the Jeep. "You basically saved Christmas."

"I saved your mom from a bathrobe. There's still the problem of your dad. A hat and gloves are not good enough, buddy."

"He's a simple guy," Landon argued. "But I'll think of something to add. I hope they'll be able to take all this home if they fly out here."

"They totally can. Just pay for another checked bag for them. I've got extra suitcases."

"Maybe I'll get her a gift certificate to a garden center back home," Landon said. "I could order one online, right?"

"Totally." Casey nudged him. "Look at how excited you are."

Landon *was* excited. He knew a few premium gardening items weren't going to make up for years of selfishness, but it was something.

Casey was smiling at him. His cheeks were pink from the cold, and snow swirled around him. He was achingly cute, and Landon wanted him to keep smiling.

"You know what?" Landon said. "I think meeting Dougie Hicks would be a pretty great Christmas present for Dad."

Casey's grin grew wider, dimples cutting hard into his rosy cheeks. "I think Dougie Hicks would like to meet, uh…"

"Mike," Landon said. "Mike and Joanna Stackhouse."

"Love them already."

Landon realized he was smiling right back at Casey. Everything he could think of saying in that moment would be too much. Too honest. Things like "This was the best day I've had in maybe years" or "I love spending time with you" or "You make me want to be brave."

Instead, he said, "Let's go home. I'm starving."

"Figures. You haven't eaten in like an hour."

Chapter Nineteen

"So," Landon said, "we've been invited to spend Christmas with the Hicks family."

"Oh," Mom said. "That's nice. Are you going? We can cancel our plans."

"No!" Landon said quickly. "I mean all of us are invited. You guys too."

He was video calling them from his bedroom two days after his shopping trip with Casey. He still wasn't sure joining the Hicks family for Christmas was the right move, but he needed to at least give his parents the option.

"Invited where?" Dad asked. "Don't they live in Florida?"

"They rented a cabin near Banff, in the mountains. I guess it's huge and fancy, so there's room for us. That's what Casey said, anyway."

He saw the change in Dad's expression, from confusion to excitement. Mom didn't seem convinced.

"We don't need to intrude on their Christmas," she said. She'd always been more like Landon, his dad more like Erin. "But if you want to, we can stay here. It's all right."

"I want to spend Christmas with you." Landon meant it. He hadn't spent many holidays with them over the past eight years. But for that reason, he would understand if they'd rather not bother flying out to Alberta. It's not like he deserved it. "If you want," he added.

"Do you really think the Hickses won't mind if we join them?" Dad asked.

"If they're anything like Casey, they definitely won't mind. Casey loves meeting new people."

"He sounds very nice," Mom said.

"He's great. He's…been a good friend."

Landon had been working through a lot of thoughts and feelings about Casey over the past couple of days. When Casey had touched his sleeve, Landon had been overcome with a shocking bolt of lust. It wasn't something he was used to feeling, and it wasn't something he wanted to feel about Casey. So he'd been distancing himself from Casey, as much as he possibly could, anyway, which basically amounted to spending a lot of time hiding in the basement. He needed the space to think, and to figure out how he was going to stop crushing on his roommate.

"Christmas with Dougie Hicks," Dad said wistfully. "Wait 'til I tell Craig and Bruno. Do you think if I brought my Toronto jersey, that Dougie would sign it?"

Landon smiled, excitement bubbling in his chest at opportunity to give his parents some good memories. "Yeah, Dad. I think he would."

Mom was smiling now too. "I've always wanted to see the Rockies."

"I haven't seen them properly yet either," Landon said. "Just in the distance. I think a cabin in the Rockies at Christmas would be cool, right?"

"With Dougie Hicks," Dad reminded him, clearly still processing that part.

Mom laughed. "It all sounds too good to be true. Like a dream."

"I know," Landon said, because he'd felt that way a few times since moving in with Casey.

They chatted for a bit about what various friends and neighbors were up to back home, and about how much colder it was in Calgary. About the storm that was supposed to hit that night in Calgary. Then Landon shared his other reason for calling.

"So, um. I'm going to be starting tomorrow night. Against Detroit. Just found out this morning." He wondered how obvious his anxiety was about it.

"Atta boy!" Dad said. "That's great!"

Mom clapped excitedly, then asked, "Are you nervous?"

"Trying not to be."

"I'm sure you'll do great," Mom said. Landon knew she meant it as encouragement, but he could hear the *I'll feel better when the game is over and I know you're safe* in her words. It made him angry and sad at the same time, and then guilty for feeling either of those things. It all must have shown on his face because Mom added, "We'll be sure to record it. Everyone here is so excited for you, Landon."

"You're the toast of Eastern Passage," Dad agreed. "Maybe they'll name a street here after you someday."

"As if," Landon scoffed. Besides only very technically being an NHL player, he hadn't spent a significant amount of time back home in years, and there were much bigger stars in the league from the Halifax area than him. Though it was nice to think about his parents' friends and neighbors being excited for them, rather than always looking at them with sympathy. He wanted the Stackhouses to be known for more than tragedy. "I'll try to give everyone there something to cheer for tomorrow night."

A silence fell between them, during which Mom's lips formed a tight smile, then fell before she said, "I've been trying. We both have. We tried to watch your first game that you started, but it's hard. I hate that it's hard, but it is and we're working on it. I promise."

Landon's throat felt tight. "Mom..."

"We just want you to know that we're trying," Mom said.

"It's okay if you can't watch. I get it." He mostly did. It made sense that his parents were terrified of seeing him get hurt. Of anything happening to their only remaining child. He'd accepted it years ago, and he tried not to imagine an alternate reality where his parents and his sister were at his games, Erin cheering louder than anyone.

"We love you," Dad said.

"I love you too." He loved them both so much, and he decided, right then, that he wouldn't waste the opportunity to finally have the big in-person conversation they'd all been avoiding for years. He would apologize to them, for everything, and maybe they could move forward together.

He forced his voice into something cheerful and said, "So I'll tell Casey that we'll go to the cabin with them?"

"Absolutely," Dad said at the same time Mom said, "If they're sure."

"Okay."

"We really can't wait to see you," Mom said. "It will be so nice to be together."

Landon's forced smile softened. "Yeah. It will be."

Casey couldn't sleep.

He'd tried everything, including attempting to read a *book* for fuck's sake. An actual paper book that Brooke had given him with a bunch of boring words in it. He hadn't absorbed any of it, because his mind wouldn't stop racing.

He wasn't even thinking about anything useful. There was the usual anxiety about being in a room alone at night, and a bit of excitement about the game tomorrow night. Usually he could sleep through that stuff, but there was more going on in his brain tonight.

He wondered if Landon was having trouble sleeping, like the last time he'd gotten the start. Casey hoped he was sleeping like a baby because he wanted him to be a wall tomorrow night.

Casey had been thinking a lot about their shopping trip two days ago. In particular, about Landon in that cashmere sweater, and the way he'd let Casey touch him. His arm had felt so warm and solid through the soft fabric that Casey had wanted to crawl inside the sweater.

And, of course, he was still thinking about Landon being a virgin. And then hating himself for thinking about it.

Did Landon *want* to have sex? Not with Casey, obviously, but with anyone? If he did, then what was stopping him? And what if he found someone he wanted to have sex with, and then that person was mean to him? Or was bad at sex? Or wasn't patient and respectful and cool? Landon deserved someone good.

If Landon asked, Casey would find him someone good.

Casey flopped onto his stomach. Then rolled to his back. This sucked.

The wind was howling outside, which wasn't helping things. It was loud and creepy. A few seconds later, it got a whole lot creepier when the power went out, plunging the room into blackness.

"No," he whispered shakily as he fumbled for his phone. "Fuck."

He turned on the flashlight on his phone, but it only made the room scarier looking. For several minutes, he was nearly paralyzed with fear. He wanted to leave the room, but he couldn't make himself move. He knew the rest of the house would be just as dark, but maybe he could get to Landon.

And then what?

Fuck it. He'd figure it out when he got there. He forced himself to his feet and walked quickly to the door.

His flashlight beam bounced around in front of him as he made his way to the stairs. His heart was racing, his throat bone-dry. He felt like screaming, but there was no reason. He knew that. The house was safe, he told himself. It was just dark.

God, it was so fucking dark.

He carefully made his way down the stairs and into the living room. He swung the flashlight beam around the room, just to reassure himself that no one was lurking there.

And then he really did scream. Because there was a fucking monster sitting on his couch.

Casey's back hit the wall before he'd even realized he was walking backward. He was still screaming. The monster stood up with his hands held palm-out in front of him. He was wearing a goalie mask.

"Casey," the monster said. "Jesus, I'm sorry. It's just me."

He removed the goalie mask, and of course it was Landon.

Casey crumpled to the floor. He felt like his circuits were all fried, overwhelmed by too many huge feelings at once: terror, relief, and now humiliation.

"Hey, it's okay," Landon said softly. He was crouched next to Casey, one big hand on his shoulder. "It's me. It's Landon."

"Okay," Casey said in a voice that didn't sound okay at all. "Fucking hell."

For a few minutes, they both stayed there, Landon's hand never leaving Casey's shoulder. Casey pressed against it, seeking comfort and wanting to wrap himself in Landon's arms. It was so fucking stupid, this fear. He concentrated hard on slowing his breathing, at getting himself under control because he was probably scaring Landon. It had to be freaky seeing your roommate reduced to a quivering ball. Casey had never wanted anyone to see him like this.

Finally, his breathing slowed to something close to normal and his heart felt less like it was going to explode. "I'm okay," he said.

"You want to sit on the couch, maybe?" Landon asked.

"Yeah. All right."

They moved to the couch, Casey scrunching himself into the corner, and Landon sitting one cushion away, the Santa-shaped pillow that Casey had impulse-bought at Costco between them.

"The power went out," Landon said unnecessarily.

"I know. I was coming to find you."

"Why?"

Casey chewed his lip, trying to decide what to say. Since it seemed like the cat was out of the bag anyway, he said, "I hate the dark. Like, *really* hate it."

"Oh."

"I couldn't sleep anyway, and then the lights went out and I just needed to find you. I couldn't be alone."

Landon didn't say anything for a moment, probably processing the fact that Casey was a baby. Then he stood up and walked toward the window. Casey wanted to beg him to come back, but a second later the Christmas lights around the window were on, and then the ones on the shelf under the TV.

Landon gave him a soft half smile in the glow of the multicolored lights. "Good thing you got battery-powered ones."

Casey exhaled slowly. He was so glad he wasn't alone.

Landon was wearing a white long-sleeve T-shirt and plaid pajama pants and he looked so cozy and cute that Casey forgot to be scared for a few seconds. "Is there a reason you're scared? Did something…happen?"

"No, nothing. That's the embarrassing part. It's just a phobia, I guess. It makes no fucking sense."

Landon sat on the sofa again, this time a little closer to Casey. "I'm sorry. That sounds awful."

"It's stupid. I hate it." Casey stared at Landon's knee. It was so close to his own. "I thought I'd outgrow it, y'know? I mean, parts of it, I did." He hesitated, unsure how embarrassing he wanted to get here. Then he just went for it. "When I was a kid, I could barely be in a room by myself, like any time of day. At night, I always slept with a light on. As I got older, I got a little better at being alone, but the dark still terrifies me. My imagination goes wild. I don't even know what I'm scared of."

Landon's lips quirked up on one side. "Masked men on your couch, maybe?"

Casey managed to smile back at him. "Yeah. You, um… Hang around in the dark wearing a goalie mask often?"

Landon laughed, just a tiny bit. "Yeah. Kind of."

Casey nodded. For some reason it made sense.

"It calms me, I guess," Landon explained. "On nights before games, especially. I think I'm more comfortable wearing the mask than I am without it."

"Oh." Casey uncurled and placed his feet on the floor. He was still jittery, so he hunched forward and took a few deep breaths.

"You okay?" Landon asked.

"Yeah. Keep talking. I like your voice." It was probably a strange thing to say, but it was true. Landon's soft, deep voice was soothing.

"I have trouble sleeping sometimes," Landon said, "and it helps if I put the mask on and kind of meditate."

"In the dark?"

"Usually, yeah. No distractions in the dark."

Casey huffed out a shaky laugh. "Everything distracts me in the dark."

It felt weird to actually be talking about this, to have shared his most closely guarded secret with someone. But Landon didn't seem to be judging him at all. He was just quietly observing him with those sad brown eyes, looking sympathetic rather than disgusted by Casey's childish fear.

Casey grabbed the Santa-shaped pillow and hugged it against his chest. "So yeah. I'm kind of a mess."

"You're not a mess."

"I'm a total mess."

Landon tapped his bare foot against Casey's ankle. "If anyone here is a mess, it's probably the guy who needs to sit alone in the dark wearing pajamas and a goalie mask the night before games."

That made Casey smile. "So you couldn't sleep this time either, huh?"

Landon sighed. "No. Same thing as last time. Just…spiraling. It happens a lot."

"That sucks."

"It does."

"Do you want to talk about it?"

"No."

Casey knew he should take him at his word, but he couldn't ignore how obvious it was that Landon needed to talk to someone. To share some of the weight he lugged around. "I'm not trying to push," Casey said carefully, "but if there's something you want to share, I want to listen. If you think it would help."

Several seconds of silence passed, then Landon said, "My sister died when I was sixteen. She was eighteen."

Casey's stomach felt like lead. "Landon," he said softly, because he didn't know what else to say. It was the same age difference as his own sister and him, and he couldn't imagine losing Brooke.

"Yeah. It was awful. It's still awful. We were really close. Her name was Erin."

Casey set the pillow down, then turned so he was facing Landon. "I'm sorry."

Landon nodded, sniffed, and then fell silent. Casey waited. He'd wait for as long as it took for Landon to share more. Here, in a room illuminated only by Christmas lights, and with the wind howling outside and Landon's body warm beside him, Casey felt like time had stopped anyway.

Finally, Landon said, "It was right after I got drafted to a junior team in Quebec. The whole family had been so excited for me, and for Erin because she'd just graduated high school. We were all so happy, y'know?" His words were clipped and sounded automatic, like he was trying to get the information out as quickly as he could. "And then she was gone. It was so sudden. A car accident. She had to swerve out of her lane, I guess. We don't even really know what happened, but it killed her. Instantly."

Casey's eyes were burning. He knew words were never easy for Landon, and these words would be difficult for anyone to get out. He took a chance and placed a hand on Landon's forearm.

Landon didn't flinch. "That's awful," he said, using Landon's own word because he couldn't think of one better.

Landon surprised him by continuing. "I felt...shattered. I can't really describe it better than that. And then just empty. My parents were barely functioning. And I left." His voice broke on the last word. "I left them alone. I was all they had, and I chose to play hockey in another province."

Casey squeezed his fingers around Landon's arm. "You didn't do anything wrong."

"I *left*," Landon said, loudly enough that it startled Casey. It seemed to startle Landon too. More quietly, he said, "I lived with another family, in Quebec. One that wasn't torn apart by grief. And it felt good to not have to think about Erin every second of every day. It felt good to just live for hockey, and pretend Erin was still okay back in Halifax. That my parents were okay."

"Of course it did. That doesn't mean that—"

"I was selfish. I was so fucking selfish and I'm *still* selfish. My relationship with my parents has never been the same. It's like we don't know how to talk to each other, or maybe we're all holding back what we really need to be saying. Sometimes I want them to yell at me or something. Let me know exactly how much I hurt them. But they're so *nice* to me. I don't know how they can even stand me."

"Because you're their son, and you're amazing." Casey inched a little closer to him. "I'll bet they're proud of you. They wanted you to be exactly where you are right now, in the NHL. If you were that good at sixteen, then your parents must have been supporting your dream a hundred percent."

"They do support me. They always have, but they're scared to watch me play live. In case I get hurt. Or worse."

That sent a chill through Casey. Of course hockey was a dangerous sport, and he'd seen his share of terrifying injuries. He could understand why Landon's parents would worry, but it was also heartbreaking to think about them not watching his games.

"I'm all they have left," Landon said quietly, "and I'm a terrible son."

"You're not. You're just..." Casey searched for the right words. "You're just dealing with something really fucking terrible in whatever way you can."

"Badly."

"No. Like someone who needed to figure out a way to keep going."

Their gazes met, and then Landon seemed to notice Casey's hand on his arm. He looked at it curiously but didn't pull away.

"Tell me about Erin," Casey said, barely above a whisper. This moment seemed so fragile, but he wanted Landon to have the chance to talk about someone he loved. Someone he never had a chance to talk about.

Landon's lips turned up. "She wasn't much like me at all. She was...fun. Popular. She had lots of friends, but she always made time for her awkward younger brother. I could always talk to her." He turned his gaze to the couch cushions. "I still do. That probably sounds weird, but it helps, sometimes."

Casey very gently squeezed his forearm. "It makes sense." He could add that he himself talked to inanimate objects all the time just to feel less alone, but he decided to stay on topic.

"It's been over eight years since she died, but it still feels fresh. Maybe because I never talk about it, I don't know."

Casey was sure that was at least part of it, but he stayed silent.

"Sometimes I get hit with these...feelings," Landon explained. "Like running into a wall. I'll be fine, and then something will remind me of her, and remind me that I got to live and she didn't. And it hurts so much."

Casey quickly wiped away his own tears with his free hand. He should have guessed the sadness in Landon's eyes had been caused by something like this, but it was crushing, knowing that it wasn't something Casey could take away.

"It's just..." Landon huffed out an exasperated whoosh of air. "She wanted to experience the whole world. She complained to me once that it was so unfair that there were so many things to see and do on this planet, and she wouldn't be able to—" He paused, and swallowed before continuing. "That's the part that makes me so angry. She never even had a chance to get started. She had no time at all."

"It's fucked," Casey said, with feeling. "Sorry. That wasn't the most sensitive thing to say."

"No, it is. It's fucked," Landon agreed. "Just totally fucked." He sighed. "So I guess I like to imagine that she's seeing the whole world now, or maybe the whole universe, in the afterlife or whatever. I know that's probably not how death works but…"

"It's a cool idea. I like it."

"It's selfish, maybe. Pretending she's hanging around me. Still ready to listen to my problems whenever I need her."

Casey didn't know how Landon managed to move through life carrying this much pain and guilt. The fact that Landon felt guilty for even imagining that his sister was still listening to him was too much.

"I mean," Landon continued, "if my idea of the afterlife is real, then hopefully she's at the top of a mountain somewhere, or behind a waterfall. Somewhere amazing."

Casey had a long history of letting whatever thoughts popped into his head fall out of his mouth, and he continued that tradition now. "I know there's no waterfall here or anything, but I think being around you is pretty amazing."

Landon stared at him, huge dark eyes glistening in the rainbow of colors from the Christmas lights. His lips parted, as if he were about to speak, but he stayed silent.

Casey wanted to hug Landon so bad, but he didn't think Landon would be into that. *Hug* probably wasn't the right word anyway. He wanted to pull Landon into his lap and hold him. He wanted to cradle Landon's head against his chest, stroke his hair, and tell him he'd be okay.

Landon pulled his arm away, as if he'd been reading Casey's

mind. "Thanks. For listening. Sorry I unloaded on you like that."

"Don't apologize. You can talk to me anytime, about anything, okay? I like talking to you."

Landon gave him a small smile and nodded. "We need to go to sleep."

"Yeah. Fuck." Casey picked up his phone and saw that it was after three AM. They were going to be wrecked tomorrow for the game if they didn't sleep.

Except the power was still off and Casey would never be able to sleep alone tonight. He tried to think of a solution, but Landon beat him to it.

"Do you—would you maybe want to sleep…together?" Landon said.

A million thoughts rushed into Casey's head. "You mean—"

"Just sleep. I wasn't suggesting we—"

"Right! No. Of course."

"I thought since we're both having trouble sleeping, and the power is still out, maybe you'd be okay with some company?"

Now Casey *really* wanted to hug him. "I'd be more than okay with that. Wanna go up to my room?"

"Sure." Landon stood. "Do you want to bring some of these Christmas lights?"

Casey considered it. "No, I'll be okay if you're there. It's being alone that…scares me." His cheeks flushed with embarrassment and maybe a bit of excitement from being able to admit that. He picked up the goalie mask Landon had left on the coffee table. "Do you need this?"

"No."

"You don't sleep in it?"

"No."

"It doesn't help you get in the *zone*?"

"Shut up and come to bed."

Those words sent a jolt of inconvenient arousal through Casey. He forced himself to ignore it, focusing instead on turning his flashlight back on and psyching himself up for another scary journey through the dark.

As they walked up the stairs together, Landon put a hand on Casey's back, as if to simply let him know he was there, and Casey's heart swelled. It was very dark upstairs, but it was okay. He wasn't alone.

They managed to find Casey's bed and lay down with plenty of space between them. Casey had shared beds with tons of guys for nonsexual reasons over his many years of playing hockey. It wasn't a big deal.

What was kind of a big deal was that Landon fell asleep immediately, and Casey quickly followed.

Chapter Twenty

It was probably rude to watch someone sleep. Landon had shared beds and rooms with plenty of guys, and he hadn't found a single one of them fascinating when they were sleeping. He hadn't been enchanted by their sighs, or tempted to gently adjust a lock of dark honey hair that was in danger of getting caught between parted lips. He'd never felt perfectly calm just being near one of those guys, hoping simultaneously that they would sleep forever and never ruin this moment, and that they would open their eyes and smile when they saw him.

So he was probably being rude.

It had been a weird night, but Landon couldn't regret any of it. If Casey hadn't come downstairs, Landon would likely have battled insomnia for the rest of the night and lost. Now it was late morning, and he'd been able to get a decent seven hours of sleep.

He couldn't even regret revealing the worst about himself to Casey because he found he felt lighter this morning. He'd never really spoken to anyone about Erin, or his parents, or the guilt he'd been carrying for years. Right after Erin died, he'd had a couple of appointments with a grief counselor, and he'd hated every minute of them. He'd barely said a word, and everything the counselor had said made him angry. They'd had plenty of gentle, sympathetic words for Landon, and had seemed to think it was important that he talk about his feelings, but no amount of talking was going to bring Erin back. It had been, he'd decided at the time, an agonizing waste of time, and he'd never since visited another therapist outside of the team-employed ones, who he only discussed hockey-related problems with. He still had no interest in therapy, but talking to Casey had felt good. It was useful practice for the conversations he wanted to have with his parents when they came for Christmas.

His chest felt tingly, now, remembering how earnestly Casey had defended Landon. How sure he'd been that Landon was a good person, despite everything. Landon didn't feel that he'd provided much evidence of that, during the few short weeks Casey had known him.

Casey obviously trusted Landon enough to tell him about his fear of the dark. Landon suspected he'd never told anyone about that before, and had been surprised to learn it, because Casey didn't seem like he was ever bothered by anything. But everyone had their secrets.

Casey's terrified reaction to finding Landon was going to be hard to forget. It had been awful, seeing Casey like that. *Screaming* like that. Landon wished he was better at comforting people.

Now, Casey looked anything but terrified, all peaceful and relaxed in the lamplight.

Landon closed his eyes. He shouldn't be staring at him like this. He kept his eyes closed for as long as he could stand it, then opened them. And again. And again until he opened his eyes and found Casey looking back at him.

A slow, shy smile spread across Casey's face. "Hi."

Landon swallowed. "Hey."

The smile grew until a dimple appeared, and Landon could only helplessly smile back at him.

"Did you sleep okay?" Casey said. His voice was huskier than usual. Softer. Landon loved it.

"Yeah. You?"

"Must have. I don't remember anything after we got into bed. Is the power back on?"

"Yeah. The lamp was on when I woke up."

Casey rolled to his back and ran a hand through his hair. Landon felt an odd pang of jealousy. "We should probably get up, I guess."

It made sense. Why would they linger in bed together like lovers?

On the other hand, why did that sound so appealing?

"I'll make breakfast," Landon offered.

"I'll make coffee."

"Deal," Landon said, then, with enormous effort and a lot of confusing feelings, he left the bed.

Landon felt invincible.

Almost invincible. He'd let one goal in, but it had been a tough one. Detroit had managed to get the puck past him on a third rebound. Landon had almost had it too.

Maybe it was for the best. The pressure was off for a shut-out now, Calgary was ahead by two goals, and Landon had stopped twenty-eight shots with six minutes left in the game. Not bad at all. Certainly a huge improvement over the last game he'd started.

But six minutes was a lot of time in hockey, and Detroit proved it by scoring a goal a minute later, bringing them within one goal of tying.

"Bring it," Landon muttered as both teams set up at center ice of the face-off. "Fucking try me."

Lee won the face-off, and the play traveled to the far end of the ice. Landon relaxed a bit and left his crease to get a better view of the action. Casey was battling for the puck in the corner. Landon could see his pink laces sticking out from between the skates of a Detroit defenseman.

"Get it, Casey," Landon said.

Casey did get it, but then he lost it, and suddenly Detroit

had a breakaway. Landon watched the puck, watched the stick, watched the hands, watched the skates. The skater was coming in at an angle from the left, moving fast, and he didn't have solid control of the puck.

Landon decided to take a risk.

Before he could second-guess himself, he gripped up on his stick, lunged forward and jabbed at the puck. If he missed, it would be an easy goal because he'd left the net wide open.

He didn't miss. The wide blade of his stick made contact with the puck, pushing it away from the skater and back toward the blue line. The skater tripped over Landon's sprawled body and slid toward the boards behind them. Landon scrambled to his feet because another Detroit player had snatched the puck and was about to shoot. Fortunately the shot was weak and Landon was able to trap the puck easily, causing play to stop.

He heard two things at once: the crowd going absolutely nuts cheering for him, and Casey screaming over it.

"Fuck yes, Stacks! Are you *kidding me*?" Casey bumped his chest against Landon's arm. "Poke check king!"

"Did it look good?"

"It was fucking epic! Look." He pointed up to the giant screen on the scoreboard. Landon flipped his mask up and watched the replay of himself attacking the puck like he was in a battle to the death with it.

It did look pretty awesome.

"Shit, that's so hot," Casey raved. "I wanna watch it forever."

"You've got a face-off to get to." Landon tried to sound stern, but he was smiling. And probably blushing, though he was already flushed from playing hockey so it hopefully wasn't noticeable.

"I'm gonna watch that all night when we get home," Casey said as he skated backward away from Landon. "All night."

"Whatever. Score a goal or something."

Landon was trying to be playful, but he really would like his team to score a goal. A little insurance for these last few minutes of game time would be nice.

Calgary didn't score, though, and when there were about two minutes left in the game, Detroit pulled their goalie for the extra attacker. Now Landon had to keep track of *six* Detroit skaters, four of which were forwards, two of which were all-stars.

Landon's teammates did a good job getting in Detroit's way, blocking passing and shooting lanes. Ross MacIsaac had planted himself in front of the crease, and was making sure no one would be able to tip a puck in.

Detroit did get some good shots in, though. A fast wrister from the left that Landon was barely able to see, and when he couldn't control the rebound, a quick shot came from the right. Ross got that one.

Unfortunately, when Ross tried to clear the puck, it was intercepted by a Detroit player, and Landon had to hope he shot it because he didn't have time to look around at other possibilities.

He didn't shoot it. He made a quick, clean pass to a Detroit sniper, who fired it toward the net. Landon wasn't in position to stop it at all, but he made a desperate dive toward the puck and then watched with wonder as it bounced off the tip of his glove and out.

Lee got the puck and fired it toward the empty net at the opposite end of the ice. The crowd, already loud after Landon's desperation save, absolutely lost their minds when the puck slid cleanly into the net.

Less than a minute later, the game was over, and the entire Calgary team was racing toward Landon to celebrate.

"Holy shit, kid," Ross said. "That was big-time."

His other teammates said similar things, between lots of whooping and cheering. Most of them hugged him or patted him in some way. And then Antton stopped in front of him, nodded once, and said, "Fucking right."

Landon smiled so wide it made his cheeks ache. He was out

of practice. "Fucking right," he agreed, then accepted Antton's quick hug.

When Casey got to him, he looked giddy. His eyes were huge and bright, and his dimples looked like craters. "I am so fucking proud of you, Stacks. That was... I don't even know. I'm fucking speechless."

Landon laughed. "That would be something."

Then, Casey placed a hand on either side of Landon's mask and kissed him.

Well, kissed the mask.

But in the chin area, in the vicinity of Landon's mouth.

Landon's eyes must have been as big as pucks, but fortunately Casey was already skating away and didn't notice his disproportionate reaction. Landon began skating to the bench too, telling himself to get a grip even as he kept touching his glove against that spot on his mask.

Chapter Twenty-One

"I think that's enough," Landon said.

"Okay, but. One more time." Casey hit play on the short video clip of Landon's poke check that had been making the rounds on hockey social media. They'd watched the glove save a few dozen times too.

"See, this guy is coming in like, 'Gonna light this goalie up no problem,'" Casey narrated. "But then Landon 'The Assassin' Stackhouse is like, 'Poke, motherfucker,' and the other guy—"

"Greene," Landon supplied. "It was Cal Greene."

"Fine. Greene is like, 'Oh no, where's my puck?' and the puck is like, 'Bye.'"

Landon gave Casey a playful shove. They were sitting right next to each other on the couch, both watching Casey's phone screen. He'd expected Casey to rally the guys together for a group celebration at a bar after the game, but Casey had seemed keen to go home.

He'd made sure Landon had gotten one of the chicken parmesan subs after the game, though. He'd actually guarded the table and loudly announced that Landon got first dibs on the food, which had been embarrassing, but kind of sweet.

The sandwich had been so fucking good.

They'd stopped at a McDonald's drive-through on the way

home to get McFlurries, and now those empty cups were sitting on the coffee table, bothering Landon. Normally he'd take his to the garbage right away, but he didn't want to leave Casey's side. He was worried he wouldn't be able to reclaim this spot right next to him if he got up.

"So in conclusion," Casey said, "you're a pretty good goalie."

Landon shrugged. "I'm all right."

"Do I need to read the comments again?"

"Please no."

Casey laughed and ran a hand through his long hair. It had dried super curly tonight. He had a stain on his light blue T-shirt where he'd dropped a glob of McFlurry. They weren't watching a video anymore, but they were still sitting close enough that their knees were almost touching.

"So," Casey said, "is that the difference a good night's sleep makes?"

He sounded a bit nervous, and suddenly Landon was too. "Didn't hurt."

"Would, um… Do you think you'll have trouble sleeping tonight, or…"

Landon stared at him until Casey looked away. He wanted to sleep with Casey again. He'd been thinking about it all day. Hell, even during the game tonight he'd gotten flashes of Casey's slow, sleepy smile from that morning. He hadn't expected Casey to want it too.

"Never mind," Casey mumbled. "Sorry."

"No, I'd like to. If you want to. It was…nice." It had been the most comfortable Landon could remember being in a long time, which was extra remarkable given the fact that he was generally uncomfortable around other people.

Casey's gaze returned to him, and there was that shy smile Landon loved. "Cool."

After that, there didn't seem to be any reason to stay awake. Landon rinsed and tossed their McFlurry cups, and then followed Casey upstairs. He could feel the bone-deep exhaustion settling in as the postgame adrenaline left him. He definitely had some fresh bruises too.

When he got upstairs, he realized all of his stuff was in the basement. Important stuff, like his toothbrush and his pajamas. "I gotta run downstairs and brush my teeth and stuff," he said. "Are you gonna be okay here?" He realized as soon as he said it that it was a ridiculous question. And insulting, probably. Of course Casey would be okay alone in his room for a couple of minutes. He'd been alone in his room most nights before last night.

Well. Except for the nights Casey had *guests*. Because of course Landon was far from being the first person to share Casey's bed, and he'd be wise to remember that.

Casey didn't look insulted by Landon's question. He looked touched, actually. "I'll be okay. But you're coming back, right?"

And then Casey pulled his shirt off and Landon forgot the question.

Casey made a face that suggested Landon was being amusing, then he went to his dresser to get a fresh T-shirt.

Landon snapped out of it. "Yeah. I'll be right back."

There was nothing, Landon reminded himself, absolutely nothing sexual about what was happening right now. This was a comfort thing, and he was *glad* that it was a comfort thing. He couldn't even imagine what he'd do if it wasn't.

He couldn't, for example, imagine digging his fingers into Casey's long curls, tugging slightly until Casey's head tipped back and his lips parted on a gasp. He couldn't imagine kissing him, hard and hungry and maybe against a wall. Or, scratch that, gently kissing that shy, sleepy smile until Casey laughed and kissed him back. Maybe crawled on top of Landon while he kept kissing him. Maybe rocked against him, showing Landon how turned on he was...

Impossible to imagine.

And, goddammit, Landon was hard now.

Arousal was something he rarely had much use for. When

it happened, he either ignored it, or dealt with it quickly and privately if circumstances allowed it. It wasn't much different from having something stuck in his teeth.

Landon didn't want to keep Casey waiting any longer than necessary, so while he brushed his teeth he tried to figure out if it would take longer to will his erection away, or to jerk off. He certainly couldn't return to Casey's bedroom in this state.

He worked through a list of pros and cons, then ultimately decided that jerking off would be the best defense against unwanted future erections tonight.

He'd need to be quick, though.

He stepped out of his pants, then tugged the waistband of his boxer briefs down just enough to free his cock. There was no time or reason to be fancy about things, so he leaned over the bathroom sink and went to town on himself. He jerked himself hard and fast and without lube, keeping his gaze locked on the sink so he wouldn't look in the mirror. He didn't close his eyes because he was sure he'd think of Casey.

It took about three minutes. He watched as his release splattered the porcelain, and embarrassment crept in before his orgasm had even finished.

God, he hoped he'd be able to forget this moment, and not forever link it to his first NHL win.

At least it was done now, and he could relax and hopefully fall asleep quickly. He cleaned the sink with a facecloth, then thoroughly rinsed the facecloth. He changed into pajama pants and a T-shirt and, after a few centering breaths, went back upstairs.

Casey was already in bed, and smiled when Landon walked in. "I was thinking about that guy in the grocery store. The dude whose hat we signed. He must be bragging to everyone about having Landon Stackhouse's autograph now."

Landon huffed. "As if." He pulled back the covers on his side of the bed and climbed in.

"You can turn off the lamp," Casey said.

"You sure?"

"Yeah." Casey yawned, then snuggled under the comforter in a way that was so cute Landon wanted to rewind it and play it back. "It's cool."

"Goodnight," he said, and turned off the lamp.

"Goodnight, superstar."

The king-size bed put a lot of space between them, which was good, obviously. It was a comfortable bed, and not having to worry about crowding Casey was a plus. But. It wouldn't be so bad, Landon thought, if Casey's hand found its way to Landon's arm under the blankets. If it rested there, warm and reassuring and sending confusing but exciting tingles into Landon's bloodstream.

He could probably live with that. If it happened.

Chapter Twenty-Two

Two days later, Casey's brain woke him up and immediately reminded him that he hadn't mentioned something important to Landon. Something he had promised to mention to him.

He rolled over and saw that the other half of the bed was empty. The sheets had even been neatly tucked and folded, as if Landon had never been there at all.

He had been there. Casey had crashed hard after their brutal loss to New Jersey last night, but he remembered the warmth of Landon's body, and the way his lips had looked extra kissable.

Casey left his side of the bed unmade, and ventured downstairs to look for Landon. He found him in the gym, doing a full side split with his face almost touching the floor.

Casey completely forgot what he was going to tell him.

It shouldn't even have been interesting; goalies did stretches like this all the time. He'd seen *Landon* doing these sorts of stretches lots of times. It wasn't a big deal.

"Wow," Casey blurted out.

Landon glanced up, and then slowly lifted his torso until he was upright. He held the split as he stared at Casey with a placid expression.

Right. The thing Casey was supposed to tell him. "There's a thing this afternoon."

"I'm going to need more information."

"It's a charity thing." Landon's shorts were stretched so tight across his groin. Casey could see everything.

"What kind of thing?"

Casey blinked. "Oh. It's fun. We did it last year and it was a huge hit. It's like a Christmas thing to raise money for the local food bank."

Landon closed his eyes and exhaled slowly. "Casey..."

"Right. Okay, so a bunch of Outlaws players set up at this booth at the mall and we wrap presents for donations. Fans love it because they get a gift that's wrapped by their favorite player."

Landon's brow pinched. "So what would I be doing?"

Had Casey not explained this well enough? "You'd be wrapping gifts. The players—" he pointed to himself and then to Landon "—wrap the gifts."

"I get that, but why would anyone want a gift wrapped by me?"

"Because," Casey said slowly and clearly, "you are a Calgary Outlaws hockey player."

Landon held his gaze for a long moment, then said, "I mean. Sort of."

"Not sort of, you fucking goof. And I'll bet you're great at wrapping presents."

"I've never wrapped a present in my life."

"Yeah, I hadn't either until the thing last year. I am so fucking bad at it. Everyone wanted a gift wrapped by me because they were so hilarious looking."

"No one asked me to take part in this."

Had Landon hit his head somehow? He hadn't played last night, but maybe during warm-up? "I just asked you, dude."

"I meant—never mind." Landon finally released his pose and shook his legs out in front of him. "I need to finish my stretches."

"Okay," Casey said, and didn't move.

Landon raised his eyebrows at him. "Did you need something else?"

"Um, nope. Nope. I'll just…" Casey pointed at the stairs. "But you'll come to the thing, right?"

"If you want me to."

"I want you. I mean…" Casey took a step backward. "Cool. Yeah. I'll just be…upstairs."

When he got to the top of the stairs, he laughed at himself. "Smooth, Hicks."

"Are you sure I should be going to this?" Landon asked as they were getting ready to leave the house.

"Totally."

"Maybe I should stay here."

"Fine," Casey said. "I'll just tell the organizers that you hate the food bank."

Landon's eyes narrowed. "Again, I was never officially invited by anyone involved in organizing this event. And I obviously don't hate the food bank."

"You do love food," Casey agreed. "And you were totally invited. I *explained this*. I just forgot to pass the invitation on to you. Anyway, the whole team goes, basically. We do shifts. And we can do some shopping while we're there."

Landon kept frowning at him.

"Come on. I'll buy you a coffee on the way."

"Fine. But if it feels even a little bit like I'm not wanted there, I'm going to the food court until you're done."

When they got to the mall, Landon was surprised to learn that he *was*, in fact, wanted at the event. He was enthusiastically greeted by the event organizer—a woman from the food bank— and she even raved about the game he'd played against Detroit.

So now he was *trying* to wrap a jigsaw puzzle. It wasn't going well.

"How the hell," he grumbled, "do you do the ends?"

"Dude, don't look at me," Casey said cheerfully. He was standing beside him, making a mess of whatever he'd been asked to wrap.

"You just, like, tuck them," offered Clint. He was doing a decent job of wrapping a large square box. "Make a little triangle."

Landon had no idea what he meant by that. He taped down the ends of the gift as best he could, but the paper was pretty lumpy.

"Oh man," Casey said, laughing, "that's rough. Maybe slap a bow on there."

"It's fine," said the woman who had brought the gift. "My friend will love it. She's a big fan."

"Of puzzles?" Landon asked.

"Of you! She lives in Saskatoon, and she's thrilled that you're getting your shot here. She definitely misses you there, though."

"Oh. Cool. Well, tell her thanks." He did stick a bow to the present, and then signed one of the special gift tags that had been printed for the event. They had a festive illustrated border that incorporated the logos of both the Outlaws and the food bank, and they said *Wrapped with love by* above a space for the player's autograph.

"Thank you so much!" the woman said when Landon handed her the horrible-looking gift. "It was so nice meeting you. Good luck this season."

"You too," Landon said. "I mean, it was nice meeting you. Um. Have a nice day."

After she left, Casey nudged him. "See? Told you you'd have fans here."

"Look at this!" Clint bellowed as he held up his finished present. "A work of art."

"Damn, Nosey," said Casey, "how'd you get the corners so tight?"

"I've got kids! And I love Christmas! I wrap a lot of damn presents." The Santa hat he was wearing, paired with his dark beard, did make him look like a rugged Christmas elf.

Landon was wearing a Santa hat too—they all were—but his was kind of fucked and the pompom kept falling in his face. He blamed his narrow head.

The next person who approached Landon had a hockey stick. "Oh. No," Landon said. "How the hell?"

Casey laughed. "Oh man. Good luck."

"Give it here," Clint said, "I accept all challenges."

It turned out that a lot of people made a game of bringing the most awkwardly shaped items they could find. A few minutes after Landon had dodged having to wrap the hockey stick, he was handed a soccer ball. Casey was laughing at him the whole time he tried to wrap it, even though Casey was simultaneously doing a shit job of the frying pan he was wrapping.

"I'm so sorry," Landon said as he handed the wrapped soccer ball back to the grinning man who'd brought it. The gift looked like a mangled lump of paper and tape.

"This is exactly what I was hoping for, honestly," the man said.

"See?" Casey said. "Terrible wrapping jobs are part of the fun." He stuck a bow to the wrapped frying pan, which somehow looked worse than the soccer ball.

For their next items, Casey got a book, and Landon got a rolled-up yoga mat.

"Race ya," Casey challenged.

"Seriously? You have a bit of an advantage."

"Coward."

Landon huffed. "Fine. Go."

Their shift was ninety minutes, which had seemed like a long time when they'd started, but the time passed quickly. Landon found he was having fun, smiling and laughing more than he had in a long time. It was nice meeting fans too. He wasn't the best conversationalist, but being flanked by Casey and Clint—two absolute chatterboxes—had helped.

What the day hadn't helped was Landon's crush on Casey. Listening to him charm every person who approached the table, all while wearing a Santa hat and flashing dimples all over the place, had been a lot to deal with.

"You wanna do some shopping?" Casey asked when they were done.

"The mall is super busy."

"Yeah, it's nuts. But we're already here, and…" He trailed off as he must have noticed something in Landon's expression. "You know what? Let's go home. That was a lot of people and I'm beat."

Landon knew Casey was saying that for his benefit, and he was grateful. He needed some air and to get away from these crowds. "Okay. Thanks."

"You hungry?" Casey asked. "Gonna guess yes."

"Yeah. I can make dinner."

"Cool. Do you maybe wanna…teach me?"

Landon's brow furrowed. "You want me to teach you how to cook?"

"Yeah. Not, like, everything. But maybe one thing?"

Oh no. Cooking together was not going to help squash this crush. "How about spaghetti with meat sauce? That's easy."

Casey grinned. "Fuck yeah! Let's get Italian up in here."

"Cooking is easy!" Casey declared an hour after they got home. Landon nearly rolled his eyes because in that time he'd narrowly prevented Casey from doing four things that would have either poisoned them both or started a fire.

He didn't want to point that out because Casey looked so damn happy pointlessly stirring the sauce with a wooden spoon. It had truly been the simplest meal Landon could think of: a package of ground beef and some jarred tomato sauce with a few herbs and seasonings added. It was the sort of thing his own parents used to throw together for dinner between work and driving Landon to hockey.

They certainly hadn't had this top-of-the-line stove and cookware, though.

"So the water is boiling now," Landon said, keeping up the educational component of the activity so he wouldn't focus too hard on how cute Casey was. "We can put the pasta in."

"On it."

Before Landon could stop him, Casey dumped the contents of the box of dry spaghetti into the pot from much higher than Landon would have recommended. Boiling water splashed everywhere, and dry noodles landed on the stovetop and on the floor.

"Whoops," Casey said.

"It's okay," Landon said as he carefully extracted a noodle from the open flame under the pot. "But maybe closer to the pot next time. And slower."

"Got it. So how long do these cook for?"

"The box has the recommended time on it," Landon said. "But about ten minutes."

Casey studied the empty box. "Hey, it does say the time! That's helpful. Do other foods tell you how to cook them?"

"Yeah. If you peel a banana there's a whole recipe for banana bread inside."

Landon didn't miss the fact that Casey's gaze shot to the bananas on the counter before he realized Landon was joking.

"That would be cool," Casey said with a grin.

Landon pressed his lips together, and then he gave up and let himself smile instead. He wanted to live in Casey's head. It seemed fun.

They ate and Casey chatted throughout the meal, marveling at how good the pasta was, clearly proud of himself.

"We're a good team," Casey said happily.

The thing was, that against all odds, they *were* a good team. Casey was the first person Landon had been this comfortable with since…well. Since Erin.

Not that he was comparing Casey to his sister. No one would ever be able to replace Erin in that way, but he didn't want Casey to either. What Casey did was fill some of the emptiness inside Landon with something…nice. He made Landon feel like someone worth knowing.

He couldn't say any of that, so instead he said, "You have tomato sauce on your chin."

"Where?" Casey's tongue darted out and began sweeping

the area below his bottom lip. Ridiculous, because he had a napkin right next to him. Landon had put it there.

"No," Landon said. "Lower."

Casey made an inquisitive noise that sounded like "Here?" while he kept searching with his tongue.

"Jesus Christ," Landon muttered, and reached out to swipe at the spot with his thumb. So now Casey had him doing two things he would normally never do: touch someone else's face on purpose, and wipe away a gross food blob with his bare flesh.

The smile he got from Casey made it worth it. Landon busied himself with wiping his thumb off on his own napkin, and tried not to think about how he'd almost—*almost*—licked the sauce off his thumb.

Who even was he anymore?

"Did you talk to your parents today?" Casey asked.

"Yes. This morning."

"Did they watch the game the other night?"

"Yeah. Not live, but they recorded it. They were pretty pumped." Landon smiled at the memory of both his parents talking over each other in their excitement during the phone call. He'd never had a phone call with them like that before, and he wanted to keep winning just so he'd get more of them.

"I guess there are probably lots of parents that don't watch games live, right? I know Sylvia, Lee's wife, never watches the games. She can't handle it. She watches highlights later."

"Oh yeah?"

"Yeah. I think she's looking forward to Lee's retirement, not that I think that's gonna be soon. Dude's a machine." Casey exhaled. "Anyway, I hate thinking about retirement. I want to play hockey forever."

Landon knew, as a goalie, that he'd be lucky to still be playing at Lee's age. Hell, he'd be lucky to still be playing by his thirtieth birthday. "Same," he said.

"It was rough for my dad, when he retired. He kind of shut

down for a while. I think he was depressed. Then he got that commentator gig in Tampa, and he liked that."

"But he stopped doing it?"

"Yeah. He announced to the family a few summers ago that he wanted to step back and see what life was like without being tied to a hockey team's schedule."

Landon almost shuddered. Having his life scheduled was possibly his favorite part of being a hockey player. "How does he like it?"

"He loves it. Mom and him have been traveling all over the place, living it up."

"Do they watch your games?"

"Yeah. All the time. Usually they come to Calgary at least once each season to see some games, and they always go when we play in Tampa."

"That's cool. Is it hard for Dougie Hicks to cheer against Tampa?"

Casey laughed. "He doesn't."

That made Landon laugh too, just a little.

They cleaned up the kitchen together after dinner, which Landon knew was also a learning moment for Casey, but they both pretended it wasn't. Landon stealthily rearranged the dishes Casey had dumped haphazardly into the dishwasher.

"So," Casey said once everything had been put away. "Movie? Unless you want some alone time, which I totally get."

Landon found, surprisingly, that he didn't. "Movie sounds good."

Much later, they were in bed together.

The lamp was still on because Casey was sitting up, texting his sister. Landon was curled on his side, facing away, trying not to wish he could be doing the same.

He wondered if Erin would have been able to help him with his inconvenient crush. Would they have had that sort of relationship, as adults? Maybe Erin would have traveled the world, like she'd always talked about, and Landon would have barely seen her. Maybe they would have drifted apart as adults.

He was still lost in thought when, a few minutes later, Casey asked, "You still awake?"

"Mm."

"Brooke is excited to meet you."

Landon couldn't imagine why. And also, what on earth had Casey told her about him? "Why?"

"Why wouldn't she be? She knows you've been living with me, and I told her you're cool and funny and smart."

Wait. Landon rolled over to face him. "Casey. Are you trying to set me up with your sister?"

Casey's brows pinched. "What? No. Of course not. You don't even like girls, do you?"

"I don't know, but don't set me up with men either."

"No, I'm just confirming—you're a hundred percent gay?"

"I don't *know*."

"How do you not know?"

Landon had reached the end of his patience. "How do *you* not know how to cook? Maybe I need to put some effort into learning."

That awkward statement hung in the air between them for a few seconds.

"That makes so much sense," Casey finally said.

"It really doesn't. Forget I said that. Sorry."

A long moment passed where they just looked at each other. Landon suspected Casey was working up the courage to ask something, and that suspicion was confirmed when Casey said, "When you say you've never had sex…do you mean you haven't done…anything?"

"Right."

"Because Brooke says virginity is a myth and—"

Landon raised his head. "Were you talking about my *virginity* with your *sister*?"

"No! Stacks, I swear, no. I would never do that. But she gets on these rants sometimes about, like, sex…stuff. Like, society, y'know? And women?"

He looked so panicked and desperate to explain something he didn't quite understand that Landon took pity on him. "Okay. I get it."

Casey smiled with obvious relief. "Cool. So, yeah. She said virginity isn't real."

That was a nice thought, if a confusing one. Landon traced one of the thin stripes on Casey's bedsheet with his fingertip. "It feels pretty real. Sometimes."

He kept staring at the bedsheet while he waited for Casey to reply. And then kept staring when Casey said, "So you'd like to…do something about it?"

Landon felt like his blood was lava. This was such a strange conversation to be having in bed with his roommate. Who he had a crush on. "Not…often. But sometimes, yeah. It would be nice to…get it over with. I guess." He glanced up quickly at Casey, saw his interested expression, and dropped his gaze back to the mattress. "I wish I was the sort of person who could just…go for it. With someone. Seems like I'm the only one who doesn't go out looking to hook up with someone. Thinking about doing that…scares me. I don't want to do it."

"What if," Casey said slowly, and Landon's heart stopped as he waited for the rest of his sentence. "What if you met someone you really liked, in a bar or somewhere? Like, really hit it off. Do you think you could then?"

Landon shrugged the shoulder that wasn't supporting his weight. "It's never happened before. I'm not a great conversationalist." He sighed. "Anyway. It's not a big deal. I'm not, like, dying to have sex or anything." This time when he glanced up, he saw the softness in Casey's eyes, and the slight flush in his cheeks.

Maybe *this* was that feeling; what everyone else felt when they wanted someone. When they thought they would die if they didn't get to touch this person, and be touched by them. He didn't know how far he would want that touching to go, but god he wanted *something*. Casey's hair between his fingers, his breath against Landon's skin. He wanted to kiss his smile.

"I just think," Casey said quietly, "you're really awesome."

And then his fingers brushed against the hand that had been tracing the stripes. Landon wasn't sure what the gesture meant, but it was so tentative—so *considerate*—that Landon couldn't help returning it. For a few electric seconds, their fingers exchanged the gentlest caresses while tingles raced through Landon's body.

It was too much. It was the barest of physical contact and he couldn't breathe. He covered Casey's hand with his own to stop it, and Casey took it as an invitation to flip his hand over and tangle their fingers together.

Casey was staring at him with an expression Landon didn't recognize; his eyes looked darker than usual, his mouth tighter and more serious.

"Landon," he said, just above a whisper. Had Casey ever even called him that before? Landon couldn't remember. He'd definitely never looked at him like this before.

Landon's heart started racing, suddenly terrified. In a panic, he turned toward the lamp, releasing Casey's hand. "We should get some sleep. Vegas tomorrow."

He turned off the light so he wouldn't have to see Casey's face. In the dark he heard Casey sigh, and then say, "Okay. Goodnight, Stacks."

"Goodnight."

Landon felt like he wouldn't be able to sleep for hours, if at all. Too many confusing feelings were churning inside him. But as soon as he heard Casey's steady breathing next to him a few minutes later, he drifted off effortlessly.

Chapter Twenty-Three

Casey's brain had to be ninety percent Landon thoughts at this point, which sucked because he was trying not to think about him at all. Or at least was trying to only think of him as a team-mate, a roommate, and maybe a buddy.

He hadn't been thinking of Landon that way last night, when they'd been in bed together, basically holding hands. He'd really wanted to kiss him, and maybe...lie on top of him? Like, just be as close as possible to him and not even try to have sex with him. Casey totally *would* have sex with him, if Landon wanted that. No problem at all. But it wasn't what he wanted the most with Landon, which was a very new and weird way to feel about someone Casey was attracted to.

Anyway, Casey had fucked things up. His face must have given him away or something because Landon had shut the fucking door on any potential kisses. He'd kind of shut the door on Casey completely, actually. Things had been awkward that morning. Landon had gone right back to barely talking, either at home or during their morning practice. Now they were on a plane to Las Vegas, and Landon was sitting several rows away from Casey, with West.

It fucking sucked.

Casey was sitting with Lee, who had earbuds in and his

eyes were closed. Casey was buzzing out of his skin. He really wanted to talk to someone.

He sent his sister a message: im bored

Brooke: Must be nice.

Casey: What did you get mom fr xmas

Brooke: That yoga bag she wants.

Casey: gtfo i bought her that too!!!!

Brooke: Well, you'll have to return it then.

Casey: y me???

Brooke: Because I probably bought it first.

Dammit. She probably did.

Casey: pls?? i need a win this week has sucked

Brooke: It's Monday.

Well, that was depressing. Not that days of the week had much meaning to Casey. Everything was just game days, practice days, and days off. He sent a sad-face emoji.

Brooke: Why has this week sucked?

Casey didn't want to get into it. He didn't need his sister to know that he was crushing hard on his roommate, and that his roommate was clearly not feeling the same way. There were less painful ways to embarrass himself.

Casey: bunch of little stuff

Brooke: Aren't you in Vegas right now?

Casey: otw

Brooke: Maybe your luck will change.

That would be nice, except luck had nothing to do with his situation. He sighed and rested his head on Lee's shoulder.

"Dude," Lee said.

"Just let me have this."

Lee sighed and leaned against the window, allowing Casey to get more comfortable. He removed his earbuds. "You've been mopey all day."

"I know."

Lee dropped his voice to a whisper. "Did you and Stackhouse have a fight or something? Why aren't you sitting together?"

"Thought he could use some space from me."

"How come he gets that courtesy but I don't?"

Casey smiled. "Because you're team captain and this is your job."

"It definitely isn't."

"Your arm is comfortable," Casey murmured. "So beefy."

An easy silence passed before Lee said, "I like Stackhouse. He's good for you."

"He's too good for me."

Lee's arm tensed, and then relaxed. "Ah," he said. "It's like that."

"It's not like anything. We're friends. Teammates. Roommates. Whatever."

"But you want more."

Casey glanced around for eavesdroppers, but as usual nearly

everyone on the team had earbuds in or was having their own loud conversations. "It doesn't matter what I want. He doesn't."

"Sorry," Lee said. He sounded sincere.

"Yeah."

"It's probably for the best, though. Dating a teammate would be messy, and besides, he's going back to Saskatoon as soon as Morin is healthy."

"I know."

"But the heart wants what it wants, I guess."

"That's really pretty."

"Yeah, I didn't make that up."

Las Vegas was no place to mope about unrequited crushes. The team had one night off in Vegas this season and Casey was going to make sure they made the most of it.

He sent a message on the group chat, and wasn't surprised at all when most of the team were down to hit a club or two. Everyone had been looking forward to tonight.

Everyone except Antton, who had booked an early tee time for himself and some of the training staff. Then Landon sent a message saying he'd probably be staying in and Casey got annoyed.

He was annoyed while he showered, and he was annoyed as he got changed into his sexy club outfit. Landon had never been to Vegas before, and Casey had thought he'd been looking forward to it. Casey certainly had. He wanted to show Landon a good time, and he hated how bummed out he was at the prospect of going out without him. Casey *should* be seizing this opportunity to find someone hot who will help him forget all about Landon.

Ten minutes later, Casey was knocking on Antton's door. "I need to borrow a shirt."

Antton placed a hand on top of his own head, then moved it in a flat line until it was hovering half a foot over Casey's head.

"It's not for *me*," Casey said. "It's for Stacks. Just, like, a nice button-up. Something dark. Do you have that floral print one?"

Antton's eyebrows shot up. "The Tom Ford one?"

"Oh shit, is it? Yeah. Do you have it?"

Finally, Antton stepped back and let Casey into his room. His clothes were all hanging in the closet, because Antton was an actual grown-up, and Casey could see the sleeve of the shirt he'd been thinking of.

"Sweet, you brought it."

Antton carefully removed it from the closet, handling it as if it could shatter. "I want it back. And I want it dry-cleaned first."

"No problem."

"It might be loose in the shoulders on Landon."

"It'll be okay. Thanks, Antton. I owe you."

"You owe me that shirt back in perfect condition."

"Love you, pal."

"My love is conditional on getting that shirt back," Antton said flatly.

"Yeah, yeah." Casey left the room and marched down the hall on a mission.

Landon was stretching when he heard knocking on the hotel room door. Planes really did a number on his legs and back.

West was in the shower, so Landon grumpily got off the floor and answered the door. Of course it was Casey.

"West isn't ready yet," Landon said.

"Huh? Oh, right. I forgot you're roomies. No, I came to see you. Here." He held out a very fancy-looking shirt.

"I didn't order that."

"Just—" Casey let out an exasperated sounding sigh. "Can I come in?"

Landon let him in. "Why are you bringing me a shirt?"

"So you can wear it out." There was a challenge in Casey's tone.

Landon folded his arms. "I'm staying in. Didn't you read the group chat?"

"I want you to come out."

"Why?"

Casey's mouth hung open for a minute, then he closed it.

Landon huffed. "Just go have fun. I'm not a club guy. You know that."

"I won't have fun if you don't go."

Now it was Landon's turn to let his mouth hang open. Casey's statement didn't make sense at all, but he sounded so earnest it made Landon's heart flip.

"Again, why?"

"Because..." Casey glanced around the room, as if the answer was hiding somewhere. "Because you've never been to Vegas and you should experience it. And I want to be with you when you do that for the first time. I want to make sure it's a good time for you, and that you're safe and relaxed and..." He trailed off, probably realizing in the same moment Landon had that he *really* sounded like he was talking about something else.

"I want to show you an amazing time," Casey finished, then locked his gaze with Landon's.

The air in the hotel room felt thick with tension, and something brighter. Possibility, maybe? Excitement?

"Fine," Landon said. "I'll go."

Casey's whole face lit up, dimples on full display. "Yeah?"

"Yes. You want me to wear that weird shirt?"

Casey held it out. "It's not weird."

"It's purple and it has flowers on it."

"It's *plum* and the pattern is subtle. Put it on. What are our pants options?"

Chapter Twenty-Four

Landon felt like he was in a movie. The Las Vegas strip at night was like nothing he'd ever seen in person, like every inch of it was designed to overstimulate. The entire place pulsed with energy that invited people to forget that anything bad ever happened in the world. Landon wasn't immune to it, thrumming with excitement, even as he felt, at the same time, like he was in the first act of a cautionary tale.

"Where'd you get the shirt?" he asked for the third time that night. Casey had dodged the question every time.

"Don't worry about it."

"Please tell me you didn't buy it for me."

"I didn't buy it for you."

"Then where—" He was interrupted by Clint draping an arm across his shoulders.

"Stacks! I'm fucking pumped you're coming out with us."

"Oh. Thanks." Clint's arm was huge and heavy and Landon felt trapped, but he didn't want to seem uncool by stepping away.

"Hey," Casey said as he playfully removed Clint's arm. "You'll wrinkle the fabric. Don't mess with Stacks's drip."

Landon attempted to gratefully acknowledge Casey's intervention with a look. Casey just shot him a quick smile and glanced away.

"You do look good," Clint said. "Hey, isn't this Antton's shirt?"

"Yep," Casey said at the same moment Landon said, *"What?"*

Clint burst out laughing. "Damn, Stacks. You're coming for Antton's job *and* his closet?"

"I'm not—" Landon glared at Casey, who at least looked sheepish. "I'm not *coming for his job*. I'm just helping out. And I didn't know this was his shirt. Oh my god."

"Yeah," Casey said. "That's on me. So, it's Antton's shirt. I thought it would look good on you and—" his gaze traveled over Landon's torso "—I was right."

Landon was blushing and he hated it. "I can't wear this."

"You *are* wearing it."

Jesus Christ, what was Landon doing? Going to a nightclub wearing what had to be a thousand-dollar shirt at least—he hadn't missed the label inside—that belonged to Antton Niskanen? What if he sweated in it? What if he spilled beer on it, or snagged it on something?

"I can't—"

"It's a fucking shirt, brother," Clint said. "Relax. As if Antton doesn't have enough of them. I'm surprised the plane can even take off, all the fucking clothes he packs."

Landon exhaled. He needed to let this go. He really didn't want to be angry at Casey all night, or panicking over a shirt. He would thank Antton tomorrow. It would be fine.

"Okay," Landon said.

Casey beamed. He looked so good tonight, wearing an ice-blue silk T-shirt that clung in all the right places and made his eyes look incredible. The neck had a wide V that, paired with the soft tumble of Casey's hair, looked almost feminine, contrasting with all of his hard muscle and masculine torso in a way that Landon found fascinating.

Casey led the group to the Aria Hotel, then to a nightclub

inside, and then to the private booth he had apparently booked in advance. No one in the group seemed surprised in the least, so Landon figured private booths in fancy clubs were a regular occurrence for superstar hockey players.

He perched on the edge of a leather bench seat and tried not to be overwhelmed by everything. It was really fucking loud and crowded in the club already, even though it was a Monday night. He was grateful for the small slice of privacy Casey had arranged for their group.

Their group was pretty loud, though, and got louder as the bottles of vodka, rum, tequila, and bourbon that had been delivered to their table got emptier. Guys had left to dance or explore the club, and some of them had returned with young women who'd become part of their group.

Landon wasn't having a terrible time. For one thing, he was on his third vodka soda, and everyone seemed thrilled that Landon had joined them. It made him feel good, like he truly was part of the team.

Also, Casey had stayed with him, but had managed to do it in a way that didn't make Landon feel like Casey was babysitting him, or that he was making any kind of sacrifice. Casey was talking to everyone, joking with his teammates and getting to know the women who'd arrived. Landon enjoyed the way his cheerful, slightly hoarse voice wafted over the noise of the club as Casey asked people questions and delighted in their answers. He also enjoyed the way Casey's T-shirt kept riding up as he made enthusiastic hand gestures while he talked. Landon was sitting next to West, who had been texting his girlfriend, Allison, all night and dutifully avoiding the dance floor. Gio and Pete had been sitting with them, but they'd left in search of dance partners a while ago. Landon was able to sit in silence and simply observe, which was his preferred party mode. Overall, he was pretty comfortable.

Needing to stretch his legs, he stood and leaned on the railing that lined their private booth and gazed down at the dance floor. He tried to imagine himself down there, but the thought of being bumped into and touched by that many people made his skin crawl.

But it also looked like it could be…fun.

"Stacks!"

Landon turned toward the sound of Casey's voice, and saw him walking over, his arm looped around a young woman's elbow.

"This is Kelly! She's from where you're from!"

"Really?" Landon asked, legitimately surprised and interested. Nova Scotia was a small place.

"Well, close," Casey said. "Same ballpark."

"I'm from Maine," Kelly said with a smile that suggested she had already explained the difference to Casey.

"Oh. That's cool," Landon said. "Pretty close."

"Yeah," Casey said enthusiastically. "Boats and lobsters and shit, right?"

"That's our state slogan," Kelly said.

Landon smiled. He liked Kelly already. "What brings you to Vegas?"

"I'm here for a super-boring convention."

"About what?"

She leaned in as if she was about to tell him a secret. Landon bent lower to make it easier for her. "Groundwater," she stage-whispered.

"Seriously?"

"Right? I'll bet I'm twice as attractive now. Those are my friends." She pointed at three women who were sitting with some of the other guys. "We like to think of ourselves as the gorgeous gals of groundwater."

Landon laughed, more easily than he usually did. Casey had taken a step back and was watching them with a smile that seemed a bit…off. Landon couldn't quite figure it out. When Casey noticed Landon staring at him, he said, "You guys want a drink?" He gestured to the table where all the bottles were.

"I'd love a vodka soda," Kelly said.

Landon nodded. What the hell. "Me too. Thanks."

Casey left, and Kelly leaned against the railing next to Landon. They were facing one another. "So you guys are the Calgary Outlaws?"

"Most of them, yes."

"And your name is... Stacks?"

Oh god. He hadn't even introduced himself. "Landon. Stacks is a nickname. Short for Stackhouse. Hockey, y'know?"

"Landon," she repeated with a flirty smile. She was very pretty, with long, light brown hair and big blue eyes. Her dark blue dress hugged her curves, and her bare arms looked strong, like she was maybe an athlete herself.

"Do you play any sports?" he asked, and hoped it didn't sound like innuendo.

"I used to play varsity volleyball," she said. "Now I mostly do Pilates and distance running. I'm training for a half-marathon."

They talked about running for a while, because it was something Landon was into as well. He'd like to do a marathon someday, if his body wasn't a complete trash heap by the time he retired. They talked about Maine and Nova Scotia, and the best places to get fried clams. Landon's voice was growing hoarse from shouting over the music, but he was enjoying the conversation. He only flinched a little when Kelly's hand brushed his arm.

"Casey is taking his time with those drinks," Landon observed after what must have been twenty minutes.

Kelly laughed. "I think he was just trying to leave us alone."

"Why?" Landon said, before his brain caught up. Jesus Christ. "Oh. I get it." Heat crept up his neck.

Kelly looked confused, which was understandable.

"Sorry," Landon said. "I'm not good at this stuff."

"At talking to girls?" she teased.

"To anyone, really. But, um. I'm not..." He had no idea how

to finish that sentence. *Interested* would sound mean, while *into women* would be kinder, but would make Casey look like an ass for wasting her time.

"Got it," Kelly said, saving him the effort. "It's okay. Too bad, though. You're hot."

Landon coughed out a very weird laugh. "I am?"

"Totally. I like tall boys. Your friend is cute too, though."

"Casey? Yeah, he is," Landon said without thinking. Stupid vodka.

Her smile shifted from flirty to *knowing*. "So we have something else in common, maybe?"

He shook his head, and then lied his ass off. "No, not like that. I'm just saying that, like, objectively, he's attractive." He attempted a smile. "Just ask him."

Her gaze shifted toward Casey, who was at the far end of the booth talking to Lee. "Maybe I will."

Landon's stomach twisted with something that he refused to acknowledge as jealousy. "How about I get those drinks?" he offered.

"Sounds good. And by the way—" she touched his arm again, briefly "—I like talking to you. It's okay if that's all you want to do."

Something unclenched inside Landon's chest. "Thanks."

About fifteen minutes after Landon fetched their drinks, Casey returned. "Let's go dance."

"Okay," Kelly said immediately. Landon didn't blame her. He'd started asking her about groundwater.

"Stacks?"

His first instinct was to say no, and he was sure Casey was expecting it. But the man whose shirt Landon was wearing— his fucking hero—had advised him to have more fun. Landon was twenty-four, an NHL player, and at a Vegas nightclub. If he didn't cut loose now, then when?

He could try.

"Sure," he said. "Let's dance."

★ ★ ★

Casey was pretty psyched about how the night was going.

Operation: Get Landon to a Club had been a success, the borrowed shirt was an even bigger success because Landon looked sexy as hell in it, and now Landon was *dancing*, which hadn't even been part of the plan.

Well, maybe it had secretly been part of the plan, but Casey had barely dared to hope for it.

Operation: Find Landon Someone Nice to Maybe Kiss and Whatever was going pretty well too. Landon was dancing with Kelly, and he didn't seem to be having a terrible time. He was trying, and that made Casey feel oddly proud. Maybe this plan would work out. He knew Landon had said he probably wasn't into women, but *probably* wasn't *definitely* and maybe Landon needed some practice talking to girls. Kelly was smart and funny and pretty and she was more or less from Nova Scotia. Casey had decided quickly that she'd be perfect for Landon.

Casey was dancing with Hailey, one of Kelly's friends, but he kept checking on Landon. Which meant he kept *looking at* Landon.

Hailey noticed. "Would you rather dance with Kelly?" She sounded annoyed, but it was hard to tell because everyone had to shout in this place.

"No," he said quickly, because Landon was dancing with Kelly, so why would Casey want to?

She looked skeptical but kept dancing. Casey glanced at Landon and found him staring right back at him.

God. He really was sexy. Landon had opened another button on his shirt, and sweat glistened on the V of skin there, and in the hollow of his throat. His neck was so long. Every part of him was so long. Casey could get lost exploring the miles of his body.

Or, Kelly could. Kelly *should*. If Landon wanted.

Hailey seemed cool. Hot for sure, and she seemed to be into Casey. If he invited her back to his hotel room, she'd probably be into it, which would be rad because Casey hadn't gotten laid since that Zach guy and he would really like to do something about that. Maybe that would keep him from thinking sexy thoughts about his fucking roommate.

Landon was a pretty good dancer. He had good control of his body, and his movements were fluid and graceful. Sensual, really, and Casey wondered if Landon was trying to be, or if he was just letting his goalie powers guide him.

Probably just goalie powers because Landon didn't even seem to be paying attention to what he was doing. At the moment he was gazing up at the laser light show above their heads. Purple, blue, green, and pink reflected off the sharp lines of his face, making him look even more beautiful than usual. The dark stubble on his jaw—he hadn't shaved because he hadn't planned on going out—was a good look too.

When Casey turned his attention back to Hailey, she was dancing with another guy. Yup. Made sense.

No worries. Casey could dance with himself until someone new came along.

After about a minute of dancing alone, Kelly tugged on his arm and hauled him beside herself and Landon. "Dance with us!" she shouted.

Casey smiled in reply, though he was a bit disappointed that Landon didn't seem to be enough for her. And he hoped he wasn't getting in Landon's way. Three's a crowd and all that. Except sometimes three was a really fun and sexy number. Not that things were going in *that* direction.

He tried not to face Kelly directly, so it wouldn't seem like he was boxing Landon out, which meant he was mostly facing Landon, but kind of to the side. This gave him an excellent view of Landon's profile, still painted by the changing lights.

"Having fun?" Casey yelled.

Landon gave him a half smile, then rolled his eyes, which was stupid hot for some reason.

Casey wasn't sure when he'd moved closer to Landon, or

when they'd ended up fully facing each other. He also didn't notice when exactly Kelly had left. Whatever had happened, the result was that he and Landon were definitely dancing with each other. Landon was still mostly watching the lights and scanning the room in general, so maybe he hadn't noticed yet. Casey felt like he should maybe point out the situation, but he decided to be a little selfish and enjoy this while he had the chance.

He wanted to put a hand on Landon's hip and pull him closer. He wanted to loop his arm around Landon's neck. He wanted Landon to look at him, and see if anything ignited in those dark eyes.

He wanted to grab Landon's shirt and kiss the hell out of him.

When Landon noticed he was dancing with Casey, his brow furrowed and he stopped moving. Casey stopped too, then offered a smile and a shrug that he hoped said, *You wanna?*

Landon began to move again. His long torso rolled in time with the beat, and he tipped his head back to gaze at the ceiling, exposing his throat. Casey didn't look anywhere except directly at Landon, even though it meant fighting a small war with himself to keep from touching him.

He moved in closer, only slightly. Only enough that their bodies brushed against each other accidentally from time to time. Only enough that he could smell what was left of Landon's bodywash, and watch a droplet of sweat trail into the open collar of his shirt.

But not close enough that Landon could feel how hard Casey was getting.

Okay, his personal mission, Operation: Stop Being Horny for Landon, was not going great.

Landon rolled his head back down and locked eyes with him. Casey's breath caught because he'd never seen this expression on Landon's face before. He looked…hungry. He watched Casey with burning eyes and parted lips, and for a moment Casey really thought he was about to get kissed. Or devoured.

Then, in a blink, Landon's face changed. His lips pressed together, jaw tight, and his eyes extinguished.

"Stacks?"

Landon turned and began squeezing through the mass of dancers, seemingly trying to make as quick an exit as possible. Casey watched him leave, momentarily stunned and still reeling from that heated look Landon had given him. Then he followed, because there was no way he could let Landon leave like that.

He caught up with him as he was climbing the stairs that led back to their private booth.

"Stacks! Wait."

Landon didn't stop, or even look back. Casey followed him back to the booth, which had emptied out quite a bit between the guys on the dance floor and the guys who had probably left already.

Casey put a hand on Landon's forearm, but Landon pulled away like he'd been burned.

"Stacks?"

"Just don't. Don't touch me. Not right now." Landon closed his eyes, then sighed. "That was a lot of people."

Casey put his hands behind his own back. "I know. You okay?"

Landon opened his eyes. He looked exhausted. "I'm going to go back to the hotel."

"Okay. Yeah. Just give me a second to—"

"No. You stay. Find someone to dance with, okay?"

Casey almost said that he'd already found someone, but he bit his lip instead.

"You shouldn't walk back alone," he tried.

"It's really not that far. And this street is like the brightest place on earth."

"That's why I like it so much." Casey smiled. "It's never dark."

Landon's eyes softened, and Casey wanted nothing more than to walk him home and tuck him into bed. Or crawl into bed with him.

"Have fun," Landon said.

Casey was still processing the fact that the tucking-Landon-into-bed scenario was more appealing than finding someone to have actual sex with.

Lee interrupted the processing. "I'm heading out," he announced. "I tried to keep up with you kids, but I am old."

"I'll walk with you," Landon said quickly.

"Cool." Lee glanced at Casey, asking a silent question with his eyes that was probably something like *Are you boys fighting or flirting?* Casey ignored him. Landon was leaving and Casey didn't like it and also a woman he'd been chatting with earlier—Claudia—was making eyes at him from one of the bench seats and he *did* kind of like that but not as much as usual.

He was just really, really confused.

Landon noticed him looking at Claudia. He smiled, just slightly, and said, "Have a good night, Casey." Then he walked away, following Lee to the exit.

Okay, so Casey could go after him and...what? Seriously, what? Landon was fine. He was tired, and being escorted back to their hotel by their very capable and responsible team captain. He didn't seem to be mad at Casey, and he didn't seem to need Casey either. If Casey ran after him, it would be weird.

If Casey stayed, he could have fun with Claudia—sexy fun that he desperately needed and wanted. That option made way more sense, but for some reason Casey couldn't commit to it.

"Did Lee steal your boyfriend?" West asked. Casey hadn't even noticed him approach.

"Huh?"

"Stackhouse. He left with Lee," West said, as if that was the confusing part.

Casey narrowed his eyes at him. "What do you mean 'boyfriend'?"

"You obviously have a crush on him." West seemed a bit tipsy, his words slurring slightly. Also he was loudly talking about something he really shouldn't be.

"No I don't," Casey lied. It was such a fucking lie.

West laughed. "Okay."

Suddenly Casey was being hugged from behind. "Hicks, you fucking animal. What's up?"

Casey tilted his head back onto Clint's shoulder and smiled. "Having a good time?"

"I'm drunk."

"Really?"

"Me an' Westy are going to play blackjack."

"Wow. That is a really terrible idea."

Clint released him and took a step back. "Yep. Let's go get rich, Westy."

West shrugged at Casey, then followed Clint. The booth was getting really empty, but Claudia was still there. And Landon was long gone. And Casey didn't want to gamble with his drunk teammates, he wanted to fuck. That was the whole point of this night, right?

He smiled at Claudia, and went to sit next to her, and thus ensured the success of Operation: Get Laid.

Chapter Twenty-Five

"Oh shit, hey, Chuckie. I forgot you play for Colorado now."

The man who was paired with Casey for the face-off huffed and shook his head. "Figures. I'm surprised you remember what team *you* play on."

"Hey now. You gotta be nice to me. I'm mic'd up."

"Jesus. They seriously put a microphone on you?"

"Yep! National broadcast too. The whole country is gonna hear my fucking wit."

"Not if you keep swearing, dickhead."

"Oh right! Whoops. Having a good time?"

"Eat my ass."

The puck dropped, Lee won the face-off, and Casey had the puck a few seconds later. Since the face-off had been in the Colorado zone, Casey was able to rip a dangerous snap shot right away. Their goalie stopped it but couldn't control the rebound. Casey happily retrieved the puck and fired it over the goalie's right shoulder.

"Hey now! There we go," he said as he raised his arms in celebration. "Kids, if you miss the first time, try again. That's an important hockey lesson."

"Who the fuck are you talking to?" Clint asked as he hugged him.

"He's mic'd up," Lee said. "So he's giving a fucking TED Talk."

"Cool it with the potty mouth, Captain," Casey scolded. "I don't want all my shit censored."

He skated to the bench to high-five his teammates. Landon was at the end of the bench.

"Nice one," Landon said as Casey slapped his outstretched goalie glove.

"You would have stopped that."

"Sure."

The score was now 3-1 for Calgary, which was excellent because they'd lost 5-1 against Vegas (probably Casey's fault for planning the night out, which had led to a pretty rough afternoon practice the next day, which had led to an even rougher game the following night). Now they had three games in three cities in four days to get through.

He hadn't spent much time with Landon since the club in Vegas. Not that Landon had seemed upset with him or anything, they'd just been separated a lot. Maybe some of it was on purpose, at least on Landon's part, but Casey understood his need to be alone sometimes.

Casey had hoped that having sex with Claudia—which had been awesome, five stars—would clear his head a bit when it came to Landon. It hadn't. His heart still bounced around in his chest whenever he looked at Landon, and he really hoped the microphone didn't pick that up.

Landon got the start in Minnesota.

The decision had been made shortly before the game, so Landon hadn't had a chance to lie awake all night worrying about it. As a result, he was cramming twenty-four hours' worth of panic into the twenty minutes between warm-ups and the actual game.

Casey noticed. Of course he did. Landon was crouched in the tunnel, staring at nothing and trying to calm himself with deep breathing when Casey's head tipped sideways into his field of vision.

"Hey, Stacks. I have good news and bad news."

Landon exhaled. "Okay."

Casey crouched in front of him. "Good news—this is gonna be the best game ever."

"For who?"

"You. Me. Us. I can feel it."

Landon took a moment to process how much he'd enjoyed Casey saying, "You. Me. Us." Then he said, "What's the bad news, then?"

Casey smiled. "Oh, the bad news is for Minnesota. They're gonna lose."

Landon actually laughed at that. A short burst of surprised amusement.

Casey laughed too, then stood up and gently bopped Landon on the top of his mask. "You should poke check someone again. That was sick."

Landon stood too. "Anything else?"

Casey pretended to think about it. Or maybe he actually was. "Score a goal? That would be so rad."

"No problem."

"Have you ever scored a goal?"

"No."

"Oh. It's fun. You should try it."

"Okay."

Casey dropped his voice about an octave to match Landon's. "Okay."

A huge, ridiculous, and frankly unprecedented smile spread across Landon's face. Then he laughed in a way that probably counted as giggling.

"You suck," he said, and jabbed Casey in the chest with his blocker pad. "I don't sound like that."

"Yes you do," Casey said, even deeper than before. "I'm a goalie and I'm way too tall."

"Wow. Hit me where it hurts."

Casey leaned up and tapped the front of his helmet to the

forehead of Landon's mask. "You're gonna fucking crush it to-night," he said in his normal voice. "I can't wait."

Landon closed his eyes, just for a moment, and enjoyed Casey's closeness. The fact that his proximity relaxed Landon instead of making him anxious was probably important, but Landon didn't have time to think about it right now. "Kick ass tonight, Casey."

Casey took a step back, breaking their contact. He was smiling when he said, "Best game ever, remember?"

It was pretty damn close to being Landon's best game ever. By the time the third period had started, he had stopped over thirty shots, and had only let in two goals. He hadn't poke checked anyone, but he'd made some pretty decent saves. One glove save in particular that he hoped would end up on some highlight reels.

Calgary had scored four goals, so they were in good shape. Minnesota came hard in the first half of the third, keeping the action in front of Landon most of the time. Landon could sense his teammates getting frustrated, and sloppy. With about ten minutes left in the game, West tried to clear the puck but a Minnesota forward intercepted and took a shot from the point. Landon stopped it, but was then run over by another Minnesota forward (and a little bit by West) who was trying to grab the rebound.

Chaos broke out. West and whoever had run Landon over were wrestling on the ice next to Landon, another fight broke out to his left, and he could hear Casey yelling from the bench.

"You're dead for that, asshole! Fucking dead."

It was honestly kind of cute.

Landon extracted himself from the net and took a little skate to show that he was okay. He checked in with his body and didn't notice anything worse than a probable bruise on his upper back.

Eventually the fights were broken up and order was restored.

Both teams received matching penalties for fighting, and no goaltender interference was called. On his next shift, Casey skated up to Landon during a break in play.

"You okay? Really?"

"Yeah," Landon said. "I'm fine."

"I still might kill that guy."

"Don't. Score a goal instead."

Casey nodded, but he wasn't smiling. "Okay. Yeah. Okay. But...you're not hurt?"

"Not hurt."

Casey exhaled. "Good. Sorry, that looked bad. Reminded me of what happened to Morin."

Right. That made sense. The Outlaws really couldn't afford to lose another goalie. "Part of the job."

Then Casey touched his forehead to Landon's again, and the bad mood that had been creeping in disappeared. Casey didn't even say anything before skating away, leaving Landon feeling a bit touched and a lot smitten.

Somehow, even after an exhausting game that had required Landon to make forty-three saves, and a flight to Winnipeg immediately after, Landon couldn't sleep.

He still felt adrenaline from the game, mixed with a million thoughts racing through his head. He thought about his parents coming to visit soon, about meeting Casey's family, about going back home to Calgary, about Casey. Always about Casey.

West was snoring a bit, too, and that wasn't helping things.

Landon felt around for his phone on the nightstand, picked it up, and took a chance. He didn't expect Casey to reply—he was sure he was asleep—but he had to try.

Landon: You awake?

The three dots appeared immediately.

Casey: yep u

Landon grinned and shook his head, then wrote: Nope. I'm fast asleep.

Casey: lmao

So now what? Landon knew what he wanted—to crawl into bed beside Casey and let his nearness lull him to sleep—but he didn't know how to ask for it. It was an embarrassing thing to need.

Casey: wanna sleep here w me???

Well. That was easy. Leave it to Casey to make something like this seem simple.

Three minutes later, Landon was outside Casey's door. He knocked once, softly, and the door opened. Casey was wearing only a pair of bright purple boxer briefs, and his hair was rumpled. Landon had not been mentally prepared for any of that.

"Hey," Casey said with a sleepy smile. He stepped back to let Landon in.

Despite the fact they'd only checked in a couple of hours ago, Casey's room was a mess. It looked like he'd tossed every single thing in his suitcase over his shoulder.

"Jesus. Were you robbed or something?" Landon asked.

"No, I was just checking to see if I had pajama pants. I don't, by the way. I can put on a shirt and some sweats, though, if you want this to be less weird."

Would it be weird if Casey only wore underwear? The bed was a king size; they wouldn't be touching and this wasn't *like that* anyway. They were only sleeping.

"It's okay," Landon said. He was wearing pajama pants and a T-shirt himself. He got cold when he wore less than that to bed.

Casey got into bed, which was a relief because Landon was having a hard time not staring at him. Landon pulled back the sheets on the other side and got in, leaving as much space as possible between them. "You can leave the lamp on," Landon said.

"Don't need it now," Casey said, and turned it off.

Silence fell between them, then Casey said, "You were amazing tonight."

Landon smiled. "You mentioned it a few times."

"Yeah, well." Casey yawned. "One more time, just so you know for sure." He squirmed on the mattress, probably getting comfortable.

Then he squirmed some more. Then he said, "Can you do me a favor?"

"Mm?"

"Can you scratch my back? It's itchy right in the fucking middle. Been driving me nuts."

"Sure."

Casey slid closer and rolled, presumably onto his side to give Landon access to his back. Landon reached out in the darkness until he found the warm, smooth skin of Casey's back.

"Here?" Landon asked, scraping his fingernails lightly against the bumps of Casey's spine. He swore he felt Casey shiver. He should probably be wearing a shirt.

"Lower," Casey whispered.

Landon brushed his fingertips down a couple of inches. There was nothing erotic about this, obviously, but he was still holding his breath. He scratched a patch of Casey's skin, and Casey let out a moan of pleasure that made Landon's cock jump.

"Fuck yes. God, that's so good, Stacks."

Landon pulled his hand away quickly. He swallowed and said, "Better?"

"Fucking perfect." Casey let out a long, happy sigh. "Thanks, buddy."

Buddy. Right. Landon hoped his dick heard that.

Landon rolled to his back and stared up at the darkness. He wasn't sure he'd be falling asleep anytime soon.

"Hey," Casey whispered.

"Yeah?"

"Was it okay that I asked you to do that? I know you're not big on touching people."

Landon's heart fluttered. "It was okay."

"You sure?"

"Yeah. I—" Landon wasn't sure how to finish that sentence. *I only hate touching people who aren't you* or *I liked it more than I should have* were both weird. He decided to go with, "It didn't bother me."

"Okay." There was a long silence, and then Casey said, "Sorry I made a sex noise when you did it."

Landon snorted—actually *snorted*—as laughter burst out of him. He covered his mouth with one hand, but his whole body was shaking.

"Oh my god," Casey said as he shifted and possibly moved closer. "Stacks, do you have the giggles?"

That only made Landon laugh harder. He rolled onto his stomach so he could bury his face in a pillow. Casey turned his lamp on, and when Landon peeked at him, he saw that Casey was sitting up and grinning from ear to ear.

"This is the best," Casey said.

Landon laughed harder. He felt like something had malfunctioned inside him, but he didn't care. He wanted to be in a room forever where Casey said ridiculous, adorable things that made Landon laugh until he couldn't breathe.

"That was supposed to be, like, an earnest fucking apology," Casey complained, though he was laughing too. "I didn't mean to make a noise that, y'know, horny."

"Am I—" Landon gasped "—am I still a virgin? Or did that count as sex?"

Then they both dissolved into another fit of laughter. When Landon finally composed himself, his stomach hurt from laugh-

ing and he noticed Casey was gazing at him with an oddly intense expression.

Landon held his gaze and didn't say a word. Probably didn't
breathe.

"I really like you, Stacks."

The words were basic, but Landon still wanted to collect each
one like a treasure. "I like you too." It sounded automatic, like
a nervous reflex, so he tried again. "I don't make friends easily.
Or at all, really. But it's been…easy. With you."

Casey's expression softened. "That's nice to hear. Thanks."
He flopped down, resting his head on his pillow, still facing Landon. He was closer than he needed to be, but Landon
didn't mind.

Casey yawned again and closed his eyes. The lamp was still
on, and Landon should probably reach over Casey and turn it
off, but then he wouldn't be able to see him.

"Glad you're here," Casey murmured sleepily, eyes still
closed. "Missed you."

They almost couldn't possibly spend more time together than
they already did, but Landon knew what he meant. He felt the
same way. "I missed you too."

Chapter Twenty-Six

Five nights later, Casey and Landon were getting ready to go to the team Christmas party at Nosey's house.

"This party would be better if it had a theme," Casey grumbled as he descended the stairs. "We had plaid one year, black tie another year, and ugly Christmas sweaters last year. This year? Nothing! Nosey really dropped the ba—"

He stopped talking, stopped walking, stopped *breathing* when he saw Landon standing in the living room.

Landon was wearing the sweater. The light purple—lilac? Lavender?—cashmere sweater that Casey had felt guilty about pushing him to splurge on right up until this very moment. Landon could have paid twice as much for this sweater, and it would have been worth it.

"That's, um," Casey tried. His throat felt dry. "That's not an ugly Christmas sweater."

Landon's mouth turned up on one side. "Neither is that."

Casey glanced down at his own outfit. He was wearing his new green velvet suit, paired with a wine-colored dress shirt that he'd left open at the collar. The suit was perfectly tailored and he knew he looked classy as hell in it. "I wanted to be a little fancy."

"Should I wear a suit too?"

"No!" Casey nearly screamed the word. "No way. You

look…" He blew out a breath. "You look really fucking good, Stacks."

"Thanks." Landon brushed a hand over his own chest. "I'm kind of nervous about this party. I know that's stupid."

Casey walked toward him. "Not stupid, but nothing to be nervous about either. It will be chill and fun. I mean, you're gonna see some shitfaced teammates, for sure. Not gonna lie, I was bombed at last year's party. Not planning on doing that this year, though."

"No?"

Casey stopped right in front of Landon. "No. I don't want you to have to cart my drunk ass home."

"I could leave you in a snowbank."

"Yeah, but you wouldn't."

Landon locked their gazes. "No. I wouldn't." A moment long enough for Casey to talk himself out of putting his hands on Landon's chest passed, then Landon said, "Seriously, though. Get drunk if you want. We're taking a cab anyway, so…" He shrugged.

Casey dropped it, because he didn't want to explain that he didn't want to drink more than Landon did tonight. That he wanted to just be with Landon at the party, and then be with him some more when they got back home. And then later in bed. And then next morning. And maybe every day and night after that.

"We should get going," he said instead.

"Okay," Landon said, but neither of them moved. "You look good too. I like this." He brushed a finger along Casey's right shoulder.

"Told you," Casey said quietly. "Samir doesn't miss."

Landon was definitely *looking at him* right now. His eyes were even darker than usual, and his hand was twitching at his side as if he wanted to touch Casey again.

Casey wanted him to.

"We should go," he tried again.

This time Landon blinked, and his brow pinched briefly. Then he stepped around Casey and said, "Yeah. Let's go." He grabbed the bag holding the four bottles of wine they'd bought as a hostess gift from the kitchen counter then continued toward the front door. Casey gave himself a moment to pull himself together. If Landon kept raking those big brown eyes all over Casey while wearing a soft sweater, he was gonna get himself kissed.

Yeah. Casey definitely had to watch his alcohol intake tonight. That was his top mission. Operation: Don't Get Drunk, which was part of the larger mission, Operation: Don't Kiss Landon.

But first, Operation: Bundle Up because it was fucking cold outside.

Twenty minutes later, Landon was getting out of a cab in front of one of the most elaborately decorated houses he'd ever seen.

Every edge of the giant two-story house was lined with red and green lights. A nearly full-size model of Santa and his reindeer was installed on the sloped roof. An assortment of large inflatables, some animatronic, covered the yard.

"Holy shit."

"Yep," Casey agreed. "Nosey doesn't fuck around when it comes to Christmas."

Casey didn't bother with the doorbell, throwing the front door open and announcing, "Let's get jolly, fuckers!"

Several guys yelled "Hicks!" in response. There was a view to the large living room area from the front hall, and Landon could see it was packed. Christmas music blared, but plenty of laughter and conversation could be heard over it.

Casey shed his coat and shoes, tossing the coat on top of the large pile that had formed near the door. Landon did the same, then shoved his shoes as close to the wall as he could. A very beautiful blond woman appeared in the hallway. She was wearing a short red velvet strapless dress with fluffy white trim and a matching Santa hat.

"Casey!" She hugged him, then smiled at Landon. She extended a hand toward him. "Hi, I'm Theresa, Clint's wife. Landon, right?"

"Yes. Hi." He shook her hand, then held up the bag he was carrying. "We brought wine."

"That's sweet of you. We might need it." She laughed. "Things are already getting nuts here."

"No doubt," Casey said.

Theresa quickly ran through where all the various drinks could be found, finishing with, "You've been here plenty, Casey. You know where everything is. Show Landon around."

"You don't have to," Landon said, as soon as Theresa left.

"Good, because I don't remember where anything is at all. I think there's a bathroom that way." Casey gestured vaguely to the left. "Anyway, there's definitely a party *that* way." He pointed forward and started walking toward the living room.

Landon followed, and tried but failed to not notice how great Casey's ass and thighs looked wrapped snugly in green velvet. Checking out butts wasn't even Landon's thing, usually, but he'd been having a lot of new thoughts when it came to Casey.

The one at the top of his mind, almost always now, was what would happen if Landon kissed him. Worst-case scenario, obviously, was Casey being horrified and never wanting to talk to him again. Unlikely, Landon thought, but not impossible. Definitely worth avoiding. Best-case scenario, Casey was very into it and they kept on kissing each other for the rest of their lives. Lofty, perhaps.

But not impossible.

Most-likely scenario: Casey kissed him back a bit, was sweet and cheerful as he indulged Landon's needs, then gently told him he'd be into fooling around but that he wasn't into Landon *like that*.

Landon didn't think his heart could take that scenario. The worst-case scenario would be kinder, in the long run.

For now, he was happy to be led around the room by Casey, and be introduced to anyone he hadn't met yet. Casey handled most of the talking, which meant Landon only had to insert a few polite words here and there. It was ideal. It also, he realized after the first hour, really looked like he and Casey were a couple. Casey hadn't left his side for even a minute.

They were beckoned over by a group of three women, all wearing festive cocktail dresses. Landon didn't know any of them.

"Landon, right?" said the woman with big, blond curls who'd invited them over. "I'm Lee's wife, Sylvia. This is Mandy, Ross's wife, and Kat, Antton's wife."

Landon was immediately intimidated. "Oh wow," he said stupidly. "Hi."

Sylvia laughed. "He has felt our power."

"We are the elder wives," Mandy joked. "Tremble before us."

"Aw, come on," Casey said. "You're not scary or old."

"How dare you? I am both scary and old," Kat said. She was Finnish and stunning, like her husband, and had very straight dark brown hair.

"How are you liking Calgary?" Mandy asked Landon. "This is only our second season here, so it's still pretty new for us too."

"It's nice," Landon said. "I hope to see a lot more of it."

Suddenly the room erupted in cheers, and when Landon turned he saw that Gilbert Morin had arrived.

"It's like you summoned him," Kat teased.

Landon's cheeks heated. "I didn't mean—"

"I know. But of course you want his job. It's nothing to be ashamed of."

Landon wasn't sure what to say, so he nodded once and changed the subject. "I think I'll get a drink."

"Cool," Casey said. "I'll go with you."

Landon didn't miss the look Sylvia and Mandy shared, as if Casey had said something amusing.

"Avoid the eggnog," Sylvia warned. "It's mostly rum."

"Clint's secret recipe," Kat said.

Landon felt it was a good general rule to avoid open bowls of anything at parties, especially hockey player parties. "I'll stick to beer."

Instead of heading to the kitchen, Casey made a beeline for Gilbert with his arms outstretched. "He fucking lives!"

Gilbert engulfed Casey in a hug. He was shorter than Landon but taller than Casey, and his dark hair was flecked with gray. "Got cleared to start working out again too. Might be coming back ahead of schedule, baby!" He spoke loudly, excitedly, and with a French-Canadian accent.

Landon managed a weak smile. "That's awesome."

Gilbert turned to him, grinning broadly in return. He gave Landon a quick bro hug and said, "Stackhouse. Saw that game against Minnesota. Impressive stuff."

"Thanks."

Gilbert animatedly told them both about the progress he'd made healing his shoulder and groin. That his shoulder was mostly healed now and the other injury was lingering a bit but the medical staff felt optimistic about an early return. Landon may have been imagining it, but Casey's smile looked a bit forced too.

"I'm not kidding myself," Gilbert said. "I know this is probably my last season, but I want to end it on my own terms, you know? Not because of an injury."

Now Landon felt bad for clenching his jaw while listening to Gilbert's happy news. "You deserve that," he said. "You've had an amazing career."

"Were you even born when I was a rookie?" Gilbert joked.

"I think I was ten."

"Gross. Well, I made it to thirty-seven as a professional goaltender. Not too bad. When I got plowed into last month, I thought that was it. I was on the ice, in pain, and thinking, 'I guess it's over.' But I get another chance!"

"Hell yeah you do," Casey said. His smile seemed more genuine now. "You're gonna be hoisting the Cup with us this year."

"Fucking right. Hey! Nosey, what's up, rock star?"

Gilbert walked away to hug Clint. Casey glanced at Landon with a sympathetic smile.

"I'd like that beer now," Landon said.

Chapter Twenty-Seven

It's not like Casey hadn't known.

Of course Landon wouldn't be in Calgary much longer. Saskatoon wasn't *far*, but with both of them playing for different teams with different schedules, it may as well be on another planet.

Landon would be gone soon, and Casey would be alone in his too-large house again. And in his too-large bed.

It's probably for the best, he thought glumly as he nursed his second beer. If Landon left, Casey could get over this crush and move on with his life.

He was sitting on the sofa in Nosey's living room, wedged between Gio and Westy. He could see Landon standing on the other side of the room, talking to Antton. He looked nervous and adorable.

Casey was going to miss him so fucking much.

"You okay, Case?" Westy asked. "You've been quiet for like a whole minute."

"Yeah," Casey said miserably. "I'm good."

"Just staring longingly at Stackhouse for fun, then?"

"I'm not!"

Westy laughed. "Okay."

"Fine. I am. So what?"

"Nothing. He looks nice tonight."

"*Right?* That sweater." Casey groaned. "He's killing me."

"Have you tried…talking to him about any of this?"

"Nope."

Westy sighed.

"What are you guys talking about?" Gio asked. His words were slow and thick with alcohol. "Hicks being in love with Stacks?"

"Hey! Your couple name could be Sticks," Westy said unhelpfully.

"I'm not in love with him," Casey grumbled. It felt like a lie. Oh no. It *was* a lie!

"I might be in love with him," Casey amended.

"Have you told him?" Gio asked.

"No he has not," Westy said.

"Well, that's fucking stupid. He's obviously in love with you too."

"Exactly," West said. Then he reached across Casey to high-five Gio. It was sloppy.

"He's also leaving soon," Casey said. "Going back to Saskatoon."

"Oh no. An impossible barrier," Westy said flatly.

"You know about cars and planes, right?" Gio said.

"And, like, the internet?" Westy added.

"Saskatoon is in the next province over, dude," Gio said. "Do I need to get you a fucking map for Christmas?"

"I *know* where Saskatoon is," Casey said, because he sort of did. "But we'll both be busy and it won't be like it is now and also he probably *doesn't even feel the same way.*"

Gio clapped him on the shoulder and said, with all the confidence of a drunk man, "Look, I don't get what he sees in you, obviously, but that dude is crushing big-time. So even if he leaves next week, you should probably shoot your shot. At least bone down a few times, y'know?"

Casey pressed his lips together to keep himself from explaining why that would be a pretty huge deal for Landon. And for himself, honestly.

At that moment, Landon glanced over at him and smiled when their gazes met. Casey smiled back, and even waved. He was so fucked.

"I think I have to tell him," Casey said. "Like, I physically can't stop myself from telling him. It's just gonna burst out, so maybe better sooner than later?"

"Tell him," Westy said. "Do it tonight."

"Yeah," Gio said. "Confess your undying love now, then go home and get poke checked by the goalie until morning." He laughed at his own terrible joke.

"Inappropriate," Casey scolded, though now he was imagining Landon fucking him and it was pretty excellent. "But maybe I'll tell him."

"Rad," Westy said, then stood up. "Let's play ping-pong. I'm in the mood to kick your ass, Hicks."

Landon never in his life imagined he'd be in the position of trying to remove himself from a conversation with Antton Niskanen, but here he was.

It was just...the thing was... Antton was kind of boring. Landon knew he wasn't exciting himself, but he'd been listening to Antton describe different golf courses for at least twenty minutes now. Landon suspected Antton was happy to have found someone to talk to who wasn't drunk.

The conversation had started okay, talking about goalie stuff. Mostly gear, and then a bit of gossip. It had been a dream come true, really, talking shop with his hero. And all the while Landon had been able to glance over at Casey and catch him smiling at him.

But Casey had left the sofa a while ago, and Landon had no idea where he was. Now Landon was stuck listening to Antton talk about the speed of the greens at some course in Arizona or maybe California.

"Nice," he said, hoping it made sense, then he made his move. "I just need to go to the bathroom. Um. Yeah."

Antton made a gesture that said *be my guest*, and Landon made a quick exit. He slipped into the bathroom down the hall, used it, because he may as well while he was there, then inspected himself in the mirror. His hair was damp with sweat at his temples, and his cheeks were flushed. The house was hot with so many people packed in, and the sweater Landon was wearing wasn't helping matters. He really didn't want to take it off because his undershirt was probably noticeably damp, and besides, Casey liked the sweater. Landon would wear it until he was an actual puddle if it made Casey think he was attractive.

He left the bathroom and nearly ran into Gio, who had been waiting to get in.

"Oh, hey," Landon said. "Have you seen Casey?"

Gio blinked at him, swaying slightly, then he smiled. "He wants to get poke checked."

"Huh?"

Gio waggled his eyebrows. "You're fucking *in*, bro. Go get him."

"Where is he?"

"Oh, he's down." Gio burped. "Down there. Basement. Playing fucking..." He flapped a hand back and forth. "Ping-pong."

"Thanks." Landon headed for the basement, trying to make sense of what Gio had said as he went. Maybe there was no point in trying to decipher what a man that drunk was saying, but Landon was having a hard time ignoring *Go get him*.

Because that was exactly what he wanted to do.

He found Casey playing ping-pong, as described. He'd removed his suit jacket and had opened at least one more button on his shirt. He was laughing, eyes bright and lips pink and shiny. His hair was also slightly damp with sweat, and was curling aggressively at the ends.

Landon had never wanted anything so badly in his life. What

he wouldn't give to be the kind of person who could cross the room and kiss him.

Was there any truth to what Gio had been babbling? Did Casey want to get…poke checked? By Landon? In a sexual kind of way?

Landon had no idea what to do with that information. That was advanced. He was still mostly focused on kissing Casey. Maybe holding him in his arms. Maybe touching each other in bed, seeing where things went…

Casey was looking at him with a confused, maybe amused, expression. God, Landon's face was probably pure, blatant desire. He really needed some air. It was freezing outside, but just for a minute.

He spotted a darkened hallway that seemed to lead outside, and a moment later found himself in the Noseworthy's enormous backyard. He closed his eyes and began counting in his head.

He'd only gotten to six when the door opened behind him.

"Stacks? What the hell? You'll freeze out here."

"It's just for a second. It's hot in there."

Then Casey was standing beside him. He'd put his suit jacket back on. Smart.

"It is kind of nice," Casey conceded. "But you should get your coat if you're gonna be out here for more than a minute or two. I can go get it if—"

"No. Just stay." He turned so he could meet Casey's gaze. "Please?"

Casey smiled at him, slow and uncertain. "Okay." His breath puffed out in a cloud. "Are you having a good time, though?"

"Yeah. It's a good party. Are you?"

"Totally. It's always fun, y'know. Parties. But the thing is…" He frowned as he trailed off. Then he exhaled an enormous cloud and said, "Would it be a really terrible idea if I kissed you?"

Everything stopped: Landon's heart, his breathing, possibly

the world stopped spinning. There was nothing except Casey's nervous smile, and his huge, hopeful eyes as he waited for Landon's answer. For Landon's permission to *kiss* him. Casey wanted to *kiss him*.

"What?" Landon finally said, the single word trembling with disbelief.

"I need to know. I'm sorry. I was trying not to blurt that out but then I went and did it anyway, so now it's out, and yeah. Good idea, bad idea? What are we thinking?"

Landon was already leaning in. "Good idea," he said, so quietly he almost didn't hear himself. Then, a little more confidently, "Great idea."

Casey beamed at him, dimples and all. Landon smiled back, and before he even had a chance to worry about what was about to happen, he was being kissed.

The warmth of Casey's lips was almost shocking in contrast with the frigid air, and Landon parted his own lips instantly, seeking more heat. Casey laughed into his mouth, and then tilted his head to deepen the kiss. Landon forgot what cold felt like because nothing existed beyond Casey's teasing little licks, or his minty sweet taste. Landon never thought he could actually have this, had barely dared to fantasize about it, but now he'd always know how it felt to have Casey in his arms, to have his heart-stopping smile pressed against Landon's own bewildered one, making the kiss ridiculous and sloppy and perfect.

Landon placed a hand just above Casey's hip, brushing his palm against soft velvet. Casey had one hand on Landon's bicep, and another tangled in Landon's hair, which was a lot of physical contact at once, but Landon didn't mind at all. He sighed happily, which made Casey laugh again. Landon pulled back just enough to look at him. Casey's eyes were sparkling in the patio lights, his dimples still on full display.

"You're laughing," Landon said.

"Sorry." Then Casey laughed some more. "I'm just really happy."

"Oh." Landon didn't seem to have control over his lips anymore. They kept shifting nervously between a smile and a frown, and they already missed Casey's lips. "So you're not laughing at me?"

"No! I promise. I'm just, like—oh man. My brain has checked out. Can I kiss you again?"

Landon answered him by leaning down and kissing him. This time he cradled the back of Casey's head in one hand, scooping up all that glorious hair and kissing him with everything he had. Everything he'd been wanting to say for weeks.

Casey groaned and tilted his hips forward, his arousal bumping firmly against Landon's thigh. Landon gasped and broke the kiss, and Casey immediately took a step back.

"Sorry," Casey panted. "Too much, right?"

Landon honestly wasn't sure. It had been new and a bit scary, but also exciting. He liked that he could make Casey feel that way. All he knew for certain was that the foot of space between them right now was way too much. He tugged on Casey's lapel and pulled him back against him, kissing him again.

"You taste good," he said against Casey's lips.

"I ate a candy cane."

Landon laughed, then kissed him some more.

"It's really cold," Casey said after a minute.

"Yeah."

"We should probably go inside."

Landon's heart sank. Inside meant people, and no more kissing. But it also meant avoiding hypothermia, so that was a consideration. "Okay."

"But um." Casey's smile was shy and sweet, his lip plump and shiny from being kissed. "We could maybe head home soon?"

Landon's heart somersaulted. "Yeah." He'd like to leave immediately, actually. Get Casey home and then…well. He wasn't sure what exactly.

But he wanted to find out.

Chapter Twenty-Eight

They immediately bumped into Westy in the mudroom just inside the door.

"Oh," Westy said. "I was gonna join you outside. Were you smoking a joint?"

"No," Casey said at the same moment Landon said, "Yes." Both of their voices were higher than usual.

Westy narrowed his eyes at them. "Is there weed that I can smoke with or without you?"

"Um," Casey said. Like, probably. But he didn't have any on him.

"Wait. Were you guys…" Westy pointed at Casey, and then at Landon.

Casey glanced at Landon, who was blushing enough to give them away.

"Nice," Westy said. Then, in classic West Ackerman fashion, immediately became disinterested. "Maybe Petey has weed. I'm gonna go find him."

He left, and Casey turned to Landon, who was still flushed with embarrassment. "You good, Stacks?"

"Was everyone expecting us to…do that?"

"Make out in Nosey's backyard? Probably not."

"No, I mean was it obvious to everyone that I…"

Casey really wanted him to finish that sentence. When it became clear that he never would, Casey helped. "Probably my fault, mostly. I was very obviously crushing on you."

That got him one of the most adorable shy smiles he'd ever seen. "You were?"

Casey nudged him. "I thought goalies saw everything. I'm fucking bananas about you, Stacks."

"Oh." Landon's smile was twitching like it was deciding whether to grow larger or disappear completely. "I'm pretty bananas about you too."

Casey wondered if it was possible to be *too* happy. "Score! So here's the plan. Operation: Don't Kiss Landon was a bust, so—"

"Operation *what*?"

"Forget about it. The mission failed. I'm now launching Operation: Get the Fuck Out of This Party and Kiss Landon All Night and Maybe All Day Tomorrow."

Landon's smile grew into a wide grin. His nose even wrinkled. "Maybe tomorrow?"

"Well. I'll leave that part up to you."

"I really want to kiss you right now, but we might never make it out of this mudroom if I do."

Casey threw his shoulders back. "Right. We need to stick to the plan. Let's move."

In the taxi on the way back to the house, Casey reached across the back seat and held Landon's hand. Landon thought his heart might burst before they got there. He felt giddy and a bit sick and a lot like he was dreaming.

And he couldn't stop smiling.

Casey's hand was so warm. His thumb was brushing over Landon's, and it felt like sparks were shooting down Landon's arm from it.

They let go of each other when the taxi pulled in front of the house, and Casey walked behind Landon to the front door. Once they were finally inside with the door locked behind them, Landon wasn't sure what to do. He removed his boots, then took off his coat and hung it up in the closet, trying to appear calm and as if his entire world hadn't just changed.

"So, um," Casey said. He still had his boots on and was holding his coat. "We were kissing back at the party."

Landon pressed his lips together. "Were we?"

Casey smiled and dropped his coat on the floor. "Unless it was someone else. I think it was you because my neck is sore from stretching up to reach whoever I was kissing. But I was pretty messed up on candy canes, so I could be remembering things wrong."

"Was the guy you were kissing any good at it?"

Casey kicked his boots off and stepped forward. "Yeah. He was fucking great at it."

"It had to be someone else, then."

Casey slid a hand into Landon's hair. "Lemme check."

They kissed, and Landon marveled at how easy it was. How he didn't have to wonder what to do with his hands, or his tongue, because his body took over. Everything shut down except his need to keep kissing Casey.

"I don't know how hot and heavy you want things to get tonight," Casey said breathlessly, "but could we move to the couch maybe?"

"Okay."

Casey grabbed his hand and led him to the living room. "Sit," he instructed when they reached the couch. Landon sat, and Casey immediately straddled his lap and resumed kissing him.

It was so...*sexy.* Landon was completely surrounded by Casey, the solid weight of him pressing against his thighs, his warm tongue teasing Landon's own. He didn't think he would like being so *surrounded* by another person, but he wanted more. He moaned helplessly and slid his palms over soft velvet, down Casey's back, pausing just above the swell of his ass.

"Yeah," Casey said. "Please."

Landon let his hands complete their journey, spreading his fingers to firmly hold Casey's muscular ass cheeks and squeezing slightly.

"Fuck, Landon. Yes."

Landon's cock was rapidly filling, and he knew Casey would notice, the same way Landon couldn't help but feel Casey's hardness pressing against his stomach. It was a lot, and he wasn't sure what he wanted to do about any of it.

"Is this okay?" Casey asked.

"Yes," Landon said, because it was. So far it was good.

Casey pulled back so Landon could see his eyes. "I don't want to do anything you aren't comfortable with, all right?"

Landon nodded. "Thank you."

"So you can ignore my excited friend down there."

Landon laughed. "Are you going to ignore mine?"

"I'll try, but your friend is a lot more noticeable."

"It's really not that big."

"Sure, buddy." Then Casey kissed along Landon's jaw, and Landon's vision almost whited out. He had no idea being kissed there would feel so good, like there was a direct cable from his jaw to his dick.

He'd barely been kissed before. There had only been a couple of awkward attempts at making out at parties with confident girls who were happy to take charge. Those kisses hadn't felt anything like this. Like every press of Casey's lips was waking up Landon's skin and nerve endings, making his heart race and his blood fizz like champagne. Casey moved slowly across the line of Landon's jaw, to his ear, and then below. He trailed sweet kisses down his neck that tickled and made Landon moan softly. Landon squeezed Casey's ass again, almost helplessly as the unfamiliar thrill of arousal pulsed through him.

"This sweater," Casey murmured against Landon's neck, "is so fucking soft. It's like making out with a cloud."

Landon snorted, and then laughed at the noise he'd made. So much for being sexy. Casey leaned back to look at him, which briefly made their erections rub together. Landon let out a surprised, punched-out gasp while Casey groaned.

"Sorry," Casey said. "Accident. Fuck."

"It's okay. Maybe you could…do that again?"

Casey smiled. "What? This?" He rolled his hips, and holy fuck. Landon nearly lifted off the couch when Casey's hard bulge slid against his own.

"Y-yeah," Landon said shakily. "That."

Casey did it again, and again, falling into a steady, slow grind that Landon dimly realized was a lap dance. Casey was giving him a lap dance. He'd basically asked Casey to do this. Was that a weird thing to ask someone for? God, Casey was good at it, though, giving Landon the exact right amount of pressure on his cock with every pass.

Landon's hands were still on Casey's ass, so he kept squeezing and kneading. Casey's eyes were hooded and hazy, his shiny lips parted. Landon wanted to kiss him, but didn't want to move at all because everything felt perfect.

Too perfect. Landon realized with some panic that he was suddenly very close to coming. "Casey…"

"Yeah."

"I'm too close."

"Mm. Do you want me to stop?"

It was a really tough question. Landon honestly wanted Casey to keep doing this forever, but he also really didn't want to come in his pants. He hadn't thought much about how he wanted his first orgasm in front of another person to go down, but he was sure he could do better than that.

The fact that he was even thinking about getting off with Casey without spiraling was incredible. He was still nervous, but he trusted Casey, and he wanted to do this with him. Also, he was more turned on than he'd ever been in his life.

Casey slowly rolled his hips again, creating more urgency. "Stop," Landon shuddered. "Fuck. You gotta stop."

Casey stopped, then stood so he was gazing down at Landon.

"Holy shit. You look so fucking wrecked." He bit his bottom lip as he openly ogled the press of Landon's erection against his pants. "No pressure, but there are like a million things I want to do to that."

Landon eyed the matching bulge in Casey's velvet pants. He could only come up with about three things to do to it, but he was willing to hear new ideas. "Yeah?"

"Wanna go upstairs?"

Landon nodded. That question, at least, was easy.

Casey extended a hand, and Landon took it, allowing himself to be pulled up to standing. Their chests bumped together when he stood, making Casey laugh. They kept holding hands as they walked upstairs and into Casey's bedroom. Once inside, Casey looped his arms around Landon's neck and kissed him.

"I have an idea," Casey said.

"All right."

"I'll tell you what I want to do, and you say stop when I get to something you don't like the sound of."

Landon swallowed. He loved how easy Casey made this. "Okay."

Casey kissed the corner of his mouth, then said, "I want to get us both undressed, and get into that bed."

"I'm good with that."

"Then I want to lay on top of you and make out some more."

Oh. Landon liked that a lot. He imagined the warm, comfortable weight of Casey's body on top of him, of being able to explore all that exposed skin as they kissed. "Yes," he said.

"And maybe I keep doing what I was doing downstairs, just kind of." He rolled his hips against Landon's crotch to demonstrate. "Until one or both of us gets off."

That sounded easy. And hot. But… "Would that be enough for you?"

"It would be more than enough for me. It's, like, the number one thing I've been wanting to do with you."

"Really?" Landon was still skeptical. Someone with Casey's

sexual history couldn't possibly be into Sex 101 with a virgin who wasn't even sure he liked sex.

"Buddy," Casey said, "you have no idea. But if you're not into it—"

"I'm into it. Just, um. You know. Manage your expectations."

"Nope. No need." He stepped back, then removed his suit jacket and tossed it on the floor, then started on his shirt buttons.

"Oh. So. Just get undressed, then?"

"Unless you want me to take your clothes off all sexy. Or I could do a striptease for you." Casey began thrusting into the air as he ran his palms over his own chest.

Landon huffed and pulled his sweater off. "Just get naked, weirdo."

Landon Stackhouse was naked in Casey's bed.

Actually more like *on* Casey's bed, which was even better because Casey could see all of him. He could see his long, muscular legs, his defined abs and obliques, the dark hair on his pecs and under his sexy little belly button.

And he could see that fucking log of a cock that was resting solidly against Landon's stomach. Jesus fuck. He'd only seen it soft before, obviously, and just brief glances, but now that it was fully filled out Casey was kind of losing his mind about it. Could he fit it in his mouth? Maybe. Casey had a big mouth and good control of his gag reflex, but it would be a challenge for sure. A challenge he'd be more than willing to—

Nope. Stick to the plan.

"Are you going to join me?" Landon asked. "I'm freezing."

"Yup." Casey yanked his own socks off then dived into the bed, immediately blanketing Landon's body with his own. "Hi," he said when their noses were inches apart.

Landon wrapped his arms around him, making Casey feel cozy and safe and ridiculously happy. Casey tilted his head and kissed him, taking it slow and letting Landon know there was no urgency. They had as long as they both wanted, and there was no need to rush this perfect moment.

Big, strong hands explored Casey's back, one sliding up to his shoulder while the other brushed fingertips over his right ass cheek. It all felt so good, and Landon was being so sweet and shy, but also so brave.

Cautiously, Casey gave a slow, controlled thrust, sliding their bare cocks together. Landon gasped into his mouth, and Casey broke the kiss. "Okay?"

"Yeah. Just...wow."

Casey smiled and thrust again. "That's exactly what I was thinking."

Landon's eyes were so dark and full of wonder and surprise as Casey found a rhythm.

"Holy—Casey. So good."

"I know. Fuck, I knew it would be. You're so beautiful. Like, so fucking beautiful, I ca—" Casey's breath hitched on a particularly good thrust. "I can't stop looking at you."

Landon squeezed his eyes shut. "Oh god."

"What?"

"I don't know how to react when you say something like that."

Casey gently kissed his nose, and Landon's eyes opened again. "You fucking dazzle me, Landon."

The confusion left Landon's eyes, replaced by something softer as his mouth stretched into a wide smile. "Casey," he whispered, "you—" His smile disappeared. "Shit. *Shit!* I'm close. God, sorry, I—"

Casey could stop, or slow down, but he was surprisingly close too and he really wanted to watch Landon come. Maybe it was selfish, but he sped up his thrusts, imagined he was fucking deep into Landon's body even as he couldn't remember feeling anything as good as what they were actually doing right now. It was perfect, and so hot, and about to be over in about three seconds because—

"Ah. Casey. I'm—" Wet heat splashed against Casey's stomach as Landon's head tipped back, his neck straining. Casey dipped his head and kissed him, right under his jaw, as his own orgasm ripped through him.

He collapsed on top of Landon, and for a long while they stayed like that, panting quietly together while Landon absently stroked Casey's back.

"Was that okay?" Casey finally asked. He was pretty sure it was, but sometimes feelings changed after climax.

"It was…" Landon exhaled slowly. "It was wow."

Casey grinned and nuzzled Landon's neck. "So fucking wow."

"Thank you."

"No thanks necessary."

"I'm serious. That was…not something I could have done with just anyone. You made it easy."

Casey's heart felt like it was glowing. He wanted to make everything easy for Landon. "Is it something you might want to do again with me?" he asked hopefully.

"Now?"

Casey kissed his chin. "Damn, Stacks. Give me a minute."

"I wasn't saying I wanted to now! I was just clarifying."

Casey folded his arms on Landon's chest and rested his chin on his hands. "Okay. I'll clarify. I would like to have as much sex with you as you want, whenever you want, however you want."

Landon tilted his chin so he could meet Casey's gaze. "Right now might be ambitious."

"Might be."

"But, um…kiss me?"

Casey didn't need to be asked twice. They kissed in a sweet, sleepy way that Casey absolutely loved, and loved even more when Landon started threading his fingers through Casey's hair. They needed to get cleaned up, probably, though they were already cemented together. Leaving the bed seemed like a terrible idea, anyway.

Eventually, Casey felt the unmistakable swell of Landon's erection returning. "Ambitious, huh?" he teased.

"He's just happy to have something to do," Landon joked. His laugh turned into a soft moan when Casey deliberately pressed his weight against Landon's crotch. "Oh."

"You want me to keep going?" Casey was wiped, but he was also very interested in trying to make Landon come a second time.

"No," Landon said, after a long moment of thinking about it. "I'm tired. And I don't think it would work anyway."

"Okay." Casey kissed him. "For the record, sex still 'works' even if you don't come. I mean, if you want to tap out before coming. Not that it's cool to not even try to make someone come, or to give up on them when they still want to. As long as everyone is feeling good and gets what they want, it totally works."

Landon seemed to consider this. "Would you call what we just did sex?"

Casey raised his head. "Hell yeah it was. Technically, I would call it *amazing* sex."

Landon smiled, all shy and adorable. "Amazing?"

"Uh, yeah. You think I was bananas about you before? Bananas times a thousand now, bud."

Casey carefully, and reluctantly, detached himself from Landon and went to the bathroom for some damp facecloths. He cleaned them both up, tossed the facecloths on the floor because that was a tomorrow problem, then crawled into bed, pulling the blankets over them both. Landon rolled to face him.

"Not to make things weird, but this was the best night of my life."

Casey's stomach flipped. "Aw, Stacks. Just wait until tomorrow night."

Chapter Twenty-Nine

Casey had been disappointed to find himself alone when he'd woken up the next morning, but his disappointment only lasted until he registered the smell of food being cooked.

He threw on some sweats and bounded down the stairs like a kid on Christmas morning, because that was the level of giddiness and joy he was at. He wanted to run in circles in his living room gleefully shouting Landon's name. He wanted to throw open the windows and announce to the world that he'd had sex with him and that he maybe would again. Maybe *today*. They'd been given the whole day off to allow for Christmas party recovery.

Instead, he went to kitchen and found Landon making pancakes. Fucking *pancakes*!

Casey took a chance and kissed the back of Landon's neck. "Good morning."

"Hi." He turned to smile at Casey over his shoulder. "Hungry?"

"Starving. I can't believe you're making pancakes!" Casey moved to stand next to Landon, and leaned on the countertop. "How do you know when to flip them?"

Landon gestured with the spatula. "They get little bubbles. When there are enough of them, you flip it."

Casey leaned in to examine the bubbling batter. "How many is enough?"

"I don't know. Just, like, more than a few." He flipped the pancake with the spatula. It was perfectly golden brown on the other side.

"You should open a pancake restaurant," Casey said. "Stacks's Stacks!"

"Oh my god."

"Can you do the thing where you flip the pancake into the air and catch it in the pan?"

"No."

"Aw, come on."

Landon sighed heavily, and then *did the thing*. The pancake did a neat little flip in midair, then landed dead center back in the pan.

"Happy?" Landon said flatly.

"That was so sexy." It really was. Maybe Casey had a competency kink. He filed that away to contemplate later.

"Sexy," Landon scoffed.

"Yup. You know what else was sexy?"

Landon's whole neck and most of his face was pink now. "What?"

"That sex we had last night."

The rest of Landon's face turned pink, but he smiled. "Yeah?"

"Probably going to be thinking about it like ninety-nine percent of the time. So when we're playing against Philly tomorrow night, I'm gonna be doing some sick stickhandling, but I'll also be thinking, 'Landon is so fucking hot when he comes.'"

"Jesus," Landon mumbled as he moved the pancake from the pan onto a plate.

"So, yeah. Anytime, Stacks. You can assume I'm down pretty much 24/7, so whenever you wanna get ravished, lemme know."

Landon laughed. "Ravished?"

"I like that word. It sounds fancy and hot. And also exactly what I want to do to you."

Landon was quiet for a long moment. He flipped the newest pancake (the boring, spatula way), then quietly said, "I'd like to do that for you too. Learn how to make you feel good. But…"

Casey's smile fell. "But?"

"I mean, I'm leaving soon."

Even though Casey knew it already, hearing Landon say the words was still a punch to the gut. The truth was easier to ignore if no one said it aloud.

"You're not leaving today," Casey argued.

"I know."

"So let's enjoy today, and any other days we get, and we'll deal with the leaving thing when it happens, okay?"

"Okay."

Casey leaned in and kissed him. They kissed until they smelled something burning, then Landon swore and frantically flipped the pancake that was now much darker than the others.

"Worth it," Casey declared.

A phone started ringing. Landon's phone.

"No," Casey moaned.

"It's my mom." He accepted the call. "Mom?"

Casey was able to decipher, from Landon's side of the conversation, that the Stackhouses' flight had to be changed for some reason, and that they would be arriving today instead of Wednesday.

Well. So much for a relaxing and sexy day alone with Landon.

When Landon ended the call, Casey said, "Today, huh?"

"Sorry. There's a storm coming to Halifax on Wednesday and this was their only option."

"Why are you apologizing? I told you I can't wait to meet them. I just wish the cleaning service was coming today instead of tomorrow."

Landon turned to face him. "I think I can handle it."

"I'll help."

Landon raised his eyebrows.

"What?" Casey said, affronted. "I can help!"

Landon poured the last of the pancake batter into the pan. "This is weird timing."

Casey yawned. "Weird timing for what?"

"For—" Landon paused, and had that confused look on his face like he thought Casey was fucking with him. "Okay, remember how we kissed for the first time last night?"

Casey grinned. "Yeah, it was awesome. And then we had sex."

"Right. And now my parents are coming today, and that's a lot on its own, but the thing with you and me is also a lot."

"A lot of what?"

Landon closed his eyes. "I'm not ready to tell my parents that we're, y'know...whatever."

Casey was silent for a long moment. He waited for Landon to open his eyes, then he said, "*Are* we whatever? Like, do you want to be?"

Landon's mouth opened and closed a couple of times. "That's...something we can figure out later. Right now I have to focus on my parents, and then meeting your family later this week."

It wasn't the "yes, of course we're together now" that Casey was hoping for, but he tried to be understanding. "Right. Okay."

Landon slid the last pancake onto the plate. "So which room should my parents sleep in? I'll make sure it's decent."

Okay, so Casey thought this was an easy question. "The basement, obviously."

It took Landon a moment. "I don't think we should share a bed while they're here."

"Oh," Casey said, shoulders slumping. "Sure, yeah. I get it."

"I just—" Landon scrubbed a hand over his face. "*Fuck.* I'm sorry. Let's eat and then I'll clean and...think. I need to think."

They ate, and the whole time Casey was confused and vaguely hurt. But, he supposed, there were more important things than his and Landon's...whatever. Landon's parents were coming and that was a big deal. Their *whatever* could wait.

Casey couldn't wait to meet Landon's parents.

He liked meeting people's parents in general, but he was especially interested in the Stackhouses. Landon's relationship with them seemed so *complicated*. Casey wanted to figure it out.

So of course he went to the airport with Landon.

"Is that them?" Casey asked, pointing to a man and a woman who looked about the right age.

"No."

He and Landon were standing together in domestic arrivals, and Landon kept unfastening and fastening the snap on the cuff of his parka. He'd been obviously nervous all day, frantically cleaning and second-guessing every decision he made, like whether to make chili or pasta for dinner (he'd decided on chili because he could make the whole thing in advance).

Casey wasn't much help when it came to cooking or cleaning, but he was good at mellowing Landon out. And at making him smile.

"Do you know how I picture your parents?" Casey asked, now.

"How?"

"Your mom is you, but with a bow. And your dad is you, but with a top hat."

Landon's lips curved up. "He doesn't wear a lot of top hats."

"I'll try not to judge him for that."

Landon was silent for a moment, then said, "I never got him a better Christmas present. All I have are the gloves and stuff."

"Oh, don't worry about that. My dad's got you covered."

Landon's brow pinched. "What do you mean?"

"I told him your dad is a fan, so he's bringing all sorts of shit. Signed jersey, puck, probably some other stuff."

Landon's brow unpinched. "Oh. Thank you."

"No problem." Casey bumped his hand against Landon's,

but didn't try to hold it. He supposed he wouldn't be touching Landon at all for the rest of the week at least. Not even in *private*, apparently. Casey tried not to be bitter about it.

But he was definitely bummed out. He'd been so happy when he'd woken up that morning, and he still was mostly happy, but it was spiked with a shot of confusion. And maybe another shot of worry that he was going to lose this thing with Landon before it even started.

He didn't blame Landon for not wanting to tell his parents about them. Of course it was too soon. Any reasonable person would agree with that. It made sense, which was why Casey was worried that he'd maybe made a bad call when he'd texted Brooke today to tell her that he'd kissed Landon, and that they were maybe together now, and that Casey was super in love with him.

He was *excited*, okay?

He'd also told her not to tell anyone, and to be cool about it at Christmas. So he was probably fine.

"There they are," Landon said, and then he was walking away from Casey and toward two people who, yep, looked like they could be Landon's parents.

Casey stayed where he was, and smiled as he watched Landon get hugged by a decently tall man with dark hair, and a woman with shoulder-length ash brown hair who only came up to Landon's chest.

His mom was crying. Smiling, but crying. His dad looked a little misty too.

Landon talked to his parents for a moment, then pointed to Casey. Casey waved and waited for them to walk over to him.

"You made it," he said cheerfully when they arrived. "Welcome to Calgary." He kind of wanted to hug them, but that might be a bit much. Instead he reached to take Mrs. Stackhouse's carry-on suitcase from her.

"You don't have to—oh, all right," she said. "Thank you. It's so nice to finally meet you, Casey."

"And thank you for giving Landon a place to live while he's here," his dad added.

"You definitely don't have to thank me for that," Casey said. "Best decision I ever made."

Landon looked away, but Casey could tell he was smiling.

His dad extended his hand. "I'm Mike, this is Joanna."

"Rad," Casey said, as he shook Mike's hand, then Joanna's. His parents both had brown eyes, like their son.

"You guys must be tired," Landon said. It was late afternoon in Calgary, and Casey guessed the flight from Halifax wasn't short.

"Exhausted," Mike said, "but very happy to be here."

"Are your parents in town already?" Joanna asked.

"No," Casey said. "They arrive Thursday afternoon with Grandma. They're all staying at a hotel that night, then going to the cabin. My sister, Brooke, is flying in on Friday and meeting them at the cottage because she had to work until then. But the rest of them will be at the game with you on Thursday! We got you guys tickets together."

Mike's face lit up. "We'll be sitting with Dougie Hicks?"

Casey laughed. "You're gonna be doing a lot of things with Dougie Hicks. But if I were you, I'd sit next to Grandma. She knows her hockey."

"There's a game tomorrow night too," Landon said, "but I figured you guys might need a day or two to adjust to the time difference." Casey knew his real concern was that it would be pushing his luck to expect his parents to go to two games.

"We'll probably be tired tomorrow evening," Joanna agreed. "But we're looking forward to Thursday night."

"Yeah?" Landon said.

She squeezed his arm. "Of course."

"You'll have lots of time to rest up," Landon said. "We've got a busy schedule this week."

"But we'll still show you around Calgary," Casey added quickly. "It'll be awesome. And you can come to one of the practices if you want. We can give you a tour of the locker rooms and stuff."

Mike and Joanna both looked excited about this, but Joanna said, "We don't want to be in the way."

"Of course you're not in the way," Casey said. "I'm looking forward to getting to know you. It's going to be a fun week."

"Totally," Landon agreed, a bit cautiously. "It'll be great."

"Well, first we need to get our bags," Joanna said. "I may have overpacked."

His parents started walking toward baggage claim, and Casey lagged behind with Landon. "They seem happy to see you."

"I know. It's not that we don't get along or anything like that. It's just... I don't know. Something we need to figure out, I guess. Too many years of avoiding saying things that need to be said."

Casey touched his fingertips to Landon's elbow, just for a second. "You gonna say them this week, do you think?"

Landon nodded, once. "I need to."

Chapter Thirty

Landon woke alone the next morning in the guest room down the hall from Casey's room. He'd set an alarm, knowing his parents would be up early because they were on Nova Scotia time. When he walked downstairs in his trackpants and Calgary Outlaws hoodie, his parents were already in the kitchen. Mom was cooking, and Dad was closely inspecting the coffee maker. Landon's heart lurched because it had been so long since he had woken up to a morning like this: his parents awake before him, in the kitchen together as they prepared for their separate days. Even in someone else's house it was painfully nostalgic, and god, he'd missed them.

"Good morning," Landon said.

Mom turned away from the stove to smile at him. "I'm making oatmeal. This kitchen is something else!"

"Unreal," Landon agreed. He nodded at Dad. "Need help?"

"What kind of degree do you need to work this thing?"

"It's easier than it looks. Here." Landon hit the correct buttons in the correct order, and the machine came to life. "Now we just wait."

"The world is passing us by, Jo," Mike joked. "We're too old to make a cup of coffee in these modern times."

"Speak for yourself. I got this stove working just fine."

Landon smiled. It was nice to hear them joking around. His family had always liked to tease each other, before. Erin had been especially talented at lovingly roasting them all.

"Is Casey still in bed?" Mom asked.

"Probably. I don't know. I wasn't in his room. I have my own room." Wow. Okay. Landon needed to shut up.

Mom stared at him in the same confused, slightly amused way he knew he did to others. Dad laughed and said, "I think every speck of dust gets its own room in *this* house."

"Yeah," Landon said. He rubbed the back of his own neck. "Anyway. He'll be up soon because we've got practice in an hour."

"Does he like oatmeal?"

"Yeah. With lots of brown sugar, though. Like, a *lot*."

"So you have something in common, then."

More than you'd think, he wanted to say. Instead, he grabbed a banana off the counter and peeled it. He ate it in three bites, then grabbed another. He honestly had no idea how or if he was going to tell his parents about Casey. Or what exactly there was to tell. Would he say, *"Hey guys, Casey and I have been making out and stuff, but that'll probably stop soon because I am heading back to Saskatoon any day now"*? Or maybe, *"You know what's stupid? I fell in love with my roommate and I think it's going to kill me when I have to leave"*?

If what he and Casey had seemed like something that could last, it might be worth telling his parents about it. As it was, it didn't seem worth the risk of potentially making this Christmas visit weird. Landon didn't think his parents were homophobic, but it would still be a lot of big revelations at once, and it was likely the case that none of those revelations was important anyway: Casey and Landon would most likely go their separate ways after Landon was sent back down, and as for Landon's sexuality, he still wasn't sure what he even was. He wasn't even sure he cared.

Just as Landon was finishing his second banana and had decided to go the rest of the week without mentioning anything about Casey and him to his parents, Casey came downstairs and scrambled Landon's brain.

He didn't even look any different from usual—athletic clothes, hair in a messy bun, sleepy eyes and a friendly smile— but Landon wanted to grab him, hold him, kiss him in front of the whole world.

"Morning," Casey said, then yawned. "Is that oatmeal?"

"It is," Mom said cheerfully. "Lots of brown sugar, right?"

"You got it." Casey made brief eye contact with Landon, who was probably staring at him with naked desire. Casey didn't return the look, which was understandable; before bed, Casey had tried to kiss him goodnight, and Landon had dodged him. Landon had regretted it for hours afterward, but not enough to go to his room and apologize. Or to give him the kiss they both wanted.

They all ate oatmeal and drank coffee at the kitchen island, chatting pleasantly. Casey did most of the talking, excitedly describing local restaurants and attractions the Stackhouses should check out.

"Tomorrow we have an optional skate, so you guys should come along and we'll give you a tour of the place," Casey said. "The rest of the day is free, so we'll show you the city."

"That sounds wonderful," Mom said. "I think today we're just going to walk around downtown a bit."

"That's cool. You should take my car. I have two."

"Oh, that's all right," Mom said. "We can take a taxi."

"Why, though? My car is just sitting there. It's got winter tires and all-wheel drive. My mom did a bunch of research into the safest cars for winter driving." He paused. "Don't tell her I almost never drive it." He paused again, and this time his eyes widened with horror. "Oh god. Sorry. I shouldn't be talking about unsafe driving. I'm so sorry."

Landon's stomach clenched, but Dad smiled at Casey. "That's nice of you to think of that, but don't worry about it. You don't need to tiptoe around what happened to our daughter."

Mom nodded. "We did that for a long time." She met Landon's gaze. "It wasn't doing any of us much good, I don't think."

Landon was stunned to the point where he wasn't breathing, but then he gave a slow nod. Under the table, Casey tapped his foot against Landon's ankle.

By the time breakfast was over, Casey had convinced Mom and Dad to take his car, and to go wherever they liked in it. Landon jogged upstairs to grab his phone and his wallet, and to brush his teeth. When he stepped out of his bathroom, Casey was standing by his bed, looking uncharacteristically anxious.

"Am I doing okay? With your parents?"

Landon didn't understand. "Of course."

"Yeah? I really want them to like me." He looked adorable, the way he was nervously twisting his sleeve cuff.

"I think they love you," Landon assured him.

Casey's lips formed a tentative smile. "Good. I want them to think I'm good enough for you. I know they don't know about…whatever. But still. I want them to like me. And I want them to know that I really like their son."

Landon's heart thudded against his ribs, then he crossed the room before he'd realized he was moving. He took Casey in his arms and kissed him. Casey responded immediately, kissing him back and sighing happily.

"I missed you last night," Casey whispered.

"Me too."

"So tonight, could we maybe—"

"I don't know. My head is still a mess right now. My parents being here on top of…this. It's a lot. And we've got to get to practice now, and focus on the three games this week, okay?"

Casey sighed as he stepped away. "Got it. Let's roll, Stacks."

"This is going to be weird," Landon said.

Casey removed his coffee from the cupholder between them. "What is?"

"Practice. Seeing everyone." Landon couldn't believe he

needed to explain this. In a few minutes they would be seeing their teammates for the first time since the Christmas party two nights ago. For the first time since Landon and Casey kissed.

Casey took a sip of coffee and returned the cup to the holder. "It won't be weird."

"You've hooked up with a lot of your teammates, then?"

Casey took his eyes off the road for a moment to look seriously at Landon. "No. Never."

"Because," Landon explained slowly, "hooking up with a teammate is *weird*."

Casey's face relaxed into an easy smile. "Yeah, but. This is us. It's different."

"Why? Because I'm not really on the team?"

"You're on the team, Stacks. And no. It's because we didn't *hook up*."

"Then what did we do?"

"I don't *know*." Casey sounded irritated. "Because someone doesn't want to talk about it."

Landon took a sip of his own coffee. The arena came into view ahead of them. "I do want to talk about it. But later. There's enough going on this week already. And, obviously, we shouldn't tell our teammates about it."

"Got it," Casey said. "It's just…some of them know already, probably."

"Well. West does. But he was pretty drunk. Maybe he forgot."

"I mean, everyone knows how I feel about you."

"What?"

"Yeah. I think I was pretty obvious about it. The guys have been teasing me."

"Oh my god," Landon moaned. "This is going to be so weird."

"Nah, I'll play it totally cool. No tongue."

"No kissing at all, you fucking doofus."

"I *know*. Don't worry, I won't even talk to you. Won't look at you. Who are you, even?"

"Thank you."

They pulled into the players' parking lot. "Except," Casey said, "I'm totally going to be ogling you during practice."

"Ogling."

"Yep. Great word."

"I'll be wearing full goalie gear."

Casey waggled his eyebrows. "But I know what's underneath."

So now Landon had a new and exciting reason to be awkward at practice.

Practice offered bigger problems than who was saying what about Landon and Casey. For one thing, Coach Patrick was gruffer than usual, stressing the point that the Christmas break hadn't started yet, and they still had three games to win. He worked them hard, especially for a game-day practice.

For another thing, Gilbert Morin was there. He'd cheerfully announced that he'd been cleared to start practicing again, and that he was feeling almost normal. He proved it by making some solid saves in practice, and generally showing that he could move quickly and fluidly. He really did look game-ready. Landon wanted to be happy for him, but fuck.

At least no one said anything to Landon about Casey. As usual, Landon mostly kept to himself in the locker room, while Casey chatted it up with everyone. It was all very normal, besides Morin being there. Some of the guys still seemed to be recovering from the party, so Landon had a pretty easy time making saves. It didn't bode well for the game that night, though.

When Landon wasn't battling Morin-related dread, he battled parents-related dread. He needed to talk to them. Soon. And maybe that small revelation at breakfast was the open door that would lead to a bigger conversation. Maybe it wouldn't be so hard.

He was so distracted by his thoughts that he didn't realize which shower stall he was in until he heard Casey yell, "Stacks! No!"

The warning came too late. Landon was pelted with what felt like ice-cold pebbles. Or sandpaper? Or acid? "Ow, fuck. What the fuck?"

Casey slid into the stall, completely naked, and grabbed Landon's arm. He hauled him to safety, then bravely went in the stall and turned off the tap.

"I told you!" Casey scolded. "Don't use this one!"

Landon stared at him, at the concern warring with disappointment on his face, at his rapid way his chest was rising and falling, at his balled fists and his limp dick. Then Landon cracked up.

"What?" Casey asked.

Landon waved a hand in Casey's direction because he was laughing too hard to speak.

Casey looked down at himself, which made Landon laugh harder. Casey started laughing too, but probably mostly at Landon.

"You're naked too," Casey argued.

"You just," Landon panted, "ran naked across the shower room to rescue me."

"Dude, I know."

Landon had to brace himself on a wall to keep from collapsing from laughing so hard.

"What the fuck is happening in here?" Clint asked as he exited his own shower stall with a towel around his waist.

"Stacks used the bad shower," Casey explained.

"Oh shit," Clint said, with real concern. "Are you okay?"

Landon was worried he'd never be able to stop laughing.

"I think he might be broken," Casey said.

"Well, fix him. We're probably gonna need him Thursday night."

That sobered Landon up. "What?"

Clint shrugged. "Back-to-back games. I'm guessing you'll be starting on Thursday, right?"

"I thought since we have a break after Friday that Antton might start both games."

"Maybe. Anyway, we can gossip about possible lineups when your dicks aren't staring at me." He left, and Casey put a hand on Landon's shoulder.

"I hope he's right. I want my parents to see you play."

"Yeah, but... My parents were going to go too."

"You don't think they'll want to go if you're starting?"

"I don't know." All of the giddiness that had consumed Landon a minute ago had evaporated. "I should shower for real, though."

"Okay. I'll see you out there."

Landon dragged himself, and all the guilt and anxiety he was carrying, into a safe shower stall.

Chapter Thirty-One

The game *was* a disaster. Boston smoked them 6–1, and Casey had been on the ice for three of those goals. Not great.

He and Landon had come home to a quiet house, Mike and Joanna probably fast asleep downstairs. Casey was exhausted and miserable, and dragged himself up to his bedroom.

"Goodnight, Stacks," he mumbled, wishing Landon would follow him into his room, pin him to the bed, and kiss him until he forgot bad feelings existed.

Instead, Landon said, "Get some sleep," and headed for the room down the hall.

Casey closed his door, stripped, then put on his favorite pair of briefs. He slid between crisp bedsheets that had been changed by the cleaning service that day and tried not to hate that Landon wasn't there with him.

It didn't work. He fucking hated it.

A few minutes later, he heard a soft knock, and then the doorknob turned. Landon poked his head in.

"Want some company?" he whispered.

Casey had never been so happy to see anyone in his life. "Yeah. Come in."

Landon was wearing his usual pajama pants and a T-shirt to bed. He closed the door behind him and gave Casey a sheepish smile. "I, um… I don't like being away from you. And maybe I'm punishing myself for no reason."

"You? Never."

Landon laughed, and crawled in beside Casey. He kissed him, then said, "Sorry about the game."

"It's okay," Casey said. "I have a good feeling about the next one."

Casey woke up in the dark.

Cold fear flooded his veins, even as he reminded himself that he wasn't alone. Landon was beside him, breathing steadily.

It was just *so dark.*

He blinked a few times, trying to get his eyes to adjust so he could at least make out the shapes of his furniture. Anything familiar.

He didn't want to wake Landon, but he felt like he wouldn't be able to breathe unless he got closer to him. He shuffled over a few inches, and carefully wrapped an arm around him, spooning against his curved back. Landon stirred, then sighed, and Casey thought he'd managed to not wake him, until he said, "You all right?"

"Yeah," Casey whispered. "Just got a little…scared. Sorry."

Landon rolled over to face him, though they couldn't see each other in the dark. "It's okay. Want me to turn on the lamp?"

Casey was too embarrassed to admit that he really did want that. He was even more embarrassed that he was too scared to reach out into the darkness to turn his own lamp on. A few seconds later, Landon shifted and his bedside lamp was on. Casey exhaled with relief, heart still racing.

"Thanks."

Landon's eyes were full of concern. He brushed gentle fingers through Casey's hair, removing a strand that had fallen across Casey's nose. "Can I help?"

"Kiss me?" Casey asked shyly.

Landon dipped his head and kissed him, slow and achingly sweet. Casey was obsessed with kissing Landon. It wasn't even sex he was craving, it was more kisses. More of simply being close to Landon. Casey was letting him take the lead when it came to sex. He didn't want to pressure him, or make him do anything that he'd regret. Instead, he focused on learning the places Landon seemed to like being touched.

He put a careful hand on Landon's hip and kissed him until he stopped feeling scared. Landon's lips were so soft and warm, and his hands were so strong, Casey sank into the comfort of the moment, his mind going blissfully blank. It wasn't until Landon moaned into his mouth that Casey realized Landon was rocking against him a bit. And that he was super hard.

"You, uh. You need something from me, big guy?" Casey pressed his own bulge against Landon's, just to make things clear.

Landon exhaled shakily. "I think I was dreaming about you."

Casey smiled. "What was I doing?"

Landon turned his head and buried his face in the pillow. "Never mind."

Uh-uh. No way. Casey playfully poked Landon's shoulder and said, "Come on. Was it hot?"

Landon nodded into the pillow.

"Where were we?"

Landon's voice was muffled. "Don't make me talk about this, please."

"Fine." Casey rolled away, onto his back. "I'll just imagine the dream."

Landon turned his head far enough in Casey's direction that Casey could see he was smiling. "Stop."

"Too late. Thinking about it."

"We were in the locker room, okay?"

Casey was delighted by this piece of information. "Alone?"

"Yes."

"Did we have gear on? Just towels? Nothing? Was I wearing gear and you were naked? What are we talking here?"

"We both had our gear on, but you were on the floor, between my pads and somehow you…" Landon bit his lip as color rushed to his cheeks.

"Somehow I…" Casey prompted.

"You had my…my dick out. And you were…stroking it."

Casey inched closer. "You had all your gear on, pads, mask, everything? But your cock was on display for me?"

Landon nodded.

"God, that's hot," Casey said. "Did it feel good, me stroking you?"

"Yeah," Landon whispered. Casey didn't miss the way he jerked his hips against the mattress.

"Roll over," Casey said.

Landon didn't hesitate. He rolled on his side to face Casey, eyes huge and dark.

Casey kept their gazes locked, watching for any sign that Landon didn't want this, as he slipped his hand under Landon's shirt, spreading his fingers on his bare stomach. Landon shivered, just from that. Casey loved how responsive he was. He loved that this man, who could barely tolerate being touched most of the time, was trembling under Casey's fingertips, and pressing his skin up against his palm.

Casey teased Landon's waistband, letting his fingers slip just inside. "You want me to?"

"Yes," Landon said on an exhale.

Casey smiled, then tugged Landon's pants and underwear down his thighs, letting his cock spring free, huge and heavy. Casey kept his touch light and teasing, experimentally brushing over Landon's cock and watching it twitch and jump. When he glanced up at Landon's face, he saw that his eyes were closed, and his jaw was slack.

"Good?" Casey asked.

Landon nodded, loose like his head was too heavy for his neck.

Casey knew his way around a cock, so he was confident he could make this really fucking good for him. He gave him a proper stroke, and Landon moaned louder than he'd probably meant to. He covered his mouth with his hand and muttered, "Shit."

Casey laughed.

"We shouldn't be doing this," Landon said. Then moaned again when Casey gave him another stroke.

"It's okay," Casey said. "No one can hear us."

"This house," Landon gasped, "is like one giant room."

"The walls and doors are solid, though. I made sure of it."

"We should still try to be—*fuck!*" Landon bit his lip.

Casey kissed his neck. "You can try to be quiet if you want." He twisted his hand around the head of Landon's cock, causing him to thrust into the air.

"Oh god," Landon said, voice shaky. "Stop. Please." Casey stopped, and Landon exhaled heavily. "Sorry."

"Never apologize for letting me know what you want," Casey said, and moved a few inches away, giving Landon some space.

After a few deep breaths, Landon said, "Can I touch you, maybe? For a bit?"

Casey scrunched up his face as if he was thinking hard about it. "All right."

Landon laughed, then kissed him. Casey felt the hard press of Landon's cock against his thigh, and then Landon's big hand cupped Casey's bulge through his underwear. Landon's curious fingers traced the outline of Casey's cock, and down to his balls. The combination of his shyness mixed with his determination to learn how to do this was making Casey's brain melt.

"I like this," Landon said softly. "Touching you."

"That works out because I love being touched by you."

"How do you do it?" Landon asked. "Normally?"

Casey exhaled a short burst of laughter. "Normally without my underwear on, but this feels pretty fucking good."

"Your underwear is soft."

Casey wasn't going to tell Landon how much his briefs cost. Honestly, even *he* was a little embarrassed by it. "Your pajama pants are sexy."

Landon laughed. "Costco's finest."

"What if we were both naked, though?"

"I'm good with that." Landon removed his T-shirt and pulled his pants and underwear the rest of the way off, then settled back on his side, facing Casey.

He was breathtaking. Every excessive inch of him. The long lines of his torso, his defined abs, the stiff nipples that peeked out from his dark chest hair, his big hands and his narrow feet. All of him, perfect.

He realized, after an uncertain amount of time, that Landon was waiting for instruction. "Go gentle at first," Casey suggested.

Landon stared at Casey's cock like it was a complicated puzzle, then lightly traced one fingertip over the swollen head. Casey's cock twitched.

"I like that," Casey said, whispering because it felt right. "I like being teased a bit."

"Okay," Landon whispered back, then added another finger and a thumb, but kept his touch light.

Casey shivered with pleasure. "That's perfect. Just like that." He almost let a lazy pet name slip out of his mouth. Baby, or sweetheart, or something else that didn't suit Landon at all. He'd have to do some brainstorming about that.

He reached for Landon's dick, but Landon stopped him. "Just let me touch you. I want to learn."

"You sure?"

"Yeah." Landon stroked him tip to base and back again, featherlight and electric. "You want lube?"

"In a sec. I like to…to get a little precome going first. I like to—*ah*—I like to watch it come out, y'know?"

This was probably way too much information, but Landon only said, "Oh. Yeah," and swiped his thumb over Casey's slit.

"If you want," Casey said, "I love having my balls tugged a little. And rolled around. That always gets me leaking real good."

"Jesus," Landon murmured, then shifted so he could more easily use both hands on Casey. He cradled Casey's balls so gingerly that Casey almost wept.

"You can squeeze 'em a little. Not rough, but, like...oh, fuck. Yeah, like that."

Landon squeezed and rolled Casey's balls as he gently stroked his dick, the whole time watching what he was doing with intense focus.

Casey laughed. "You're using your goalie eyes on me."

Landon blinked. "No I'm not."

"Yeah you are. It's hot. Love having that much attention on me. Turns me on." As if to prove it, precome began to pearl at his slit. Landon licked his lips, which just about killed Casey. "Keep going. Get me fucking dripping."

Landon did, working Casey with careful fingers until his cockhead was glistening. Casey was losing the ability to give instructions.

"You can—*fucking hell*—you can go faster. And maybe... lube...oh god."

Landon didn't move. He was still staring at Casey's dick like he'd never seen anything so fascinating. Then, in a quiet rumble, he said, "Could I—would you mind if I tried to... suck you? A bit?"

"Oh shit. Yes. Please do that."

Landon leaned in slowly, then surprised Casey by giving the head of his cock a sweet little kiss. Then he began lapping at his slit, and Casey was in heaven. He groaned and rolled to his back, and Landon followed, positioning himself between Casey's legs and taking him in his mouth.

"God, you look good doing that," Casey said. He could barely think anymore; he could only state facts. "Your eyes are so pretty. You're so pretty."

Landon moaned around his cock and kept sucking, harder now, more confident. He returned his hand to Casey's balls and must have felt how tight they were getting already. There was no way Casey was going to last much longer, but that was okay because he really wanted to get his hands on Landon.

"Keep going like that and I'm going to come," he warned. "Like, hard. Holy fuck."

Landon hummed.

With the last scraps of coherent thought, Casey tried to spell out the situation. "In your mouth. If you don't pull off I'm gonna—shit, fuck. *Fuck!*" He gripped Landon's shoulder with one hand and grabbed a fistful of bedsheets with the other. Landon kept sucking, the stubborn fucker.

Well, Casey had warned him. And now all he could do is gasp and swear and writhe on the bed because he was riding the edge. God, he loved sex. It was so awesome.

"Coming," he managed to pant, and then he was. Landon stayed on him, letting Casey empty himself into his hot mouth. Casey wasn't quiet about it at all, so he hoped he was right about the thick walls.

Landon pulled off slowly and drew himself up until he was kneeling between Casey's boneless legs. He pressed his lips together, brow furrowed.

"Thoughts?" Casey asked.

"I could use some water."

"There's a—" he waved a hand toward one corner of the room "—thing over there."

He had a fancy crystal decanter of whiskey and two glasses sitting on a table by one of the windows. He'd never used it. Landon grabbed a glass and took it to the bathroom. A minute later, he emerged with the glass at his lips.

"You good?" Casey asked. Landon's cock was hard, so that was a plus.

Landon nodded. "I liked that. Just, you know. The taste is a bit...weird."

"Yeah, sorry. I thought the lemonade would help."

Landon sputtered his next sip. "Wait. You think drinking lemonade will make your jizz taste better?"

Casey shrugged. "Can't hurt."

Landon smiled and shook his head.

"What?" Casey said. "It's not the only reason I drink it."

"Sure."

"By the way, that was fucking amazing. I can't believe how hard you made me come."

Landon set the water glass on the nightstand and sat beside Casey. "Yeah?"

"I mean, you heard me."

Landon poked his arm. "All of Calgary heard you. Probably Edmonton too."

"Sorry."

"No you're not."

"Nope." His gaze dropped to Landon's erection. "So what about you? How do you touch yourself?"

Landon took his time answering. Finally he said, "I don't, very often. And when I do it's usually hard and fast, I guess."

"Really? You don't jerk off, like, all the time?"

"No."

Casey had assumed that Landon would have replaced having sex with other people with an epic amount of masturbation. Casey had sex a lot and he still jerked off every day. "That's cool," he said, to reassure Landon that he wasn't weird. Just… surprising. "So I can freestyle it here?" He wrapped a hand around Landon's cock.

"Uh-huh." Landon's breath hitched. "But maybe just your hand? For tonight?"

Casey nodded, even though he didn't quite understand why Landon didn't want his mouth on him; he was missing out on some expert shit. Landon was in charge, though, and Casey was happy to follow his instructions. "Lucky for you I'm really good with my hands."

★ ★ ★

Landon didn't think it was possible to feel so many things at once. He was nervous, definitely, as well as uncertain and a bit scared. He was also embarrassed about feeling any of those things, and embarrassed about the moans that Casey was wringing out of him. But with each magical stroke of Landon's cock, those feelings were fading into the background, replaced by thundering arousal and a single-minded need to come.

He felt so fucking *good*.

It was different, like this, with all of Casey's attention solely on him. Landon felt exposed, laid out for Casey to play with. For Casey to observe every involuntary shift in Landon's face, and to hear every desperate sound he made. But Landon didn't want Casey to go down on him; he wanted him right here with him.

"You're so beautiful," Casey said. "So fucking beautiful. Like an angel."

Landon could only gasp, eyes rolling back as Casey twisted his hand around his cock. Casey was the one who looked like an angel, with his unreal eyes and the long blond hair that was now damp and curling around his face.

Casey kissed his throat, his collarbones, his chest. He lapped at one nipple, making Landon tremble as an entirely new jolt of pleasure shot through him. Casey did it again, and then gently caught the nipple in his teeth.

"Oh, fuck," Landon said, too loudly.

Casey grinned, then went back to attacking his nipple. Landon had played a bit with his nipples before while jerking off, but it had never felt like this.

Casey kissed his way back to Landon's ear. "Do you like having your balls played with?"

"Pr-probably."

Casey kissed a spot behind his ear that made Landon's spine melt. How did Casey know his body better than he did? Then Casey was cupping his balls, massaging them gently.

"Always heard that goalies have big balls," Casey joked. "Guess it's true."

They were whatever. Proportional. Landon didn't think they were anything special, but Casey was sure handling them like they were special.

"They feel so full," Casey murmured. "So heavy and aching to come."

Scientifically, that was probably nonsense. But it was also fucking hot, so Landon went with it. "Yeah. Want to come."

"I want that. I want you to come all over me."

Landon let out a sharp exhalation like he'd been gut punched because those words pushed him right to the edge. "Oh fuck, Casey."

"Here. Straddle me." Casey rolled to his back. Landon scrambled on top of him, no longer feeling nervous or embarrassed or anything except the need to come. "That's it. God, you're tall," Casey said as he poured lube into his hand. "I love it. Love looking at all of you."

Landon let Casey look. He planted both hands on the bed behind him, arching his back and thrusting his cock forward like an offering. Casey took it, moving his hand hard and fast while Landon bit down hard on his own lip to keep from crying out.

It only lasted seconds after that. Landon felt like his entire body was pulsing, white hot and wonderful, as wave after wave of intense pleasure crashed over him.

When he opened his eyes, he saw the mess he'd made of Casey. He also saw Casey's wide smile.

"That was so fucking hot," Casey said.

Landon barely managed to stop himself from collapsing on him, catching himself with a hand on the mattress as he leaned down to kiss Casey. "Thank you," he murmured between kisses.

"Literally any time."

Eventually, Landon flopped on his back beside Casey, giving himself a moment to catch his breath.

"That was so good," Casey said.

"Mm."

"Just wondering, do you always come like a fire hose or what?"

Landon glared at him. "It's a normal amount. Shut up."

Casey waved a hand over his own chest and stomach and, oh, his neck. "No, dude. This is a fucking monsoon."

Landon left the bed before Casey could notice him blushing. "I'll get you a cloth if you promise to stop talking about it."

"I might need two or three."

"Oh my god." He walked toward the bathroom.

"Hey," Casey called after him. Landon paused and turned, then everything went fuzzy when he saw Casey lazily dragging his fingers through the fluid on his chest. His cock was hard again, resting on his stomach. Casey smiled at him, looking relaxed and so fucking sexy. "I'm really happy right now. Don't be embarrassed, okay?"

"Okay," Landon managed. He'd done that. He'd made Casey look that wrecked and messy and turned on. He'd made Casey come, and then he'd made him want more.

He carried these thoughts to the bathroom, and tried to sort through them as he cleaned himself up and wet a cloth (one was surely enough) for Casey. He'd never thought of himself as a sexual being, but he liked how powerful he felt right now. He liked that he could be sexy, when he wanted to be. That he could make Casey feel good, and give him what he needed.

When he returned to the bedroom, Casey's eyes were closed. He was still smiling, though, and still hard. Landon decided to wash him himself, rather than hand Casey the cloth. He was careful and thorough as he removed the traces of himself from Casey's skin. When he finished, he stared at Casey's erection, wondering what the etiquette was here.

"Don't worry about that guy," Casey said sleepily. "He'll chill out eventually."

Landon was relieved to hear it. He was exhausted. "You sure?"

"Oh yeah. I'm half-hard most of the time. I can't let this guy boss me around or else I'd never stop jerking off."

That was...an image. "Oh."

"Woulda had to whip it out after that poke check you made, right there in the middle of a game."

Landon choked on a laugh. "Fuck off."

"No lie, Stacks. I was at half-mast for the rest of that period. It was distracting."

"Don't make me worry about that when I'm trying to make saves."

Casey laughed, then looped an arm around Landon's neck, pulling him down for a kiss. "Don't worry about it. It's a me problem, anyway."

"So I'm a problem?"

"Best problem I ever had."

Chapter Thirty-Two

The next morning, Landon woke with Casey wrapped around his back like a cuddly squid. It was the sort of thing Landon never would have expected to be comfortable with, but it made him deliriously happy. Everything about Casey made him deliriously happy.

God. Last night had been unexpected and perfect. Yes, he'd been scared, and yes, he was still anxious and unsure about the whole sex thing, but Casey had been so patient and had made Landon relax enough to enjoy himself. There had never been anyone Landon had trusted enough to relax that way. To experience pleasure in being touched, and in being watched. In sharing something intimate with another person. Casey had made it easy. Or, easier, at least.

Now, Casey was warm and soft and all around him. His left hand was hanging in front of Landon's chest, so Landon took it in his own, tangling their fingers together. Behind him, Casey sighed sleepily and shifted. The hard length of his morning wood bumped against Landon's ass, and then again with more purpose. Casey groaned softly and did it again.

Landon's state of pure comfort and contentment began to crumble. It wasn't that he didn't like how this felt—he did—but it still brought on a fresh wave of anxiety. There was something important he needed to tell Casey, even though it might mean the end of their...whatever this was.

"Morning," Casey mumbled, and kissed Landon's bare shoulder. They were both naked, which was also new for Landon. He found he liked the way his bare skin felt against Casey's, and against the sheets. He felt safe, in this bed. Which was how he found the courage to share what was weighing on him.

"I need to say something, and I know it might be a deal breaker. If it is, I understand."

Casey stopped rocking against him. "Deal breaker? What?"

Landon stared at the wall in front of him and kept his tone as neutral as possible. "I don't want to—" He stopped, then tried again. "I don't think I'm into, um. Anal."

Casey exhaled. "That's cool. Lots of people aren't."

"But isn't that sort of, like, the main event? For two guys?"

Casey actually laughed. "For two guys who love anal, maybe. Not when one or more of them isn't into it."

"I mean, I've never done it. Obviously. But even thinking about it..." Landon felt like a fucking baby, but he continued. "Touch is weird for me. You know that already, I guess. There will probably be times I don't want to be touched at all, even by you. And there are places on my body I'll probably never want to be touched. I can't explain why. It's not for any reason, really."

"You don't need a reason," Casey said, then kissed behind Landon's ear. "You can always tell me not to do something. And if you ever want to try something that was off the table before, that's cool too."

Landon rolled to face him. "You wouldn't mind if we never...fucked?"

Casey's eyes looked a little dazed, but he recovered. "I won't mind. I..." He blew out a breath. "Sorry. Hearing you say 'fucked' kind of fried something in me. But for real, I'm happy doing whatever with you. To be honest, anal isn't my favorite thing either. Too much work. Like, don't get me wrong, I love getting fucked when I'm in the right mood, but I've got toys."

"Oh," Landon said, suddenly dazed himself.

"You could watch," Casey offered, "next time I fuck myself with one."

Landon swallowed. "I'd like that, I think."

"Fuck yeah, you would. I'd put on a show."

Landon could imagine it, Casey on display, fucking himself with a dildo while Landon was fully clothed and just watching. No pressure to touch or be touched. It sounded ideal, actually. "And that would be okay with you? If I just watched you and didn't want to be touched sometimes?"

"Uh, yeah. I'd fucking love it. I'm kind of a showoff."

Landon's dick was surprisingly interested in all of this, especially considering everything Landon had just said. Casey seemed to notice the change in his expression, because he said, "You want me to get one of my toys right now?"

"No," Landon said, meaning it. "I just want to stay like this for a while." He slid a palm along Casey's side and rested it on his hip.

"You're so sexy," Casey said, his voice husky with sleep and lust. "Love being with you, however you want. Just want to make you feel good."

"You do." Casey made Landon feel good in every way, far beyond physical pleasure. Casey lit Landon up, filling all his dark caverns with sunshine. He made him happy in a way that Landon had forgotten was possible.

"Can I kiss you?" Casey asked.

Landon answered by closing the gap and kissing him, morning breath be damned. They kissed for a long time, hands exploring lazily. Eventually, Landon realized he'd been absently rubbing his erection against Casey's thigh, and that Casey was doing the same to him.

God, it was easy. Sex could just be something that *happened* if they both felt like doing it. There didn't need to be pressure or expectations. Landon knew he could choose to stop right now, or keep going until they both climaxed, and Casey wouldn't mind either way. Landon wasn't embarrassed or scared, because this felt right. And in that moment, it was something he *wanted*.

Casey moaned into his mouth, which made Landon pick up the pace. He crawled on top of Casey, still kissing him, still thrusting, welcoming the exhilarating tension that was building inside him.

"Fuck, Landon. You're so hot. Wanna do this all day."

Landon did too. He wanted to stay in this bed all day, kissing and touching and learning each other's bodies, and listen to Casey call him sexy. He wanted to gaze at Casey's face without having to pretend he wasn't. He wanted—

Something clattered downstairs, startling Landon, and then he heard Mom say, "Oh, shoot."

Landon glared at Casey. "Thick walls, huh?"

Casey laughed. "I mean, I think between here and the basement they are."

"They'd better be," Landon grumbled. He left the bed and threw his pajamas back on. Then, as stealthily as he could, he opened the door and slipped out. He hoped his parents wouldn't look up and see him leaving Casey's bedroom.

They were both distracted by cleaning up whatever Mom had dropped. When Landon got closer, he saw that it was a broken plate that seemed to have been piled with French toast.

"I'm so sorry," Mom said when she saw Landon. "It just slipped out of my hands."

"Don't worry about it," Landon said as he crouched to help clean up. The plate, at least, had broken neatly in half, so there weren't any shards. "I'm sad about losing the French toast, though."

"You and me both," Dad said.

"I'll make breakfast sandwiches," Landon suggested. "That'll be easy."

Casey bounded down the stairs, dressed in sweats with his hair pulled back. "Aw, man. French toast down."

"We can pay for the plate," Dad offered.

"Oh my god, no," Casey said. "I barely even use my dishes. Ask your son."

"It's true," Landon confirmed. "I think he just ate food out of his hands before I moved in."

Casey ruffled Landon's hair. "Everything got better when you moved in."

Landon scurried to the garbage can with a handful of French toast, hoping no one could see the color in his cheeks. He made breakfast sandwiches while Casey made coffee and poured orange juice. It was nice, working together in the kitchen, entertaining his parents. It felt...homey.

"So," Casey said after they finished eating. "You guys ready to see the best arena in the world?"

"Can't wait," Mike said. "I've never been in an NHL locker room."

"I've been in way too many of them," Casey joked. "Ours is the best, though. And after, I'm gonna be your guide to the city."

"You don't have to do that," Landon said. It was a reflexive reaction, because despite everything that had happened over the past few days, he still couldn't imagine Casey actual Hicks wanting to spend his time showing Landon's parents around.

"I want to," Casey said. Then his smile faded. "But I get it if you guys want to be alone. No worries."

Landon glanced at his parents and saw a definite *Please let Casey Hicks show us Calgary* look in Dad's eyes.

"I don't really know the city very well," Landon conceded. "If you want to join us, that would be cool."

Casey lit up. "Sweet! I know a fun country bar that has decent food for lunch. You can get the cowboy experience. And we can go up in the Tower, and check out the Christmas decorations downtown. It's gonna be awesome. Do we have time for the zoo?"

Landon laughed. "The *zoo*?"

"Yeah! It rocks."

"It's December."

"The zoo is year-round, Stacks. But I like to set a whole day aside for that. Give all the animals the time they deserve, y'know?"

"Sure. Of course."

Casey beamed at him, and Landon had to turn away to stop himself from kissing him. As fun as the day sounded, he found he was already looking forward to bedtime.

The locker room tour and practice went smoothly, right up until the moment Coach Patrick told Landon he'd be starting tomorrow night's game. Landon began spiraling, wondering if his parents would even want to go to the game now. Would it be too stressful to watch live?

He waited until they were all headed back to Casey's car to tell them.

"So. I'm starting tomorrow night. Coach just told me." He glanced over at his parents, then back at the ground, and added, "Sorry."

He knew Casey was staring at him, and pretending not to stare at him. Landon was acutely aware of how weird this was. Most NHL players didn't apologize to their parents for having to play in the games they attended.

After a long, horrible silence, Mom said, "I told you he'd get the start."

Landon looked up and saw his parents smiling at each other. They looked...excited? "You guys are okay with that?"

"We're thrilled," Dad said. "I know we've been...well. A lot of things, but let's say not very supportive."

"No, Dad, I—"

Dad held up a hand. "We can talk later, and I think that's

long overdue, but for now just know that we're both very proud of you, and we can't wait to see you play tomorrow night."

Landon didn't know what to say. He glanced at Casey, who was smiling, of course.

"Okay," Landon finally said. "Cool."

He kind of wanted to go straight home to have the conversation now, but he didn't want to rob his parents of their celebrity-guided tour of Calgary.

Casey bounced on the balls of his feet. "So. Calgary Tower? You guys good with heights?" He smiled at Landon, all dimples and twinkling aqua eyes and boyish excitement. Landon couldn't believe he was ever allowed to kiss him. That Casey wanted him.

And that Landon knew, if they went home now, he'd be robbing Casey too. Because Casey wanted nothing more than to do this for Mom and Dad. For Landon.

Something weird happened in Landon's chest. He felt like he might start crying, which would be an intense way to react to Casey wanting to spend time with his family.

Maybe this was how his body dealt with unfamiliar emotions, like happiness. Because Casey made him happy. So fucking happy Landon's chest hurt from it, too full of warmth, and when Casey smiled at him like he was doing now, he felt like he might split open.

Landon tilted his head back for a moment to give his heart a rest from having to deal with Casey's dimples. The sun was starting to peek through the clouds.

They didn't get home until early evening. Casey had been an enthusiastic, tireless tour guide, showing them everything from his favorite downtown boutiques to his favorite views in Nose Hill Park. Every place they went, Casey was recognized and approached for autographs and photos, and he'd always cheerfully obliged.

Now, Landon and his parents were relaxing in the living

room. He knew they would want to go to bed soon—they were still adjusting to the time difference—but he was determined to have the talk with them that he'd put off for too long.

He'd quietly told Casey his plan at the park, and Casey had said he'd make himself scarce when they got home. About ten minutes after they all walked through the front door, Casey, with no subtlety at all, announced that he needed to go to "the store." To Mom and Dad's credit, they at least pretended it wasn't weird.

Now Landon needed to figure out how to get the conversation started.

"It's a nice house," Dad said. He tapped his socked foot on the floor. "Good floors. Top-quality stuff."

Landon nodded. "Yeah. Nice." This was ridiculous. He decided to dive in. "So you guys don't mind watching me play tomorrow night?"

His parents shared a look. Landon could only see Dad's face, but he imagined Mom's was similar. His expression said, *Should you tell him, or should I?*

Mom turned back to face Landon. "Part of the reason we wanted to visit you was to…well. I think we're long overdue for a conversation. As a family. And we wanted to have it in person."

"We need to talk," Landon agreed. "I know. I want to."

Mom gave him a small, sad smile, and continued. "We've been working really hard on a lot of things. A few months ago we started seeing a couples counselor." She held up a hand. "Don't worry. Our relationship is just fine, but friends of ours suggested it. They lost their son, so they understood, you know? And the thing is, sometimes you get so lost in your own grief when you lose part of your family, and you don't realize that you're damaging your relationships with the people who are still here." She took Landon's hand. "I regret a lot of things, Landon, but one of my biggest is that we haven't been there for you for years."

Landon could only stare at her, speechless. Her words didn't make sense.

"We are," Dad said, "so sorry."

Finally, Landon whispered, "What?"

"We're sorry," Mom repeated. "I know that isn't enough, but we hope it's a start."

"No. Why are you apologizing to me? You didn't—*I'm* the selfish one. I've been the worst son in the world."

"No," Dad said sternly, "you haven't."

"I *left*," Landon said, louder than he'd meant to. "I left you both alone after—" He swallowed. "After Erin died."

"We weren't alone," Mom said. "We had each other, and your aunts and uncles. Our friends, Erin's friends. They were all there for us, and they all loved Erin. You were the one who was alone with your grief, and we let you stay that way."

Her words hit Landon like a truck, and suddenly his eyes were burning with tears. "Don't say that, Mom. I chose to leave. I chose hockey over you."

"If you hadn't gone to Quebec," Dad said, "if you hadn't taken that opportunity you'd worked your whole life for, it would have killed us, Landon."

Landon shook his head. "I abandoned you because I couldn't deal with losing her. I didn't want to deal with it. I wanted to pretend it hadn't happened, but I never—" His voice broke. "I never forgot. Of course I didn't."

"You were sixteen," Dad said gently. "A kid. We should have done more to make sure you were okay, but..." He exhaled. "This is hard, but we were relieved, I think, that you had something else. That you were being taken care of by another family and doing something you loved. That you had a chance to be happy."

"And," Mom added, "it meant one less thing for us to have to deal with. That was selfish of us, and I'm sorry."

Landon had to cover his mouth with his hand. He felt like

he was crumbling apart. All he could do is shake his head, and stare at their blurry forms with disbelief.

"Of course it was hard to watch you go," Mom continued. "But knowing you were chasing your dream, that maybe you were happy—that was the only thing getting me out of bed some days."

Landon lurched forward and wrapped his arms around her, burying his face in her shoulder. He loved his parents so much, and he couldn't believe they'd been carrying the same guilt as him all these years.

"We are so proud of you," Dad said, tears streaming down his face now. "The boys back home are sick of hearing about you."

They all laughed soggily.

"So what we're trying to say," Mom said, patting Landon's back as he lifted his head, "is that we've been watching your games this season. Not always live, because of the time difference, but we've been watching. Our therapist has been working with us on our fear of losing you. Of seeing you get hurt. It's silly, really, that I worry about you stopping pucks more than I worry about you driving to the arena, since that's how—" She stopped. She didn't need to finish the sentence.

"It's not silly, Mom. It makes sense. Hockey is dangerous, and I'm sorry I didn't pick a more boring job."

"Don't ever be sorry about that," Dad said. "I can't brag to Craig and Bruno if my son is an accountant."

Landon hugged his dad then, wishing they could have talked like this years ago. But maybe it had to wait. Maybe none of them had been ready.

As they all wiped the last of their tears away, Landon admitted, "I'm going to be so nervous tomorrow night knowing you're there."

"You think *you'll* be nervous," Dad joked. "I have to sit with Dougie Hicks!"

Chapter Thirty-Three

Landon went up to the bedroom hours later than he'd expected. He and his parents had stayed in the living room for a long time after their big talk, catching up and chatting about lighter topics. He hadn't wanted it to end, but eventually his parents couldn't ignore how often they were yawning.

Casey had come home sometime in the middle of it all. He'd given them a quick greeting, shot Landon a questioning glance that Landon had replied to with a nod, then made himself scarce upstairs. Landon appreciated it, but now he was dying to see him.

"Hey," he said quietly as he closed the door behind him.

Casey was rummaging through a duffel bag that Landon had never seen before. He had it open on the bed, a few objects strewn on the mattress beside it. He abandoned whatever he was doing as soon as he saw Landon, crossing the room to meet him. "Hi. How'd it go?"

"Good. Really good. I feel…" Landon shook his head. "I don't even know. Lighter, I guess. Relieved."

"That's great!" Casey took his hand and rubbed his thumb in soothing circles over the back of it. "You wanna talk about it?"

"No, I've talked enough for one night. My mind is reeling

a bit, though." He exhaled, long and slow. "I hope I'll be able to sleep tonight."

Casey placed his other hand on Landon's cheek. "I could maybe help with that."

Landon closed his eyes and checked in with himself. He was full of something close to adrenaline: jittery, but with exhaustion creeping in. He wasn't sure what he was up for, but he wanted Casey near him.

To buy himself some time, he kissed Casey, slow and sweet. Thanking him for abandoning his own house to give Landon space to talk to his parents.

"What did you get up to out of the house?"

"Not much. Drove around, got a McFlurry, ate it in the car while I texted Brooke."

"That explains why you taste so good."

Casey smiled. "Christmas flavor. Candy cane fudge."

"What's with the duffel bag?"

Casey's brow furrowed, then he seemed to remember what he'd been doing before Landon interrupted. "Oh! I was looking for something. But, um, it doesn't have to be a right-now thing."

Landon glanced at the bed and realized at least one of the objects on the bed was a Fleshlight, or something similar to one. Another object was definitely a dildo. "Is that whole bag full of sex toys?"

"Yup! Those are the backbench ones. I keep my starting lineup in my nightstand."

Landon, who owned zero sex toys, blinked. "Starting lineup?"

"Yeah, so—" Casey jogged over to the bed "—we were talking about you maybe watching me sometime, and I remembered this steel wand I have with a really long handle and a good curve to it. Thought it might be the right toy for the job."

Landon moved to stand beside Casey, peering down into the bag. It was crammed full of toys of all shapes and colors. A rainbow of silicone. "You've used all of these?"

"Some of them only once because they didn't do much for me, but yeah. Sometimes I get bored and I go online and fill a cart, y'know?"

Landon did not know. He spotted something shiny near the bottom of the bag, and reached in to grab it. He pulled out a long, curved metal dildo.

"You found it!" Casey said happily. "Goalie eyes, right?"

"Good for all sorts of things." Landon inspected the dildo. "This is heavy."

"A bit, yeah. I like that about it. Feels great inside me."

Landon envied how easily Casey could talk about sex. His own mouth was dry and he felt slightly feverish. "So, you want to use this on yourself? While I watch?"

Casey took the toy from him. "I really do. But we can do it another time if you—"

"No. I want to. Watch you. Right now."

Casey smiled, then kissed him. "Give me a few minutes in the shower to get ready and I'll put on the best show you've ever seen."

Landon almost lost his nerve while Casey was in the shower. He paced the bedroom, wondering if he should remove some of his clothes. Wondering if Casey would expect him to jerk off while he watched, and if he'd be insulted if Landon didn't.

Casey was singing to himself in the shower, and that was what convinced Landon to see this through. Casey was getting ready to pleasure himself for Landon's entertainment, and he was relaxed enough to be happily singing off-key.

Landon was sitting on the edge of the bed when Casey emerged from the bathroom, wearing a towel and holding the steel wand. "Me and my costar are all clean and ready to go," he said cheerfully. "But you're in my spot."

"Oh," Landon said, and stood up.

"I was thinking we could pull that chair over to the end of the bed here, and you can just chill in that."

Landon wouldn't be *chilling* no matter where he sat, but he nodded and went to get the armchair that sat next to the window. When he returned, Casey had laid the towel he'd been wearing on top of a pillow that he'd placed near the end of the bed, and was standing completely naked, skin flushed and gleaming from the shower. He began piling more pillows behind that one.

"So how do you want this to go?" Casey asked as he grabbed a bottle of lube from his nightstand. "Wanna make out for a bit to get me fired up, or do you want me to just get to it?"

Casey wasn't hard, but his cock was plump and slightly raised. Landon tried to embrace his inner Casey and said, "I want to watch you get yourself hard."

Casey looked delighted by this announcement. "Damn, Stacks. That's kinda mean and I like it."

"I'll kiss you later. I promise."

Casey bit his lip, as if he were imagining it. "Like a reward?"

"Yeah," Landon said, then sat in the chair. He'd decided to keep all of his clothes on for now, and a dark part of him liked the power he felt from that.

Casey sat on the pillows, legs spread wide, and began to fondle himself, keeping his gaze fixed on Landon. "You do look happier," he observed. "Like a cloud is gone, y'know?"

Was Casey really going to continue their conversation from earlier *now*? Landon tried to steer things back to the present. "I'm happy when I'm with you. I know it's hard to tell."

Casey's smile was soft and unguarded. "Yeah?"

"Yeah."

"Can I tell you a secret?"

Landon held his breath instead of answering.

Casey told him anyway. "I can tell. And it makes me feel good, making you happy."

It was making Landon feel good watching Casey make *himself* feel happy. He watched him scoop his balls into his palm and gently tug at them, mesmerized. "I feel like I should be taking notes."

Casey laughed. "Nah. Just watch. I like you watching me."

"Okay."

"We know from last night that you can make me come like a fucking hurricane, so you're good. No notes."

Landon swallowed. "That was good, last night."

"Mm," Casey agreed. "Oh. Here we go." His cock straightened in his hand, jutting out eagerly as he stroked it.

This whole situation seemed advanced for Landon's third sexual encounter, but it also felt exactly right. He relaxed into the chair, letting himself enjoy the luxury of not having anything to do but watch.

Casey stroked himself until he was rock solid, his foreskin pulled back to expose the purple head of his cock. Landon didn't have any strong opinions about dicks, but he liked Casey's. He liked the shape of it: not huge but thick, with a bit of a curve. He liked his neatly groomed pubic hair, darker blond than the hair that fell around his shoulders.

"Gonna lube up," Casey said, then did it, smearing his length with a healthy amount of lube. "Usually I would wait longer before using lube, teasing myself more, but I've got work to do here."

Landon's gaze dropped to Casey's asshole, which was on shameless display now that Casey had planted his feet on the mattress, legs still wide. It was so small, so tight, barely there. Landon *had* watched porn, so he knew basically how this worked, but he was still fascinated.

Casey was sprawled luxuriously over the mountain of pillows he'd built on the bed, sighing and moaning softly and looking perfectly happy and relaxed as he stroked his glistening cock and balls. "Feeling really good right now," he said.

"You look good," Landon said, trying to look everywhere at once.

"*You* look good," Casey said. His voice was thick and deep, like he was drunk. "Blue looks good on you."

Landon laughed and brushed a hand over his royal blue hoodie. He certainly hadn't chosen it to be sexy. "Maybe I should play for Toronto."

"Don't you—" Casey grunted and jerked his hips off the bed. "Don't you dare."

The hand that had been massaging his balls trailed down, pausing just above his hole to tap and then press slow circles into the skin there.

"Mm," Casey said. "S'good." He stopped and reached for the lube, then coated his fingers. He gave a breathless little laugh and said, "I'm excited."

"I can tell."

"I mean about fucking myself. It's been a while."

"Oh."

Casey pressed the tip of his index finger to his hole and began circling it, getting it shiny with lube in the process. "God, I fucking love this."

Landon apparently did too. His cock was painfully hard in his jeans, but he didn't want to do anything about it. Not yet. He just watched, transfixed by the way Casey was able to work himself open, slowly and carefully. By the time he sank a finger inside, Casey seemed to be out of his mind with pleasure.

Landon had never tried this. He'd touched his hole a bit, on the outside, to see if it did anything for him. He certainly hadn't felt anything close to what Casey was experiencing as he writhed on the bed. He worked a second finger in, and the tip of a third, and then said, "Okay. Time for the main event."

He picked up the steel wand and pressed it between his palms. "Warming it up," he explained with a lazy grin. His gaze landed on Landon's crotch. "Enjoying yourself?"

"Yeah," Landon whispered.

"You can join in, if you want. Jerk off a bit."

"Later. Maybe."

Casey laughed. "You're so mean to yourself."

"I'm not," Landon argued. "I'm being very selfish right now."

Casey coated the wand with lube and pressed it against his hole. "You ready?"

Landon was pretty sure *Casey* was the one who needed to be ready, but he said, "Yeah. Do it."

The round head of the wand slipped inside easily, and Casey moaned at the sensation. Landon still couldn't imagine enjoying it himself, but he loved watching Casey work the toy deeper. Loved the sounds Casey made while he did it.

"Oh shit," Casey panted. "Yeah. Okay. That's the spot." He blew out a breath. "So now I just kinda rock it against my— *fuck*—my prostate and—ah, fuck. Okay. I need to stop talking." A giddy little laugh escaped from him. "Wow. Forgot how good this can be."

Precome was streaming down Casey's dick as he rocked against the toy. His balls were tight and twitching, ready to burst, and Landon had never seen anything so hot in his life. No porn was this good. No fantasy.

He palmed himself through his jeans, but it wasn't enough. With a muttered curse, he opened his fly and gripped himself through his underwear.

Casey noticed. "Oh fuck, Landon. That's so hot. You couldn't stop yourself, huh?"

"N-no," Landon said shakily. God, his underwear was damp where his cockhead pressed angrily against the cotton.

"I'm not gonna last much longer. But I wanna get you off after, if you want. Want you to come on me. Would you do that? You could jerk yourself off or I could help or—oh fuck. Fuck. I'm gonna come."

Landon squeezed his dick hard and gave Casey his full attention. He watched Casey's hole clench around the toy, and the muscles above pulse as Casey erupted. The first long rope spurted high into the air, landing on Casey's chest. Then more dribbled over his fingers, down his cock. Though it all, Casey moaned and panted and swore, keeping one hand on the base of the wand to hold it inside.

When it was over, Casey removed the toy, then collapsed bonelessly against the pillows, arms spread.

Landon stood and stripped off his clothes. There was no way he could resist jerking off now. Not with Casey offering himself as a canvas, all pink with exertion and glistening with lube and sweat and come.

"Shit," Casey rasped when Landon loomed over him, cock in hand. "Yes. Please."

Landon worked himself hard and fast, his usual style. Except this time he wasn't sadly spurting into a bathroom sink. He brought himself to the edge quickly, then grunted and said, "You want it?"

"Fuck yes. Give it to me."

Landon curled forward with the force of his orgasm, but managed to keep his eyes open so he could watch his release streak Casey's torso. Then he dropped down and kissed Casey messily, hungrily.

"Thank you," he said.

"You gotta stop thanking me after sex, Landon."

"That was more than sex. That was…a whole experience."

Casey grinned up at him. "Sex with me is always a whole experience."

Landon laughed and kissed his temple. "You make me so happy," he said, in case Casey had forgotten.

"That's all I want." Casey stretched beneath him, arching his spine. "I hope I also made you sleepy."

"I feel like I could sleep for a week."

"Awesome. But we should probably be at the game tomorrow night."

Landon smiled at him and stroked his hair. "We're gonna win."

"Obviously. It's going to be the best game ever."

Chapter Thirty-Four

It was just a game.

Landon had been repeating that in his head for the past five minutes as he waited in the tunnel with the rest of his team. He tried not to think about the fact that his parents were here to watch him play for the first time in his professional career. He tried not to think about Casey's family, who Landon still hadn't met, being here. Their flight had been delayed, so they'd barely made it to the arena in time for the start of the game, but Casey had happily announced that they were here when he got a text from them.

But anyway. It didn't matter that Casey's parents and grandmother were here. It didn't matter that they were sitting with his own parents, *meeting them*. He needed to try not to think about any of that now.

He needed to not to think about how this would likely be the last game he started for the Calgary Outlaws this season, and possibly ever.

None of that mattered. What mattered was beating Washington.

"Hey," said Landon's favorite voice in the world. "I've got good news and bad news."

Landon smiled behind his mask. "What's the good news?"

Casey poked him in the chest with a gloved finger. "This is gonna be the best game ever."

"That's a relief. What's the bad news?"

"I can't kiss you properly with that mask on."

Would Landon ever get used to Casey just saying stuff like that? "Does that mean you'd kiss me right now if I wasn't wearing it?"

"Probably. But it would serve you right for flaunting your super-cute face."

Landon shoved him lightly. "You're so weird."

"Nope. Just lucky."

Scientifically speaking, Landon knew it wasn't actual sunshine that was filling his chest, but it sure felt like it.

Landon was still smiling when he stepped onto the ice. He automatically looked to where his parents were sitting. Casey had made a show of waving to both of their parents during warm-ups. There was no doubt that the broadcast would be showing Dougie Hicks sitting in the stands at least once, and Landon wondered if his own parents would be visible next to him. Dad would definitely get a thrill from the boys back home seeing that.

By the time the national anthems had finished, Landon felt settled. Washington had opted to start their backup goalie, Mats Norberg, for this game, too. Landon knew Mats from a goalie training camp they'd both attended in the summer. He was a nice guy, and Landon was happy that he'd become Washington's main backup goalie. Good for him.

Landon also hoped that Mats would get lit up tonight. Nothing personal.

The puck dropped and Landon needed to make a big save almost right away. He stopped the dangerous wrist shot with his chest, managed to keep control of the puck, then passed it to Lee. It was a good save, a solid save. The kind that showed his teammates that he was dialed in, and he would do his job so they could do theirs. If this was his last game in Calgary, he was going to put on a fucking show.

The first period was tough. Washington was relentless, with shots coming from all angles. Landon had scrapped his mantra of this being just a game and was playing like the whole world was riding on Calgary winning. Like winning this game would mean Landon could stay on this team, in this city, in Casey's bed.

His teammates were playing hard, too, as if they knew what this game meant to him. Despite the efforts of both teams, the period ended 0-0.

Landon's teammates knew not to speak to him about how the game was going in the locker room, but he definitely noticed Casey beaming proudly at him. Landon rolled his eyes as his heart bounced around.

In the middle of the second period, still scoreless, Washington got a breakaway. One of their star forwards, Garth Fraser, streaked toward Landon, with West close behind. West reached out with his stick and hooked Fraser's hand with the blade. Fraser went down, probably with more gusto than necessary, and Landon swore under his breath.

Penalty shot.

Landon glanced up to where his parents were sitting, and saw his mom covering her mouth with one hand. Dad had a hand on her shoulder.

Time to show them what their son could do.

"Bring it," Landon said as Fraser got ready at center ice. "Fucking try me."

Fraser did the usual zigzagging when he started, trying to confuse the goalie. Landon stayed with him, and predicted that Fraser would cut left and shoot low. Fraser cut left, held the puck for as long as possible, and tried to shoot it into the bottom corner of the net. Landon extended his leg and stopped it easily.

He made it look good, though.

The crowd erupted, and there were even some sustained

chants of "Stackhouse! Stackhouse!" for a minute or so after the save. Landon hadn't heard that since Saskatoon.

It felt fucking great.

The next time Casey was on the ice, he skated up to Landon during a stop in play and said, "That was the sexiest thing I've ever seen."

"Shut it."

"Seriously, Stacks. I'm hot and bothered right now. Gonna seduce the shit out of you later."

"Go play hockey."

Casey pointed his stick at him. "It's happening. Consider yourself seduced."

God, Landon liked him.

The game continued to be a goalie battle until the very end. When the siren blared to end the third period, there was still no score, and the shots on both sides were in the forties.

The two goalies skated to the opposite ends of the ice for overtime, but stopped briefly in the middle. "Good game," Landon said.

Mats smiled at him. "No matter what happens, the goalies won tonight, baby."

"Fucking right."

Landon was running on pure adrenaline as overtime started. It ended up being a pretty easy five minutes for both goalies, exhaustion obviously affecting everyone. When no goals were scored in overtime, a shoot-out started to decide the winner.

Mom and Dad were certainly getting a show.

Shoot-outs were basically a series of penalty shots. Goalies hated them, and Landon was no exception. He'd generally done well in them back in Saskatoon, though, and tonight he felt invincible. Like the net was a tenth of his size.

He stopped the first attempt, and Mats did the same, stopping Casey cold. Then Landon stopped the second Washington shooter, and Mats didn't even need to stop the Outlaws' next attempt because Clint lost control of the puck.

Hoo boy.

It ended up going to a seventh round, when West got the puck just over Mats's extended leg. The building went absolutely wild, and seconds later Landon was engulfed by his entire team.

Casey had got there first, of course, and had his arms *and* legs wrapped around Landon's torso, forcing Landon to wrap his arms under Casey's butt to support him. "Best game ever!" he yelled. "You fucking beast! What the fuck!" He kissed the side of Landon's mask, then finally dropped his legs back to the ice.

"Holy shit, Stacks," Lee said. "That was a fucking clinic. Beautiful."

The crowd was chanting Landon's name again, and everything kind of slammed into him at once: he'd recorded an NHL shutout. In front of his parents. This was his moment. Right now. He knew he would always look back on this exact moment for the rest of his life, no matter what happened.

Landon looked up to the rafters. "Did you see that, Erin?" He laughed, feeling overwhelmed by too many emotions at once.

It only got worse when Antton approached him, hugged him close, and said, "They'll be talking about this one in Calgary for a long time. Legendary stuff, kid."

Landon had to bury his face in his giant glove for a minute, trying to bring his emotions back under control. He registered Casey's hand on his shoulder, and his husky voice saying, "You did so good. I'm so fucking proud of you."

Later, in the locker room, Landon was surrounded by reporters. It was a scene he wasn't used to, but he didn't hate it. He was modest, praising both teams, and especially the amazing performance by Mats Norberg. Then someone asked how it felt to have his parents in the crowd.

"It, um." The lump returned to Landon's throat, and he tried to swallow it down. "It really means a lot, that they're here. I haven't seen them in a while and I hope—" He paused as his voice cracked. "I hope I made them proud tonight."

Casey found him, after that. After the press had left, and Landon was alone in his stall with his feelings.

"Hey," Casey said softly. He'd stripped from the waist up, chest still glistening with sweat, his hair a damp curly mess. Landon wanted to pull him into his lap.

"Hey."

Casey tapped Landon's calf with the side of his ankle. "Best game ever."

Landon nodded as the lump in his throat came roaring back. He looked away, blinking. It really had been the best game ever; the best *weeks* ever, and he didn't want them to be over.

Casey squeezed his shoulder. "Let's get cleaned up. Our families are on their way down here."

"Oh. Yeah. Okay."

"But Landon?"

When Landon turned his gaze back to Casey, he was shocked to see tears in his eyes too. "Yeah?"

"This is only the beginning, okay?"

God, Landon wanted to believe that. He wanted to shake the feeling that tonight was the end of everything: his time in Calgary, his NHL career, living with Casey, being with Casey.

He managed to nod, even if it felt like a lie. Then, Casey surprised him by kissing his forehead. It wasn't a particularly remarkable thing for a hockey player to do to his teammate, but Landon knew it meant something. He knew it was a place-holder for the kiss Casey really wanted to give him, and he tried to focus on that so he wouldn't think about how much it felt like a goodbye.

Much later, he and Casey left the locker room and found their families waiting for them in the hall. Casey ran for his, practically jumping on them as he hugged all three people at the same time.

Landon approached his own parents more calmly.

"Our son the superstar," Dad said, then hugged Landon tightly.

When Landon turned to Mom, she looked like she was going to burst with excitement. All she said was, "Landon!" and then she wrapped her arms around him.

"Did you guys have fun?" Landon asked.

"Oh my god," Mom said. "I won't lie—I think my heart stopped a dozen times. But we are so proud of you."

"Landon," Casey said excitedly. "Meet my parents! And Grandma! Guys, this is Landon. He's awesome."

And then Landon was being approached by Dougie fucking Hicks. "That," Dougie said, "was some of the best goaltending I've ever seen. No joke."

"Th-thank you, Mr. Hicks." Landon awkwardly extended his hand. "Nice to meet you."

"I'm Dougie to anyone my son likes this much," he said as he heartily shook Landon's hand.

"Dougie," Landon repeated. "Hi." Oh god, what had Casey told his parents about him?

Dougie Hicks was still an attractive man. He'd kept in shape, still had a thick head of dark blond hair, and exactly the right amount of dark stubble. And he had the same blue-green eyes as his son. "This is my wife, Michelle."

Casey's mother—short, blond, and stunning—went for the hug over the handshake. "We've really been looking forward to meeting you, Landon. And we love your parents already. We're so glad we'll all be spending Christmas together."

"It was really nice of you to invite us," Landon said earnestly. "Thank you."

She stepped back and smiled at him, and Landon saw where Casey got his dimples from. "The more the merrier, right?" she said.

"This is Grandma," Casey said, looping his elbow with the short woman wearing an Outlaws jersey with her grandson's name and number on it.

"Hi, um." Landon wasn't sure what to call her.

"Eleanor," she supplied. "I like your goaltending style. Old-school and a little scrappy. I especially enjoyed that double pad stack in the third against Beaumont."

"Oh. Thank you." Landon was feeling the weight of having too much attention on him, so he said, "Casey played great tonight. Lots of good chances."

Eleanor patted Casey's arm. "He promised to score me a goal, so I'm not speaking to him right now."

Casey laughed. "I'll score three tomorrow night for you."

"I won't be at that game, because *someone* said it's more important to get to the cabin tomorrow."

"Well," Dougie said sheepishly, "we do have the place rented starting tomorrow, and there are things to prepare."

Eleanor sighed. "I suppose it's only against Anaheim."

Everyone laughed, but Casey said, "Way to jinx us."

They chatted for a bit longer, then Casey asked, "You guys want to come back to the house for a bit?" He pointed to his dad. "I've got Heineken."

"You've also got a game tomorrow," Dougie said sternly, though his eyes sparkled.

"I don't know how you can even hold your eyes open," Michelle said. "Especially Landon."

"Adrenaline," said Casey, Dougie, and Landon all at once.

"Well, that won't last," Michelle said. "Go get some sleep. We can drink and be merry on Christmas Eve."

Dougie nodded in agreement. "Besides, the time zone is messing with us and it must be even worse for Mike and Joanna."

"It should be," Mom said, "but I am just buzzing right now."

"Okay," Casey said. "Heineken for Joanna, sleep for the rest of us."

They all laughed, then Michelle pointed to Mom and Dad and said, "You guys still want to come up with us tomorrow?"

"Well," Mike said slowly as he turned uncertain eyes on his son. "If Landon and Casey don't mind."

Landon could tell Dad *really* wanted to spend more time

with Dougie, so he nodded and said, "Of course. You should go. I'm not even playing tomorrow night, anyway. And we'll meet you there on Christmas Eve."

"Are you sure?" Mom asked.

"Totally. Have fun." He wanted them to have fun. And, if he was being honest, he wanted some alone time with Casey before a couple of days of even more family.

"We need to leave early because Brooke is going be getting to the cabin in the afternoon," Michelle said. "And I have to hit a grocery store and a few other places before we leave town. We can get those chowder ingredients." She turned to Landon. "You should have seen the way Dougie's face lit up when your mom mentioned seafood chowder."

"I can help make it," Landon offered quickly. "I mean, I'd like to, if that's okay."

Mom smiled at him. "I'd love that."

Chapter Thirty-Five

"Okay, so this is not a cabin," Landon said as they arrived at the house in Banff on Christmas Eve.

Casey winced. He'd been expecting something big, but even for his parents, this was lavish. "Yeah. It's a bit fancy."

It was a mansion. It had rustic cabin-inspired design, but only in that there were some exposed logs trimming the stone walls, and it had the shape of a mountain lodge. If that mountain lodge ate five other mountain lodges.

"How did they even rent a place like this?" Landon asked.

"I think Dad's friend owns it. Or stayed here once. I dunno."

Casey parked, and was barely out of the car when he heard his name being screamed. He glanced toward the house and saw Brooke charging toward him with her arms spread wide. "Yay! It's my gross brother!"

"Merry Christmas, dipshit," he said before she crashed into him, wrapping him in a tight hug. He'd missed her a lot.

"Ugh, it's like hugging a statue," she complained. "You're too ripped."

"Yep. Your hair looks rad." He flicked her short, white-blond bob. She used to have long, dark blond curls like him.

"Aw, thanks." She stepped back and turned her attention to the man standing behind him. "So this is the famous Landon

Stackhouse. Jesus, you're tall. How do you guys even kiss?" She slapped a hand over her mouth, eyes wide. "Shit. Sorry, Casey."

Casey glanced sheepishly at Landon. "So, um. Okay. The thing is—"

"It's okay," Landon said, though his wide eyes and his pink cheeks suggested it probably wasn't. He stuck out his hand, "Hi, I'm Landon."

Brooke shook his hand, still looking like she wanted to die. "Hi. As you can see, my brother and I have the same lack of filter. But for real, I am so psyched to meet you because Casey has never brought anyone home ever. Well, this place isn't *home*, but you know what I mean. It's just awesome that he likes you so much. And that you sound so great. So, welcome to the family!"

"Oh my fucking god," Casey groaned. "Welcome to the *family?*"

Brooke cringed. "Too soon?"

"Yeah, it's too fucking soon. We're not *engaged*." Landon coughed. Casey turned to face him. "I'm not helping, am I?"

Landon shook his head.

Casey took a breath. He couldn't believe he was fucking this weekend up already. They hadn't stepped inside the house yet. "Sorry. Let's, um. Let's get our bags and shit. Brooke, help us carry gifts inside."

They opened the back of the Jeep, which was packed with (badly) wrapped presents.

"Oooh," Brooke said. "Is that big one for me?"

"No, it's for Landon's mom because she's nice."

"She is nice! Landon, your parents are adorable. I love them."

"Oh. Thanks."

"And I heard there's going to be seafood chowder for dinner, so now I super love them."

Landon smiled. "It's kind of a tradition in our family, for Christmas Eve."

"That's awesome. We do different stuff every year. Dad loves to show off in the kitchen."

Casey noticed Landon gazing around at their surroundings. There was a thick blanket of snow on the ground and covering the boughs of the endless evergreen trees that surrounded the house on all sides, except for a clearing that framed a spectacular view of a frozen lake. And then, behind all of that, were the majestic, jagged, and snow-covered mountains that Casey always thought looked like they'd been Photoshopped into the background. They were too incredible to be real.

"Wow," Landon said.

"Ideal Christmas setting, right?"

"It doesn't look real."

"Right?" See? Landon got it.

When Brooke headed back to the house carrying a bag of gifts, Casey tugged on Landon's arm. "Hey. Sorry about telling Brooke about us. And not telling you I told Brooke about us. That was shitty of me."

"Thanks. But I guess it's okay. I mean, I've been thinking maybe we should tell our families."

Casey lit up. "Yeah?"

"I don't know. Maybe it's not a good idea, since…y'know."

Casey didn't know. "I think we should tell them, but if you need to talk to your parents first, that's cool."

"But isn't it too soon? Or too…" Landon sighed. "I'll be gone soon."

"We could make it work, though, right?" Casey asked.

"How?"

"We can still see each other sometimes, probably. And we can talk."

Landon was silent a long while. "I don't want to do that. It's not fair to you, and it wouldn't work, long term."

"But what if—"

"Casey. Think about it. We literally won't be in the same city for months once I'm gone. And then maybe we can see each other a bit in the summer, but then what? I could end up anywhere: the East Coast, a different league, *Europe*. Who knows?"

"Or," Casey argued, "Morin retires at the end of this season and you take his place."

Landon shook his head. "They won't do that. They'll sign someone better. Trade for someone. It won't be me."

Anger flickered in Casey. Landon didn't even want to try? "I don't want this to be over when you go."

"Sometimes life is just really unfair and there's nothing you can do about it." That hung in the air for a moment before Landon said, "I'm sorry. There's just a lot going on with me at once. I don't mean to be an asshole. Let's just—" he gestured at the house "—have a good Christmas. We can figure stuff out later."

"Okay," Casey said, though his heart felt much heavier than it had a few minutes ago.

They carried everything from the car through the giant double front doors, which both had wreaths on them, and into an actual Christmas explosion. Like Casey's own house, the layout of the cabin was very open. The living room, dining room, and kitchen were all enormous, and all visible from the front entrance. Garlands, wreaths, lights, and other festive decorations were everywhere: around the windows, draped along the solid wood railing that ran around the mezzanine-style second floor, on the walls, on the floors, and on every other surface. And to cap it all off, a massive, lavishly decorated Christmas tree stood in the very center of the house.

"Casey! Landon! Welcome!" Mom said. She had a glass of wine in her hand, which she set down next to a figurine of a moose wearing a Santa hat so she could hug them. "Merry Christmas."

"Did you do all this decorating?" Casey asked.

Mom laughed. "Oh, Casey. No, it came like this."

He supposed it had been a stupid question. He was sure he'd ask a lot more of them over the next couple of days, and get a similar fond-yet-mocking response every time.

Landon bent and put his lips close to Casey's ear. "I was wondering the same thing."

Casey pressed his lips together to stop himself from kissing him.

"Should we put the gifts under the tree?" Landon asked
Mom.

She waved a hand. "Yes, and wow! You boys did some shopping, huh?"

"A bit."

"What can I get you to drink? We have everything. Like,
literally everything. I challenge you to think of something we
don't have."

"We can get our own drinks," Casey said. "You relax." He
waved at Dad, Grandma, Mike, and Joanna, who were sitting in the living room in front of a roaring fire in the massive stone hearth.

"Sorry I only scored two for you last night, Grandma," he
called out.

"You should be," she joked. "Absolutely terrible."

Casey and Landon put their gifts under the tree, then went
to the kitchen. Brooke was there, adding thinly shaved meat
slices to a large charcuterie board.

"This is my contribution to the festivities," Brooke said. "'Tis
the season to consume way too much salt."

For all of Mom's bragging about drink selection, there was
no lemonade. When he complained about it, Brooke said, "Mix
limoncello with soda water and thank me later."

So he did. And after he'd downed his second one, he thought
maybe the ratio in the glass shouldn't be 50/50.

Landon was drinking beer, slowly. Everyone else was drinking wine and plenty of it. Dad was telling hockey stories that
Casey had heard a million times before, but that Mike, Joanna,
and Landon were enthralled by. So Casey just watched Landon.
He was wearing his lavender sweater. Casey had gotten it dry-
cleaned with his own clothing so that Landon would have it

for this weekend. Obviously he didn't *need* Landon to wear expensive cashmere sweaters to turn his head, but he just looked so fucking cuddly in it.

At some point the Stackhouses went to the kitchen to get the chowder started. Casey was well into the wine by then.

It was *fun* being with his family like this. Being with Landon's family. Eating cheese and meat and little pickled red things that looked like berries but tasted like vinegar. Drinking wine that was really delicious. Casey wondered if he should become a wine guy. Landon would be a good wine guy. He already looked so classy.

If Casey wasn't sure he'd only be in the way, he'd go to the kitchen to help. And to be closer to his wonderful, mostly secret boyfriend. He missed him.

Seriously, what were these little red things? They were like little baby red peppers. Holy shit. *Were* they? "Hey, are these little baby red peppers?" he asked the room, holding one up between pinched fingers, squinting at it as if it might reveal its secrets.

"Sort of," Brooke said. "They're sweety drops. Tiny pickled peppers from Peru. Aren't they good?"

"Sweety drops," Casey repeated, whispering the words like they held power. Then he popped the pepper in his mouth.

He stood up to go to the bathroom and the room tilted slightly. Maybe he should cool it on the wine. He roamed around the main floor until he found a bathroom, used it, then went to the kitchen.

"Hey, sweety drop," he said to Landon.

"The hell?" Landon said. He turned away from the scallops he was doing something with to study Casey. "Oh. You're drunk."

"Nope. Just…hey, is there any lemonade?"

Landon pressed his lips together and shook his head.

"That's cool. Brooke showed me the recipe." He grabbed the limoncello bottle from where he'd left it on the counter.

Landon snatched it out of his hands. "How about some water?"

"Boooooo." Then he noticed something on the counter. "Are those fucking *biscuits*?"

"They are," Joanna said. She seemed to think something was very funny.

Whatever. Everyone always laughed at Casey. He was used to it. Everyone but Landon. Landon was awesome, and very soft.

Landon gently removed Casey's hand from his chest. "Why don't we take our bags up to our bedrooms?" he suggested. "We haven't done that yet."

"Bedrooms?" Casey asked sadly. He didn't like the plural. "Can't we stay togeth—"

"Okay," Landon interrupted. "Upstairs. Let's go."

Casey heard Mike and Joanna laughing behind him as Landon practically pushed him toward the stairs.

"This tree is so big," Casey said as they walked past it.

"Yep." Landon gathered their two small weekend bags and prodded Casey again toward the stairs.

"Turning in already?" Grandma joked. "Can't keep up with us, huh?"

"Just going to put our bags away," Landon said. "And maybe, um, freshen up."

"The two rooms at the end of the hall on the right were the ones we were thinking you'd take," Mom said.

"Sounds good," Landon said.

They found their rooms, and they were very nice and conveniently next to each other, but still sucked because there were two of them instead of one.

"I'm gonna sleep with you anyway," Casey announced.

"Not here, Case."

Casey rubbed his face against Landon's chest. "We should just tell everyone right now."

"You're drunk."

"Only a little. Hey, you should let me suck your dick."

"Shh!" Landon darted over to the bedroom door and closed it. "Casey, seriously. Get it together."

Casey pouted at him. He hoped it was sexy. "I'm really good at it."

"I'm sure you are," Landon whispered. "But not right now."

"Oh yeah. You're making soup."

Landon stared blankly at him. Then his lips twitched, and then he laughed. Casey laughed too, though he wasn't sure why. He liked it when Landon laughed. It never felt mean.

"Casey," Landon said softly as he stepped toward him, "I like you so much."

Casey beamed. This was great news. "Aw, I like you so much too!" No, that wasn't right. "Actually, I think I—"

"I gotta get back down there," Landon interrupted. There was a definite note of panic in his voice. "So, yeah. Why don't you rest for a bit? I don't want you to be sick on Christmas Eve. Drink some water." He put his hand on the doorknob.

"Okay," Casey said, feeling like he'd done something wrong.

"I'll come up to check on you soon. I'll tell everyone you wanted a quick nap."

"I'm not sleepy."

"I know. Just try to rest, okay? For me?"

Casey nodded. "For you." Then, very seriously, he said, "You won't make me miss dinner, right?"

"Of course not."

"Okay good. I want some of those biscuits."

Landon smiled. "They're the best. And, um, for the record. When we get home, I wouldn't mind finding out how good you are at...that thing you mentioned."

It took Casey a moment. Right. The dick sucking. "You got it, buddy. Anytime."

Chapter Thirty-Six

Landon closed the bedroom door behind him and jogged down the stairs. Maybe he'd been too bossy about insisting Casey stay upstairs for a bit—*everyone* was drinking, after all—but Casey was a lightweight and Landon really didn't want him to be sick for Christmas. And, more urgently, he didn't want him to blurt out their secret to everyone, and that seemed like a definite possibility. Landon *really* didn't want to come out to his parents via his drunk possible boyfriend. If Casey couldn't be contained, Landon would have to have an emergency talk with them.

Everyone downstairs was as they were before: his parents in the kitchen, the Hicks family lounging in the living room. It would have looked rude, except Dougie and Michelle had insisted this would be the only meal they wouldn't prepare themselves, and Landon appreciated having a bit of alone time with his parents.

He nodded at the Hickses, hoping his expression said, *Your son is fine and I was not just negotiating future blowjobs with him*, then headed to the kitchen.

"Everything okay?" Mom asked.

"Yep. Casey is just having a bit of a rest."

She kept her eyes on the potatoes she was chopping, but she smiled. "Too hard too fast, was it?"

Landon fumbled the scallop he'd picked up. "What?"

"He's not a big guy. Probably doesn't take much for him to get drunk."

"Oh. Yeah, he's a bit tipsy. And he's still tired from the back-to-back games, so he's going to have a nap."

"Must have been a short one," Dad said.

Landon turned and saw that Casey was back in the living room. And he was holding a glass of wine. Nuts.

Okay. Emergency talk, then. It wasn't ideal, and he wasn't sure he was ready for it, but his parents deserved better than to be shocked in front of everyone. Landon quickly surveyed the kitchen and decided this would be as good a time as any, because the chowder needed to simmer for a bit before they added the more delicate ingredients. "Hey, do you guys want to go outside for a bit with me? I haven't seen much of the scenery and the sun is setting."

Ten minutes later, the three Stackhouses were bundled up and standing together at the edge of the clearing, gazing at the frozen lake far below. This place was really fucking beautiful.

And now Landon was going to make it weird.

"I need to tell you guys something."

He felt both of his parents' concerned gazes on him, but he kept staring straight ahead. Mom put a hand on his arm. "Of course. What is it?"

Landon hadn't planned this conversation out. He probably should have. He supposed he'd hoped it wouldn't be a conversation at all; just a statement, followed by acceptance. He decided to try for that. "I'm attracted to men."

There was silence, and then there were arms around his shoulders, and bodies pressed against his, Dad saying, "That's just fine by us," into Landon's toque.

Then Mom said, "I'm glad you found Casey. We both really like him."

Landon's heart came to a skidding halt. "How'd you know?"

Mom laughed. "We've been living with you for almost a week. You boys are clearly over the moon for each other."

Landon blinked, and then blinked again because the lake was getting blurry. "I didn't think we were being obvious."

"I don't think you could help it."

"We're happy for you," Dad added. "And for him. He got a good one."

Landon laughed and then sniffed. "It isn't going to work, though. I'm leaving soon. Back to Saskatoon."

"That will be hard," Mom agreed. "But it can still work."

Dad said, "I'm no expert in romance—you can ask your mother—but I think all three of us know you need to make the most of the time you have with the people you love."

Landon blinked some more. *Love.* That was the word he was trying not to think about. "We'll both be so busy, and then I could be anywhere. Any team."

"Or," Dad said, "you could be in Calgary. Morin must be thinking about retirement."

"I'm not good enough."

Mom moved to stand directly in front of him. She didn't look impressed. "Excuse me, but I was at that game the other night. Was that not you in the goalie gear?"

Landon managed a small smile. "It was me."

"You're not wrong," Dad said, more sensibly. "Your job is uncertain, and it will always be a fight to earn your spot on any team. But I know you'll always fight like hell for your spot on those teams because it's important to you."

"I will."

"So maybe," Mom said, "fight like hell for the relationship that's turned the light back on inside you."

Landon didn't know what to say. He couldn't promise to fight because he still didn't think there was any point. It would only prolong the inevitable. It would only increase the pain. But, "I want to enjoy the time I have left with him, however long that is. And with you guys too." He wiped at his eyes. "I don't want to be sad anymore this weekend."

"Agreed," Mom said. "I can almost hear Erin scolding us for crying in the middle of all this beautiful scenery."

"I hear her all the time."

Dad put a hand on his back. "We all do."

"What kind is this?" Casey asked as he poked at a chunk of cheese with a breadstick.

"It's still smoked gouda, same as last time you asked," Brooke said.

"It's good."

"You said that too."

Casey frowned at his wineglass. "Am I drunk?"

"Yes, sweetie," Mom said. "Would you like some water?"

Casey nodded. "Landon told me to drink water."

"He's a good influence." Mom got up and went to the kitchen.

"Where *is* Landon?" Casey asked.

"He's outside with his parents," Grandma said. "If it wasn't so cold, I'd be out there too. It's some view."

"Maybe I should go out there," Casey said. He stood, but Brooke tugged him back down by his hand.

"I think they're having a *talk*," she said meaningfully.

"About what?" She stared at him so hard that for a moment she reminded him of Landon. "Ohhhh. About us."

Grandma laughed. Casey wasn't sure why.

Mom returned with a pitcher of water and a stack of glasses. She poured him a glass and handed it to him. "Drink."

Casey drank. It was really good water. Cold and clean tasting. "Thanks."

"Maybe that will keep you from spilling your terribly kept secrets," Mom scolded.

Now Casey was really confused. "What secrets?"

Brooke started laughing too. Wait, was everyone laughing?

"All right, I'll say it," Dad said. "You and Landon. You're an item, right?"

Oh no. Landon was going to kill him, but he couldn't lie to his parents. Not directly. "I mean, yeah."

Mom fist-pumped and said, "Yes!"

"He's way too good for you," Brooke said fondly.

"Oh yeah. Way too good," Casey agreed.

"So we can all stop pretending those two aren't a couple?" Grandma said. She raised her glass. "Thank goodness. Life's too short for that nonsense."

Casey knew she was thinking about Grandpa. This was their third Christmas without him, and it still felt strange. He smiled at her. "You're right, Gran." He refilled his water glass and raised it. "To not wasting time."

Everyone toasted that, and as Casey took a big gulp of water, he silently gave thanks for his awesome family.

"So, does that mean I can share a room with my boyfriend here? Because, full disclosure, I was gonna sneak into his room anyway."

"God above, Casey," Dad said in his gruff hockey voice. "We don't need to know everything."

"Sorry," Casey said, though now he had an even better reason to sober up.

Landon beckoned Casey upstairs just before dinner.

"I told my parents about us," he said when they were in his bedroom. "They seemed to know already, but still. I told them."

Casey grinned. "Mine knew too! I guess we're bad at secrets."

"They did? They know about us?"

"Yep. So, good news, we can share a room now!"

"Bad news: it's still weird to do that when we're surrounded by family."

Casey leaned into him. "It's fine. Everyone is cool. And I didn't mean sex. I like sleeping next to you. And I wanna wake up on Christmas morning with you."

Landon couldn't help smiling at that. "Oh god. What are you like on Christmas morning?"

"You'll see tomorrow." Casey kissed him, then kissed him again. They kept kissing until Dougie shouted, "Chowder!" up the stairs.

Landon laughed against Casey's lips. "He's really excited about that chowder."

"Mm."

"You seem less sloshed."

"I've been drinking water," Casey said proudly. "I'm such a lightweight. It's embarrassing."

"So am I. That's why I don't drink very often." They kissed again, then Landon did the responsible thing and opened the bedroom door. "Let's go eat."

"Biscuits!" Casey ran past him out the door.

Later that night, Landon was in bed, staring at the ceiling while Casey stroked his chest. They'd left a lamp on because Casey had admitted he didn't like waking up in the dark in strange places.

"I can hear you thinking," Casey said. "Are you still mad about Uno?"

"No," Landon said. Then, "It's a stupid game for kids."

Casey laughed and kissed his shoulder. "I should have warned you that we take Uno pretty seriously in my family."

"I'm not even thinking about it. I don't care."

"I can tell. What's up, then?"

"Your family kept making fun of you."

Casey looked momentarily confused, then he smiled when he realized what Landon meant. "Oh. For being stupid. Yeah. Well."

"Doesn't it bother you?"

Casey shrugged, but he didn't say no.

Landon placed his palm on Casey's hip. "You're not stupid."

"According to pretty much everyone, yeah, I am. Well—"

Casey covered Landon's hand with his own "—not you. I know I'm annoying, and let's be real, I'm not a genius, but you make me feel...worthwhile? I dunno. Is that the right word?"

"God, I hope not."

"See? Stupid."

Landon leaned in. "Casey," he said seriously, "you're amazing. Every day I feel so lucky to be around you. You're interesting and funny and I hate that it's going to end soon. I fucking hate it, because I know I'll never meet anyone like you again."

Casey held his gaze and said, "Definitely not."

They both laughed, though it sounded sad. Then Landon kissed him, slowly, as he wished things didn't need to be so complicated for them. The day had been so incredible, with both of their families together and all of them treating Landon and Casey like a couple. It had been overwhelming and wonderful, and Landon would cherish the memory of this weekend forever.

"Thank you," he said, now. "For inviting me. And my parents. I'm really glad I'm here."

"I'm really glad you're here too," Casey said. "You're not the only one who feels lucky."

Landon's heart wobbled. "Come here," he said, and pulled Casey on top of him. They kissed in an unhurried way that didn't lead anywhere, and Landon loved it. Loved the weight of Casey on top of him, loved the way he smiled even as he kissed him, loved the way he made Landon smile right back at him.

Eventually, Casey rested his head on Landon's chest, and Landon stroked his hair until neither of them could hold their eyes open.

By midmorning on Christmas Day, Mike Stackhouse was wearing a Toronto jersey and ball cap, both signed by Dougie Hicks, and a huge smile. Landon couldn't have been happier for him.

"Unbelievable, Mike," Casey complained. "Your actual son plays for Calgary!"

"And, God willing, someday he'll play for Toronto," Dad joked.

Casey booed him. Dougie laughed and said, "The man's got taste."

Casey gasped. "My own father!"

"Well, *I* like my gifts," Eleanor said. She was wearing a ridiculous oversize novelty chain with a big foam Outlaws logo hanging off it, along with a new Outlaws pompom toque.

"Grandma's loyal," Casey said.

"As if she wouldn't be at the front of the crowd at a Toronto Stanley Cup parade," Dougie said.

"Like that's ever going to happen," Eleanor quipped.

Everyone laughed, even as Dad kept saying, "You never know. You never know."

It had been the best Christmas morning Landon could remember, full of laughter and teasing and really fucking good cinnamon rolls that Michelle had ordered from a local bakery. Mom had been thrilled with her gardening gifts, and Dad had been disproportionately excited about his new gloves. Apparently he'd been looking for some just like them.

And Casey was pressed against him on the sofa, his socked foot slightly overlapping Landon's own. Landon was trying to be cool about it, even though he felt like his blood had been replaced by champagne: bubbly and excited.

"I got you something," he murmured into Casey's hair.

Casey's head whipped around to face him, his lips stretched in a delighted smile. "Yeah?"

"It's stupid. But, uh, just a sec." Landon stood and went to the tree. He grabbed the horribly wrapped box he'd hidden behind all the other gifts, then handed it to Casey.

Casey tore the paper off then smiled even wider. "Christmas Cap'n Crunch! Where'd you get it?"

"Minneapolis."

"This is the best gift ever!"

"I mean, it's a box of cereal."

Casey stood and wrapped him in an enthusiastic hug. "This makes my gift for you look terrible."

"Again, it's a box of cereal."

"One sec." Casey practically dived under the tree and emerged with a lump of wrapping paper. He thrust it at Landon and said, "I just thought...since you liked mine so much."

Landon had no idea what the gift could be, but heat flooded his face as soon as he got the paper off. Because Casey had really just given him expensive underwear in front of *both of their families*. After announcing that Landon had *liked Casey's underwear.*

"Uh, thanks."

Brooke face-palmed herself. "Seriously, Casey?"

"They're *nice underwear*," Casey insisted earnestly. "Super soft. Remember how soft you said they were, Landon?"

Landon nodded, gaze fixed on the three pairs of underwear and not on anyone else in the room. "They are. Soft."

"Oh, hey," Dougie said. "Those *are* nice. I wear those too."

"Yeah," Casey said cheerfully. "You're the one who told me about them."

Landon was in actual hell. This was hell. Everyone was either laughing or talking very enthusiastically about the underwear he was holding.

"Thank you," he said, hoping to end this. He put the underwear on the couch beside him. Honestly it was a thoughtful gift, and he'd certainly never owned underwear half that nice before. And maybe it was a little thrilling, getting a somewhat sexy gift from his...guy. But not in front of so many people.

Casey sat next to him, pressing against him again. He leaned in close and whispered, "Sorry. I should have thought that one through."

Landon's lips twitched. "It's okay. I'm being weird. It was a nice gift."

"I guess it's sort of a selfish gift," Casey said with a cute little smile. "I just wanna see you wearing them. And I thought, when you're gone...it would be nice to think about you wearing them sometimes." He frowned. "Okay. This sounds stupid as I'm saying it."

Landon put his hand on Casey's forearm and squeezed. "No. You're right. I'll wear them all the time."

"And think of me?"

Landon couldn't help himself. "Or your dad."

It started snowing late in the afternoon, and kept snowing through dinner. The beef tenderloin roast had been delicious, and there'd been lots of teasing and laughter and wine. A typical Hicks family Christmas.

Now Casey was lounging on the couch, gazing at the tree, capping off his meal with a bowl of Christmas Cap'n Crunch.

"How is it?" Landon asked as he entered the living room. He looked so beautiful, backlit by the tree.

"So fucking good," Casey said with his mouthful of sugary cereal.

"Isn't it just regular Cap'n Crunch but with food coloring?"

Casey swallowed. "No, *Landon*. There are stars and trees."

"Yeah but…" He smiled. "Never mind. You look cute, by the way."

Casey had changed into the fleece onesie Brooke had given him. It was basically a panda costume, complete with ears on the hood and a little tail. "She thought this was a gag gift, but joke's on her: I fucking love it."

Landon kept smiling at him.

Casey put his bowl on the coffee table and sank a little deeper into the couch. "Wait, is this doing it for you? Are you into this?"

"What? No!"

Casey slowly pulled the zipper down a few inches. "How about now?"

"Oh my god." Landon covered his face with his hand. "Stop."

"Too sexy?"

"Too weird."

Casey laughed. "Wanna get in the hot tub with me?"

"It's snowing."

"I know! That's the best time to hot tub!" He stood. "Come on, Stacks. Christmas hot tub."

"Maybe I'll get a hot tub," Casey mused. "For the backyard. Makes more sense than a pool."

Landon sank lower in the hot tub and rested the back of his head on the edge so he could gaze up at the snowflakes falling all around them. "That sounds good."

"Maybe a sauna too. Antton has one and it's sweet."

"You've used Antton's sauna?"

"Jealous?"

"Of course I'm fucking jealous. Of you, I mean." He paused. "Maybe also of Antton."

Casey laughed, and Landon smiled up at the sky. The contrast between the frigid air and the hot water was exciting. It was exciting being here with Casey.

They sat side by side, even though they were alone and the tub was big enough for eight people. They were holding hands under the water.

It was truly a perfect moment, and Landon wished he could see a future where there'd be many more moments like this one.

"I should get an ice bathtub too," Casey said. "A lot of the guys are getting those. You'd like that, right?"

Landon didn't want to ruin the moment, but he had to say it. "You're talking like I'm going to be there. Living with you."

Casey was silent for a long moment, the water churning between them. Then he said, "There has to be a way."

There wasn't. Landon would always be grateful for everything that had changed in his life these past several weeks—talking things out with his parents, making peace with his past behavior, meeting Casey, kissing Casey, learning that he could, in fact, enjoy sex with another person. These were incredible things, and he loved that Casey had been there for all of them, but Landon knew he'd be moving forward with his life alone.

"You okay, Stacks?"

Landon blinked, and realized his eyes were wet. "Yeah," he said. He let go of Casey's hand to scoop some of the hot water and press it to his own face, hoping the evidence of tears would be camouflaged if his entire head was red and wet.

Casey wasn't fooled. "What's up?"

"Just thinking." He knew that wouldn't be a good enough answer, so he added, "This has been the best Christmas I've had since I was a kid."

Casey took his hand back, and squeezed it. "I'm glad."

Landon considered stopping there, but then words started spilling out of him. "I've spent so many years trying to be perfect, or trying to disappear. Trying to cope with being the one who got to—" He took a breath and continued. "To *live* without ever believing that I was worthy of it. It's…lonely."

Casey pulled Landon's hand out of the water and kissed his knuckles. "I won't let you be lonely anymore."

Landon blinked away fresh tears, and held Casey's gaze. "You can't promise that. Not when I'm going—"

Casey shushed him, then kissed him. "We're here now, okay?"

Landon nodded, his forehead rolling against Casey's. "I'm ruining Christmas hot tub."

"Impossible. Christmas hot tub is a journey."

Landon laughed. Despite everything he was feeling, Casey made him laugh. "Let's talk about something else. Please."

Casey kissed him again and said, "Do you want to hear how jelly beans are made?"

Landon absolutely did.

Chapter Thirty-Seven

Boxing Day was a long day of goodbyes. First to Casey's family, as he and Landon had to drive back to Calgary, and then to Landon's parents when they took them to the airport late in the afternoon. There had been lots of promises to keep in touch, an invitation to the Stackhouses to visit Florida, and a lot of frantic packing.

And now, finally, Casey and Landon were alone. At home.

Casey knew Landon was probably emotional after seeing his parents off, so he gave him space after they walked in the door. Casey went to the kitchen, thinking he might take a stab at making sandwiches.

Landon followed him.

"You hungry?" Casey asked, his hand on the fridge door handle. "We could—"

Landon spun him around and kissed him. It was a wild, urgent kiss, catching Casey off guard. He would have stumbled if Landon didn't have such a firm grip on him.

Then, like a dam bursting, Casey let all of the want he'd felt for Landon over the weekend flood through him. He kissed him back, then turned them one more time and pressed Landon hard against the fridge.

"All fucking weekend," Casey rasped between kisses.

"I know."

They'd kissed, at the cabin, but not like this. Not when it was clear path to *more*. Not with Landon grinding against him, his fingers in Casey's hair and his tongue sliding against Casey's own.

"Want you," Landon panted.

Casey palmed Landon's erection through his pants. "You know what I want?"

Landon shook his head.

"I want my mouth on this. Will you let me?"

"Yeah. Yes. Please."

Okay. Casey's kitchen floor was *hard* and his knees wouldn't thank him if he spent any time kneeling on it. But he liked the idea of Landon standing over him, all tall and sexy. "Living room," he decided, out loud.

The living room floor wasn't soft either, but he had a shit ton of pillows on his couch. He led Landon by the hand to the living room, set him up against a wall, then grabbed a pillow.

"You've got a plan," Landon said, laughing.

"If you think I haven't imagined this moment, you're wrong, bud." Casey dropped to his knees, then began opening Landon's jeans.

"Just a reminder," Landon said as he watched him. "I've never done this before. So."

"So?"

"Anything I should know?"

Casey smiled. "Just that I'm better at this than anyone else in the whole world."

Landon huffed.

"Seriously, Stacks. You'll never have better."

Landon gently brushed aside a lock of Casey's hair. "I already believe that."

Casey began fondling Landon's hard length through his sexy new underwear. "Okay, so, I guess just, y'know, relax and enjoy the ride. If you don't like something, tell me. We can stop anytime and, um…oh! Try to keep still if you can. You've got a monster cock, so I need to experiment a bit before I let you fuck my throat. Cool?"

Landon looked dazed. "Uh, yeah. Cool."

"Awesome. Blowjob time." Casey leaned in and pressed open-mouthed kisses against the fabric, getting it wet. He slid Landon's jeans down, and ran his palms up his thighs. Above him, Landon shivered and made delicious little noises of surprise and happiness.

Casey teased him like that, mouthing his cock through cotton, until Landon's sweet noises turned to desperate whimpers.

"You want these clothes out of the way?" Casey asked.

"Yes. Fuck."

Casey helped him out of his clothes, then removed his own shirt. He kept his sweatpants on for now, even though they were already tented. Landon's cock bobbed in front of his face, huge and heavy and so fucking hard.

"Fucking gorgeous," Casey murmured before he wrapped his lips around the wide head.

"Oh fuck," Landon whimpered. "Oh fuck. Oh god."

Casey wanted to smile. He tried to remember the first time he'd gotten blown, how overwhelming it must have been. He was going to make sure Landon never forgot this first time.

He attacked on all fronts, flicking his tongue and sucking hard, stroking the inches he couldn't reach with his mouth while he rolled Landon's balls in his other hand.

Landon kept stroking his hair, which Casey was extremely into. He rubbed against Landon's palm like a cat while he sucked him. It was heaven.

"Casey," Landon said. Even just the one word sounded wrecked. "Close. Really close."

Casey knew it. He pulled off for a moment but kept stroking. "How do you want to finish, big guy?"

Landon gazed down at him with glazed eyes. "Like this. Jerk me. I'm so close."

"Yeah? You wanna make a mess of me again?" Landon groaned

as his cock jumped in Casey's hand. That was a good enough answer for Casey. "Come on, then. Fucking give it to me."

"Oh fuck. *Fuck!*" Landon shot hard, blasting Casey's chest and neck and chin. Casey smiled up at him, pleased with himself for a job well done. Landon was breathtaking when breaking apart like this, his chest flushed, abs clenched, lips slack. He gazed at Casey like he couldn't believe he was real. Like he hadn't known he could feel this good.

It was exciting, knowing Casey could make Landon feel that way. And then watching the tension leave his body, muscles relaxing, eyes soft and sleepy, lips shifting into a sloppy grin. He was beautiful, and so hot that Casey couldn't stop himself from sliding his hand into his own pants to stroke himself. It shouldn't take long...

"No," Landon said, chest still heaving. "Let me." He got on the floor in front of Casey, then tipped him onto his back. Then he was on him, pulling his waistband down and taking Casey's cock into his mouth.

Within seconds, Casey was reduced to mindless babbling. "Shit, Landon. God, that's—yeah. Just like that. You're so fucking sexy. Love how hard you came. Love the sounds you make when you're wrecked like that. Fuck, yeah—tug my balls. Love that. Love it so much. Love—" He bit his lip hard to interrupt himself. Landon grabbed his hand and held it tight as he kept sucking him. "I'm right there. Landon. Fuck. I'm gonna come." He had the thought that he wanted to shoot on Landon's chest, but it was too late. The first burst of his release went down Landon's throat, and then more and more until there was nothing left of him. Just a lovesick blob sprawled out on his living room floor.

Landon pulled off and flopped beside him, and for a minute or so they lay there side by side, panting at the ceiling.

"I can see why that's popular," Landon said.

Casey cracked up.

Chapter Thirty-Eight

It happened at the end of their second practice back.

"Stackhouse," Coach Patrick said, gesturing for Landon to come talk to him near the bench.

Landon went. His stomach was one giant knot, but he tried to appear calm. He knew what was coming.

"Morin has been cleared to play tomorrow night," Coach said. He delivered the news in a straightforward manner, but with a bit of sympathy too.

"Right," Landon said. "Okay."

"You were great. Really, I was impressed. We were all impressed, and you should be proud. And from what I hear, Saskatoon is excited to get you back."

Landon nodded. His gaze landed on Casey, who was messing around with West at one end of the ice.

"Bill's expecting you in his office. He'll let you know about your flight and all that," Coach continued. He put a hand on Landon's shoulder. "Good luck with the rest of the season, Landon. And keep working hard. You've got what it takes, you just need your shot. It'll come."

"Thank you," Landon said. He felt hollow, all the old crevices splitting open inside him. And Casey wouldn't be there to fill them with sunshine. Not anymore.

He met with the GM, as instructed, and got his marching orders. He'd be on a plane to Saskatoon at seven o'clock that evening, and was expected at practice for his new (old) team tomorrow morning. He wouldn't even get a final night with Casey.

Casey found him in the hall outside Bill's office. He looked as miserable as Landon felt. "When?"

"Today. Flight's at seven."

"Fuck."

"Yep."

Casey threw his arms around him and squeezed him tight. Landon hugged him back, and refused to let himself cry. Not here.

"I thought we'd have New Year's Eve together," Casey said.

"Nope." He let go of Casey. "I need to pack."

Casey nodded vigorously, the kind of frantic head bobbing someone did when they were trying to appear like they were fine. "I'll help."

Landon gathered his gear first and packed it all into his giant Calgary Outlaws bag that would be a nice souvenir. He gathered his sticks together, and began saying quick goodbyes to whoever was still around. He wanted to make a quiet exit.

"Oh shit, are you leaving us?" Clint boomed. "Guys, Stacks is out of here."

Well. So much for that.

Landon was immediately surrounded by everyone in the room. He knew he hadn't gotten to know any of them very well, but they all seemed sincerely sad to see him go.

Antton walked into the locker room, looking handsome and slightly menacing in a bespoke black wool coat and perfectly arranged dark gray scarf. Landon had been sure he'd left a while ago, but he strode over to Landon and put a hand on his shoulder, the same way Coach had done. "Sorry to see you go."

"I thought you'd left," Landon said stupidly.

"I did. I came back when I got the news from Morin."

"Oh. Thank you." He'd never been entirely sure what Antton thought of him, or if he thought of him much at all, but this gesture meant the world to Landon.

"You're an excellent goalie. I'll be seeing much more of you, I think, either in here or from the other end of the ice."

Landon swallowed and tried to hold Antton's blue-fire gaze. "I hope so." He knew which one he hoped for more.

Antton nodded. "Until then, good luck in Saskatoon."

He turned and left so quickly, Landon wondered if he'd imagined him being here.

"So—" Casey put his hand on his back "—we should probably head home and get you packed."

Landon's heart sank as he realized this would be the last time he could think of Casey's house as home.

Casey chatted nervously the entire drive home. He knew Landon wasn't really listening, and he certainly wasn't responding, but Casey couldn't help himself. If he stopped talking, he might shatter apart.

"I never did take you out for a steak," Casey was saying now, as if it was important. "Seems wrong to be in Calgary this long and not have a proper steak."

"They have steak in Saskatchewan," Landon said, his first words during the entire drive.

Of course Casey knew Saskatchewan had steak. Probably the same steak, except theirs was stupid and far away and hard to spell and...oh no. Casey was crying.

"Hey," Landon said softly. "Pull over."

Casey pulled into the parking lot of a strip mall, parked, then rested his forehead on the steering wheel. "I don't want you to go."

"I wish I could stay."

At least they were on the same page about that. "When will I see you again?"

"I don't know."

Something occurred to Casey that made him brighten enough to lift his head and look at Landon. "We have our week off coming up at the beginning of February."

Landon smiled sadly. "The Bandits are on the road that week. I checked."

"Oh."

Landon took his hand and held it tight. "I think this might be it."

Casey shook his head. "Don't say that."

"I'm being realistic. I don't expect you to wait for me."

"I will, though," Casey said quickly. "Of course I will."

Landon choked out the most miserable laugh Casey had ever heard. "How long? Months? Years? We both know that's ridiculous."

Casey sniffed. "It sounds like you're breaking up with me."

"I'm—no. I—fuck. I don't know. I just don't see how it will work, and I think it would be less painful if we part as friends, y'know?"

Casey could understand the logic of it, but he didn't care. He didn't want to part as friends. If they had to part at all, he wanted it to be as a man who was going to miss the man he loved, and who couldn't wait to see him again. "We wouldn't be the first long-distance relationship ever," he argued.

"I know. But it's different."

"How?"

"I told you before, I could be anywhere next season. I could be traded *this* season. I don't have a long-term contract like you do. I'm a goalie who isn't quite NHL-caliber. I go where I'm needed until no one needs me anymore."

"I need you." Casey sounded pathetic, but he didn't care.

Landon squeezed his hand. "Like I said, I wish I could stay."

A selfish part of Casey wanted to tell him to stay, then. Quit hockey. Live in Casey's house and let Casey pay for everything and…be miserable. Landon would be miserable.

"You need to pack," he said instead.

"I do."

They drove home.

"I thought I'd drive you to the airport," Casey said, two hours later. He sounded hurt.

"It will be easier this way," Landon said. He put his phone in his coat pocket after seeing the confirmation that a taxi was on its way. His heart was in a million tiny pieces, but he tried not to let it show.

"Can I kiss you goodbye at least?"

Landon had been wrestling with this himself. Of course he wanted to kiss Casey, but would it only make it more painful to leave him?

Maybe just a quick one.

"Okay." He tilted his head and leaned down, meeting Casey's lips in a sweet kiss that was exactly as devastating as he'd expected.

Then Casey placed his hand on Landon's jaw, and Landon opened automatically, moaning and pulling Casey hard against him. He backed Casey against a wall, lifting him until Casey wrapped one leg around Landon's thighs. They kissed wildly, breaking every rule Landon had mentally set for this farewell.

"I'm going to miss you so much," Casey said against Landon's lips.

Landon kissed him again to stop him from talking. Before his heart broke into even tinier pieces.

They kept kissing in a storm of sadness and regret and longing. Landon tried to savor the taste of Casey's mouth this one last time, tried to ignore Casey's hardening cock, and especially trying to ignore his own. There was no time, and no point.

A horn sounded from outside.

"Shit," Landon said, pulling away. "Gotta go."

Casey looked at the floor, sniffed loudly, then said, "I'll help you with your bags."

When all the bags were in the trunk, and Landon was about

to get in the car, Casey put a hand on his arm and said, "Call me when you get there? Or text me at least?"

Landon nodded, though he knew he'd have to kick that habit pretty quickly if he was going to survive the heartbreak that he knew was about to slam into him like a train.

Casey must have seen something in Landon's eyes—a pre-emptive apology, maybe—because his tentative smile fell away.

"Living with you, and everything we've done since I came here…it's been the best time of my whole life," Landon offered. It seemed like too much to admit, while also being a massive understatement.

Casey looked both sad and touched. Then, without any of the hesitancy that had been in Landon's voice, he said, "You're my favorite person, Stacks."

Landon shook his head in disbelief. "You love people."

Casey stared at him, all wide blue-green eyes that glistened with unshed tears, and kiss-bruised lips that seemed to barely be holding back an important declaration. Something Landon absolutely couldn't hear right now.

"Goodbye, Casey. Thanks. For everything."

He got in the car.

Chapter Thirty-Nine

Casey decided pretty quickly that having a broken heart fucking chomped.

It might have been easier, he thought as he exhaled a vape cloud into his living room, if Landon had dumped him cleanly. Maybe Casey could accept that and move on. Maybe he could even find a way to hate Landon for it.

A week had passed since Landon left, and Casey didn't hate him at all, and he definitely hadn't moved on. Barely a minute had gone by without Casey wanting to drive to Saskatoon, except he didn't know what he would say when he got there. He didn't have any new information, or any solutions. All he had was an unending ache in his chest, and a certainty that he and Landon were perfect for each other.

Casey should have fought for them. He should have convinced Landon to give them a real chance, even if it would be hard.

"Maybe," he said to his living room, "I should have told him I love him."

Landon had basically been ghosting him, only sending the occasional short reply to Casey's texts. Casey had called him once, and Landon had answered, but had ended the call after a minute, saying someone was waiting for him. Casey suspected

Landon's behavior was more about self-protection than anything, but maybe not. Maybe Landon really had realized, once he'd put some distance between them, that he didn't even like Casey all that much.

Casey stood and paced his living room, angry that the sun had set and that his house was so big and empty. Angry that he'd be sleeping alone again tonight. He was angry at himself for being weak, at Landon for putting himself last and, most irrationally, at Gilbert Morin for healing so fast.

A loud crash from the kitchen startled him, and then he was angry at his ice maker too.

"You know what?" he said to the fridge, and the house, and the dark. "I'm not afraid of you. I'm done. Nothing even fucking matters anymore." He stomped over to the living room window that was now a black rectangle with his own reflection in the middle. He stared out of it, defiant with his hands balled into fists at his sides. "Fuck you, window. All that's outside of you is my yard. It's not scary."

But the tightness in his chest, his quickening heart rate, and the way he suddenly felt like he couldn't move, said otherwise. With a gasp, he managed to take a step back and then he turned and ran to his kitchen. He planted both hands on the counter, head down, and let out a long, ragged breath.

"Very cool, Hicks," Casey said.

It had been a shit week, no question. Even being named to the All-Star team again hadn't cheered him up because Casey couldn't enjoy anything lately. He felt like he'd never be happy again. Even more out of character, Casey didn't want to talk to anyone about Landon. He'd been drifting through life like an exhausted, grumpy zombie, miserable and alone.

Needless to say, he hadn't been playing the best hockey of his career.

God. How did people do this? How did they get their hearts stomped and then just…keep going? How was he supposed to pretend that waking up alone—if he even managed to get to sleep at all—felt like a gut punch every morning? How was he supposed to forget about the way Landon had laughed against Casey's lips, or the sweet way his breath would hitch when Casey would brush his fingers over Landon's bare skin? Casey had friends who'd gotten their hearts broken, and he'd always offered as much comfort and support as he could, but he'd had no idea how painful this was. Again, he wondered if it would have been easier if Landon had just dumped him. Landon's "I wish we could but we can't" farewell was far more devastating.

Hours later, Casey was wide awake. His brain was unhelpfully presenting him a greatest hits reel of his and Landon's brief, world-changing time together.

"Fuck, Stacks," Casey said to no one. "Why won't you try?"

It wasn't the distance that was killing Casey; it was the uncertainty. Uncertainty that was rapidly dissolving into a gut-wrenching certainty that things between them were well and truly over. That the thing they'd shared had been brief, and would now only be a memory. If Landon had been open to a long-distance relationship, they could be having phone sex right now, or at least texting and sending each other cute photos.

Instead, Casey was blinking back tears next to a row of pillows he'd assembled as a terrible Landon substitute.

Saskatoon was…fine.

Landon had been back for three weeks, and it was good, being a full-time starting goalie again. No question. And he was playing well, despite the fact that he felt like a black hole of sadness every minute of every day. And being around his old teammates was nice. Comfortable. So things were okay.

But, man, Landon sure missed traveling by plane.

He was on a bus, now, heading for Des Moines, his knees pressing uncomfortably into the back of the seat in front of him. He'd been staring out the window for hours, even though there wasn't much to see besides blackness. It was after two AM, and most of the men on the bus were asleep. Felix, the other goaltender and Landon's current seatmate, had been dead to the world since they'd left Winnipeg three hours ago.

Three hours down, seven to go.

Maybe, Landon mused, he would get traded to an East Coast team. The cities would be closer, the bus trips shorter. And he could see his family more often. It wouldn't be bad. And maybe it would make things easier, being farther away from Casey. Saskatoon was frustratingly close to Calgary, and he may as well be in New England or somewhere else that was far enough that he'd stopped hoping Casey would show up at his door.

It was a ridiculous thing to even fantasize about because their schedules would never allow it. And besides that, Landon had been pretty committed to being a huge asshole to Casey since they'd parted. Not in an obvious way, but in a pretending he was too busy to call or even text him back kind of way, even when Landon was dying to hear Casey's voice.

It was easier this way.

Well, no. It was fucking excruciating. But it *would* be easier. Someday. Landon had to believe there would be a morning when he would wake up and not instinctively reach for Casey, only to be crushed by the weight of reality. There might be a day, far in the distance, when he didn't imagine Casey making a joke about something, or gently teasing Landon, or being excited about some ordinary thing. Maybe a day when Landon didn't miss Casey so fucking much.

But that day would never come if Landon didn't force himself to forget.

"I think my biggest mistake," Casey said as he set his empty pint glass on the table, "was falling in love with him."

"So it's that bad, huh?" Lee said, then popped a piece of fried cauliflower in his mouth. He'd insisted on having lunch with Casey after their practice in Philadelphia because he wanted to address the constant state of misery Casey had been in for the past month. Casey knew there was no point in denying the reason for it.

"Yeah. It's really fucking bad." Casey drummed his fingers on the table. "But it was so *good* before he left. I mean, he was, like, I dunno. Guarded, I guess." He huffed. "Makes sense. He's a goalie."

"Guarded against what?"

Casey shrugged one shoulder. "He knew he was leaving. We both knew; I just thought we could make it work."

"And he didn't?"

"I guess not. He won't even talk to me."

"I'm sorry," Lee said.

"I think he's trying to protect himself. I'm not smart enough to do that, so I'm lugging around a broken heart while he's… doing whatever."

Lee rested his elbows on the table and leaned in. "If he's trying to protect himself, it must mean he's got some pretty big feelings for you."

Casey picked up a piece of cauliflower, then set it down on a side plate. He wasn't hungry. "Even if he does, I don't think it matters. He wants to forget about me. And I…" Casey had to swallow the lump that had formed in his throat. "I can't forget about him. I don't want to."

Lee looked at him seriously for a long moment. "Damn. You really are in love with him."

Casey nodded. "He *got me*, y'know? And I think I got him too. We're good for each other." He swallowed again. "We *were* good for each other."

"You were," Lee agreed. "I could see it. And there's something else you said back there that I want to address: you're not stupid, Casey."

Casey huffed. "Since when?"

Lee shook his head and swore under his breath. "This is my fault. We chirp you all the time, and I told myself that we do it out of love."

"You…what?" Casey had no idea what Lee was looking so upset about. "Everyone teases me. It's okay. I get it."

"It's not okay if you take it seriously. I should have noticed, and I'm sorry. Because I mean it: you're not stupid." He stared at Casey, waiting for something. When Casey nodded, Lee nodded back, and continued. "The truth is, you *notice* people, y'know? You always seem to know what everyone in the room is feeling, or what they might need. That's big-brain shit, Hicks. That's emotional intelligence. The important stuff."

Casey was rarely at a loss of words, but he truly didn't know what to say. No one had ever said anything like that to him before.

"You're going to make a great captain one day," Lee said.

That shocked Casey into speaking. "Me? I'm not captain material. I haven't been team captain since I was twelve, and even then I think it was because of who my dad was."

Lee spread his arms dramatically. "You think I don't know about captain material? You care more about your teammates than anyone I have ever known. It's why Stackhouse was living with you in the first place."

Casey dragged his fingertip through the condensation on his beer glass. "I like people. That's all."

"That's what I'm saying!"

Casey couldn't take much more of this. They were here to talk about Landon, not Casey being fucking *captain*. Though he appreciated everything Lee was saying, and he would definitely think about it all later.

"Anyway. Back to my broken-heart situation."

"Right. So assume he never plays in Calgary again. I'm not saying that's what's going to happen, but let's assume that. What then?"

Casey did have an answer ready for this, because it had been all he'd been thinking about since Landon left. "I could do long distance. I know it would suck, but I would do it. If I knew we were together, no matter the distance, I'd be happy. Even if we went months without seeing each other, it would be worth it."

Lee raised his eyebrows as he swallowed a sip of beer. "So I'm just going to say it: you have sex with a lot of people. You're just gonna stop?"

"I mean," Casey said slowly, "we never talked about monogamy or whatever, but yeah. Of course, if that's what he wanted." He poked at the cauliflower on his plate. "I haven't had sex since he left."

Lee blew out a breath. "Wow. Maybe *that's* the problem?"

"No," Casey said quickly. "I haven't even wanted to. I've definitely been taking care of myself, like, *a lot*, but—"

Lee held up a hand. "Okay. That's cool. So have you told Landon that you want to do long distance and commit to him and all that?"

"Basically, yeah."

"Basically," Lee said flatly. "And what did he say?"

Casey thought about it. "He doesn't think it would be fair to me. I guess because of the sex thing you mentioned."

"What about to him?"

"He doesn't seem too concerned about his own happiness, to be honest."

Lee pointed at him. "But you are."

"Yeah. Of course." Casey's brain was getting all scrambled. "Could you tell me exactly what you're trying to say, please?"

"I'm saying that *you* have to tell *Landon* exactly what *you* want. And if he starts talking like he doesn't believe you, you've got to make him believe you."

Casey blinked. "Shit, Lee. That's good advice."

Lee nodded and took another sip of beer.

Casey picked up a coaster and flipped it over a couple of times. "So how do I do that?"

"Nope. That's your job. Figure it out."

"But I suck at figuring shit out," Casey whined.

"You can do it. I believe in you."

Casey knew that Lee meant it, and that made him feel lighter. He rested his chin in his palm and said, sincerely, "I love you, Lee."

Lee rolled his eyes. "Yeah, I'm not the one you need to be saying that to, bud."

"Did you watch Casey in the skills competition last night?" Dad asked.

Landon managed a small smile. "Unfortunately."

"I felt so bad for him," Mom said. "It's a sin that they make them keep shooting until they hit all the targets. There should be a time limit."

It had been a bit painful to watch. Casey must have taken at least twenty shots on the final target in the shot accuracy competition. But, in typical Casey Hicks fashion, he'd been entertaining about it. The broadcast had even had him mic'd up, so viewers at home could hear Casey's amusing, but increasingly frustrated, remarks as he'd been shooting. When he'd finally smashed the foam bull's-eye target, Casey had raised his arms in celebration, then did a little victory dance as if he'd just accomplished something impressive. It had been adorable, and so perfectly Casey that Landon had found it painful to watch for a whole new reason.

Also adorable had been the selfie Casey had sent Landon from the ice after, cringing at the camera. Beneath it, he'd written: Harder than it looks.

Landon, after a lot of deliberation, had sent back a laughing-face emoji. Then he'd spent more time than he wanted to admit staring at that photo.

But now he was in a hotel room in Colorado, on a video call with his parents. Calls like this one had become a regular thing since Christmas, which had been nice, but also difficult because his parents could tell he was miserable, but he didn't want to talk about it.

So they mentioned Casey in little ways, like this. Safe ways.

"He seemed to be a good sport about it," Mom said.

"Yeah," Landon agreed.

Mom smiled sympathetically at him. "Have you talked to him lately?"

"Not really, no."

"Do you think," she said carefully, "you're making this harder than it needs to be, maybe?"

Landon tensed. "I don't have a choice."

"You do, though."

That ticked him off. "I *don't*. He deserves better than a long-distance relationship with me. He...he hates being alone. He should be with someone who can actually *be with him*. I can't promise him anything, and I can't..." Landon sighed. "Why would he even want a long-distance relationship with me? It makes no sense. We never made sense. It was just...a thing that happened. And now it's over."

"Did he tell you that he didn't want to have a long-distance relationship with you? That he wanted it to be over?" Mom asked.

Landon looked away from the screen when he said, "No. He said he wanted to try."

"Well then," Dad said, "what's the problem?"

"The problem is..." Landon had to think about it. "He deserves better."

"The hell he does," Dad said, which shocked Landon into looking back at the screen. "You keep beating yourself up, Landon, and it breaks our hearts. *You* deserve better."

Landon blinked as his eyes began to burn. "I'm a mess."

"You're not," Mom said. "You're sad. And maybe you don't need to be. We saw how much you mean to each other. What you two have is special, and you should give it a chance."

"How?"

"Talk to him," Mom said simply. "And, more importantly, listen to him."

"I miss him so much."

"We know," Dad said. "And I'll bet he misses you just as much."

"I don't know."

"You can't keep carrying all this pain," Mom said. "Let yourself be happy, sweetheart."

Landon blew out a breath. "I need to think about it. What to say."

"Of course," Mom said. "But don't overthink it. You know what you need to tell him."

Landon nodded. He did. And he wanted to.

"And, Landon," Dad said gently, "have you thought about finding a therapist to talk to?"

Landon put his hands on his knees and curled his fingers. "I don't know. I hate talking."

"I was skeptical," Dad said. "I didn't think it was for me. But, like your mother said, it helped a lot."

"It can really help put things in perspective," Mom added. "Make things more manageable."

Landon nodded. "I'll think about it." He knew he should, and not just for his own sake, but for anyone who had to deal with him. For Casey, if there was a future there.

Could there really be a future there? Landon still couldn't see a way it would work. Even a best-case scenario, where Landon earned a permanent spot on the Calgary roster, would come with its own challenges. Workplace relationships were supposed to be a bad idea, right? And Casey was a high-profile player—did he really want to have the whole world know that he was dating his teammate? Did Landon want that? There were other openly gay and bisexual players in the league; not many, but any number more than zero was significant progress for men's hockey in general. None of those guys were dating their teammates, though. At least not publicly, and certainly not that Landon was aware of. Their relationship would get some attention for sure, if they decided to go public with it.

Landon was getting way ahead of himself. And had totally zoned out while Dad was talking.

"You're not listening at all, are you?" Dad said with an affectionate smile.

"Sorry. My brain kind of took off running."

"Did it take you anywhere good?"

Landon furrowed his brow as he worked out his next words. "I think I need to talk to Casey. When I get back to Saskatoon, maybe. I'll call him. I want to...try. If there's a way we can make this work, I want to try."

Both his parents were smiling broadly now. "I'll bet he's dying to hear from you," Mom said.

Landon hoped so. He wouldn't blame Casey if he'd given up on Landon by now. Except he'd sent that selfie last night. That meant something, right?

Landon would be home in two days. Between now and then, he was going to figure out what he wanted to say to Casey. And then he was going to tell him.

Chapter Forty

Casey was flying back to Calgary, via Toronto, after the All-Star weekend in Raleigh, and, as usual, all he could think about was Landon. He'd been all Casey could think about during the skills competition, which was probably the reason Casey had missed all the targets a million times, and was definitely the reason he'd sent him a selfie immediately after. All he'd gotten back was an emoji, but he'd fucking cherished it.

He'd kept sending occasional texts to Landon, but none of them said what he really needed to tell him. They were playful and light, just letting Landon know Casey was thinking about him. Landon's replies were brief, but lately he always answered, and that was something.

Lee's advice from a few days ago kept echoing in Casey's head: he needed to make Landon believe Casey would fight for them. Would wait for him. Would do fucking anything for him because Casey was in love with him.

But how?

He was still thinking about it as the plane descended into Toronto. He had three fucking hours to kill before his connecting flight to Calgary. Maybe a great idea would come to him, though he was doubtful that many people had romantic epiphanies in Pearson Airport.

An hour later, standing in front of the giant timetable in the domestic departures terminal, he got an idea. It was probably not a good one, but in that moment he was jacked on a Venti Double Chocolaty Chip Frappuccino and anything seemed possible.

What if he didn't fly to Calgary? He had the next four days off and there was a plane leaving for Saskatoon in three hours. He knew Landon was in Colorado tonight, because he always knew where Landon was, but his team would be arriving back at home sometime tomorrow.

Casey was going to do it. He was going to meet Landon at the fucking...bus place...and it was going to be romantic as hell.

Okay, so it turned out a lot of people flew from Toronto to Saskatoon. Casey wasn't able to get on the flight he'd been hoping for, but there was one leaving in *six hours* that had room.

So now Casey was lounging sideways in a big leather armchair in the fancy Air Canada VIP lounge, enjoying his fourth complimentary cookie. He'd booked a hotel room in Saskatoon for three nights, just in case he needed more time to convince Landon that he was super in love with him.

Landon must be getting ready for his game in Colorado right now. Casey decided to send him a selfie, even though he looked like a guy who'd spent the entire day in two airports and one plane.

Feeling bold, he wrote: I miss you.

Deal with it, Stacks, he thought. *You're missed.*

To his surprise, three dots appeared less than a minute later. He sat up properly in his chair in anticipation, but the dots disappeared. Then they reappeared briefly before disappearing again.

"You're killing me, Stacks," Casey said.

Finally, after several agonizing minutes, a message came: It hurts even more than I thought it would.

Casey's heart stuttered. He knew how hard it would have

been for Landon to type that. Landon kept his feelings fiercely guarded at the best of times, so this honest admission had to mean he was at his breaking point.

Casey replied quickly: It's not just me then?

Landon: Of course not.

Casey smiled at that, even though he hated thinking about Landon hurting. He considered telling Landon that he was coming to Saskatoon, and had started typing it out when another text came from Landon: I have to go. Game soon.

Casey deleted what he'd written and replaced it with: Kick ass.

Landon replied with a thumbs-up emoji.

Casey had so many things he wanted to say, so many questions he wanted to ask.

Tomorrow, he reminded himself. He could unload a month's worth of conversations on Landon tomorrow, and hopefully an equivalent amount of hugs and kisses too. If Landon was into it.

Casey really hoped Landon would be into it.

Fuck, was this a terrible idea?

He'd find out tomorrow.

There was a particular type of exhaustion that came from spending over fifteen hours on a bus that Landon was far too familiar with.

They were finally home, later than they were supposed to be, thanks to snow in Wyoming. They'd left in the dark, and now it was dark again in Saskatoon. Thankfully they had tomorrow off. Landon had big plans to sleep for the entire day.

He stepped off the bus with his backpack slung over his shoulder, then went to wait for his suitcase to be unloaded from the luggage compartment. It had to be at least twenty-five below zero outside, but even frigid fresh air was a welcome change from recycled bus air.

He swore he heard one of his teammates murmur the name "Casey Hicks" as he waited, but he ignored it. He was probably hearing things. God, he was so tired.

Then he heard it again. And then, clear as day, Morgan Dillon said, "Why is Casey Hicks here?"

Landon turned around, and there he was, standing between the bus and the arena and wearing a jacket that wasn't nearly warm enough. He waved at Landon, or maybe he didn't. Maybe he hadn't moved at all, or maybe he wasn't even here. Maybe this was another fantasy about Casey walking back into his life. Landon dropped his backpack and walked over to him, just in case he was real.

"Hi," Casey said in that voice Landon had been missing so much.

"How are you here?" Landon blurted. It probably sounded rude, but his brain wasn't in top form.

Casey's eyes were more nervous than Landon had ever seen them. "Like I said, I miss you."

The weirdest, most unhinged laugh ever burst out of Landon. Then he wrapped his arms around Casey, pulling him tight against him. Casey exhaled against his neck, then said, "So this wasn't a terrible idea?"

"No. I don't know. Even if it is—god, I'm so happy to see you."

Landon's brain came back online enough to remind him that all of his teammates were probably watching, and that this hug had crossed over from "what a pleasant surprise" to "my husband is back from the war" several seconds ago. He loosened his hold, then stepped back. Casey was smiling at him, and Landon smiled right back.

"When did you get here?" Landon asked.

"Last night. Changed my flight in Toronto. I'm staying at the Hilton."

"Not anymore you're not."

The last of the tension left Casey's smile. "Are you gonna show me your place, Stacks?"

"It's nothing special."

"Oh, okay. I'll just head back to Calgary, then."

Landon laughed. "I missed you so much."

"Dude, I know. That's why I'm here. Let's get your bags, swing by the hotel real quick to get my stuff, then go warm up in your bed."

Landon felt warmer already.

"It's nice," Casey said as he examined Landon's small apartment for the first time.

"It's fine," Landon said, because he knew it wasn't particularly nice. "It smelled like a dumpster when I first got back from Calgary. Morgan was supposed to take all the food out of my fridge—he lives down the hall—but he didn't. I feel like I can still smell it."

Casey went to the window by the kitchenette table and peered out. The apartment's best feature was its view of the river, but there was nothing but darkness and scattered city lights out there right now. Casey was wearing light pink jeans and a T-shirt with an octopus fighting a bear on it. His hair spilled out from the black toque he was still wearing.

Landon couldn't believe Casey was really here, in Saskatoon, in his kitchen. He was still processing what it all meant.

Then Casey crossed the room and placed one palm on Landon's cheek. "Can I kiss you?"

"Yes," Landon whispered, with no hesitation.

"Okay, but just to warn you: I might not stop. Ever."

"I'll risk it."

When Casey's lips brushed his, he forgot every reason he'd been clinging to for denying himself this man. He forgot that their relationship was probably doomed, or that Casey was only here for a couple of days, at best. He forgot that nothing had changed. He forgot about how exhausted he was, or how badly he'd wanted a shower. All he cared about was kissing Casey with everything he had. Because he was *here*.

"I need to tell you something," Casey said when they broke for air, their chests heaving against each other.

"Good news or bad news?"

Casey smiled. "I don't know yet."

"Tell me."

Casey closed his eyes, and when he opened them again, they blazed with determination. "I know all the things you said, about why us being together wouldn't work. That it's too hard, or too…okay. I actually forget what you said. But it doesn't matter because I came here to tell you I don't care and I want to be your boyfriend anyway."

Landon's heart was pounding. "Why?"

"Because I'm in love with you."

He said it so simply, like it was obvious instead of wondrous. And Landon didn't say anything, just stared at him like a weirdo until Casey brushed a thumb over Landon's road-trip stubble and said, "You don't have to say it back, but could you say, like, literally anything?"

"Yes," Landon whispered. "I mean, yeah. Yes. I love you."

Landon only got the briefest glimpse of Casey's dimples before they were kissing again. Landon tugged Casey's toque off and let it fall to the floor so he could dig his hands into his soft hair. He smelled like hotel bodywash and tasted like breath mints and he was in love with Landon.

"I love you," Landon said again as he kissed along Casey's smooth jaw.

"I love you too. Fuck, I love *that*," Casey said when Landon nibbled at the hinge of his jaw.

"I really need to take a shower."

"You say that like it's not something I would enjoy."

Landon laughed. "Come on."

The one thing about the apartment that Landon liked better than the view was the shower. The showerhead was high enough even for him, and since it was a shower/tub combo, it was big enough for two. Not that he'd ever tested it before.

"Jesus, Stacks," Casey said when Landon pulled his shirt off in the bathroom. He placed a hand on a large bruise on Landon's right pec. "They firing cannons at you in the AHL?"

"That wasn't a puck," Landon said. "I got slammed into after I covered the puck last night. Fucking hurt."

"I'll bet." Casey brushed a kiss over the purple skin. "The bus ride after probably wasn't comfortable, then."

"Never is."

"You need to come back to the big leagues."

"Okay. Who should I ask to trade places: Gilbert or Antton?"

Casey pretended to think about it. "Is there golf in Saskatoon?"

"Not much in February."

"Maybe not Antton, then."

Landon huffed and stripped off his sweatpants. He'd been dressed for comfort on the bus.

"Oh wow," Casey said. He gripped the edge of the ceramic countertop behind him, as if he suddenly needed support.

"What?"

"Nothing." He shook his head. "I guess I forgot about your giant fucking cock."

Landon was in too good a mood to be embarrassed. "First of all, it's not *giant*. And second of all..." He leaned down, brushed his lips against Casey's ear, and in a low rumble said, "No you didn't."

"Oh fuck," Casey said shakily. "I wasn't expecting that. Say something else in that voice."

Landon's lips curved up. He kissed the hinge of Casey's jaw again, now that he knew how sensitive he was there, then said, "Take your clothes off." He waited several heartbeats, psyching himself up, then added, "And show me how much you missed me."

Something crashed to the floor, and Landon pulled away to see that it was his toothpaste.

"Sorry," Casey said, removing his hands from the vicinity of Landon's other toiletries. "That was, um." He blew out a breath, then pulled his T-shirt off. "Yeah, let's get in that shower."

"Mm." Landon reached out and turned the shower on, but then crowded Casey against the sink and kissed him until Landon's cock was a solid rod caught between their stomachs. Landon couldn't remember ever feeling this turned on in his life. The combination of the surrealness of Casey being here mixed with excitement and relief and blue-green eyes and dimples to create a heady aphrodisiac.

"Say it again," Landon breathed against Casey's swollen lips.

"I love you," Casey said automatically. "I missed you. I want to be with you."

"I love you too," Landon said with his whole heart. "I'm with you." He rocked against him, letting his erection glide along the ridges of Casey's abs. "I want you."

Casey let out a choked laugh. "I can tell." He tipped his head back, and Landon kissed his neck, his throat, his chin. One hand held a fistful of Casey's silky hair, and the other gripped his hip. "Landon," Casey rasped. "I haven't been with anyone since you left."

Landon stilled. "You haven't?" He would never have expected that, knew he had no right to want it, but knowing Casey had believed enough in them to wait was huge.

Casey dropped his chin and looked Landon in the eye, expression serious. "No one. I want you to know that." His smile returned. "For two reasons, really: one, I want you to know how serious I am about you, and two: so you aren't surprised when I shoot off, like, the moment you touch my dick."

Landon smiled back at him. "That bad, huh?"

"You have no idea. I mean, I've been jerking off a lot. Like, *a lot* a lot, but it isn't the same, y'know?"

"It isn't," Landon agreed. "And I always thought about you. I tried not to, but…"

Casey's smile grew. "I definitely want to hear more about that later, but if I think too much about you stroking yourself to thoughts of me, I really will bust in my jeans right here." Landon…kind of wanted to see that. And he could tell Casey knew it because Casey laughed and shoved him toward the shower. "This'll be better. I promise."

When they were both in the shower, naked and kissing and pressed against each other while hot water streamed down Landon's aching body, Landon could see how it was better.

It got even better when Casey took both their cocks in his hand and stroked them together. He set a quick pace that hurled Landon to the edge in no time.

"I want to spend hours touching you," Casey said, close to Landon's ear. "Want to take my time later. But right now I need to come."

"Yeah," Landon said, the familiar pulse already starting behind his balls. "Fuck. Come on."

He heard Casey groan as the first splash of Landon's release hit his chest, then Casey was coming too, painting Landon's abs while Landon watched.

For a long moment after, they both panted under the running water, foreheads pressed together. In the afterglow, some of Landon's usual worries about the impossibility of this relationship working tried to speak up in his head. He silenced them. He'd much rather listen to Casey's happy sighs and murmured "I love yous."

Eventually, they used the shower for its intended purpose, then went to Landon's bedroom. Casey sat now on Landon's bed, wearing sweatpants and one of Landon's Saskatoon Bandits hoodies, with his back against the cheap headboard and knees tucked under his chin. Landon lay beside him, stretched out on his side with his head propped up on an elbow.

"So you just, what, switched your ticket to Saskatoon in the Toronto airport?"

"Yep."

"Was that hard?"

"Not really. Probably being a hockey star didn't hurt. The woman I was talking to seemed excited to be helping me."

Landon huffed. "You probably didn't flirt with her at all."

"A little. Maybe. But I flirt with everyone."

Landon slid his hand into the pocket of Casey's hoodie, then began absently rubbing his belly through the fabric. "You're good at it. You make people feel like they're...important. Interesting. I don't know. It feels nice."

"Y'know, you were the first person I tried not to flirt with, because I liked you too much."

"That doesn't make sense."

Casey rested a hand on the pocket, on top of Landon's hand. "I'm just saying. You've always been...more."

Landon processed this. "But you *did* flirt with me."

Casey smiled. "Yeah. I said I *tried* not to. I'm not made of stone, Stacks."

Landon removed his hand from the pocket and held Casey's hand directly instead. "I don't know what I did to be *more*, but... I'm glad."

"You didn't have to do anything. You just had to walk into my life and, like, exist." He squeezed Landon's hand. "Next thing I know, I'm waiting six hours in the Toronto airport for a flight to Saskatoon."

"Six hours?"

Casey shrugged. "Would have waited longer if I'd needed to. Would have rented a car and drove if it came to it."

"I think you're underestimating that drive time."

"Definitely. I barely know where I am right now."

Landon lifted himself until his lips were close to Casey's. "You're with me."

Casey smiled and leaned in. "Yeah I am."

★ ★ ★

They spent an entire, magical day together. They never left the apartment, and barely left the bed. It wasn't all sex; Landon was still exhausted from the road trip, and Casey had admitted he'd been sleeping terribly all month, so they napped too. When they woke from their second nap, the sky was getting dark. Landon ordered pizza and made out on the couch with Casey until it arrived.

They talked, but not about anything heavy. Landon was content to pretend, for that one perfect day, that they wouldn't be separating tomorrow morning. That soon he'd be alone again.

It wasn't until late in the evening, when they were sitting on the couch with a couple of beers that Landon had dug out of the back of his fridge, ostensibly watching an Edmonton vs. Chicago game that Landon wasn't paying any attention to, that Casey broached the subject.

"So we probably won't see each other for a while."

"Probably not." There was still a lot of the regular season left, and both their teams were heading for the playoffs. It was time to focus on their jobs.

"But after," Casey continued, "in the summer, I want to be wherever you are."

God, that easy offer. That Casey would follow Landon, instead of expecting him to spend the summer in Calgary. "I was planning on going home for a bit," Landon said. "Halifax, I mean."

Casey smiled, wide and bright. "I'd love to see it."

"It's mostly boats and lobsters and shit," Landon said dryly.

Casey nudged his thigh with his toe. "I wanna see where you're from. And maybe we can go to Florida too. Or anywhere. I don't even care. You ever been to Italy?"

Landon laughed. "No."

"Let's do that, then."

"Just...go to Italy?"

Casey looked confused. "Yeah. You buy a ticket and you go."

Landon supposed it was that simple, when you had money and time and someone to do that with. It was staggering to realize he had all of those things.

"I usually train in Minnesota," Landon said. "In August."

"I love Minnesota. I could train there."

Landon smiled at the thought of them spending the summer together, visiting different places. Sharing things with each other. But he had to ask, "And after the summer?"

"Too soon to say. But all I need is to know that we're a couple, okay? The distance will suck, but it's the not knowing where we stand that's been killing me all month. I'm yours. You get that, right?"

Landon swallowed. "It just…still feels like too much to ask of you. You shouldn't have to be alone so much. You hate being alone. You could be with someone who—"

"Except I'm in love with *you*. Bananas, remember? There's not gonna be anyone else, no matter how far apart we are."

Landon reached out and took Casey's hand. "I'm sorry I'm so…me about everything. My parents told me I beat myself up too much, and I really don't want to anymore. I want to be happy, and I want to make you happy. I want to be the best boyfriend. Even when we're apart, I want you to know that you're…" He searched for the right word, and landed on, "Loved. I love you so much, and I could probably live with it, if you wanted to have sex with other people. I mean, we'd be so far apart for so long, and you—"

"I don't need to," Casey interrupted. "I appreciate the offer, but I don't. Seriously. I mean, my Fleshlight is gonna be exhausted, but…"

Landon laughed, then pulled Casey on top of him. They were still laughing as they kissed.

The next morning was awful. Landon knew it would be, but he still hadn't adequately braced himself for the pain of saying goodbye to Casey.

"It probably would have been easier if I'd never shown up at all," Casey said sheepishly.

"Don't say that," Landon said, and hugged him tighter. "I'm glad you came. Even if it hurts now."

They were standing by the door of Landon's apartment, trying to squeeze out every second of privacy before Landon drove Casey to the airport, and then drove himself to practice.

"I'm going to call you as soon as I get home," Casey promised. "And probably every single day after that."

"Okay."

"Are you any good at sexting?"

Landon laughed wetly. "Probably not."

"It's okay. We'll do video stuff. I can do all the talking."

"Sorry in advance for how weird I'm going to be in those videos."

Casey kissed his jaw. "No way."

They held hands in the car while Landon drove. Landon had to keep blinking tears out of his eyes. He tried to focus on the positives: Casey loved him, and they were together. No matter what.

"Are we going to be, um, public?" Landon asked.

"We can kinda halfway it, if you want. We don't have to make a whole announcement, but I don't want to hide, if you're cool with it."

Landon had no doubt that a lot of hockey fans—and players— would not be cool with him dating Casey. But ultimately, it didn't matter, because, "I don't want to hide either."

Casey smiled. "Cool. We're going to melt Instagram with our hot summer selfies."

Landon laughed.

They kissed in the car after Landon parked in the drop-off area at the airport. Maybe people could see them, and recognize them, but Landon didn't care. He put everything he was feeling into that kiss.

"Jesus," Casey said when they broke apart. "I'm just supposed to walk away now?"

Landon cradled Casey's face in one palm. "Listen to me: I'm going to work so hard. I'm going to make Calgary want me."

Casey looked at him seriously. "You're the goalie we need. I know it."

Landon nodded back. "Yeah. I am."

Casey kissed him quickly, one more time. "I fucking love you," he said.

"I love you."

Then, with a parting smile, Casey got out of the car, grabbed his bags from the trunk, waved, and went into the airport.

Landon smiled all the way to practice because he had a fucking *boyfriend*.

Chapter Forty-One

It was the first week of March, and things were getting real.

Calgary was in a battle with L.A. for the number one ranking in their division, and the playoffs were only five weeks away. Casey was buzzing with adrenaline, pretty much 24/7. Calgary had been a good team last year, but they were a great team this year. They were contenders.

He knew it was only his fourth season, and that it was maybe greedy to be so hungry for his first Cup win when guys like Lee had been waiting for almost fifteen years, but damn, he wanted it. He wanted it bad.

"This is going to be the best game ever," he told himself as he got ready to charge out of the tunnel in San Jose. It should be an easy win—San Jose was at the very bottom of the entire Western Conference now—but he knew better than to treat any game like a sure thing. They were taking this one seriously. They even had Antton starting.

Landon's team had been doing well too. Number one in their division, and the favorite to win their championships. Casey had been watching as many of their games as he could, and Landon was a fucking rock star in Saskatoon. It made him wish they'd left the apartment when he'd been there, gone out for dinner maybe, seen how the locals treated their star goalie.

A whole month had gone by since that visit, and even though Casey missed Landon a lot, it had been a good month. They'd called each other almost every day, usually video calls, and usually at bedtime. It helped, being able to talk to Landon when Casey was alone in his big creepy house. He'd been sleeping well.

It was nice, being in love. Casey was into it.

"You ready, Hicks?" Nosey asked, bumping his chest against Casey's shoulder.

"Fuck yeah."

They did their usual pregame routine: crosschecking each other's sticks like they were in a swordfight, then bumping hips, then doing a little shimmy.

"Let's go shut this crowd up," Nosey said.

The game was going great. Casey had a goal and an assist by the middle of the second period, Antton hadn't let any pucks past him, and the score was 3-0. The crowd had been silent for a while.

It was late in the second period—less than three minutes left—that everything changed.

San Jose had a two-on-one, two forwards charging toward Antton with Westy between them. Casey was on the bench, so he didn't get the clearest look at what happened next, but something made the forward on the left go down hard, and at top speed, and he crashed into Antton.

Casey could see the way Antton's arm got caught between the forward and the goalpost. Then he could hear Antton cry out in pain.

Oh fuck.

The entire Calgary bench was standing, watching with their hearts in their throats as the medical staff crouched on the ice beside Antton. Finally, Antton was helped to his feet, then he skated slowly to the bench as the crowd applauded in support.

Antton was cradling his arm, his face twisted in pain. It didn't look good.

Beside him, Nosey had his forehead on the boards. Casey put a hand on his shoulder. "It'll be okay," he said, though he knew he wasn't selling it.

"We're fucked," Nosey moaned.

And yeah. Okay. They probably were. If Antton's injury was as bad as it looked, then their chances in the playoffs just got a whole lot worse.

Gilbert stepped on the ice with his mask in place, shaking himself out. He'd only started two games since his return, and he hadn't been great in either of them. He *could* be great, though. There was a time when he'd been one of the best in the league. And right now, he was all they had.

"You got this, Gilly," Casey said, and hammered the boards with his stick. "We're gonna win this one."

Others joined him, though Clint was hammering the boards with the front of his helmet instead.

"Cheer up, Nosey. We've got a game to win."

Nosey lifted his head. "You're right. Let's do it."

Casey smiled. "That's better."

He sighed. "I guess we'll be seeing Stackhouse again."

Casey was trying not to think about it. Obviously, yes, if Antton was hurt, then calling up Landon would be the next move, but now was not the time to get excited about seeing his boyfriend again.

Not when their best hope of winning the Stanley Cup had just disappeared down the tunnel.

Landon was in Milwaukee when he got the news.

He'd been asleep in his hotel room when he was awoken by aggressive knocking.

"Stackhouse," boomed the voice of Coach Hayes through the door. He sounded angry, and Landon couldn't imagine what this was about.

Landon groggily went to the door and opened it. Coach was standing with his hands on his hips.

"Pack your stuff," he said. "You've got to catch a flight to L.A. to meet the Outlaws."

"I…what?" Landon had checked the score of the Outlaws game before falling asleep last night. It had been 3-0 for Calgary and it seemed like nothing notable had happened by that point in the game. "Is Morin hurt?" Morin hadn't even been playing, but maybe something flared up when he'd been working out or—

"Niskanen broke his arm. He's out for the season."

Landon's stomach dropped. "What?"

"Arm. Broken. It's shit luck for Calgary, and for us, frankly, because we're losing you." He sighed. "Being an AHL coach is bullshit sometimes. But that's not your problem." He put a hand on Landon's shoulder. "Get dressed, get packed, get to the airport, and kick some ass, okay? We're gonna miss you. Again."

"Okay," Landon said, trying to focus on one thing at a time even as a million thoughts crowded his brain. "I'll just be a couple of minutes."

Antton was out for the season? Landon was going to be with Calgary for the rest of the regular season *and* the playoffs? Landon was going to be in the *Stanley Cup Playoffs*. Landon was going to be in Calgary again. Landon was going to be with *Casey* again.

It was too much to process in that moment, so instead he focused on putting on socks.

"Can you believe this, Erin?" he said, because he had to let out some of his giddiness. "Mom and Dad are going to be pumped."

He'd have to call them from the airport. He couldn't wait. He couldn't wait for so many things; he was determined to keep moving forward, chasing happiness instead of hiding himself from it. And right now happiness was waiting for him in Los Angeles.

★ ★ ★

Casey was waiting for him in the hall outside the locker room. When Landon saw him, he sped up his walking, resisting the urge to run into his arms.

He'd needed to go straight from LAX to the arena so he could dress for the game that night. It had been a long day of flights and a delayed connection, but he was here now, and Casey was smiling at him.

"Oh my god," Casey said, and wrapped Landon in a hug. "It's really you."

"It's really me." Landon assumed they weren't kissing here, but he let himself bury his nose in Casey's soft hair. He'd missed his smell. He'd missed everything about him. "Is Antton—"

"He's okay. I mean, no. His arm is broken and I'm sure he's mad as hell about it, but he's back in Calgary now."

"Yeah. Fuck. How's everyone else doing?"

Casey huffed. "Not great. Antton getting hurt is a pretty huge blow."

"No shit." He released Casey and stepped back. "I don't expect anyone to be excited to see me."

"Well, *I* am. And the rest of the guys will be too. We need you, Stacks."

Landon nodded. "How's Morin?"

Casey immediately grimaced, probably without meaning to. Then he said, "More playing time will probably help. I sure wish we had Antton tonight, though."

Landon knew how important tonight's game was. L.A. was one point ahead of Calgary in the standings. A win tonight would put Calgary in the number one position, which would be a much-needed confidence boost right now.

"I should get in there," Landon said, nodding at the locker room door. "Is there food? I'm starving."

Casey smiled. "There's food. And also, I really missed you and I'm fucking psyched that you're here. And I love you."

Landon smiled back at him. "We're going to the playoffs together."

Casey glanced around, then gave Landon a quick kiss. "We're going everywhere together."

By the end of the first period, the score was 3-0 for L.A., and Landon was surprised the score wasn't even higher, the way Morin was playing. After the third goal, Gilbert had attacked his goalposts with his stick, so it was fair to say his head wasn't in the right place tonight.

Now Gilbert was hunched forward in his stall, head in his hands as everyone gave him space.

Landon decided to take a chance, and crouched in front of him. "Hey."

"It's not working tonight," Gilbert said, unnecessarily. He tapped his head. "It's all fried."

"I get it. It happens."

"Bad timing, though." Gilbert sighed. Then shook his head miserably. "I don't know, Stackhouse. I don't know."

Landon was pretty sure Gilbert's uncertainty was about more than just tonight's game. He'd only wanted to come back from injury and finish his career with some dignity, backing up Antton. Now he had to *be* Antton, and he hadn't been anything close to that for years.

Pep talks weren't Landon's strength, but he tried. "My dad still moans about that save you made on Davidson in OT. Stopped Toronto from going to the next round."

Gilbert smiled at that. "That was a great moment." His smile faded. "But it was a long time ago."

Okay, Gilbert clearly wasn't up to stopping pucks tonight. Landon was exhausted after a day of travel, but he was also riding the high of being here. Of being *back*.

"If you need me to go in," Landon said carefully, "I can go in."

Gilbert raised his eyebrows. "Didn't you just get off a plane?"

Landon fixed him with a steady, determined gaze. "I can go in."

Gilbert held his gaze for a moment, then glanced at something over Landon's shoulder. "Coach is coming over."

Landon stood. "If you need me, okay?"

"Okay. Thanks."

Landon left, but made quick eye contact with Coach Patrick as he passed him. He hoped he looked more confident than tired. He returned to his own stall and sat for about three seconds before Casey came over. "How is he?"

"Not good."

"You going in?"

Landon glanced across the room and saw Coach looking at him over his shoulder. "Maybe."

"How are you feeling?"

"Good," he said, and it wasn't a lie. "Focused."

Casey exhaled. "All right. Good."

"Wouldn't hurt if you assholes scored some goals, though."

Casey spread his arms wide. "I'm trying! Did you miss that sick rebound I had?"

"No. *You* missed that sick rebound."

Casey's mouth dropped open. "Did you fly across the country specifically to bully me? Because I'm kind of into it, not gonna lie."

"I flew across the country to win the Stanley Cup. You gonna help with that?"

"Oh shit, I like *this* Landon. Where's this guy been?"

Landon stood. Coach was gesturing him over. "He's been in Saskatoon, but he's here now."

Chapter Forty-Two

Casey was legit half-hard as the final seconds of the third period ticked down, because Landon had played like a fucking beast.

He'd let in nothing—*nothing*—and the Outlaws had rallied and scored three goals to tie the game. It was taking all of Casey's self-control not to jump on Landon's back and scream about how proud he was of him.

Instead, he tapped Landon's leg pad as he skated by before the start of overtime. "Where are ya, buddy?" he called out.

He could see Landon's wicked smile, even behind the mask. "Right here."

Casey couldn't help flirting a little. "You got plans after we win?"

And then Landon *winked at him*.

Casey was actually blushing as he went to line up for the face-off.

"All good?" Lee asked.

"Oh yeah. Stacks is dialed in. Let's score a goal and end this."

It took less than forty seconds for Casey to score, and he could hear Landon celebrating from the other end of the ice. Casey met him at the blue line, arms spread wide.

"Fucking right!" Landon yelled in his ear as they hugged. "You didn't even give them a chance."

"I wanted to end it quickly. I've got a hot date after the game."

Landon laughed, loud and unguarded. He really did seem like a different person tonight. Or rather, like the same person without the self-loathing and anxiety he'd been shouldering for so long. He was fucking beautiful.

The rest of the team caught up with them and piled on. Morin tapped his forehead against the front of Landon's mask, said something Casey couldn't hear, and then Landon gave him a one-armed hug.

And Casey knew it was only one game, and also that he was a little biased, but he couldn't help thinking that maybe they'd found their goalie.

Landon didn't even pretend to go to his own hotel room. He didn't even ask which room it was. He followed Casey into his room with the suitcase he'd packed for an AHL road trip and a smile that he hadn't been able to control since the game ended.

As soon as the door clicked shut behind them, Casey was on him, kissing him against a wall.

"I'm so fucking hot for you right now," Casey said between kisses. "Are you tired? I know it's fucking late and that game was crazy but—"

"Not tired," Landon said. He knew he was about to crash hard, but until then, he wanted this. He wanted as much Casey as he could get.

"I wanna—" Casey said, then dropped to his knees and began fumbling with Landon's belt.

"Oh fuck." Landon helped him, because yes. This. Seconds later, his suit pants dropped to the floor, and his underwear was hauled down to his knees. Casey dived in, taking Landon as deep as he could right away. Landon's head hit the wall, and he groaned far too loudly. "Fuck, that's good."

Casey pulled back, focusing his talented tongue on the swollen head of Landon's cock. Landon grabbed a handful of Casey's

hair but didn't put any pressure on his head. He let Casey set
the pace and enjoyed the show. A dark part of Landon felt like
he deserved this; like Casey was paying tribute to his cham-
pion. It was a pretty ridiculous thing to think because Casey
had scored the game-winning goal.

Landon would pay his own tribute later.

They were way too close to the door for this, and Landon bit
his lip in an effort to stay quiet. Casey wasn't making it easy, al-
ternating between sucking hard and flicking his tongue over all
the spots that made Landon's spine melt. He massaged Landon's
balls with one hand, and gripped his thigh with the other.

Landon thrust, once, by accident. Casey moaned his approval,
sending delicious vibrations through Landon's cock.

"I didn't mean to," Landon said.

Casey pulled off and gazed up at him with eyes so glazed he
looked drunk. "You can, though."

"I don't want to hurt you."

"You won't. I trust you. I love you." He opened his mouth
and slid his lips over the head again, then waited.

"God," Landon rasped, then thrust again, slowly, carefully.
"I love you so much. I missed you. Don't want to leave you
again." He tightened his grip on Casey's hair and was rewarded
with another moan.

Fuck, it felt good. He embraced the challenge of keeping
a steady rhythm. Of not going too deep. Of sinking just far
enough into the wet heat of Casey's perfect mouth before sliding back and burying himself again.

One of Casey's hands fell from Landon's thighs. He was
opening his own belt, unfastening his pants, and sliding his
hand inside. It was so hot, knowing this was turning him on
so much.

"Casey," Landon panted. "Casey. I'm close. I'm—oh shit.
You gotta finish me. I can't. I'll go too hard, I—"

Casey stilled him with his free hand, placing it firmly on his
hip. Then he sucked him hard and fast, head bobbing, tongue

swirling, and Landon exploded. He felt like he actually burst apart, flooded by white heat and joy. Casey swallowed and swallowed around him, finally pulling off with a gasp. There was come on his lips, and a bit on his chin, and his eyes were watering.

Then he laughed. He wiped his mouth with the back of his hand and said, "I mean…it's a lot."

Landon let out a wheeze of breathless laughter. "Sorry." He took a moment to catch his breath then said, "Get on the bed."

Casey scrambled to his feet, went to the bed, then fell backward on it. His pants and underwear were just above his knees. He was still wearing his suit jacket. They both were.

Landon removed his own as he walked to the bed. Then he leaned over Casey, pushed his shirt up with one hand, and took his cock in his mouth.

It didn't take long at all. Casey covered his face with a pillow as his orgasm hit him, but it didn't do much to muffle his enthusiastic announcement of the event. Landon hoped whoever was next door had earbuds in.

Landon pressed soft kisses to Casey's belly while he waited for the aftershocks to pass. Finally, Casey removed the pillow and spread his arms wide on the mattress. "I love you, Stacks."

Landon smiled against Casey's skin. "I love you, too, Hicks."

"Let's win the next game too so we can celebrate again."

"Okay." Landon kissed Casey's belly button, then lifted his head. "Where is our next game, anyway?"

Casey laughed. "Anaheim."

"Short trip."

"Mm. We can sleep in."

Landon crawled up Casey's body until their faces aligned. "I think I missed waking up with you more than anything."

Casey smiled lazily at him. "Yeah?"

"Yeah." Landon dipped his head and kissed him.

"You know what I missed the most?" Casey said.

"What?"

"You."

Landon thunked his forehead against the mattress. "That was cheesy."

"Every day, Stacks."

Landon turned his head and breathed against Casey's neck. "Me too."

Landon got the start in Anaheim.

He wasn't surprised, exactly. Honestly, he'd been expecting it. He'd played well in L.A. and Anaheim was a low-ranked team anyway. But he still felt weird about it.

Casey tapped his ankle with his foot under the little round table they were eating their pregame meal at. "I hear we have a ringer in nets for us tonight."

Landon didn't smile.

"Okay, you're obviously nervous because you've barely touched your food."

"No," Landon said, too quickly. "Not exactly. I don't know."

"You know you deserve this start, right?"

Landon sighed. He couldn't hide anything from Casey. "I do know it, but I can't help feeling…guilty? Is that stupid?"

"Nothing to feel guilty about. We need to play our best players every night." He pointed his fork and the two pieces of penne he'd speared with it at Landon. "You're our best goalie right now."

Landon nodded. Casey was right.

At that moment, a hand landed on Landon's shoulder from behind. He nearly jumped out of his skin trying to get away from it.

"Shit," said Gilbert Morin. "Sorry if I startled you."

"It's okay," Landon said, fighting the urge to put his own hand on his shoulder to erase the unexpected touch.

"I just wanted to talk to you for a sec." Gilbert looked at Casey. "Can I borrow him for a minute? Goalie business."

Casey stood and picked up his tray. "No prob. Come find me after, Stacks."

"Okay." Landon watched him carry his tray to Gio and Petey's table.

Gilbert claimed the chair Casey had vacated. "You know how my career got started?"

Landon didn't answer, because he knew he wasn't supposed to.

"Ollie Beck separated his shoulder. Beck was my fucking hero—I couldn't believe I was even on the same team as him. I'd been called up to replace the backup goalie, Lewis, because he'd needed surgery. I was twenty-three years old, totally starstruck, and suddenly I was moved up to the top spot in Buffalo. And Buffalo was a contender back then, remember?"

Landon nodded.

"I got my shot. It meant two great goalies getting hurt for me to get that shot, but I got my shot. And, Stackhouse..." He tapped two fingers hard against the tabletop. "I. Took. That. Shot."

Landon's heart was in his throat. "You were one of the best."

"Fuck yes I was. And now I'm not. I'm just a backup goalie. I'm not—" he straightened his shoulders and lifted his chin "—*Gilbert Morin* anymore. I'm not the future of this team. You are."

"Antton is," Landon corrected him. "He'll be back next season."

"He will," Gilbert agreed. "His arm will be healed, but still bother him. He'll be another year older. You know he's only four years younger than me, right?"

Of course Landon knew that. But Antton seemed ageless. Invincible. Eternal.

The fact that he wasn't able to be here now proved otherwise.

"I'm not Antton Niskanen," Landon said. "Or Gilbert Morin."

"Of course not. You're Landon Stackhouse, one of the most

talented young goalies I've seen in a long time. And I've seen a lot of young goalies. Believe that."

"Thank you," Landon said quietly, unsure how he was supposed to deal with this much praise.

"Take your shot, Stackhouse. Make everyone stand up and notice you tonight in Anaheim. Show them the last game wasn't a fluke. And don't feel bad for me because I'm going to be the loudest one cheering your name, okay?" He paused. "Well, not louder than Hicks. No one is louder than Hicks."

That made Landon smile. "He's a great cheerleader. And, seriously, thanks."

"You can thank me by taking us to the finals. I wouldn't mind another Cup win before I retire."

"Hell of a finish to a great career," Landon agreed.

Gilbert smiled, then stood up. "Fucking right. Now eat your pasta. You've got a game to win."

Gilbert walked away, and Landon immediately took a bite of pasta. He did have a game to win. He had lots of games to win, and a legacy to launch.

They walked into Casey's house the following afternoon, both in great moods after their win in Anaheim. The game hadn't been as much as a challenge as the one against L.A., but the win put them more firmly in first place in their division and had made Landon feel more firmly like an NHL goaltender.

And now they were home. It felt both surreal and familiar, being back in the space where Landon had fallen in love with Casey.

"You still have your Christmas decorations up," Landon observed.

"Yeah. I like them. They make the house less creepy, y'know?"

"I think in March they start to feel a little creepy, maybe."

Casey removed his coat and boots and put them neatly in the closet, then held out a hand for Landon's coat. Landon raised his eyebrows. "What?" Casey said. "I'm *trying*, okay? The house was so much nicer when you lived here and I wanted to keep it that way because then I could pretend you were still here." He dropped his gaze to the floor. "Maybe that's why I left the lights up too."

Landon smiled and handed Casey his coat. "That's really sweet. And weird."

"No shit, dude. You make me sweet and weird. That's on you."

Landon noticed that the couch was free of the usual debris, and there were no shoes under the coffee table. "I really missed this place. Even the mess."

"You didn't miss the mess."

"I did," he said honestly. "There was nothing about my apartment that reminded me of you. Except…"

Casey wrapped his arms around him from behind. "Except?"

Landon tipped his head back onto Casey's shoulder. "You left one of your hair elastics in my bathroom. I, um. I wore it around my wrist for weeks after."

Casey spun him around. "What? That is so fucking romantic. Are you wearing it now?"

Landon dipped his head to hide the color in his cheeks. "No. I took it off before I flew to L.A. because it seemed embarrassing."

Casey pulled him down into a kiss. He tasted like the Skittles he'd been eating on the plane. "I love that," he said. "I love you. And I'm glad you're home."

"Me too," Landon said, because he couldn't deny that this house felt like home. Then his stomach growled, and they both laughed.

"Oh hey," Casey said, "I've been cooking a bit."

"You have?"

"Yeah! I don't get the premade meals anymore. I get groceries delivered instead. And I watched some cooking for beginners-type videos online, and I can make a few things now!"

That was…surprising. "I leave for a few weeks and now you can cook and clean?"

"Yup. I'm gonna be the best husband you've ever had."

Every word of that sentence was ridiculous, but it still made Landon's heart stop. "I know."

Casey's expression was pure delight, as if they'd both agreed on something important. "Can I make you dinner?" He went to the fridge and threw open the doors. "Cool. We're fully stocked. I coordinated the delivery with the cleaning service. So do you want chicken teriyaki, or sausage and pepper pasta? I'm also getting decent at omelets."

Landon was unsure about letting this happen, but Casey seemed to have all of his fingers still, and had no visible burn scars and hadn't poisoned himself, so, "Chicken teriyaki sounds good. You want help?"

"Nope. I want you to sit there and look pretty while I dazzle you with my skills." Then he pulled an actual apron out of a drawer and put it on.

"Oh no," Landon said as he settled onto one of the stools at the island. "You didn't warn me about the sexy apron."

"It's super sexy, right?" Casey tapped at his phone and then furrowed his brow adorably as he, presumably, read the recipe. "Right. Rice. Gotta start with that. You want a beer?"

Landon's chest felt tight with happiness. "You got any lemonade?"

Casey beamed at him. "Always."

Epilogue

Next December

"I'm going to propose," West whispered, much too loudly, as he leaned into Landon's personal space. "I'm going to *propose!*"

"I know. That's great." This was actually the third time West had told him, but West was very drunk and could be forgiven. He'd probably told everyone at the party at least three times about his plans to pop the question to Allison on Christmas Day, in front of their families. Landon suspected Allison wouldn't be surprised, since she was at the party too.

"You want some water?" Landon asked.

"Nah. You got any weed?"

"Totally," Landon lied. "Go drink some water and I'll get it."

"You're the best, Stacks." West drifted off in the direction of the kitchen.

"Good save," Antton said from behind him.

Landon turned and saw Antton smiling at him. "I doubt he'll make it to the kitchen without getting distracted."

"You've done all you can." Antton took a sip of wine. His pale cheeks were unusually rosy, and Landon suspected his goal-tending partner may be a bit tipsy.

"How's the party?" Landon asked. A year ago he may have

been desperately seeking his idol's approval, but now he only asked to make sure his friend was having a good time.

"Good. Great. You and Casey are excellent hosts." He lifted his glass. "Good wine."

"You can thank Casey's dad for that. He sent a case of that one."

"I will." He reached out and pinched Landon's dress shirt between two fingers. "This is nice."

Landon knew it was nice. It had cost a fortune and it was tailored to flatter his long torso and muscular shoulders. "Thanks. It's new."

"Samir?"

Landon smiled. "He doesn't miss."

Truthfully Landon had bought the shirt because Casey had loved it so much, and because Casey had wanted this party to have an ugly sweater theme. Landon had talked him out of it by promising to wear the shirt.

It had been Casey's idea to host the team Christmas party, saying it would be a cool way to celebrate the sort of anniversary of their first kiss, and also a good way to show off their new hot tub. It was the first party they'd hosted as a couple, even though they'd been living together since March, and had been more or less publicly out as a couple since the summer. They'd never made a big announcement or anything, but Casey had started posting photos of the two of them together on Instagram, with Landon's permission. Everyone who knew them knew they were a couple, and anyone who didn't know them could draw their own conclusions. If there'd been any negative comments on those photos, Casey had been happy to ignore them, and Landon didn't even use social media. Their teammates, friends, and families were supportive, and that was all that mattered.

It had been an incredible summer. He and Casey had spent two weeks in Nova Scotia, sightseeing with Landon's parents and helping out in their garden during the day, and snuggled together at night in the queen bed that had replaced the twin beds in Landon's childhood bedroom. Casey had listened while stroking Landon's skin with soothing touches as Landon shared the memories of Erin that had flooded his brain since returning home.

Then they'd gone to Tampa for a week, enjoying much more privacy in the Hickses' massive home. They'd swum in the pool, and went to expensive restaurants with Casey's parents, and had laughed their way through giddy sex in Casey's enormous bedroom.

And then there'd been Italy, which still felt like a dream. Casey had insisted they'd barely scratched the surface of the country during their two weeks there, but each day had been full of wonders and the best food Landon had ever eaten. Even against all the stunning scenery there, Casey had remained the most beautiful thing Landon had ever seen, and he'd told him so every day as he'd kissed his sun-warmed skin.

"You and Casey should come for dinner on Sunday," Antton said, now. "It's a night off, and we have elk steaks."

"I've never had elk."

"Come, then." Antton smiled. "And bring a bottle of this wine."

"If there's any left, I will." It was nice, having Antton as a friend. The two of them had formed the top-performing goaltending duo in the league, with Landon starting almost as many games as Antton.

Calgary hadn't won the Cup last season, but they'd made it to the third round of the playoffs with Landon starting every game. The run had made him a star in Calgary, and had made the entire league learn his name. He'd earned his spot in Calgary, in the league. At least for as long as he kept playing like he was now.

Landon had only been back to Saskatoon once since March, to clear out his apartment.

"I was talking to Gilbert today," Antton said.

Landon smiled. "How's he doing?" By the end of the playoffs, Landon and Gilbert Morin had been pretty close. Gilbert had been a great mentor for Landon, warmer and easier to talk to than Antton.

"Good. Planning a huge family Christmas at his place in Quebec. Have you seen that house? Unreal. Right on a big lake. He's living the dream now."

Landon honestly felt like he was living the dream himself now, and couldn't imagine life getting even better. He was really happy for Gilbert, though.

Landon excused himself to make the rounds, though really he just wanted to find Casey. He spotted him standing near the bottom of the stairs, wearing a sage-green suit with a dark green sweater underneath. He looked hot in more ways than one.

"Hey," Landon said as he stepped close. "You look like you could use some air."

"It's fucking roasting in here."

"You're wearing a tweed suit and a sweater."

Casey placed a hand on Landon's chest. "You offering to take me out of them?"

"Nope. Come with me."

He led Casey upstairs, and then to the door that led to the seldom-used patio that sat on top of the garage. It was covered in a couple of inches of crusty snow.

"Fuck yes," Casey sighed. "That feels better."

Landon wasn't sure how long he could stay out here because it was cold as hell, but he enjoyed the relief in Casey's expression. He wrapped his arms around him, pulling him close and dropping a kiss on the top of his head.

"Hey," Casey said, "did you hear Westy is gonna propose to Allison on Christmas?"

Landon laughed. "I think everyone on earth knows."

"It's nice, though. I'm happy for them."

"Me too. But being proposed to on Christmas in front of all your family would be a nightmare, right?"

Casey stiffened in his arms and didn't say anything.

"You okay?"

Casey gave an awkward little laugh, then said, "Totally. Yeah." He was silent another moment before adding, "So, is it the Christmas part or the family part that sounds like a nightmare to you?"

"Both. It's not that I don't think Allison will say yes, but having to be on display like that in front of people, and then having Christmas always remind you of that awkward moment? No thanks."

"Right," Casey said quietly. "Fuck."

Landon stepped back enough to see Casey's face. "You're being weird."

"Nope. Totally chill and regular."

Nothing about Casey's face looked chill or regular. He looked like he'd seen a ghost.

Things clicked into place.

"Wait," Landon said slowly.

"Nothing!" Casey said loudly. "I didn't say anything. I'm not planning anything. What are you talking about?"

"Oh my god." Landon had to walk away and grip the railing. Had Casey really planned on *proposing* to him? *Marriage?*

With his back to Casey, he let a goofy grin take over his face. Holy *shit!*

"Okay, fine," Casey said, behind him. "It was a bad idea. I just thought, since our families will be here at the house with us this Christmas, it would be ideal timing. I mean, I *was* worried about stealing Westy's thunder a bit, but...would you have said yes?"

"I would have died of embarrassment. But I would have said yes before that, maybe."

"How about now?"

Landon turned to see Casey on one knee in the snow. His mouth went dry, and his stomach fluttered because there was no way this could be real. But of course it was, because being with Casey meant a life full of impulsive, ridiculous moments.

Casey always offered fun, and joy. All Landon ever had to do was say yes.

But because he was still Landon Stackhouse, he said, "You're going to ruin your pants."

"Too late." Casey swallowed. "Will you marry me, Stacks?"

It was too soon. They were probably too young. Their future was too uncertain. But yes, of course Landon would marry him. Of course he wanted a life of moments like this one, and all the joy that came with it.

"I have good news and bad news," he said, speaking quickly before the lump in his throat got any bigger.

Casey smiled. "Good news first."

"Yes. I'll marry you."

Casey theatrically wiped his brow. "Phew. Rad. Okay, hit me with the bad news."

"I'm going to look hotter than you on our wedding day."

Casey burst out laughing.

"You can stand up now," Landon said.

Casey stood and then they crashed together, kissing and laughing.

"I love you so much, Landon."

"I love you too."

"Brooke said I should have a ring for this, but I wanted to pick those together."

"I like that."

They kissed again. "I thought last year's party was good, but damn," Casey said. "This is gonna be hard to top."

"Best party ever," Landon agreed. He tipped his head back, and smiled at the stars.

★ ★ ★ ★ ★

Acknowledgments

As always, I'd like to thank my wonderful husband, Matt, for his support and for giving me time and space to write even when things are hectic, and for his endless support and enthusiasm. And thanks also to my kids, Mitchell and Trevor, for their patience. Huge thanks to my editor, Mackenzie Walton, who is amazing and I hope to work on a million more books with her. To Kerri, Stephanie, Katixa, and the whole team at Carina Press and Harlequin for believing in my books. To my agent, Deidre Knight, for being a great cheerleader. To all of the fans of the Game Changers series, thank you so much for every review, kind word, piece of fan art, reel, and recommendation that you've shared. I appreciate all of it, and I hope you enjoy this book. Also, a big shout-out to my Discord fam: to everyone on my own server, thank you for all the hours of conversation and the overwhelming love and support. To everyone in my author support group server, thank you for making me feel less alone and for writing books that keep setting the bar higher.